MOON & EARTH

MOONFIRE TRILOGY BOOK 3

PATTY JANSEN

GET FREE EBOOKS

Visit pattyjansen.com
to sign up for Patty's mailing list. You get four series starter ebooks
for free!

CHAPTER 1

FOR TWO DAYS, the group of eagles and their riders followed the western coastline north. During that time, perched on the back of his bird, Isandor became reacquainted with a lot of muscles he'd forgotten he had. He usually flew in the middle of the group, free from the buffeting wind and the biting cold. The Knights were unhappy to have him in the lead, but even if he knew that they sheltered and protected him, he enjoyed finally doing something. He enjoyed being out of the palace and away from Jevaithi's tantrums. He wished that he could let Tamerane know that he was coming for her.

With all his heart, he longed for Tamerane, taken to Arania by her parents from the old nobility of the City of Glass, who were too tied up with Arania to even allow their daughter to marry the king.

If Isandor was honest with himself, he knew that he and the Knight Council had ignored the unhappiness of the nobles of the City of Glass for too long. They had called them quaint and old-fashioned. They had laughed about the haughty speeches given at dinner parties, where all the nobles came together and which informants for the Knight Council sometimes attended. They had watched how the nobles tried—and mostly failed—to prop up their family wealth with businesses.

They had viewed the struggles of the nobles as *not their problem,* because it was the nobles' own choice to refuse to work with the Knight Council, right?

They had pretended the problem might go away. And go away, it had: the nobles had sold themselves and their businesses to Arania. Even if the mission to retrieve Tamerane from the northern Aranian town of Curack was risky and ill-advised, the Knight Council could no longer watch Arania steal people, money and knowledge from the City of Glass.

And, oh, Isandor knew that the small army of the Eagle Knights was no match for the full force of the Aranian army, which consisted of people *wanting* to die for the sake of glory, and so these tiny spearhead missions was all they could manage against that overwhelming force.

One didn't need a giant net and bear-like strength to kill a bear. One needed a strong arm, a keen eye and a sharp spear. A tiny insect could kill a bear, if its poison was strong enough.

That was the thinking, at least. Whether the Knights were well-trained enough and their actions poisonous enough to do any damage remained to be seen. So far, the Aranians had cast the first stones. They had captured a patrol and when another patrol went after them, they had captured that group as well. They had coerced many nobles to move to Arania. They had forced the Knights' actions. Once he returned, the Council would have to sit down and make a plan.

A war plan.

The coastline that passed underneath them was near-deserted, almost free of ice these days. They spotted the occasional ship out to sea on its way to Arania, or little fishing boats closer to the shore, but little else. A few flocks of sheep went running at the sight of the group of eagles, but they saw no people.

This coastline was perfect ground for illegal activities, for smuggling, for amassing armies, and the Knights had no manpower to patrol it. If Arania wanted, they could just occupy this land and Peria could do nothing to stop it. There was too much land and too few people.

The thought was depressing.

For two nights in a row, they stopped at a rocky outcrop and set up camp using their saddles and saddle blankets for shelter and the birds' big feathery bodies for warmth. There were no trees, so the first task at the campsite was to press firebricks from grass and heather. The vegetation was damp from the mist, so the resulting fire produced more smoke than flames.

This was wild, majestic country, with sweeping views, rolling highlands, rocky headlands and pristine beaches and, in the distance, the craggy and snow-covered outlines of the mountains.

Because of the time of year, the sun was low during the day and hit the coastline side-on from over the ocean, where only the occasional island interrupted the eternal cloudbanks that hung offshore.

The memory of Tamerane explaining her theories shot through him painfully.

He hoped with all his heart that they wouldn't come too late. He'd heard terrible things from other men about what high-class Aranian men did to women who came to their houses. No Aranian man would take Tamerane into his house for her ideas and intelligence. Because in Arania, women were not meant to be intelligent. They were mothers.

Occasionally, they passed little fishing villages, nestled on the shoreline. Those were recent settlements, since all of this land used to be covered in sea ice, and no one was quite sure who lived in these lawless places. They were technically on Perian land, but no one in the City of Glass had the resources to monitor the western coastline. That was a matter to be addressed in the future, as were so many other things.

To avoid being spotted by Aranian spies, the scout, the rider at the front of the group, would steer inland, where a group of eagles at high altitude wouldn't attract any attention.

Mostly, those fishing settlements consisted of shacks and tents, but towards the end of the second day, the scout pointed out a larger structure.

Isandor didn't see it at first. It wasn't a building exactly, but a structure in the side of a hill, with the top of the grassy hill forming the roof. The entrance was on the side, visible through the two tracks that led to it, one from the beach below, and one from the coastal track that ran more or less along the entire coastline.

A small jetty in the bay indicated that large ships came there, even if none were there now.

The expedition's leader was a Knight Captain named Nallayo, a strong competent woman a few years younger than Isandor.

She whistled to the scout, and he sent his eagle into a circling descent. Rider Nallayo led the rest of the birds into a circling pattern over the ridge a bit further inland, where relatively warm and moist air rose from the sun-warmed hillside. All the Riders' communication was through whistles and hand signals, and it seemed that many new signals had been added to the language since Isandor had flown with the Knights.

From up here, he could see how the scout landed his bird on top of the hill, how he walked down the grassy slope, followed by the bird —scout birds were trained to do that.

The man went to the hollowed-out side of the hill where the tracks led. He disappeared for a bit, came back and disappeared again.

Then he came back and waved his blue shawl. Isandor definitely remembered that sign: all clear.

Rider Nallayo led the group to the bay.

The riders and eagles landed on a grassy field in front of the entrance to the hideout. The little bay faced northwest and the sunlight warmed it into a cosy little nook. There were even still a few flowers in bloom.

Isandor let himself slide off the bird, stamping life into his numb feet.

Nallayo was already talking to the scout, who was pointing at several features of the hideout.

The entrance was a solid wooden door. A second entrance was much bigger, like a warehouse door. The wall was made from beach boulders held together with white cement. There were two small windows, but both were covered on the inside by blinds.

"But what if people are hiding inside?" Nallayo was saying.

The scout shook his head. "No one is here, and hasn't been for a while. The chimney up there on top of the hill is cold and there is no recent soot on the sides. The windows are cold. There are no recent footsteps in the mud patches leading up to the door."

"Can we get in?"

"Depending on how much we want to destroy, yes, we can."

They both turned to Isandor when he joined them.

"It's your mission," Nallayo said to him. "Do we spend some time figuring out what sort of business goes on here?"

Isandor badly wanted to say no, but ultimately, he knew that everything in this mission, everything related to the nobles, the secretive connection with Arania and the sea trade along the western coast, was connected. The key to finding Tamerane might even be connected. House Mara was deeply involved with the Aranian sea trade, and it was what had led her father Ledor to flee the City of Glass.

"Break the door," he said. "Try to do it with as little damage as possible, but if it's not possible, break it anyway."

A couple of the Knights went to work. At first they tried the door to what looked like the office or residence, but it was quite solid and they didn't have the heavy equipment needed. They had more luck with the big warehouse door, which had a lock on the outside that could be wrenched open with the sharp point of a dagger.

They managed to open it enough for a person to get through. Behind the door was, as suggested, a warehouse. It contained a truck, a study vehicle with large wheels and a cabin that would seat twelve people.

Well . . . that was interesting.

Isandor immediately thought of Zaina's business and how the men had wanted to buy or sell a truck. The coastline track obviously existed partially because of these trucks.

The sea trade with Arania covered mainly fish and agricultural products. Isandor was sure that some of the Aranian imports bypassed the harbourmaster in the City of Glass, but most of it would be recorded in some way.

If one wanted to be really secretive, obviously, one traded overland. Maybe the princes and spies came in through this place via sea and then went the rest of the way overland to avoid being detected by the harbour authorities.

That was a chilling thought. The fledgling Knight Council was failing badly at covering all aspects of the security of the City of Glass and Aranians had found many ways in. It was something that he would have to address urgently when he got back . . . and probably would not have the manpower for. How could a small nation cope after more than half its population had been wiped out, and half of the survivors had chosen never to return? Even twenty years after the disaster, there were never enough people to get anything done in the City of Glass.

Rider Nallayo had found and lit a lamp. The lamp's metal construction with the clear glass shade was of Aranian origin, and so was the book that lay next to it.

A door was in the back of the warehouse, underneath shelves containing nets and crayfish pots and other fishing gear—most of it dusty.

The door led to a second storage area, with shelves all around containing neat boxes labelled with Aranian script.

"It's warm in here," one of the Knights behind Isandor said.

He was right. Coming in from outside, it was really warm in this room, but there was no obvious source of the heat.

From that room, Rider Nallayo led the group into a hallway to a residential section of the building. There were rooms with beds on both sides and a large kitchen at the end. All of this hadn't been used for quite some time, judging by the amount of dust on tables and shelves. It was surprisingly warm in here, also.

They passed a living room with couches. This room had a window on the far side, which, when Rider Nallayo lifted the blind, turned out to be one of the two windows they had seen from outside. The second window belonged to an office next door —a large room, with a desk, and shelves with boxes of files or archives.

Isandor looked around this room. Something in here made him feel uneasy, but he would probably need to pull things off shelves to know what it was. It wouldn't be a quick investigation.

"Well," Rider Nallayo said, standing outside the door to this room. "It's very odd. What would they do here?"

"It looks like some sort of storage and administration office," one of the Knights said.

"This place gives me the creeps," the scout said.

Isandor agreed.

Rider Nallayo said, "I don't understand why it's so warm in here. There is no fire."

"The chimney hasn't been used for a while."

In fact, Isandor had noticed only one fireplace, and it wasn't a fireplace as such: it was the cooking fire in the kitchen. This place didn't appear to use any fires for heating.

While the Knights talked about the possible purpose of the building, Isandor walked around a second time. In one of the rooms off the side, he found a little door to a storage room—empty—where it was even warmer than in the rest of the building.

"Something in the ground warms the building," he told the Knights, and several agreed, also looking disturbed.

They went on a hunt for further doors that led into the hill and found a narrow door in the back of the second storeroom behind the one where the truck stood. The door—made of metal, and rusty—was locked, but the scout made short work of the lock.

The door creaked when he pushed it open. It was very thick and heavy and as he pushed it, a bubble of golden fire burst out.

Rider Nallayo took a step back and trod on the toes of the Knight behind her. "Whoa!"

"What?" that Knight asked, looking slightly put out.

Isandor knew. He could see the golden strands, but because they belonged to the Pirosian clan, most of the Knights could not see it.

"Icefire," Rider Nallayo said, for the benefit of those who couldn't see it.

"Well, it seems we may have located the source of icefire patches on the coast," Isandor said.

One of the Knights said, "Why would the Aranians build this on top of an icefire source? Doesn't icefire kill Aranians?"

Rider Nallayo snorted. "Maybe that's why there is no one here."

Maybe, Isandor thought, the noble Perian families built this here *because* no one else could come to this building.

He stepped into the narrow passageway beyond the door. It was rough underfoot, with the walls hewn into the rocky ground and sloped down into the earth.

The strength of icefire strands almost blinded him. He had to use his hands to guide him along the wall.

After a while, the passage opened into an underground cavern where the air was warm and humid. A basin in the middle of the cavern steamed bubbling water. To his eye, the water also exuded many golden strands of icefire, which snaked into the air and were absorbed into the rocky walls and ceiling. At least that explained why it was warm in the building. It might even explain why it was so warm in the bay, and the flowers outside.

But then again, icefire usually turned the air *cold*.

He peered into the bubbling water, and gestured Rider Nallayo to come over. Even the flame on the lamp she was still holding was doing a strange dance, threatening to break loose of the wick.

The Knights were complaining that it was too dark in the room to see where they were going. This was strange, because to Isandor's eyes, the strands of icefire lit the room with blazing brightness, but it was also further evidence that this was indeed icefire.

Rider Nallayo must have a good deal of Thilleian blood, because she was peering into the water. The light from all those concentrated strands lit her face.

"Can you see what's down there?" Isandor asked.

"No, but it will be the source of the heat."

Isandor looked around the room. The wall surrounding the basin looked like a recent construction, but the stone paving around it was blackened, worn and covered in moss.

He knelt on the ground and scraped some of the moss aside. Underneath, he found the same type of smooth artificial stone that made up the walls in the buildings of the City of Glass. Well, that was interesting. He'd never heard of other places where remnants of the ancient civilisation that had built the City of Glass still survived, although he'd always considered it likely that those places existed.

"The floor in this cavern is very old," he said to Rider Nallayo.

"What's the basin for?" she asked.

Isandor rose. "I don't know. Cooling the device, maybe. I don't think anyone comes close to understanding why these people made machines that kill."

"Or why some of us have resistance to it."

He nodded, looking at the bubbling water. "I've never seen this before. The machine we called the Heart made the City of Glass a cold place. Since it has been destroyed, our weather has become so much warmer. This one produces heat. I thought icefire was cold, but here it is, lighting the cave."

Rider Nallayo also nodded, staring at the glowing surface of the bubbling pool. She offered no theories of her own—Isandor had found that Knights were highly practical and wondered about "what" and "how" much more than about "why".

So of course she said, "What are we going to do about it?"

"Eventually, the machine down there needs to be destroyed."

"Do you know how?"

"No, but the Brotherhood of the Light will be able to advise us."

Rider Nallayo pressed her lips together. Most Knights didn't like the Brotherhood, an ages-old organisation steeped in tradition and knowledge dating from before the time of King Caldor.

Isandor didn't trust them either. They were probably more closely aligned with the nobles than the Knight Council, but they were an important source of knowledge about icefire.

They decided that the building was safe enough for them, as natives of the City of Glass who were naturally resistant to higher levels of icefire, to spend the night in its relative comfort and warmth. The kitchen store held a variety of grains, and together with fish caught from the jetty, the Knights fashioned a decent meal. It was nice to sit at a proper table again.

After dinner most men retired to the bedrooms, where they rolled out their blankets over the musty mattresses. Isandor, however, felt too restless to sleep. He took the light and wandered into the office. He pulled the archive boxes off the shelf, looking for clues to the purpose of this place, as well as for something he could read. He knew the Aranian characters, but only recognised a few words here and there. Those words, like *duty* and *delivery* and *tax* seemed to indicate that this was some kind of freight handling office.

But why have it in the middle of nowhere on top of an icefire source?

The first reason—easy heating—seemed obvious.

A second reason might be to disinterest intruders. But then why was all this documentation in Aranian and not Perian?

He leafed through the papers again, mainly invoices and bills of transport. What did they transport and who were the recipients of it?

Isandor spent some time trying to decipher the writing on one particular page. Not because it was different from the rest, but because he had to start somewhere. He cursed himself that all the Knighthood's Aranian speakers had gone on the previous missions and none had been available for this one, or at least none who had skills with eagles.

If he was correct, the top section identified the transport company, underneath that was the name of the sender or recipient. The row of numbers with items spelled out was easy, if only he could read what sort of items had been sold or bought.

The next page repeated that pattern. The top ones identified the transport company. And it said . . . it said . . . something like Waifei Farlong Curack . . . if he was correct.

In the end, he grew so frustrated that he grabbed a handful of the papers and stuck them into his saddlebag. He'd ask someone at home.

But when he closed the flap on the saddlebag, his hand met with something else: the Chevakian sonorics meter. He pulled it out. The little dial said forty motes per cube.

What?

That was slightly elevated, and probably not terribly healthy for a Chevakian, but there was no way it could be correct, sitting right on top of an icefire source.

He walked down the corridor, into the storage room and through the little door into the cavern with the water basin.

Icefire was so strong here that he needed no light to show him the way. The basin and the boiling water inside it glowed with light, and the golden strands were so bright that he could barely see where he was going.

At the edge of the basin, he looked at the dial again.

It had dropped to zero.

CHAPTER 2

FROM THE OLD FARM HOUSE that was Karlen's shelter on the southern bank of the creek at Lekata, Javes and Tali made their way into the highlands in the company of the camel and the goats. The road wound slowly up the central plateau, and fields and paddocks along the side of the road were replaced by desolate forest.

The road was paved—the first part at least—and followed the telegraph line, but whenever they passed a weather station and Javes tested the line, it was always inactive. He had no idea if his message had even made it to Tiverius.

Since he had left Tiverius to go to Ysherra, everything he'd sent back to the capital seemed to have disappeared in a void. In Ysherra, he'd assumed that it was the normal state of affairs, but now they were coming into the northern central districts, and this was not an area habitually ignored by the capital.

Javes was beginning to worry whether they got his messages at all or whether the replies they had sent were reaching him. He worried if anyone had even sent replies. He began to worry that something might have *happened* in the capital.

The first night after leaving Lekata, Javes and Tali camped at the roadside. This far into the high country, where the soil was extremely poor, the vegetation consisted of hundreds of twisted and scrawny trees, mangled by drought and wind.

The weather was blustery, with a squally wind continuing well into the night. It made the flames of the fire dance so that the tree trunks threw long, flickering shadows over their neighbouring trees, making it look like the forest moved. The wind would sometimes whistle through the branches.

Tali was unfamiliar with the concept of *forest* and found it scary. Javes had to explain to her that it was just the wind doing those things, but he wasn't sold on it either. He was trying to remember from geography classes at school just how big this forest was. On the way to Watya, the train had spent an entire night going through it.

"I don't care what you tell me about the trees. I don't like it," Tali said. "Is there another path we can use?"

"We're going to Velora," Javes said. "It's on the southern end of the highlands, and it has a station. Once we get on the train there, we'll be in Tiverius in no time. This road is the shortest route to the station. The other roads are far longer, and they don't take us anywhere near a station."

The forest density increased as they travelled further south the next day. Scrawny trees made way for thick stands of tall, straight pine trees. This was logging country, and the road reflected its use by big trucks or wagons to carry logs from the forest to the towns along the railway.

They saw plenty of those trucks. You could hear the chugging engines coming from far off. The drivers usually greeted the two youths, but were too busy or going too fast to stop and offer them a lift.

Javes worried that they had seen so few other travellers on the road. Any small carts or travellers on horseback they had seen were locals—hunters taking pelts to tanneries, or mushroom collectors with their harvest on the way to market.

Javes warned the few on the way north about the floods, but most people already knew or weren't going that far.

Javes wondered about all those people who had fled Lekata at the time they passed through. A whole convoy of people had been in front of them when they stopped at Karlen's hideout. Where had they all gone?

"Is it still far to this next town?" Tali asked in the late afternoon on the third day.

"It's a fair walk. We probably need to camp for two more days. Why?"

"There is bad weather coming. It gives me the chills."

Yes, he could feel it, too. The breeze blew from different directions, one moment cold, the next warm. Low clouds chased each other through the sky, dropping occasional specks of rain.

The animals could feel it, too.

A pair of forest hares came out of the undergrowth, and charged down the road in the direction from which Javes and Tali had come. Javes grabbed his trap, but it was much too late, of course.

The hares were followed a moment later by a family of deer running in the same direction.

The goats were jumping around and bleating and head-butting each other. The camel reacted to that by frequently tossing its head which, in turn, would almost rip the rope from Javes' hand.

"See?" Tali said. "Even the animals are scared."

Javes would have loved to say something soothing, that animals didn't have the same fears or that they were just cagey because of some predator in the forest, but every bit of his training about weather systems said that she was right. The warm and cold air, the changing wind direction, the low clouds were all classic signs preceding an old-style, sonorics-induced winter storm.

Yet there was nowhere to go and nowhere to shelter.

Javes pushed on as far as they could in search of a place where they could camp without the risk of a tree falling on them.

At dusk, when it was almost too dark to continue, they found the remnants of a wooden logger's hut at the edge of what must have been a clearing, but was now a field of closely-growing pine saplings.

The wind whistled through the branches almost constantly. Wood creaked and cracked. Branches fell on the ground with soft rustling thuds.

A couple of mossy, half-disintegrated walls were all that was left of the hut. They offered little shelter against the weather.

Javes unpacked the canvas sheet. It flapped in the wind and he needed Tali's help to hold it down. The logs were so rotted it was hard to find a place to tie the canvas down, but he managed to make a shelter big enough for both them and the animals.

They ate while leaning against the camel's warm and furry side.

Making a fire was out of the question, so the meal consisted of flat-bread and dried fruit.

Javes slept for a bit after that.

At first, it was quite warm, but it got much colder during the night. He had to use both blankets. Tali was shivering so much that he put his arms around her and held her close. At first, the nutty scent of her hair disturbed him, but he kept thinking about how frightened she had been when he found her.

The wind swelled to a roar. Occasionally, it lifted the canvas and made it flap, letting in a waft of freezing cold raindrops.

Only when the storm abated and quiet returned did Javes fall asleep. Tali was a warm presence against him. He had the camel at his back and goats around his legs. He was sure the blanket would need washing, but for now, they were warm.

Morning dawned pale and blue and without a sound.

Javes crawled out from underneath the shelter, looking straight at the grey sky. That was strange. He swore they'd been in a pine forest.

The tall trees of the forest had been reduced to a mass of mangled, splintered and broken tree trunks as far as the eye could see.

"It looks like a dust devil came past here," Tali said next to him.

She was right. Not only that, but . . .

He left the shelter, stepping over fallen branches to a patch of bare ground. His boots left dark footsteps on the ground.

Snow.

He bent to touch the ground, and yes, it was snow. His hand left a dark print in the thin layer. It was already well on its way to melting. But had snow ever fallen in this area? He didn't think so.

"Can we keep going?" Tali asked.

"I don't know. I hope so."

Javes looked at the devastation behind the hut and the sea of mangled wood downhill from where they stood. The entire valley floor was covered in fallen trees. Not a single tree still stood upright. Trunks had split, branches torn off. The air was full of the scent of fresh pine resin.

He couldn't see the road. They *might* be able to keep going. Just as well they didn't have a cart.

"Do you think any people lived here?" Tali asked.

"I hope not." They would not have survived this.

They packed up and ate a quick breakfast. There was no time to make a fire, especially since all the wood was wet and fresh.

Their progress that day was painfully slow. Javes had hoped to reach Velora today, but it became clear they would need at least one more day.

It took them most of the day to reach an area where they could walk at something resembling a normal pace, without having to clamber over tree trunks, without the camel's rope becoming entangled in branches.

They were tired, scratched from climbing over fallen trees, and filthy.

At midafternoon they came to a hill from which they could see across farmland. The town of Velora would be in the dusty air at the horizon.

A sense of relief washed over him. The trek through the central highlands had been much harder than he had expected. Tomorrow, or at least the day after, they could get on the train.

"Let's stop here. We have plenty of wood. Let's cook a nice meal tonight." The past few days had been harrowing enough. "We'll get on the train tomorrow and then we'll be in Tiverius soon."

There was a copse of trees halfway down the hill. A few had fallen over, but most still stood. More importantly, a little creek with clean water ran through the gully at the back of the stand of trees.

Javes hobbled the camel so that it could graze and set up the cloth for their tent. Tali went to the creek to fill their water bags.

Javes watched her from under the cover of the tent. She swung the water bag and if he listened carefully, he could hear her singing. She had become so much more confident and less skittish and he hoped that her newfound confidence wouldn't be damaged once they got to the city.

It was hard to predict what the future would hold for her as a northern girl in Tiverius. He found that he'd come to appreciate her quiet presence, her keen eye for the animals and the things they could eat or sell. She was also—he hated to admit it—quite pretty. If she were his sister . . .

Wait—he could say that she was his sister. That would stop the odd looks people gave him.

"Why are you looking at me like that?" She ducked under the tent cloth and poured water in the blackened pan.

"I find it hard to believe that you're only thirteen."

"Nearly fourteen."

"Still. My life was very different when I was fourteen."

"Oh? How?"

"I didn't know very much." He'd been silly, childish, immature compared to Tali.

"I thought all children went to school in Tiverius."

"Of course I went to school, but school doesn't actually teach you anything."

She laughed, a sound that had become more frequent the further away they had travelled from Ysherra. "If school doesn't teach you anything, then why does everyone in the city go to it?"

"You don't learn any of the . . ." He was going to say *important things*, but that wasn't it, either. Reading and writing—not Tali's strong points at all—were important. They just weren't the only things that were important.

"Yes?" She prompted.

"You learn reading and writing at school. You don't learn much about life, about helping your parents, about carpentry, about . . ."

"Milking goats?"

"Yes, milking goats." She used to laugh at his ineptitude at milking goats when he first came to Ysherra.

"But when you go to the weather boxes and send the messages, that is when you use what you've learned."

"Yes."

"I want to learn that, too."

"Sure, you can."

There was wood to make a fire, and they ate well from their supplies, supplemented with milk and some mushrooms that Tali had found.

They would usually go to sleep soon after dark, lacking the warmth of a fire, but the fire was warm, so Javes made tea and they both wrapped themselves in blankets and sat talking, while holding steaming cups of tea.

Tali wanted to know what Javes was going to do with the maps of the location of the machine that Karlen had given him. So Javes explained about the doga and the systems of government and how he would probably apply to see the proctor and give him the maps and Karlen's notes in person. Then she wanted to know what *they* would do with it, and he said that they'd likely send a team with balloons to destroy it.

"Do they know how to destroy this machine if no one can get close because of this thing called sonorics?"

Javes gave her a sideways look. He had assumed, at Karlen's shelter, that Tali had gone to sleep and had no interest in the matters that Karlen shared with Javes. But she'd been listening all along.

"Some people can get close. They live in Peria, and they're immune to sonorics because a machine like this used to sit under the City of Glass, and these people lived on top."

And then Javes had to explain about the City of Glass and the huge explosion of the machine twenty years ago—in the year before he was born—that had brought a lot of Perian refugees to Tiverius and had led to a change in the weather in the entire world.

And then Tali said, "Like what happened in Ysherra in the last few years."

Javes was embarrassed not to be aware of this, especially since he'd spent time with Pashtan and was supposed to know about the weather. But he didn't, so she told him of how, when she was little, winter would bring rains in which farmers could grow grain; but, lately, the rain would fall in summer when it was not useful to farmers because the water dried up too quickly to be of use for crops. Dust devils were also a new addition to the climate. They used to occur just in the desert north of Red Hill, in places where no one except windwalkers ever went. She also said that big storms like the one they had come through were new, and that often the weather would get really cold during those storms and the old people would complain about it and would say that this never used to happen in the past.

"Like the storm we just came through?"

She shrugged. "I don't know. Does it ever snow here?"

Javes had to admit that the Scriptorium's weather recordings from the north and less-populated areas of the country were woefully inadequate. In the north, they only recorded data from around Ysherra and Watya. There used to be a meteorologist in Tamyra, too, but the doga had been unable to fill that position for a long time. Here on the highlands, there were few weather stations.

None that had ever recorded snow, as far as he knew, and he should know because he was studying to be a meteorologist, and being a meteorologist was an *important* task in the world. Because weather was influenced by sonorics, and it seemed that everyone in Tiverius had been ignoring the deep changes, of which he had witnessed enough to know that he shouldn't ignore them any longer, never mind the presence of weather stations.

A chill went over his spine. "The weather stations in the north are reporting all these things, but no one in Tiverius is listening."

"That's because no one ever sends anything back from the big city," Tali said. "So it seems like no one cares."

Javes balled his fists. He would set about changing that. The data about the changing climate in Ysherra had probably been buried in the Scriptorium for many years, and no one had thought to notify anyone about it. They probably wouldn't, unless the dust devils hit Tiverius.

That was a disturbing thought. Dust devils in Tiverius would definitely disturb the genteel, sophisticated lives of the citizens. He could imagine the death and devastation.

Tali then wanted to know what he was going to do when he got back to Tiverius.

Javes abandoned his horrifying thoughts of things that might come to pass, and returned to the safe *nothing is going on* bubble. "I need to finish my studies, and then I'll get a job somewhere."

"Taking measurements?"

"Probably not." Most graduates ended up as number crunchers in the Scriptorium or in the meteorology department under his tutor Viki. And he would end up helping to bury data in big books that no one ever looked at.

That was another disturbing thought. He *had* wanted to work at the Meteorology Department, but if this trip had made him realise anything, it was that those pretty maps with pressure and temperature lines represented the lives of real people in many different ways.

It also made him realise that if anyone could alert the doga to the problems with the weather, it was him.

They finally went to bed when the fire started to die down, and long after the animals had gone to sleep.

Tali seemed no longer afraid of him, and slept next to him for warmth, and he no longer had embarrassing dreams about her. She was like a sister he never had.

JAVES WOKE up when it was still dark. He had dust in his mouth. Dust was on his face, too, and on top of his blanket.

It was much later in the morning than he had first thought. The sky was covered in dark brown clouds, and most of the valley had disappeared in a brown haze.

Tali sat up, clutching her blanket around her. Her eyes were wide in panic. "They don't have dust devils here, do they?"

Javes didn't know. He didn't think so. "Better get the animals, just in case."

He crawled out from under the cover and—

"Oh, look at that!" The sky to the north was almost black with big, towering clouds. Yet another storm? How many of these storms could they cope with? What was going on with the weather?

The camel stood nearby, sniffing the wind and pulling funny faces. Javes knew that this was a sign of distress. He grabbed the headgear and led the animal to the shelter, rubbing the furry neck.

Tali tried to round up the goats, but they were nervous and kept jumping away.

Javes called, "Come on, come back here. Help me pack this up."

Wind whipped his hair to one side.

"But the goats. . . ."

"We'll make a dash for the town. The goats will come, if they want to."

Javes had never packed up so quickly. The camel, too, was keen to go. It was pulling on the rope. Javes wished they could ride, but asking the animal to carry both of them and the packs was too much.

They sped down the road as fast as Tali could walk. As Javes had predicted, the goats came bounding after them soon enough. The wind was picking up again, bringing strangely warm air laced with brown dust. It would whip branches, leaves, grit, the occasional sheet of roofing across the road. The black clouds at the northern horizon grew and came closer. The wind came alternately from the north or south. Sometimes it was biting cold, sometimes it was warm.

The big storm in the desert had been relatively normal, but nothing was normal about this weather. All his knowledge about weather patterns and rain depressions was of no use.

While taking a short break in the shelter of the wall of a shed, Javes took out his sonorics meter. The reading on the dial was four motes per cube; then suddenly, it went up to twenty-five, and then it fell again.

The world was broken. The weather was broken. This happened because people had destroyed the machine in the City of Glass, but they hadn't destroyed the one in the northern desert. That had to be done as soon as possible.

THE TOWN of Velora lay at the very foot of the central platform. The river that flowed through the town provided power for the many timber mills. In the old days, the sawmills used to fish the logs out of the river after they floated down from where they had been cut upstream, and then they would put the cut wood onto rafts that would float to Tiverius. But this made shipping on the river rather dangerous, so now the timber went by train.

For a logging town, Velora was surprisingly free of surrounding forest, because the land on the river plain was fertile for crops, which, thanks to the railway, they could sell in Tiverius.

Many years of logging and selling crops had made Velora one of the richest areas in Chevakia outside Tiverius.

Unlike the northern towns, Velora did not greet its visitors with the ugliest parts of town: the warehouses, the businesses, the scrap yards. Stately houses lined the road into town, all of them well-tended, neatly painted and cleaned.

But even here were signs of bad weather: a tree blown over, dust heaped onto a veranda, part of a roof lifted off. People in front yards were repairing the damage, and these houses of the well-off had weathered the storm quite well. The same could not be said for the much smaller houses of the workers further into town. Sometimes nothing was left of a house except a pile of mangled wood. Men and women sorted through the rubble.

Here, the industriousness of *fixing* the damage and been overtaken by the instinct to flee.

The road grew busy, crowded with families with donkey carts laden with all their belongings, and women with harried faces dragging children, looking around in the crowd, maybe for their husbands or their parents. As in Lekata, people stood by the side of the road, trying to sell belongings to fund their trip. The camel was nervous, and the goats wanted to bolt in all directions at once, which made Tali's job—hanging onto the rope that held all of them—quite interesting.

A big mass of people waited in the square outside the train station, corralled into a semblance of a queue by a handful of harried guards, too few for the task.

Javes and Tali and their menagerie got some hostile looks.

One man said, "You don't think you're going to get on the train with all those beasts, do you?"

Javes didn't say that yes, that was intention. It also didn't take him very long to realise that there was not much chance to get a spot on the train. Animals travelled in special wagons, and those would certainly be used to transport people and their luggage.

A station employee was answering questions further down. How long would it take for everyone to find a spot on the train? He didn't know. When would the next train come? There was one this afternoon. Beyond that, he didn't know. Were there facilities set up for them when they got to Tiverius? He didn't know.

And so on and so forth. Javes and Tali had arrived at the front of the queue.

"Yes?" the ticket seller said in a harassed voice.

"I'd like to go to Tiverius with my sister and the animals," Javes said.

The man shook his head. "No animals on this train."

"What about the next one?"

"No animals on that one either, or the next one or the one after that, if there are still trains after that."

Javes dug in his pocket and found the piece of ancient metal he had taken from Arukat's house. "I can give you this if you'll let us on."

The man squinted. "Whatever piece of rubbish is that?"

"It's ancient. A collector's item. It's worth a lot."

"If you say so. I have no time for that rubbish. Next!"

"But our camel—"

"*No* animals. The train is packed. We're putting people in the freight carriages. We have no room for camels. No matter how much ancient rubbish you pay. No matter how many gold eagles you pay. There is no room. Either you go without the camel or you don't go at all."

Javes took one look at his menagerie—camel and goats—and knew that they had come this far with him and there was no way he'd leave them behind. "Well, then I'm not going either."

And he grabbed the camel's rope and yanked it away.

He strode across the square, his legs trembling. He sensed Tali and the goats behind him, but didn't stop. He was furious. He could have . . . should have gone to Watya and caught a train from there. But he couldn't have known if trains were still running over the bridge across the Aramys River. He should have . . . he should have sold that piece a lot sooner while they were still in country where ancient arte-facts had value.

"What is the matter, what did he say?" A small brown hand patted his shoulder.

Javes looked into Tali's eyes. He let out a deep sigh, tucked the metal back in his packet. He took her hand and held it briefly. After having promised her a ride on the train, he felt terrible. "He said we can't go on the train with the camel and goats."

"Well, then we don't go on the train."

Javes heaved a deep sigh. He needed to get to Tiverius and fast. "It's still a very long way to Tiverius."

"Further than we have already come?"

"Probably as far." In distance, at least. They were probably more than halfway time-wise.

"I don't mind."

"But *I* do. I want to give this map to the doga as quickly as possible."

"Then let's get going—hey, there's another camel."

He turned around to see where she was looking, and sure enough, it was a smaller beast, female, with a fluffy light-coloured pelt. It wore a harness for a cart. The cart stood next to it, and two men were unpacking the contents into a railway freight trolley.

An old bent grey-haired woman sat on the driver's seat of the cart, clutching a walking stick.

One of the two men—middle-aged and quite round in the waist—saw Javes' camel and met Javes' eyes.

He jerked his head. "Oy!"

Javes gave the rope to Tali and joined the man. The two camels had noticed each other, and his camel started doing that lip thing that male camels do when they smell the ladies.

"What are you doing with your animals when you go on the train?" the man asked.

"Nothing," Javes said. "I'm not leaving them, so we're not going on the train."

"I thought there would be a stable somewhere, but there doesn't seem to be anywhere to house them."

"Sorry, I can't help you there. I'm not from here either."

The man nodded, pressing his lips together. He looked at Javes' camel. "That's a very strong beast you have there."

"We've come from Ysherra. He's a windwalker camel."

The camel was holding up its head in the haughty way only camels can. At that moment, Javes was incredibly proud of his camel.

"Oh. Plenty of camels there." The man glanced at his male companion, who now had to unload the cart alone. The group also included a couple of middle-aged and younger women, as well as a couple of children. "Well, my mother can't walk, and we can't ride that far because she needs medical attention."

"I'm really sorry, but I can't help," Javes said.

The man went back to the cart. Javes turned around to go back to Tali when the camel's owner called behind him. "Hey!"

He held out the rope of the female camel. "Take her. I'm going to have to set her loose otherwise, or give her to someone who knows nothing about camels."

Javes' mouth fell open. "How much do I owe you?" He rummaged for his belt pouch.

"Nothing. If we happen to meet in Tiverius, you can hand her back to me. She's a fine breeding animal and her wool is of high quality."

Javes didn't know how to begin to thank the man.

The camel came with a saddle with attachments for a cart, a blanket and headgear, including an ornamental headdress that consisted of strings of little metal disks attached to each other with loops of wire that fitted over the animal's head. Javes had no idea what it was for, and Tali said that it must be terribly annoying for the poor camel to have these strings of glittering metal disks dangling from its head.

There were no saddlebags, so Javes bought some and they took the animals to a vacant block on the outskirts of the town where they could graze and drink and get used to each other. His camel chased the new camel for a bit but, having been divested of his male tackle, soon conceded defeat.

The black clouds of the approaching storm still hung on the northern horizon. Javes had hopes that they would be able to outrun it.

While the two camels grazed, Javes and Tali spent some time rearranging the packs.

Then Javes tied the new camel's nose rope to the back of his camel's saddle. He helped Tali into the saddle and patted the beast on the shoulder so that it rose, first on its back legs and then the front. Tali held on tightly to the top of the saddle.

"I'll let you ride on your own once you've become used to it," he said. "First we need to make sure the new camel isn't nervous and doesn't do anything strange."

The camel turned out to be well behaved, much better than his camel. They made their way out of town, against the stream of the crowd and people still joining the queue to get onto the train.

"How far is it to Tiverius?" Tali asked.

"A long way. It will take us more than a week to get there." In a way, he didn't mind not being able to get on the train, even if it annoyed him because he wanted to deliver the map as soon as possible. On the other hand, he preferred being independent and not having to rely on the vagaries of whether the trains ran and who was waiting on the platform. He'd read the stories of chaos that followed the explosion in the City of Glass and the following refugee crisis. Many of those had arrived by train. Older people told the stories about these trains of death. The people had been wounded, and many of them exposed to so much sonorics that even people from the City of Glass died.

The city guards of Tiverius had put everyone in big camps, and had locked up important people in those camps, including people who should have been presenting their case to the doga. If there were any parallels with his situation, he did not want to become stuck in a camp where he could not deliver Karlen's message.

"We need to name the camels," Tali said, breaking his silence.

Javes turned around in the saddle to look at her.

She shrugged. "Camel One and Camel Two doesn't do much for me."

That was true. "The goats don't have names."

"Yes, they do!" And she went on to name all the animals that followed them, including the white one, which had not belonged to Pashtan, and the two kids that had been born since leaving Ysherra.

"I'm not even sure I can tell the difference between all the goats."

"Oh, you're such a boy. Useless at telling the difference between anything. Don't tell me you can't tell the difference between the two camels either."

"Of course I can."

"There you go. They need names. They're a part of our travelling family."

That was also true. "So, what would you name them, then?"

Naming a camel turned out to be more complicated than he had imagined. You couldn't, for example, give camels people names, and some of the camel names were really hokey, or so Tali informed him. You also couldn't name a camel after its physical features.

"Because how would you like to be called 'Whitey'? A name like that is an insult to such a proud animal."

And so on and so forth. Javes was happy that Tali had returned to her former self, and the subject of naming camels kept them busy for most of the day, while the dark clouds remained on the horizon and every step of those camels brought them closer to Tiverius.

CHAPTER 3

SADY REMEMBERED WHEN Viki first came to him as a student. He had looked younger than his age, was petrified of his tutor Alius, stuttered and mumbled his way through his weather reports and got terribly upset if people questioned his science.

The job of Chief Meteorologist had been thrust upon him when Sady challenged for the position of proctor and won, and Sady had fully expected the Meteorology Department to replace him as soon as they got a selection process going.

But Viki had very quickly grown into a confident young man. He was thorough, gentle, patient and kind. Most importantly, he dealt well with conflict, never showed his anger in public and shrugged off the ridiculous demands, claims and conspiracy theories that always surrounded the job of Chief Meteorologist.

He was, and Sady was biased of course, the best Chief Meteorologist Chevakia had had for a long time.

Sady never thought he would have to bury him.

But Viki's body had been brought to Tiverius by the Balloon Division yesterday, and Sady had gone over to the morgue to look at it. He had seen the juxtaposition of the terrible injuries inflicted by the murderers and the peaceful expression on Viki's untouched face.

He'd come to the morgue because he wanted to know that there

27

had not been some sort of mistake and that the body in the coffin didn't belong to some other unfortunate man, but no, it was Viki and no, no one had seen a sign of Lana who had been with him.

Sady had said his private goodbyes then, letting his tears flow, and cursing the flare-up of violence along the border and worrying himself sick about Lana's fate.

And now it was time for the public farewell, and once again, he stood in the graveyard.

Even the weather was appropriate for a meteorologist's funeral.

Little specks of rain spattered the attendants and a blustery cold wind blew over the hillside.

Fayala han Marianna, Viki's faithful wife, stood amongst her ten children, her face blank with grief. Viki's oldest daughter was eighteen, starting at the Scriptorium, and the youngest was a little chubby boy who was yet too young to understand what had happened.

Just looking at them, looking at the oldest children wipe their red-blotched faces, watching the stoic expression on Fayala's face, imagining what she must feel like, tore Sady inside. No family should have to go through this for the sake of—what? No one even knew what Arania wanted or whether this was the long-awaited revenge for the crushing defeat delivered by his brother Milleus.

Sady rearranged the blanket over Loriane's legs. Tears were running over Loriane's face.

"I feel," she said in a hoarse voice. "I feel like we will come home and Viki will be sitting in the kitchen chatting to Myra."

Viki had the rare ability to get along with anyone. He would amuse Myra with his jokes and Loriane with his knowledge of crops and growth cycles. He would talk to Myra's husband Farius about the army and about technical things.

No more.

Sady hoped that the Aranian murderer who had killed him knew what a wonderful life he had taken, that he slept badly at night, knowing that Viki had ten children who were now orphans, and a wife who needed to look after those children rather than worrying about where to get money to feed them. He hoped that the Aranian murderer would die a slow, painful death being tortured by the souls of those whose lives he had taken.

He hoped that wherever she was, Lana was giving her captors a hard time, that she would fight being taken to some important man's harem, that she would take the first opportunity to escape, and heaven forbid, even seek revenge for her tutor's needless death.

What had Viki done wrong to deserve this?

Sady felt numb.

After the ceremony, he exchanged a few words with Fayala, while they were both too overcome with emotion to say much. Most of the children were crying and some of the little ones were shivering with the cold wind.

"How can I help you? Are you all right with the financial advisor I've sent?"

She nodded. Her eyes glittered. "Once the payment from the doga comes through . . ." She swallowed. "We'll be fine for a while. I'll have enough time to brush up my teaching skills and apply to schools."

"You shouldn't have to do that."

"Someone has to bring in the money. I'd love to have a young man to live in the house to help me cope with all the jobs in the house, but we'll get there. The children can help. I'll teach them what I know to do, and get others to teach them the things I can't do."

"I'll send Farius around once a week."

"Thank you. That will help me until I get on my feet."

Sady admired her strength. He didn't know if, given the same situation, he would have the same resolve. In fact, he was sure he wouldn't, seeing how he had wallowed in inaction for all those years that he had lived alone.

She dug in a satchel that she carried at her side. "I wanted to give you this." She pulled out a stack of papers which flapped in the wind. "It was in his suitcase. I though it might be of use to you."

Sady leafed through a couple of pages. There were maps, notes, drawings and a stack of letters. Nothing seemed terribly out of place, but Sady spotted the name Ysherra several times, and that might be of interest. "Thank you. Please let me know if there is anything I can help you with. Don't hesitate to ask."

She said she would do that, and shepherded her children to a waiting coach. Sady went back to his truck, where Farius was helping Loriane into the cabin.

During the cheerless ride to take Loriane back home, the anger built inside him. He was no longer a young man, but that didn't mean that anyone could invade his country, randomly kill his citizens and abduct his daughter and that he would not get angry. That he would not want to raze the entire country to the ground. In fact, why hadn't Milleus burned the entire city of Kadrish to the ground and populated it with decent Chevakian people?

Must they wait until Arania made the first move to start this long-awaited war? No, he could surprise the troops across the border, go in with the Balloon Division and bomb all the camps to rubble—

And Lana might be in one of those camps.

He felt sick.

The truck stopped at the house's front gate and the helpers set up Loriane's chair. Sady and Farius helped Loriane down and into the chair.

Sady pushed it up the path. He said to the driver, "Just wait out here. I'll be back soon."

He wheeled the chair up the ramp that Farius had made to get the chair up the steps, and into the house.

"Sady?" Loriane asked in a soft voice when the door had shut behind them, leaving them in a bubble of silence.

An all-knowing look passed between them. She knew how he felt and with that one mention of his name was asking if he was all right or wanted to talk about it.

He sighed. "We have no option but to declare war on Arania."

She nodded. Once she might have protested because, having lived through many years of it, Loriane knew the cost of war on the normal people of the land. "Do you think she's still alive?"

Lana. He couldn't bear the thought that his only daughter might no longer be alive. He had to hope. "There is a good chance. There are many reports of Aranian soldiers taking women as presents for their highly ranked officers and princes or whomever they owe favours. In the way their culture works, there are never enough women. Men, they have aplenty, especially ones that have leadership ambitions. But women will produce more fighters."

He felt sick at the thought of his Lana, his smart and intelligent daughter, reduced to a breeding machine.

"By all accounts, she is not the first woman taken, and we will fight to get all of them back. And we will fight to stop the raids and seal the border."

Although all of this was so much more easily said than done. The women would probably bring a host of Aranian friends and half-Aranian children and the resulting mess of loyalties would be similar to the integration of the Perian refugees into Tiverius. Parts of the city still bore the scars from that time. Sealing the border was an equally impossible task. The border ran almost the full length of the continent. It petered out in the northern desert and in the southern mountains, where the location of the border had never been set or agreed on. He would have to fight battles over those pieces of land before the border could be defended. It was time to fight those battles. Arania had to be stopped, especially those units that were using sonorics weapons.

He pushed open the door to the kitchen. A pan stood on the stove, issuing big clouds of steam, but Myra was elsewhere in the house.

Sady wheeled Loriane to her usual spot at the table and poured some more tea for her. "I'm going to have to go back to work."

"I know. I'll be all right here."

He hesitated, but then turned back and said the words he'd been turning over in his mind for days now. "I'm going to ask the Balloon Division to take you to the City of Glass."

She raised her eyebrows.

"We've heard from six of your children and I think you should go to visit them."

"What about you?"

"It's going to get nasty here. If we declare war on Arania, they will come for us, like Milleus went for Kadrish. They're already gathering on the border closest to Tiverius. They could be here within a day with balloons, two on horseback. I can't guarantee your safety in Tiverius. I'll send some good people with you. Myra and Farius can come. I'll join you later."

"But what if Lana comes home?" Loriane said.

All Sady could do was shake his head. If Lana was in Kadrish, she would not come home for a long time.

Then Sady left the kitchen and walked back to the truck waiting at the gate.

He went straight into another emergency closed session of the doga. General Selidas was there with his maps and further intelligence about the position of Aranian troops. Apparently a unit of men had also been taken from Watya—news that had been delayed and overshadowed by the stories of the floods in the region. Strangely enough, the capture rated no more than a single line mention in the local news.

Sady asked why.

"This has been going on in northern Chevakia for many years," said one of the northern senators. "It is ironic that it has taken the abduction of the proctor's own daughter to finally get action on it."

Yes, Sady remembered hearing stories of rogues and bandits making life unsafe in the north. To be fair, there had never been many of these reports, nor had there been any indication that the Aranian army was involved or that there was any kind of plan to it. Without knowing those two things, the recorders at the doga had filed them in the "we'll do something about it if it gets worse" basket. They had failed the people of the region.

He knew it and he wasn't proud of it. To the contrary, he should have done something sooner, but he hadn't judged the situation clear enough to be able to act on it.

Act on it, they would.

How was another matter.

General Selidas hung up a large map and described all the routes that Aranian troops would be taking to Tiverius and how long it would take them to get there.

A major battle could be less than a day away.

But the doga's Arania expert said, "The biggest problem we face is not that Arania wants to conquer Chevakian land. Their actions are entirely driven by internal conflict. King Orik is set to choose a successor soon and each of the major princes is eager to show his military prowess. Show it to their father, that is, so that they get chosen by him as successor. It has little to do with us, other than that the princes each want to be seen as the one who will pay back Chevakia for what we did to them."

Apparently, according to the expert, Prince Nayek was not dead, as earlier reported, and this created a three-way contest for the throne, between the princes Denori, Sferuk and Nayek.

"And they would go to war over this?" a senator from the central district asked.

An older senator said, "You would not remember the civil war in Arania after the defeat by our army and before King Orik came to the throne. They went through a blood bath of successive princes who each brought their private armies and absolutely slaughtered each other."

Another senator added, "Arania has been spoiling to have a war for a long time."

"At least ever since Orik sent us the turd," a third senator said.

Yes, that object in its ornate box that stood in its glass showcase in the foyer outside Sady's office. That had made it perfectly clear that Arania didn't want to talk. A new king *could* be persuaded to talk, but Sady didn't hold his hopes up.

The Aranian expert said, "I honestly don't know anymore who would be the most favourable candidate from our point of view. We used to be in favour of Nayek, because he appeared to be interested in trade, but he is showing himself to be just as ruthless as the other two princes."

"Will it honestly make a difference who is chosen?" Sady said. "We don't have any formal contact with Arania at all." Communication couldn't possibly get any worse.

The expert said, "Failing a successor who is interested in building bridges between the two countries—and none of them seem to be— we just want the king to make a choice, to appoint one of the three, so that the princes can stop showing off their projects and curtail their threats of revenge for their loss in the last war. This issue came up in the last succession struggle, too. Orik was full of talk about revenge, but little of it eventuated. Once he was on the throne, the need for him and his brothers to show off was gone. They forgot about the projects that would potentially lose them support of the citizens. Wars usually do. It is only heroic to talk about war until the first mothers, wives and daughters start burying their sons."

Sady knew that very well, and sometimes an attack, or a defensive action, was *still* the best action to take. He thought this was such a time, but he worried that his judgement was coloured by Lana's fate. He wished he could resign and concentrate on using what few contacts he had to find her, but instead, the fate of an entire country rested on his shoulders.

General Selidas reported on the state of mobilisation of the army. Many troops were already in the western regions, and he had sent out mobilisation calls to other units elsewhere in the country. In addition, every man who had served in the past five years had received a letter to report to the local garrison.

"We need to get all the sonorics suits out of storage. We also need to ask the Eagle Knights for assistance. Once we locate the places where the Aranians are doing their sonorics work, we will request help from the Eagle Knights to destroy the installations, because they alone can come close without sustaining harm."

"Are Aranians immune to sonorics?" a senator asked.

Someone else said, "Some of them must be."

"They wear suits," said General Selidas. "I don't believe any of them have resistance."

After that, temporary meteorologist Rodi spoke briefly about the storm in the north and the current weather patterns. Winter was finally going to hit Tiverius with a cold snap that had snow falling on the highland just west of the border.

It had never snowed there in living memory, a fact that Rodi mentioned in passing, but that disturbed Sady deeply. Back in the time of the sonorics threat from Peria, the Most Learned Alius had devoted most of his life to devising systems to protect Chevakia from the deadly influence. The weather prediction patterns they had used were based on it. But after the destruction of the machine, patterns had changed, and the world was still settling. Isandor had mentioned unknown sonorics sources and the possibility that there might be another machine. Sady had thought the flare-up was caused by Aranian meddling but, in truth, he didn't believe that the couple of small devices built by the Aranians could have that much effect. The world couldn't handle another sonorics threat on top of everything else.

The meeting was over and people streamed out of the doors. A couple of confused citizens waited at the door. They'd been wanting to attend the session and had found themselves locked out.

Sady went up to the general. "I want one Balloon unit to stay in Tiverius," he said.

"Your personal action unit?"

"No, it is for my wife. I want the men to take her to the City of Glass. I fear Tiverius will become the next focus for Aranian attacks."

The general nodded and did not offer an opinion to the contrary.

SADY RETREATED TO HIS ROOM, where he sat at his desk, staring ahead, his mind in turmoil over what he was doing, what it might mean for the Chevakian people, and whether it was the best thing for him to do.

With the return of Viki's body and his possessions, Lana's bag had also come back. It had been left behind in the luggage compartment in the bus. Sady fingered the familiar clothes, hoping that somewhere Lana would be safe and that she would find a way to let him know where she was. He swore he would send the army to get her out.

Lana had brought her spyglass, wrapped in clothes so that it wouldn't get damaged. He'd been upset at how much she'd spent on it, but in hindsight, how petty he'd been. Who was he to tell Lana what she could do in her spare time and what she could spend her own money on? Secretly, he'd been afraid that her interest in the sciences meant that she would be left behind and never find the love of a partner. It had taken him so many years to muster the courage to tell a woman that he loved her. He was terrified that a similar lot would befall her. But Lana didn't seem to care about boys at all, and after all, it was her life, and he couldn't live it for her.

Freedom was what she deserved, and that was something worth fighting for. Not just her, but all the other girls who had gone missing from northern Chevakia.

Then he turned to the stack of papers and notes that Fayala had given him and leafed through. Most of them were measurements that Viki had been looking at on the train. In the long lists of temperatures, he had circled some measurements. It had been *how cold* in Tamyra?

And then he had received this morning's report of snow in Velora. The world was behaving strangely.

He now went back to those data, and noticed a big cell of cold air that had pretty much formed out of nowhere. Out of interest, he checked the other measurements, and noticed a small rise in sonorics. Nothing to get excited about on its own, but in combination with the other data . . .

He waded through pages of reporting. Apparently, on the day that Lana had travelled on the train, the whole sky had lit up with skylights at night. It had been visible in a wide band across north-western Chevakia and in Arania.

Damn it. Rodi had gathered this data. Why hadn't he said anything about it?

He debated going to the Meteorology Department but realised he was falling into his old trap of making things easy for his workers, making them think that he would run around for them. So instead he called his secretary to send a messenger to ask Rodi to come to his office as soon as possible.

Rodi came in not much later. From the way he breathed, Sady figured that he had run from the Scriptorium, and he felt irritated that Rodi had time to go to the Scriptorium while neglecting to report important data to the doga.

He bowed. "Proctor. You wished to see me?"

Sady shoved the tables and graphs over the desk. "Have you seen this?"

Rodi picked up the papers and read through. Sady studied his face. Rodi showed no emotion, but his cheeks were colouring red.

"Viki was a very meticulous worker," Sady said. "He took great pride in his work. When a major weather event happened, he would map out all the data, including temperature, surface pressure and sonorics levels. He would collate maps and present them to me the next day, and he would make efforts to predict the formation of main weather cells, hard as they have become to predict."

"I am not Viki."

"Let me assure you, I am painfully aware of that. I will tell you one thing: the fact that all this data has gone unreported does not make me happy. It looks like we have missed a major event because of this regression. Who knows what else lies hidden in this data. We know there have been strange phenomena in the north. How long since you've made a complete map of the weather data of Ysherra."

"Ysherra stopped reporting to us two weeks ago."

Sady spread his hands. "And you didn't tell me?"

"The line to the north is very vulnerable."

"You don't have to tell me anything about the northern telegraph line. It's become more unreliable than the southern one. That is telling us something right there—"

"It's just the heat—"

"The heat, or the rain, or the snow even." He gestured angrily at the piles of data on the desk. "Anything. It's *weather.* You're the Chief Meteorologist. Make the reports. Get to it!"

Rodi rose and scurried out of the room.

IN THE NEXT FEW DAYS, Sady prepared for Loriane's departure. He made sure she had enough warm clothes, that she had all the correct medicines and letters from medicos that stated exactly how she needed to be treated if problems arose. He wrote to Isandor about the reasons for sending her, about Lana's abduction, about the ultimatum. He also wrote to Rider Barton asking for assistance from the Eagle Knights in locating and destroying the sonorics devices that the Aranians had produced. Since only Perians could get close to those machines without being affected, they were going to need that help. He also wrote to Loriane's children that their biological mother was coming and wanted to see them. Loriane herself found it hard to concentrate, and her hand kept cramping up if she tried to write for too long.

It pained Sady to have to send her away, but he saw no other option. Once the Aranians were here, it would be too late. He gave the same advice to everyone who would hear it: send your vulnerable family members out of the city, if you can.

Tiverius would not be unprepared.

Loriane left a few days later.

Sady came to the balloon base with her. He helped her into her seat and folded her wheelchair. He hugged her with a feeling despair. Everything was changing and not for the better. She looked so frail.

"I'll come when I can," he said, struggling to contain his tears.

"When you hear from Lana." Her eyes glittered.

Then he did cry. They held onto each other.

This was not how he had imagined spending his old days. He

would have expected to retire to a home in the country and grow vegetables and keep ducks, not take a country to war while his wife was slowly dying of a wasting illness in another city.

He left her, looking forlorn and lonely, and watched the balloon rise into the air.

"Look after her, Isandor," he whispered.

How he wished he could go with her.

CHAPTER 4

*T*HE **TRUCK STOPPED** in front of the house, dark grey in the misty street. The door opened, letting out a couple of men in different types of military uniforms. Tamerane knew the uniform of the low-ranked guards and she recognised the face of Commander Lakrey, but she didn't remember seeing the grey uniforms of the other two men.

They spoke briefly to each other, and then Commander Lakrey entered the yard to the house.

Tamerane shifted her weight from one foot to the other so that she could see the door without having to touch the curtain.

She heard the front door open. Her father , standing in the hall-way, said something, but she couldn't make out his words through the door. Commander Lakrey replied. He laughed.

"Come away from that window, dear," her mother said behind her. She sat in the chair by the hearth with her hands nervously tending her embroidery. No, her mother didn't like it when the military men came, and she didn't even know about Zeiro who had been hiding in the back shed for the past few days.

Tamerane knew, and every time a soldier came, she was afraid that he would be discovered.

"I want to see what's going on," Tamerane said. "I don't like those men or what they are doing."

"Well, your father made a promise and he's fulfilling that promise."

Her mother's answers were always the same. *Your father is fulfilling a promise*, but increasingly Tamerane wanted to know just what her father did when he left the house for hours on end, and whether that had anything to do with the ship of death with the rows of body bags on the deck, from which she had seen Zeiro escape.

She had seen the bodies being unloaded onto carts, but had no idea where they were taken, and no idea what those men had done to justify being killed with icefire weapons out at sea.

And while that happened, her mother was just sitting here doing embroidery. *Because your father has made a promise.* Well, her father made a promise to Isandor, too.

The door opened and her father came in. "Tamerane, get your cloak. The General wants you to come."

For the briefest of moments, Tamerane hesitated. What if she refused? What if she said enough is enough? Let her go back to the City of Glass, while her parents could stay here to fulfil whatever duty they thought they had to an Aranian prince who cared nothing about duty.

But, as so many other times, she had no way to refuse, because her father and these military men held power over her. Because they controlled her means to escape. Because if she kept quiet, she would have more freedom than when she protested.

She took her cloak from the hook on the wall and followed her father into the dreary weather. One of the guards held open the door to the cabin of the truck. They entered its plush-seated interior, with wood-panelled walls and ceiling, and little oil lamps to light the dark interior.

General Pakori sat there, a thin man with a big hooked nose like a bird and short-cropped dark grey hair that always looked a little dishevelled.

He nodded at her father while ignoring her.

Tamerane sat next to the window, gathering her skirt around her knees. The general never spoke to her, and barely acknowledged that she existed. But he still wanted her to come, huh?

The Commander and the two soldiers in grey also climbed into the cabin. The guards shut the door from the outside and climbed into the front with the driver. Tamerane could see them through the little window between the two sections. Their chatting and laughing voices drifted through the thin metal wall between the two compartments.

The truck started moving through the narrow streets of Curack. The houses were built from local stone, dark grey, with roofs of black slate. Because of the frequent mist, the roofs on older houses were usually covered in moss and lichen.

Houses rarely had yards, especially in the centre of town, and stood directly on the street. This made the streets narrow and pokey.

Everything was grey and wet and the cobblestones glistened with water. The few people outside huddled deep inside their cloaks.

After a few turns, they picked up the main road inland. The vehicle increased speed here while passing the types of businesses one would find at the edge of most towns: a water mill for making flour, a horse breeder, a cart maker, a carpentry business and a blacksmith.

After that came only fields with sullen-looking cows, orchards with leafless trees and plots of fallow land.

Tamerane guessed they were going to the military base. She had been there a few times before, and those visits were always highly controlled. She would have to wear a veil so that the poor soldiers weren't subjected to her female face, and was only allowed to go a few places in the camp.

After traversing the delta formed by the river whose mouth was Curack's natural port, the road wound up a gentle slope and then down the other side into the next valley. Here, large orchards covered the rolling hillsides, the trees now clinging to the very last of their yellow leaves. Occasionally, she would see a house, usually a few interconnected blocky buildings that, from the outside, looked like an ugly, rambling shed.

But after they passed the crest of the hill that looked out over the town, the truck turned left and bumped along a narrow track, first between two stubble fields, and then through a forest with dark pine trees. Pines, of course, didn't lose their leaves in winter.

Tamerane definitely hadn't been here before. The main base was much further down the road.

The truck stopped in the middle of the forest. A soldier got out to open a gate and shut it again when the truck had gone through.

They continued up the track for a bit more, until they came to a clearing with a settlement that looked like a disused logging camp. It consisted of about ten or twelve roughly made wooden cabins. All of them looked like they were about to fall in, with moss growing on the roofs, broken windows and doors and weather-eaten walls. One even had a pine tree growing on the roof.

There was no one else to be seen. The truck stopped in the middle of the clearing. One of the guards opened the door.

Tamerane climbed down the little ladder after the general.

The ground was kind of springy, full of big—and now dead—tussocks of grass.

A few remains of the site's logging history remained: piles of logs, overgrown with lichen and moss.

It was cold enough here that her breath steamed. The air was very, very still.

Tamerane listened, but she heard no voices or other sounds that indicated that a camp was nearby.

"Follow me," the general said.

He led the way to one of the huts, walking around dew-laced tussocks. The hut's roof sagged with the weight of a huge mound of moss that supported several small saplings.

The general pushed open the door, which looked like the wood was completely rotten and would fall into pieces any moment, but had been fortified from the inside.

The air inside the single-room cabin smelled of damp earth and mushrooms.

A wooden staircase in the middle of the unpaved floor disappeared into the earth. Warm light and the sound of male voices drifted up from below.

The general preceded Tamerane and her father down the stairs.

They came out into a cavern where a group of about twenty men sat at long benches around a table. A couple of pans bubbled on a stove in the corner, blowing steam into the already steamy and earthy air.

The men greeted the general in a jovial, informal way. And then some of them spotted Tamerane, and elbowed each other, glancing at her.

All of them had that sly, oiled look that came with men from a certain class in Kadrish. Probably all of them were princes and had the same father. Maybe even the general was that father.

The general walked past the table to a door on the other side of the room, which led into an underground passage dug into the earth. It was dark and quite narrow, and the general had to be careful not to hit his head on the many timber support beams. Walking at the back, Tamerane found it hard to see. The passage was lit only by sparse oil lamps, and the ground was slippery with muddy puddles.

Wafts of unpleasantly warm air streamed through the tunnel. At times, the air was laced with a strange smell that pricked her nose and that she didn't like. It wasn't decay exactly, but for some reason she kept thinking of the dead bodies on the ships that were loaded onto carts and taken away.

The general led the way down another staircase and came out onto a raised walkway that surrounded a large room. On the floor below stood a piece of equipment in the shape of a box about twice the height of a person. Tamerane knew what this was by the way it consisted of layers of tubes folded back on themselves like multiple lengths of rope with metal plates in between.

It was an icefire machine.

During her first weeks here, Tamerane had helped improve early crude models of these machines made by the Aranians. It had shocked her to find that they were reproducing technology that up until now had been the realm of the ancient past. Magic, some said. Even King Caldor had only ever *used* the machine already available to him, the powerful one under the City of Glass, even if he had also modified it and had learned a good deal about its operation. But no one had ever *made* a new machine, no matter how weak, crude and incomplete the Aranian concoctions were.

She had learned the science of King Caldor in the classes her father had forced her to attend at the Brotherhood of the Light. She knew how to calculate how long the pipes needed to be, how much metal to use, how thick it needed to be, in order to create a field that would spin icefire from the air.

The general led the group over the walkway into a room off to the side. Apart from a normal door that opened outwards, the room had a second door, made of a sheet of metal, that closed snugly on the inside of the door frame.

The room contained a couple of seats, all of them facing a window of thick glass. Tamerane could see the fine metal gauze structure inside the glass that warded off icefire when the mesh was activated with a current. A man in uniform waited here, next to a control box with levers on the wall next to the door.

The members of the group sat down. Tamerane found a seat next to her father. She didn't like how he avoided meeting her eyes. Did he know why they were here? He definitely knew that she didn't like any of the Aranian projects.

These machines were dangerous, even if only for the simple reason that they needed a part called an igniter, which calibrated the strength of the initial current that got the machine going. It was a vital part in making sure that the machine didn't produce so much icefire that it exploded, and it still relied on ancient technology. No one could reproduce these parts, because no one had ever tried. Tamerane had once seen the inside of the device—usually a metal globe that slotted into the control panel—and it consisted of a true maze of little wires and connections that would take at least ten years of development to reproduce.

There *were* only a few of these devices, and Aranians had been circulating them to the machines they had built, which meant that at any given time, a number of them would be in operation in a site where there was no igniter to control the machine if anything went wrong.

It was dangerous and stupid, but the general had given her a blank look when she told him, and her father had made her promise afterwards never to talk to the man like that again.

Once the soldier at the door panel had given the thumbs up through the window, a door opened in the far corner at the ground level of the main room. A man in a thick, all-covering suit entered. He carried a stepladder, which he set down next to the machine. He climbed up, took something out of waist pouch and inserted it into the machine.

Well, at least they had an igniter here today.

Tamerane could feel the icefire engine turning on, a low hum in the air. Her father took in a sharp breath, but the Aranians were oblivious to it.

That was another stupid thing: most Aranians were *not* resistant to icefire, and yet their superiors were messing around with it.

The man jumped down the ladder, picked it up and ran without even folding the ladder. The bottom of the ladder was the last thing Tamerane saw before the door shut.

They waited in silence.

In the main room on the other side of the glass, the field had built up so much that the first golden threads of icefire snaked towards the top metal plate.

For a while nothing happened. Tamerane's father watched the golden strands with wide eyes. The Aranians just stared. They couldn't see it.

Then the door opened again. A small figure came out: a boy, no more than four years old, Tamerane guessed. Her stomach knotted with discomfort. She had known about the presence of children in the military camp and could have guessed that they were probably not there for family reasons, because Aranian families were even stranger than Perian ones, but she had thought that they were the children of prisoners or workers.

They might be, but this boy was a subject for experimentation. See how long he can stay in that room until he dies.

The boy wore no protective clothing at all. His expression was vacant, as if he had just woken up. He walked a few paces inside the room, staring at the golden strands that danced over the top of the machine and vanished into the room's ceiling and walls. Tamerane was sure that he could see them just as sure as she was that the general and other Aranians couldn't. Their expressions were all distant and closed, as if they knew that experimenting on children was vile, but believed it served a greater purpose.

The only one showing any emotion was her father, and his face shone with sweat. Likely he could also see the strands of icefire, and knew that any Aranian who went into that room would die within the hour. Maybe he was afraid that the boy would die, too. Maybe he didn't want to see it. Maybe he was afraid of her anger once they were alone together. She wished she understood what went on in his head.

And here were all these grown men, just *watching* as a child died, and no one *did* anything. None of these junior Aranian officers with blank faces dared speak out against that monster of a General.

How could they not care?

How could Aranian society have slipped this far?

The boy stood in the room, as if dumbstruck. He looked up at the ceiling and at the window where he would probably not see the spectators watching him.

"His resistance is remarkable," Commander Lakrey said in a dry, emotionless tone.

Tamerane swore that one day, she would hit him in the face, or knee him in the groin, or better still, turn one of his awful weapons on him and burn the flesh off his bones.

"Wait until you see this," the general said, and to the soldier at the door: "Turn up the machine."

Tamerane turned to the general's smug face. "There is a young *boy* in that room. Do you want to kill him? Would you kill him if he was your son?"

Too late, she realised that it was an irrelevant question. High-class Aranian men had so many sons, it was her experience that they truly did not care about one more or less.

The man at the panel hesitated, glancing at his boss.

The general sniffed. "Just turn it up, will you?"

Tamerane balled her fists against her sides.

Her father put a hand on her knee. His expression said *please, calm down*, but Tamerane was too angry.

Legs trembling, she got up from her seat, and crossed to the door as if she was going to help the soldier. She hesitated with her hand on the doorknob. What would going into that room do to the child inside her? She was resistant to icefire. Isandor was resistant. She believed he had even inherited some of the capabilities of his great-grandfather to use icefire as magic.

She opened the inner metal door. An alarm started ringing in the room.

Commander Lakrey swore loudly. "Shut that door, stupid woman!"

Tamerane opened the outer door and slammed the metal door behind her. That did not stop the alarm. Men's voices shouted inside the room.

She ran along the walkway, and down the stairs to the ground floor.

Golden strands of icefire flowed around her. Like most people who were resistant, the strands actively went out of her way, unless she held up her hand and called them. That was the only way to manipulate icefire that she had ever learned in those classes given by the Brotherhood of the Light, back when a lot of icefire still hung around in the City of Glass.

The boy still stood there, staring at the machine. Even if icefire didn't kill him, it seemed to affect his mind. He didn't look at her, didn't even seem to register that she was there.

First, she would turn this terrible thing off.

Tamerane opened the cover of the control panel. A second alarm started ringing. She put her forearm across all three levers that controlled the current, the flow of fluid through the pipes and the distance between the top two plates and pushed them down as far as they went. The top metal plate came to rest on the metal tubes, which shorted the current and sent a spark along the wires that linked the two plates. With a crack and a puff of smoke, the machine stopped.

The boy started crying.

Tamerane wished the suited man had left the ladder inside this room. She would have climbed up and taken out the igniter. They would get no more work out of her unless they promised not to use it on innocent children again. Better still, she would have thrown it in the ocean.

But she had no ladder. So while yet another alarm joined the first two, she gathered up the boy and ran to the nearest door. It was locked.

What? They were going to lock him in this room?

She had to keep a tight grip on the boy. He was screaming and pummelling her shoulders.

Tamerane spoke soft words to him. "Be quiet. I'll have you out of here soon."

She tried the next door and this one opened. There was another metal shield door inside, which, when she opened it, set off another alarm. Everything in the building was ringing and honking and wailing. People were now entering the large room. She could hear the footsteps on the stairs. A man shouted orders. His voice echoed so much in the chamber that the words became lost. The boy struggled in her arms.

It was dark in the room she had entered, and the air smelled unusually musty, laced with a tang of decay. She had no idea how to get out of this place. They were underground and, likely, the only way out was through the stairs that came out in the dilapidated hut.

But she wouldn't give up until the soldiers caught her. Maybe there was a second passage out, maybe—

A soft shuffling sound came from the darkness to her right. The boy jerked, almost falling from her grip.

"Be quiet, just hold still!"

This four-year-old was much heavier than she thought he would be.

Tamerane stared into the dark, wondering who—or what—was in the room.

She needed a light, needed to see where she was going. In the dark, she ran her one free hand along the wall. There had to be a door somewhere.

It was too late. A couple of soldiers appeared as silhouettes in the doorway. One of therm shone a light into the room, a white beam of pure icefire light.

The glow of the light showed the edges of glass cabinets on table legs. They were like display boxes, with glass top and sides, and there was something inside . . .

A bloodied hand.

Hair matted with blood.

Pale grey skin.

A deep hole cut through a ribcage.

The boy in her arms was making snivelling sounds and people yelled in the room, but Tamerane's ears didn't register any of the meaning of their words. Swallowing hard to keep herself from vomiting was all she could manage.

A man shouted, "For your own safety, let him go!"

Tamerane turned around, squinting against the glare. "Go on then, kill me. Isn't that why you brought us here?"

Like these poor people in this room, for their bodies to be displayed in cabinets.

"No, it's not about you. Let him go!"

Only then did Tamerane register that the boy had become even bigger and heavier and his limbs had grown longer and thinner, and that the sounds he had been making while she stood frozen, watching the bodies in the room, had not been *human* sounds.

She set him on the ground and when the light from the soldiers' torches lit him, he was not a boy at all, but some . . . creature.

His skin had gone dark and wrinkly; his arms had lengthened into big leathery wings. His feet had turned into claws, his face had narrowed and grown into a snout.

Drawn-up lips showed a row of sharp teeth.

Whoa!

Tamerane reeled back.

By the skylights, what was that?

The creature lowered its head and crouched, ready to spring at her. It hissed.

"Watch out!" a man shouted.

A soldier ran to Tamerane and pushed her down to the ground.

The creature flapped its huge wings. The air in the room whirled. The icefire light detached itself from its holder. It struck the creature in the chest and vanished.

The creature hissed and flapped its wings. Soldiers at the door screamed and dropped to the ground, covering their heads with their hands. An oil lamp fell. The shade broke and an oil stain spread over the floor. The burning wick fell in the oil, which burst into flames with a "foomp". The creature screeched. It took off, scattering the flames with flapping wingbeats, and then crashed into the doorframe with a thud. It tumbled head over wing to the ground and scurried on all fours through the doorway.

Male voices shouted in the big room where the machine stood and where more lights had come on.

A man screamed. The creature hissed. There were thunks and crashes and thumps.

Father.

Tamerane scrambled to her feet and ran to the door.

A couple of men were holding the creature down, sitting on its back and pinning down the wings. It bucked and wriggled and hissed and screeched.

Soldiers shouted to bring a cage, and people ran up the stairs to the walkway.

Tamerane joined her father on the gallery, looking down at the poor creature.

Was she imagining it, or had it become smaller?

But no, as she watched, the wings grew shorter and loose skin was absorbed into the body. The thin limbs became chubby and child-like.

If Tamerane hadn't seen this change before her eyes, she would never have believed it.

"It's a dacon," her father said to her unasked question. He didn't meet her eyes.

"They *exist?*" She had read about dacons and had seen drawings of the creatures in old books. The Brother who had taught her in her last year at the school had devoted an entire lesson to them. He had told the class full of seventeen-year-olds that dacons were the result of interbreeding people with the purest blood from the two main clans in the City of Glass: the Pirosians, who were mostly Knights, could not see icefire and could do nothing with it, but weren't harmed by it; and the Thillei, the royal family and nobles, who could see icefire and could shape it.

She had considered the shapeshifter children to be one of the many myths that the Brothers told her about icefire.

Her father snorted. "Sometimes, I wonder why we sent you to the Brotherhood of the Light for tuition."

Tamerane spread her hands. "Father, they talk about *magic.*"

He nodded at the creature that had almost changed back into a boy. "What do you think this is?"

"Well . . ." Not magic, because magic didn't exist, but . . . some very strange things could be done with icefire nevertheless.

The Brothers always said that magic and icefire were the same thing, and that magic could be used to—

—to cut out people's hearts and turn them into servitors, blue ghosts that felt no pain and blindly obeyed their makers. King Caldor used them to sow fear amongst people who criticised him.

Her cheeks burned.

Surely that couldn't be what the Aranians had tried to do with the people in that horrible dark and smelly room. And if they had, they had found that surprise, surprise, if you cut out someone's heart, the person dies.

Because magic does not exist.

Her father looked down. He could likely see her anger. Dacons, servitors, this was all stuff that King Caldor used to do. Things that scared the common people so much that, when they finally got the upper hand, with the aid of the Knights, they cut the king's body in many pieces so that he could not come back to life, no matter how much magic his supporters used.

A couple of soldiers carried the boy out of the room. He was looking around, confused. She now also remembered reading in one of the old books that these creatures were said to be incapable of communicating in any form with anyone other than their birth parents.

"Well," General Pakori said.

He stood on the gallery on the other side of her father, making another effort not to look at Tamerane.

"I am very sorry," Tamerane's father said.

Tamerane felt like slapping him in the face, screaming at him, *You are using the vile things that King Caldor was killed for, that we vowed never to allow in our world again, and you're sorry that you can't manage it?* What was wrong with him?

"Well . . ." said the general again. "That puts a premature end to the things I wanted to show you."

Her father's shoulders slumped. "I *am* sorry."

"The van's waiting outside." The general turned around and left the room.

Tamerane and her father were escorted back to ground level, where it had started raining, and where the truck stood.

Only the driver and two guards waited with the vehicle, but the latter two went into the cabin with them, so neither Tamerane nor her father said anything during the ride back to town.

She glared at him, and he sat with his hands in his lap, avoiding her eyes, avoiding the glares of the two guards.

Tamerane would have to go into the harbourmaster's office later in the day, but the truck dropped them off at the house.

She followed her father to the front door steps and into the hall.

Only when the door shut were they alone, at least until one of the servants turned up.

Tamerane gave her father a hard look.

He mouthed, *What?*

"What have you been meddling with? How long has this been going on?"

"You were most insolent today, daughter."

"I am *not* sorry about that. I thought, no, I *hoped* that somewhere through all this idiocy, you had some honour, some dignity to do the right thing, but I must have been mistaken. I'm done with this."

"Stop shouting." He jerked his head in the direction of his cold study.

Tamerane kept her cloak on inside the room. Her father sat down behind the desk, still wearing his coat. She sat on the very edge of the seat opposite him, wrapping the fur around her. Her stomach was making weird noises, as well as forming into a hard ball before softening again. She remembered that from her previous pregnancy, too. How long could she still hide it?

Her father folded his hands on the surface of his desk. He was not wearing gloves and his fingers were white from the cold.

"You have to understand. There are few of us left." He spoke in a low voice.

"Who's 'us'?"

He hesitated before answering. "We—me, my father, you—are some of the last magicians."

The last what? "Sorry, magicians?"

"The dacon and some of the other features of icefire are at risk of dying out. The art of magic is old and no one practices it anymore. It's a beautiful art and must not be forgotten. Much good can be done with it."

"But also much ill." Tamerane felt sick. "Are you saying that our family supported King Caldor when he was in power?"

"We supported his scientific and engineering projects."

"Seriously? Did you support cutting out people's hearts and filling them with magic so that they turned into servitors?"

Her father shook his head, a sad expression on his face. "That is what you've learned, what is being taught in schools. The children are made to fear and vilify the king. There is no nuance in any of the history teaching as far as King Caldor is concerned."

"Who needs nuances? The man was a butcher!"

Her father continued shaking his head. "There is so much that you don't know."

Tamerane was speechless. The history accounts of the thousands of people turned into servitors and made to terrorise the citizens did not lie. There were far too many eyewitness accounts for those stories not to be true. They didn't need "nuances" and there were no mitigating circumstances.

But, in a way she should have seen the signs: the books, her father's obsessive connection with the Brotherhood, itself an old and quaint institution. The fact that—wait. She understood in one terrible moment of clarity. "That's what we're doing here, right? There is no more icefire in the City of Glass, and the Knight Council is happy with that, so you went to a place where icefire is being created. No, you even offered me as a lure to help fine-tune the machines so that the Aranians would welcome you and let you conduct vile experiments with *children*—"

"He is a *dacon,* not a child."

"I don't care. You or someone must have *bred* this poor boy for your purposes. What are you going to do with him? Wage war on Chevakia or the City of Glass? How many people are going to die?"

"If you would just let us explain what it's about."

"Explain? Explain to me why a few days ago, I saw a boat arrive in the harbour with rows and rows of dead bodies. Most of them looked Chevakian to me. I . . ." She almost said something that would give away that she had talked to a survivor from that ship, and Zeiro still hid in the shed in the back yard. "I found that really disturbing, and none of the guards volunteered any information about it. This place is a big death trap and you have brought me here to cause more deaths."

"How do you dare say things like that about your parents?"

"Because they're true?"

"Lies. We always have the best in mind for you. But we have to consider the position of the family."

"All right. I understood when you said that Prince Denori financed your business and gave our ships preferential treatment but that it came at a price and he was demanding favours to be paid back. I really understood that, and that it put you in a position of trouble, and I wanted to help you, because I *care* about you. But we weren't forced to come here by the prince at all, were we?"

"We were."

"Maybe, but there was a voluntary component to it as well. You *wanted* to come here because you could work with people who didn't have any hang-ups about the ethics of working with icefire. You *wanted* to work with this wonderful magic, no matter that it kills so many people—"

"You are being an insolent brat. You don't understand anything."

"Then explain it to me."

"Stop yelling. You don't want to draw attention with your voice. The servants are listening and they will inform their superiors."

Tamerane snorted. "You've been giving me this hush, hush, don't talk in front of the servants ever since we got here. I'm thinking it's just a way of getting me to shut up. I don't believe you anymore."

"Daughter, out of all the things I say and you disagree with, at least believe that one. We are being watched, constantly."

She *did* believe it. There were enough guards and other hangers-on around who were in the position to do just that. She lowered her voice. "That still doesn't make everything else all right. You have not given me one good reason why you are involved in this foul project that I saw today. I am pretty sure that a dacon has feelings. And also that dacon births are so rare that you had to have been selecting people with the purest blood from the two opposing clans, the Thillei and Pirosians. These people don't just find each other by accident."

"There is a lot more to it than that. Dacons are incredibly powerful magical beings. They occur in other people as well."

"Dacons are dangerous!" She couldn't even believe she was having this discussion, after all the proof of history of the vile things King Caldor had done.

"Dacons can be trained."

"In however many days of their extremely short lives? To do what? All they can do is kill." Tamerane spread her hands.

He gave her a hard look, out of arguments. As always, her father rarely argued, and just did—and told her to do—exactly as he wanted. "The Aranians will be increasing their guard on you, after this."

"Because you tell them to?"

He didn't answer that.

She didn't need the answer. She understood. He had *sold* her ability to calculate and understand the science of icefire. She was his spearhead tactic for keeping the business alive. In her youth, she had been sent to Brotherhood schools in order to prime her for her father's opinions, and the Brotherhood had failed to convince her of his opinion.

From his point of view, she could not be allowed to fall under the influence of another family, not even if that was the royal family. An heir on the throne, that would be beneficial, but marriage, no.

She was not a prisoner of the Aranians. Her jailer was her father, and she would do well not to get him to the point where his anger would make him lock her in the house or something.

Tamerane did not want to talk to him anymore, because it would be pointless. Having thought this way all his life, and planned this for years, he would never change his mind.

Tamerane went back to her room in the harbour master's office. She worked on calculations, but entered a lot of deliberate mistakes in the figures. In fact, she went over a few old calculations and entered a factor-of-ten error in one of the machine calibrations. These people deserved to have their machines explode in their faces. She did, however, make sure to ask the same types of annoying questions to the guards who stood, bored as ever, in the room with her.

Plotting to get out of here would take a long time. She didn't have a long time, because already some of her dresses felt tight. Whether the child was male or female, there was no way that she would let the heir to the Perian throne and to the Thilleian clan fall into the hands of the Aranians, where—she realised with horror—the child would have a high value as a breeder of more dacons. If she could plan nothing else, she'd run away and hide somewhere in the mountains, with all the risks and discomfort that would entail. Her first birth had been hard enough for her to know it was not something she wanted to do alone in a cold cave, but she'd do it. If not even running away was an option, she'd prefer to kill herself and the child. But that was a last desperate option. She'd try to get out. She'd ask Zeiro to look for opportunities.

When she came home later in the day, she scoured the cupboards upstairs for useful things. She found a large fur cloak of the type that many local men wore, which she brought to Zeiro when she went to bring his food.

"I would like you to go out into town during the day, and look for ways we can escape."

"But we're going into winter. It will be hard to travel, even if we can steal a cart."

"Can you sail a ship?"

"No. I grew up near Tiverius."

"I was thinking that going over the ocean might be safer than over land." Tamerane knew some basics, although she was far from a confident sailor. It would have to do. Zeiro's expression remained doubtful. "Anyway, I want you to go into town, look for any opportunity, and any other people who might want the same and who can help us."

"You're sure you don't want to wait until spring?"

"I can't. I'm pregnant with the king's child."

CHAPTER 5

$\mathscr{I}$T TOOK THE KING a couple of days before he came to the Mothers' House to look at his new plaything.

Lana spent those two days checking out the library, talking to women in the house and looking at the garden, which was the only place that Mothers were allowed to go without reason and without escort. She discovered nothing terribly interesting in the library and, besides Selwa, who called the shots, she found only a few of the women mildly interesting; most were there only to be pampered and lead vacuous lives.

Most of the garden was on the front and sides of the house, and it contained little waterfalls, quiet ponds, clipped hedges and many flowering plants. It was lush, tropical and wonderful.

The biggest pond was at the front of the house, hemmed in by the patio and glass doors of the reception room, the lawn and the boundary wall at the far end. That wall wasn't terribly high and, rather than to keep people from getting out, served to stop people falling all the way down into the streets way below. You could lean on it and admire the magnificent view over the city: a jumble of closely built houses with white-washed walls punctuated by the many golden domes and arched temples dedicated to the Mother. She could also see the harbour, and the ships with tan-coloured sails that slowly glided past the lighthouse, took on or delivered freight and left again, always going either north or south.

Lana spent a lot of time watching those. She had no patience for embroidery, didn't want to learn Aranian songs and preferred to stand here and think of all the freedom she would have if only she were allowed out of this gilded prison. She also didn't care about fussing with her hair or painting her face, even if the latter was considered almost compulsory for Mothers.

She wondered about Nashi and the other Chevakian girls, but most of all, she worried about her parents. She asked for pen and paper, but when she got them, didn't know how she could write to her father without revealing his identity, or even how she could get any messages delivered to Tiverius. And she was afraid that if she left any draft letters in a drawer somewhere, someone would discover them and might be able to read them.

Her letter remained unwritten. Instead, she made some sketches of the house and garden and drew more fantastic representations of the Great Wanderer and its children as she imagined them from close up. The Great Wanderer was, by her surmise, a lot closer than the other stars, and this was the reason that you could see it move. It was not that stars didn't move—one of her books had spoken about Aranian star charts that were different from today—but that they did so slowly enough as to be imperceptible. The Great Wanderer moved in a certain pattern over a period of eleven years and its children accompanied it. The other wandering stars also described patterns that they repeated. To Lana's thinking, this meant that the wanderers were worlds like the earth and all belonged to the Sun. So she drew circles like the moon, and crossed out many of her drawings because they just made no sense, and eventually decided that she might not be able to write to her parents, but writing to Tamerane in the City of Glass would not arouse any suspicion.

So she did that, and spoke about her latest discoveries with the light plates. Few enough people in Kadrish could read Chevakian, and the number who would be able to read Perian would be fewer still. So she thought it safe enough to add a small note at the bottom. *Please tell my parents I am in the Mother's House in Kadrish and am safe.*

She then had to find out how one went about getting a letter delivered. There was, apparently, something like a telegraph office in town that also looked after letters which were taken on the train services. Letters to the City of Glass would go via sea on one of the freight ships that regularly made the journey. Getting something to the telegraph office involved asking the guards at the door who then contacted the citadel's administration offices, who had to approve of the communication.

The guards assured her that the letter would be delivered, but couldn't say anything about how long it would take, so she went back to hanging around in the garden, even doing some weeding, growing a lot more freckles—because her skin didn't tan at all—and wondering how to get out.

It was during one of those days that a servant came into the garden to call her into the reception room, and she followed him through the garden, looking at the back of his athletic legs. She'd been surprised to find attractive young men working here, but Selwa had told her—shamelessly—that the men had pledged service to the Mother and they went to the temple first thing every morning to "give her their seed". They did this, apparently, in a bronze bowl at the altar, and the purpose was to keep them from becoming tempted during the rest of the day. This was such a strange country, so blatant about things that were discussed quietly, if at all, in Chevakia, and openly ignorant about important things, such as provable knowledge and science.

There was a lot of activity in the reception room. Servants had come in to bring flower arrangements to every table—flower arranging was another thing Mothers were allowed to do.

Kitchen maids were walking in and out with trays laden with little cakes and dainty tarts and pieces of fruit. Women often entertained male guests in this room. Usually these were fathers and brothers of the women whose families lived in Kadrish. Occasionally someone would receive a private astrologer or some other practitioner of hocus-pocus, but these men all came alone or in small groups. Never had she seen such a large group of *men* in here.

Standing at the back wall was a row of guards in royal livery or red and yellow. There were so many of them!

The men seated on the couches were all older and dressed in rich clothing. She had seen some of them before, when they came to see women privately and went to the quiet rooms upstairs. Lana wasn't quite sure what happened there—or at least she was reasonably certain that the one thing she *could* imagine happening there in fact didn't. Those visits seemed to involve the spreading of cards over a velvet cloth and something mysterious with beads on a string and a pair of octagonal dice cut from bone.

Apparently, this was also something that Mothers did when they knew or suspected they were carrying a child, and some of those actions banished ill spirits and ghosts.

Hocus-pocus.

Amongst all these soothsayers, followers of magic and other superstitions sat one man she had not seen before. He looked fairly tall, sat upright with a straight back and was neither unusually skinny nor soft-fleshed. He had short grey hair and a short, neatly clipped beard, also grey. His eyes were light grey, and they were sharp and intelligent.

Lana estimated him to be in his fifties, although when she realised that this had to be King Orik from the way the servants treated him, she knew that he must be much older, a few years short of her father's age. The man next to him spoke in his ear, and the king turned to Lana.

He smiled.

It was a disturbingly friendly smile. His teeth were clean and straight. His hands were clean and sported a few gold rings. He wore rings in his ears, too, small ones with little ruby jewels. His skin bore the spots and marks of many days spent in the sun, and while he obviously no longer had peach smooth cheeks and wrinkle-free eyes, Lana found herself appreciating his carefully cultured looks.

But maybe, just maybe, her position wouldn't turn out to be too bad after all. If he was friendly, he might at least see sense?

He gestured at the couch opposite him, which didn't normally stand here, but had been moved in order to make a broader circle for all the king's hangers-on.

Lana sat in full view of all those people in the king's company.

"Mala, that's your name, eh?" the king said.

"Yes, Your Majesty." Lana clamped her hands between her knees. She didn't want to seem nervous and she didn't want look afraid. She also didn't want to embarrass Selwa, who was sitting on the other side of the room, behind the king.

Over the past few days, Lana had come to appreciate Selwa's frank honesty. The king would not hurt her, she'd said. He was not like Denori or Sferuk or Nayek. The king was a master in the royal art of love and would seek to pleasure her. She could rise high in his favour by letting herself be pleasured.

Did that include talking about matters of state or asking for special favours, Lana had asked, and Selwa's face had gone serious.

"If that is what you want, you might do everyone a favour and jump straight off the tower. Yes, the king will extend favours to women he likes. They could be pleasure trips on his boat or visits to markets. But he is very guarded about his safety and who knows what about him and his habits, and rightly so. With every year he refuses to retire, the chance increases that one of his sons will knife him in the back. You are the vehicle to prove his virility. You are a *Mother*. Don't forget that. Don't meddle in things that aren't yours to meddle in, because he will not forgive you."

And looking at those grey eyes, Lana believed every word of what Selwa had told her.

He leaned forward on his knees. "I hear you are interested in the arts."

Lana cast a sideways glance at Selwa. How was she supposed to answer this? Was it a good or bad thing? "I'm a meteorology student at the Scriptorium in Tiverius. We prefer to call that science rather than arts."

He cocked his head. "But meteorology is the *art* of trying to predict the weather?"

"We do a pretty good job at predicting the weather. We have a lot of things we can measure." Lana's heart was thudding in her throat. Was he deliberately trying to provoke her?

He chuckled. "Ah, Chevakians are always writing down and measuring things. Do you think you'd have much to measure here?"

"I would love to set up weather stations around the city." All around the country, if she got half a chance, not that she thought there would be any chance of that happening. "I hear that Aranians study the skies. I hear that the citadel has a famous library of star charts and books of observations."

"Did you hear about that all the way in Tiverius?"

"The Scriptorium likes to study the world objectively, setting aside differences between countries. But we only have a few Aranian works. *Star Signs and Their Meanings* is one of them."

"Ah, poor old Sizek." The author of that book.

"Poor?" Her heart jumped. Had she made a wrong choice mentioning him?

"He's very, very old and very confused."

"He is still *alive?*"

"He is, but his mind seems to be elsewhere most times."

"But that is incredible."

"Hmmm. I can see we will find plenty to talk about. I came here to see if you would be a suitable guest at my dinner table. It seems that you are. I think we will get along fine. Do make sure that you're ready before dinner this evening. I will send my guards along to collect you."

And that, apparently, was the end of the meeting. He pushed himself to his feet. The women scurried aside to make a path for him to the door. As the back of his richly embroidered tunic disappeared out the door, it struck Lana that all the women in the house, young, older, slender or very heavily pregnant, had spent time in the king's private rooms and had sex with him.

"Come," Selwa said, groaning while heaving herself to her feet. She made a gesture towards the stairs. "You passed your first inspection. We have to get you ready."

"Getting ready" apparently involved being washed all over, having her legs shaved and rubbed with scented oil to stop the itching from the scraping blade, having her hair washed and combed until it was dry. While Selwa was carefully shaving the patch of hair between Lana's legs into a narrow strip and exhorting her to "Please keep still, because if I nick you, he'll be upset with me," a young girl came to lay out a gauze outfit in bright pink. Lying on her back on a bench with her legs spread, Lana had no energy to complain about the colour. The Aranians seemed to be keen on bringing out the pale-ness of her skin, ugly though she thought the colour looked on her.

"Are you done?" she asked Selwa, who was wiping her blade on a towel.

The skin in those sensitive spots was wet and made her shiver.

"Not quite." Selwa took an earthenware pot and stuck two fingers inside. They came out with a glob of jelly-like salve. She proceeded to smear it all over Lana's sensitive parts. The smell of it—like flowers—drifted on the air.

"The king is not a young man," Selwa explained, as she had explained everything she was doing. "Certain things don't come as easily anymore to him. If he tries to enter you and your skin is dry, you will get cuts and bleed. It might get infected."

Well, thanks, that was way more information than Lana wanted, but that was Selwa. No shame about the whole process at all.

"There." She slapped Lana's thigh with a salve-covered hand. "Get your outfit on."

The singlet was horribly short and the loincloth embarrassingly revealing. You could even see the little red spots where Selwa had shaved the hair just above her legs. The gauze dress that went over the top didn't hide much at all, and the whole ensemble was horribly, eye-bleedingly pink. Lana felt like a giant pink candy. Selwa loosened her hair and tied it back with a jewelled hair band and stuck a couple of flowers behind Lana's ear.

Through all of this, Lana's mind worked to come up with ways to reduce the embarrassment, since escaping her fate did not seem to be an option. She tried very hard to feel privileged to be chosen by the king, but all she could think of doing with that privilege was think of how to put a knife through his heart while he was in a vulnerable position. Not that this would help her in any way.

She didn't, *didn't* want to be treated as a piece of meat to be presented for enjoyment by an old powerful man.

But there was no way out, or at least none that wouldn't get her killed, and she was sure that whatever defilement the king could bring on her, it wasn't worth the pain her parents would suffer if she died.

Getting out of here alive, that was her aim.

Secondly, getting out while inflicting as much disturbance on the Aranian royal family as possible, as long as that didn't threaten her survival.

It was time to go. Two guards in the livery of the king came to the door and Selwa gestured for her to go with them.

Lana rose, taking a few steps to gain her balance because her knees felt weak. She schooled her face into a proud expression.

Whatever happened to her, she would let no man take her pride.

The dry air breezed through her flimsy garment. It stroked her skin in places normally covered by clothes. Servants in the corridors stepped aside and bowed. Lana left the house for the first time since coming here. The guards led her across the large courtyard at the entrance of the house. Then into the citadel's main building, which housed the official function rooms, audience halls and offices for the public.

People were still at work, and members of the public stood in lines to complete business. All were men and gave her sly, hungry looks.

From that building, the guards took her through an ornate courtyard with mosaic tiles, and pots with little clipped bushes. An ornate entry was on the other side, which she assumed to be the entrance to the king's private quarters, since it was in the corner of the citadel where the map she had found in the library had indicated the king's private quarters to be.

A cart stood in the corner of the courtyard with a sullen-looking donkey in front. The back tray was filled with what looked like bags of laundry. A man, the cart's driver perhaps, stood at the doorstep to a side entrance talking to another man while a woman was bringing bags of dirty laundry from inside an open door.

In one instant, Lana recognised the tall, brown-skinned woman: it was Nashi.

Nashi stopped, halfway through heaving a bag onto the cart. Her eyes widened.

There was no way Lana could stop and talk. In fact, it was probably best not to show that she knew Nashi at all. But oh, how Lana's heart ached to speak to her, even if only to hear some Chevakian.

Nashi made a hand signal underneath the bag she was holding. Lana was unsure what it meant. Unsure that she could do anything about it even if she knew what it meant.

Nashi watched her progress all the way into the building's ornate entrance. Lana tried very hard not to stare back and alert the guards that they knew each other.

She entered a big and airy hall with a big set of double doors on the other side.

As soon as they entered, liveried servants on either side of those doors flung both doors open before bowing deeply.

Lana went inside, leaving the guards behind at the door. In the next hall stood a couple of servants, all attractive young men, who bowed and gestured for her to go up the stairs. She felt like a goat on the way to the altar to be sacrificed.

Lana climbed the stairs, meeting more servants at the top. They guided her to the door on the other side of the landing.

She did know the man who waited at a little table in front of the door: it was that horrible astrologer. He had his star map spread out on the table in front of him and held those coins and gemstones in his right hand, ready to spread more of his claptrap about her future, or more specifically, about the number of children she would have, or something equally ridiculous.

He bowed to her.

She didn't bow back. She had no respect for this man, none at all. She couldn't imagine, if he was as studied as he said he was, that he believed his own nonsense, and that made her despise the man even more.

In complete silence, he tossed the coins and gemstones over the map. The ruby and one of the coins came to rest in the Lion star sign, another coin in the Wagon. The two other gemstones fell between the star signs and the last coin fell in the Horse.

He smiled, showing straight teeth with bits of gold. "Go ahead inside. Your visit will be fruitful. We will have a prince before the year is out."

The doorman opened the door behind the astrologer's table. Lana walked past, ignoring the horrible man. All sorts of thoughts went through her mind when she walked past him. The deep disdain she had for practitioners of astrology, the fact that he didn't even seem to believe in his own predictions and the fact that she definitely didn't believe in them. She could be silent and tolerate this nonsense, but it would be weak to say nothing at all.

At the door, she turned around and said, "You're lying."

His mouth fell open. "You . . . how dare you? I am the king's brother."

"I bet the king has far too many brothers."

She didn't wait to see his reaction, but continued into the king's private quarters. The door shut behind her with a snick.

The first thing she noticed was the warmth of the air in the room.

Kadrish had a fairly warm climate, with cool, moist winters, where the breeze brought showers from the sea.

It had gone quite dark outside really quickly and at first, she didn't see much, because it was even darker inside the room, with only a single sparse lamp on a table set with gold-rimmed plates and glittering glasses.

The window on the far side of the room offered a magnificent view over the city and the harbour. A huge cloud mass hung over the ocean, with lightning flickering within.

Then her eyes became used to the low light level.

Most of the floor was covered in a thick red carpet. Along the wall to the left behind the dining table, there was a huge bank of bookshelves, groaning with leather-bound tomes. There was a little desk, too, full of papers and inkpots.

To the right stood two couches and a low table between them. King Orik sat here. He wore dark trousers and a simple linen tunic, unadorned except for a strip of embroidery at the hems of the short sleeves. There was no crown or circlet. The only jewellery he wore were the rings on his fingers and golden loops in his ears.

He held his hands on his knees. His upper arms bore red tattoos of the type that the younger princes had on their heads. Age had not decreased his muscles, even if it had softened his skin tone.

She had expected . . . she didn't know what. To be grabbed from behind, to see a man naked on a bed, to see a room full of instruments of sexual torture.

He gestured at the table.

"Sit and eat," he said.

Lana chose the chair closest to the door. The heavy wood felt cold on her near-naked buttocks. The king pushed himself up from the couch and sat opposite her, far enough away that she was completely out of his reach.

The servant rushed across to pour her some wine in the gold-rimmed glasses. He picked his glass up. "Dinner will be served shortly." He lifted the glass, indicating for Lana to do the same. He drank.

Lana took a careful sip. Best not to drink too much, to keep a clear head.

Aranian wine was good, and this was sure to be of the highest quality.

The servant came back with a huge tray of bowls that exuded a heavenly smell and proceeded to unload it onto the table.

As Lana set the wine glass down, it occurred to her that her father, the proctor before him, her uncle and a whole string of Chevakian men in power would kill to be in her position: facing the Aranian king in a semblance of an amicable dinner. Well, at least the only sword to come out tonight would be one of the metaphorical kind. She could handle that. Selwa said not to get political during these visits, but she was going to try anyway. Carefully, without taking it too far.

The servant proceeded to scoop little bits out of each bowl onto both plates. Lana wasn't sure what all those things were. There seemed a good bit of fish involved, an expensive delicacy in Tiverius. There were also little parcels wrapped in leaves which the servant cut in half—there was some sort of white stuff inside—and drizzled with fragrant oil. He arranged little dollops of some kind of mashed fruit or vegetable around it, and arranged a longbean in a closed circle on the inside of the circle of dollops. Then he poured orange sauce inside the bean-circle and added two drops of clear fluid out of a tiny bottle. He took a box from his pocket, flicked open the lid and *whoof* the sauce burst into flames.

Lana gasped, but the fire lasted only a few heartbeats before going out.

The servant did the same thing to the king's plate.

The king was looking at her, an expression of bemusement on his face. "Never seen this before?"

She shook her head.

"The fluid in the bottle is a strong distillate. Some people drink it, but it is my preference to burn it." He picked up a gold spoon and scooped up one of the dollops of mash.

Lana figured that it was all right to start eating. She wasn't sure how hungry she was, but the food truly looked like nothing she had ever had before. Not even at the annual Proctor's Banquet did the kitchens serve food like this.

It tasted wonderful, too, and her plate was soon empty. The king seemed to like this. He noted, "I don't like thin women. There has got to be some flesh to those bones. Soft and healthy, not scrawny and mean."

After one dish came another, each more intricate and wonderful than the previous. They all involved tiny amounts of food and took a fair amount of time to set up by the servants.

Meanwhile, the king questioned her about her age, her education, what she was doing in the place she had been captured and her background. She mostly told the truth, because lies would be so much harder to remember next time.

She was shivering in this flimsy outfit. Not just because the air coming into the open window was chilly, but because she was nervous. She still didn't know what to expect and wanted the evening to be over.

He was watching her, but not in the way she had expected. She had expected him to be leery, to stare at her breasts or her thighs or other parts of her that were uncomfortably visible through the thin cloth. But he merely studied her face.

"How much southern blood is in your veins? You're Chevakian, but you look Perian."

"My mother is from the City of Glass." A stab went through her heart. She would probably never see her mother again.

He gave her a sideways look. "Mala, hmmm?" As if he knew it was a false name.

"It's my name."

"I would have thought your mother would have given you a more southern name, like Rosane or Tamerane."

Lana's heart jumped.

"Do you know these women?"

"I've never met either of them. Lady Rosane is King Caldor's daughter in law. She lives in Tiverius and is very old. She plotted to return to her father-in-law's rule, but that was thwarted. Tamerane is . . . do you know Tamerane?"

"How could I not know Tamerane? I have never met her, but her studies in astrology are known all over the world."

Really? Lana had not known that. Tamerane definitely didn't have that fame in Tiverius. Did this have something to do with the relationship between the old noble families of the City of Glass—of which Tamerane was a member—and Arania? "She studies astronomy, not astrology."

"Small detail."

Lana didn't think it was small at all. "I have always admired the notes on features of the sky made by Aranian observers." She deliberately avoided terms like astronomy. "When you said that Sizek is still alive, I was amazed. Would it be possible for me to visit him?"

The king frowned. "He is a very old and sick man."

"Or I'd be just be happy if I could visit the astrology library. Imagine all the things I could write about when combining the Chevakian and Perian knowledge with the wealth of historical observations in the library."

"Yes. Although the last time someone attempted that, it didn't go so well."

She was surprised that he knew about that Chevakian study that sought to discredit Aranian astrology.

"This would be purely about knowledge. I believe that I and my friends are about to discover something important. Imagine if Kadrish could be credited with some of this work."

"Hmmm." He fingered his upper lip.

Lana's heart was thudding. She didn't think her request was political in any way.

"Hmmm," he said again. "Somehow, it seems that Chevakia insists on asking us questions that are rude and come from their perceived place of superiority, like that time they had the hide to tell us that Milleus the butcher of Kadrish had died and therefore the time was now ready to forgive. Well, I said I'd have forgiven them if they had executed the man the moment he came back to Chevakia, and not given him a big victory parade. Or even if they'd made him stand trial for the atrocities he committed. But they did none of that. I wrote several letters in response and never sent them, because I realised only one response would do, so I asked for a nice box, and after a particularly nice meal, deposited my excrement in there. I sent them that."

The turd that still stood in the doga foyer. "It's still there." And she told him how Chevakian children went on excursions to the doga building and would learn about the offending object in its glass case.

He snorted. "They put it on display? Really?"

"Really."

And then he started laughing, and Lana couldn't help laughing, too. Although she couldn't imagine this man doing a thing like that. He didn't seem crude enough.

Uncle Milleus had been so old that she barely remembered him. The war and the aftermath were truly events from a different era.

"Anyway, *I* have no intention to ridicule anything or anyone. If I'm allowed to work in the library and correspond with my fellow students in Tiverius, I will give Arania credit where it is deserved. It could be a better way of repairing the relationship than through old men who have too many memories of who did what."

For a moment, he stared at her, and she was afraid that she had gone too far, but then he laughed again. "You are quite the scheming little vixen, are you?"

"I use my brain. I've been taught that way. I'm sorry if I disappoint you."

"No, you amuse me."

"I want to be more than amusing. I want to discover the truth of the world. When I do, whoever helps me will get their part in the history books. Wouldn't it be good if the history books said that Arania made these discoveries possible, because the king made it possible?"

Lana's heart was thudding. She thought he looked interested, at least for a moment, until he shook his head. "You're still a woman, and I intended a specific purpose for you."

He snapped his fingers.

The servant dressed in white came in again. "You called, Your Majesty?"

"Take her next door."

The man bowed to Lana. "If you would come with me, honoured lady."

This was it: the time of her humiliation.

She rose, her legs trembling. The king made no sign of getting up. He flapped his hand. "Go with him and get ready. I'll think about your words. Excite me in the room next door and I may look upon them favourably."

He dragged the carafe over the table and poured himself some more wine.

Lana had no option.

The next room was more like what she had expected.

There was no bed, but a very large couch with a satin sheet draped over it. There was a chair raised to waist height that consisted only of a sloping chair back and two wooden platforms. It reminded her of the birthing chair that stood in the attic at home, a leftover from the days when her mother worked as a midwife. This contraption had a lot more padding, but its purpose was painfully clear. In the corner stood a huge bath full of steaming water and next to it a table with a collection of bottles containing oils.

"You can undress and leave your clothes here," the servant indicated a chair. "The king will be along shortly."

He started to fuss with the bottles, pouring syrupy content into the bath. Then he brought out another carafe of wine and two glasses.

Because he kept looking at her, Lana could see no option but to undress. The gauze dress was useless anyway, and the loincloth was rather tight and had started to annoy her because of the way it wedged between her buttocks. The singlet . . . well, it didn't annoy her, but it didn't hide very much. She pulled it over her head, shivering.

The man poured a glass of wine from the carafe. "Drink this. It calms you down." As if he could see how tense she was and how much she still hoped to find a way of avoiding what was to come.

The wine tasted sweet, and the glass was very small, so it was gone quickly. When she set it down, the door opened and shut and the king came in.

The servant bowed. "Everything is ready, Your Majesty." He scurried out of the room.

Lana sat petrified as the king crossed the room. The first thing he did was pick up the second wine glass and knocked back the contents in one gulp.

Then he slowly started undressing. First the tunic went over his head. He was wrinkled underneath with a good amount of greying chest hair. Then he took off his trousers. His legs looked strong, with a deep ugly scar on his right thigh. That looked nasty.

He kept his undershorts on.

He gestured. "Get on there."

Damn it, that terribly embarrassing chair. A wooden step was connected to one of the legs, and Lana climbed up, sat on the bottom of the sloping platform, turned around, lay down and put her feet on the two platforms. There. Naked, vulnerable, with her legs spread ready for the taking.

The king scooped a bowl of warm water out of the bath. He collected a hand towel, dipped it in the water and gently placed the warm cloth on her private parts. It was a strangely pleasant feeling. He went to get a bottle of oil, poured some on his hand and proceeded to massage her thighs. His fingers were strong and his touch confident. He worked his way all over her body, telling her to close her eyes and relax.

By this time, the wine had started to work. Selwa had said that he was good at this, and he was. Lana was embarrassed that he managed to excite her twice. The first time, it took her by surprise and she even cried out. When he entered her, she didn't mind anymore, because he had earned it. She might have been fooled that part of her even *longed* for it. Certainly her body was betraying her in that way.

When he spilled himself inside her, he clung onto her for a desperate moment afterwards, while his breathing calmed and his muscles relaxed.

He pushed himself up.

"You can . . ." He cleared his throat. "You can wash yourself and get dressed now. Write to the library for permission to visit."

Something about his voice made her take a good look at him. His eyes glittered in the low light of the lamp. A glistening tear track ran over his cheek.

Lana's heart jumped. She didn't dare ask what the problem was. She waited until he had pulled on his clothes and had gone from the room. Then she got up, washed herself, put the awkward loincloth and silly singlet back on, pulled the gauze dress over the top and left the room.

King Orik sat in the other room by the hearth. He was staring out the window into the darkness.

"Well, I'm going then," Lana said. "Thank you so much for permission to visit the library."

He didn't reply.

"I just wanted to say that it wasn't as terrible as I'd imagined."

Now he turned around and gave a snort. Both his cheeks were wet with tears. "No. A lot of things are worse than being tended by a man who knows how to be a lover. Even if you didn't ask to be here—I know that, girl, you don't need to tell me. But a lot of things are worse. When you get older, you'll know."

Lana hesitated. Did he want her to say something or not? Would he appreciate it if she did? But in the end, her desire to leave was bigger than her curiosity. She wasn't sure if she wanted to know what bothered him. For the time being, she had what she wanted.

CHAPTER 6

THERE WERE MANY TIMES since signing up with the knighthood that Zaina thought she would die of fatigue. The days were so long, and the training so arduous, that every night she went to bed early and had to be woken in the morning. Of course, it being winter, daylight was limited to a glimmer at the horizon and even in the middle of the day lights were on inside, and you could only barely see enough in the street to miss walking into other people.

Not that there was much time for walking in the street.

She had no time for anything, not her workshop, not the animals, apart from the eagles. She had to attend briefing meetings first thing after breakfast each day, and from then on it was a solid day of flying, training and looking after the birds, lessons in tactics, weapons training and strength training. At night, she fell into bed already half asleep and didn't wake up until the morning bell.

And even then she often woke up swearing.

The only time she saw Jevaithi, it was when Zaina was at the top floor of the eyrie and Jevaithi walked through the dusk-lit garden along the path lined by flickering lights.

She looked lonely.

Zaina had expected to be glad to be away from the uneasy interactions with the queen, but she found herself wondering how Jevaithi was coping with her brother's absence. She asked at dinner, and tried so very desperately to make her question casual and innocent, so that no one would suspect how her heart sped up each time someone mentioned Jevaithi's name.

A Knight told her, "She'll be attending the Knight Council meetings. Not many of the council are here, so the people who are left have more work."

What that work was, no one could tell her. Not building new projects. Because it was winter and snow would fall frequently, most building activity had stopped. Not trade. Because it was winter, everyone hid inside, trade slowed, traffic over the sea almost stopped and the workers in the shipyards spent more time chasing Legless Lions from their wharfs than servicing ships.

One day, when Zaina went out with the patrol and flew out of the eyrie, there was a lot of activity at the palace. The royal coach had just come in and guards were helping a woman down the steps and into a waiting wheelchair. Her coat hung around her like a tent, loose in the shoulders. She had long curly greying hair that gave her an elfin appearance.

She looked important.

"She has come here from Chevakia because she did a lot of work with the monument for all those who died in the explosion," said the patrol leader when Zaina asked about it.

Zaina had seen this building project, eerily similar to the wall of names on the waterfront in Kadrish. It was a circular pit, a good fifty paces across where the names of all those who had died were inscribed. A metal pole in the middle of the pit looked like a giant lance, and during the highsun night, when the sun never went below the horizon, its shadow would creep over all the names and each would be shadowed at the time of day that corresponded with the person's birthday in the year.

Zaina didn't care much about politics, but one thing struck her as important: after the disaster in the City of Glass, Peria and Chevakia had grown closer, allowing free movement of people and ideas. Arania had been left out, and the only people who came to the other countries from Arania were refugees who did low work, didn't get involved in any local business or politics out of fear, and tried their best not to draw attention to themselves. That could not be a good thing.

At dinner in the big hall downstairs, the Knights and Apprentices were talking about the woman. Apparently her name was Mistress Loriane and she had been one of the great breeders before the time of the explosion. This woman was, Zaina heard, the current wife of the Proctor of Chevakia, himself an old man called Sadorius han Chevonian, brother of the much-hated General Milleus han Chevonian, nicknamed the Butcher of Kadrish.

"I got a letter," one of the Knight Captains said, and then all the Knights at that section of the table fell quiet.

Another Knight said, "Really? That you're her son? Are going to see her?"

"Yeah, I think I will. Things have changed a lot. It's not like I never knew that the mother I grew up with was not my real mother. My parents never made a secret of that."

If the problem in Kadrish was too many children, in the City of Glass it was too few. Rich citizens would pay the fertile women to have children for them. Mistress Loriane had been one of those women.

Another Knight said, "Sure, but what would you say to her?"

"I'm sure we'll find something to talk about."

"Who else got letters?"

"I understand Rider Carro is her oldest son."

"You're kidding. He's also Rider Cornatan's son."

"No kidding. He's lucky to know who both his parents are."

The Knights around the table agreed with that.

While the discussion about parents and real mothers went on around the table, Zaina's thoughts flooded with a feeling of emptiness.

She couldn't help but think of her own mother, who would never contact her again, and all her sisters and brothers and half-sisters and half-brothers. Her father would never come looking for her. In fact, her father might have been happier had she been taken into Prince Nayek's Mothers House, or before that, had she been killed along with Xalia. Being a lover of other women, she was an embarrassment to him.

After the episode with Xalia, the few sisters who were still in contact had stopped speaking to her, because they were too ashamed to be related to a woman who loved women. That was years ago.

Zaina *pretended* not to care, because she was all grown up now, ran her own business and didn't need Arania, but if there was anything she had learned in the City of Glass, it was that people in Arania were horrible to their family members. The life of an Aranian child, unless a first or second son of a prince's favourite wife, was worthless the moment the child was born and had been tallied up to the father's list of achievements.

She had joined the Knighthood with the aim of moving forward, but every day, life in the eyrie held a mirror to her face and showed her the ugly truth about herself and her country.

ZAINA WAS STILL CONSIDERED a natural with the eagles. She got her own bird, a young male she named secretly, because Knights didn't tend to name their birds. She called it Preyo, ancient Aranian for fire. She spent more time with it than with any human.

Whenever she had a bit of time, she would go up to the stable and would groom the bird and talk to it. The bird was, she would say jokingly, the only man she would ever love.

The three birds she had brought back with her from the ill-fated expedition were assigned to other teams. Rider Jeito's bird was highly trained and such training could not be allowed to go to waste.

Zaina would often give it special treats, too, as if treating the bird well could make up for having led the team into capture by the Aranians.

One day she heard one of the hunters on the team complain about the bird's skittishness. According to that Knight, it listened poorly to commands and fussed with its food.

Zaina went to check it out.

The bird greeted her with a hiss and raised all its feathers. Whoa.

"What's wrong? Are you hurt? Give me your foot." She held out her hand.

The eagle refused to comply. Its nails looked a bit long, but not long enough to cause trouble when walking on the stone.

Did it have ticks or lice?

She tried to check, but the eagle snapped at her twice before she decided that if she intended to keep her fingers, it was probably best to stay away.

The bird pulled at the chain that held it to the bar, and then inserted the curved tip of its beak in the knot, trying to yank itself free.

"Something's up with that one," a male voice said next to her.

Zaina gasped. She had not heard the stable boy come in. He watched the bird from a safe distance, leaning on the shovel he used to remove spitballs.

"Do you have any idea what's bothering it?" Zaina asked.

He shrugged. "It's not mating season and there's no wild birds around. I don't know. Sometimes they get grumpy like this. Anyway . . ." He glanced over his shoulder, where another man waited, this one in the uniform of the royal guard. "Someone's here for you."

The guard bowed. "Yes, ma'am, if you could come with me."

Zaina cringed. He would be here to ask her to help in the palace stables, where they had trouble finding a replacement for her. They'd burned through a few stable hands already, because of those temperamental bears.

She said, "I'm very busy. There are some guys lounging at the station downstairs. Can you get one of those?"

"No, you are requested specifically."

When that happened, it usually meant one thing: there were Aranians involved. Zaina quickly washed her hands at the basin in the corner and followed the guard downstairs.

He went out the building's side door to the little path that connected the eyrie with the palace and that came out next to the palace stables where she had worked before. The coach stood, empty, under the awning before the entrance.

The guard took her into the foyer and from there into the ground-floor corridor. Instead of going to the Council hall at the very end, he turned through a doorway to the right.

They entered a smaller meeting room, with a table surrounded by a couple of chairs.

Jevaithi sat there, in the company of someone she knew well, but had never expected to see in this situation: Marek.

He looked quite dapper in his Eagle Knight uniform. When they both signed up, the Knights had placed him with the intelligence division and her in the flying squads, according to their skills. She had seen little of him lately, and he looked older and more mature.

Jevaithi, too, looked different. Instead of a thin dress, she wore a more sturdy number, and her cheeks were red as if she had been outside. Zaina met her eyes and instantly wished she hadn't looked. Blood rose to her cheeks.

She sat at the table, clearing her throat. "You called for me?"

"Yes, and I appreciate that you're busy," Jevaithi said.

Not *that* busy. And oh, how Jevaithi's voice sounded like honey.

"I understand that you know this young man here?"

"We signed up together. We're . . ." She didn't know what to call Marek. *Friend* didn't really cover the relationship. "I've known him since I came to the City of Glass."

"Yes, she's a friend of mine. Damn good mechanic."

Zaina had to do her best not to cringe. Marek was a prince, even if not a major one anywhere big enough to contend for the throne, but enough of a threat to be sent to a special part of the military designed to rid the world of potentially dangerous princes. Zaina was the cleaner's daughter. "Friendship" did not cover the huge class difference between them.

"Tell her what you have just told me," Jevaithi said.

Marek told her that a part of his task with the Knights was to infiltrate the upper class to check out what the nobles were doing and to prevent them from selling further knowledge and old items to Arania.

"Last week, a man was murdered. He was of a noble family, but ran a business—rather badly, as is common. Following his murder, on the front porch of his house, there was a lot of talk about him. It seems no one liked him much and most nobles attributed the murder to *I told you someone would stick a knife in his back sooner or later.* He was said to be an unpleasant character."

Zaina wondered if she knew this man, because some of the nobles she had dealt with in the workshop could be extremely unpleasant.

"Anyway, this morning, another man was murdered. This was a man called Erendor of House Kayati, who was well-liked and well-respected. When I heard of it, his brothers had been going through his business files and found letters of threats from a source known to be aligned with Prince Denori. This is a family who knows what I am and who I work for, and the poor man's wife and his secretary revealed a host of similar threats that were made right here under our noses to citizens of the City of Glass by Aranians. First, for switching their support from Prince Nayek to Prince Denori when it was thought that Nayek was dead—"

"Wait—*thought* he was dead? He isn't dead?"

"No, you didn't know this?"

Zaina spread her hands. "What do you mean—didn't know this? I killed the bastard. He was dead."

"Well, apparently he was only gravely wounded. They took him to Kadrish to be buried, but it turned out he was still alive. He recovered and he's back. He's angry with a lot of people for switching their allegiance so quickly to his competitor half brother. He sent his thugs back into the City of Glass to reassert his position."

The blood roared in Zaina's ears. She had thought she was *safe* from that particular threat.

"And of course Prince Denori, who suddenly found himself more popular with Nayek gone, is reluctant to give up ground he won while Nayek was supposed to be dead. *He* is in charge of the most impressive military force Arania has ever seen, and as it turns out—and this is the reason I'm here—some of them are stationed outside the city."

Zaina gave him a sharp look. "Prince Denori?"

"Probably not the prince himself, but his forces. We've flown out and seen them. They're camped in the bays to either side of the city, having taken over some of the farmhouses. There are likely to be more than what we've counted, if they've dug in."

"Does Rider Barton know about this?"

"He does. He'll be calling a general assembly a bit later."

An uneasy feeling crept over her. "Why are you asking me?"

"Because you and I are the only people with a reasonable command of Aranian within the Knights."

"So, let me get this right: where are Prince Nayek's men?"

"They're scattered throughout the city, drumming up support for Nayek in the hope that the nobles and their magic will be able to shield them against Prince Denori's much larger army."

"Why don't we tell both of them to fuck off?" Then heat rose to her cheeks at the thought of having used a profanity in front of the queen, and Jevaithi met her eyes, which only deepened that damned blush.

"The nobles tried that, but that's when they started to get killed. The Aranian princes both want the extensive collections of old artefacts and knowledge of ancient magic owned by the noble families. The nobles are going to need some help. The nobles are not friendly to the Knights and probably don't want to accept that help, so we're not offering them help, we're just helping them. To start off, we're going to root out the Aranians in the city. I need your help, because we need people who understand Aranian so that we can question them."

"What are we doing about the forces outside the city?"

"Rider Barton will talk about that."

Zaina met Jevaithi's eyes. The queen had not yet said anything during this meeting.

She now said, "I asked you to be involved, because I know how much you hate this prince so I know that I can trust that you will do whatever you can to make sure that he doesn't win the race for the throne."

Zaina was going to say that she didn't care who won the race to the throne because she hated all of them anyway, but that was not entirely true. She didn't think much of Sferuk or Denori, but only Nayek had a personal issue with her. Mostly, she wanted all of these princes to go away. She didn't understand what their obsession was with the City of Glass and wanted nothing more to do with Arania.

"I would like to kill him properly this time."

Jevaithi smiled. "Precisely. Join Marek and the team he works for."

With that, the meeting was over. Marek excused himself because he had a lot of work to do, but when Zaina moved to go with him, Jevaithi gestured that she wanted her to stay.

Zaina's heart jumped, and she both wanted to run and say *yes, please*. She wasn't even sure that Jevaithi would love another woman, or that she even knew that, if she allowed herself to love a woman, her life would be so much better.

And after Xalia, Zaina wasn't sure if she could face another relationship like it.

It was not until the door had shut behind Marek that Jevaithi spoke. "How have you been since moving from the stables to the eyrie?"

Her voice was soft, but had an edge to it. Zaina wasn't sure if it was trick question or one with a double meaning. She wasn't good at politics and always had trouble determining people's intentions when they spoke in hidden meanings, one reason she preferred machines and animals.

She decided to answer in the plainest way possible. "I enjoy working with the birds. The training is good, but very tiring."

"I can imagine."

Zaina doubted that she could imagine it, but could no longer meet those innocent eyes. "I'm sorry. I'm worried about being given special projects. My track record in this sort of thing is not exactly good. Bad things happen to people when I go with them."

"Oh, nonsense. Unless you're at risk of betraying us and going back to Arania?"

"Me? Oh, hell, no."

Again using bad language in front of the queen. "I'm sorry. It's . . . how we talk." Her cheeks grew hot. She wasn't handling this very well.

"What do you dislike about Arania?"

How about everything? "Arania is . . . I don't know how to describe it, but everyone constantly lives in fear. Not just fear for bad things to happen, but fear of their lives. Arania always has far too many people, and most of those people have nothing to live for, so those people then take little glimmers of hope offered by some fortune teller and hang their entire lives on it."

"Like astrology?"

Zaina snorted. "Astrology is for the rich. I couldn't afford an astrologer."

"If you could, would you want to?"

Was that a trick question? "I honestly don't think an astrologer would have anything to offer me. Everything I did in my life, I've done myself, including the bad things."

"That's just it, isn't it? People taking their own fate in their hands."

"Well . . . yes. I guess . . ."

Zaina had no idea where Jevaithi was going with this. She only knew that the chance she would say something stupid or inappropriate increased the longer she stayed in this room.

But Jevaithi continued. "I've been thinking a lot about this recently. I was never allowed to make my own fate because it was determined the moment I was born. I never even thought about it. I didn't know how to do it—still don't, I suppose you must think."

"I don't think that at all."

"Oh, I can hear what people say when they think I'm not listening. There is no need to hold back. I *am* clueless. I wanted to run the Knight Council, but I'm not very good at meetings. I wanted to help rebuild the city, but other people's ideas are much better than mine. I wanted to be a mother, but I guess that's not going to happen. I look at you and I see all the things you have done, and sometimes failed, and I think I want a life like that. You know how I came and helped you in the stables? I enjoyed that, but then when I got back to my room a bevy of people was waiting for me, telling me that I shouldn't do things like that. I feel guilty because I've been given a position of power, but I'm not using it. I want to *stop* being clueless. I've tried so many things. The world is fine without me. All they need me for is to be a pretty puppet at ceremonies, but everything else runs just fine without me. The Knight Council is capable, and Isandor is really good at talking to people and organising building projects. No one needs me."

"Well, I wouldn't say that."

"It's true. I'm not even useful for producing an heir." Her eyes glittered.

"Well . . ." Zaina didn't know what to do or say.

In a way, Zaina did understand what it felt like to be useless. In her early adolescent years, in General Pakori's Mother's House, she had felt like that. Uninterested in women's things, and especially in becoming a mother herself, she was constantly the subject of scorn or ridicule with the established mothers. One thing had changed her life: the day the general brought home a truck. Zaina remembered that she just *had* to understand how it worked. She would watch every time someone did anything to that truck, to the point where the men would let *her* do these things.

She said, "The only thing that will make a difference is if you actually do something about it. You can't wait for people to give you permission or approval. You have to stand up and say 'This is what I want to do' and they will just have to accept it."

Jevaithi stared at her, opening her mouth and closing it again. She blinked, as if she might burst into tears any moment.

Zaina took a shuddering breath. She remembered that difficult time so well. When Xalia had been killed, when her entire life had fallen apart a second time. She remembered coming here not knowing what to do.

Every person had times in their lives when they needed someone else to help them see the path. There never seemed to have been anyone for Jevaithi, who needed to step away from her desire to please everyone.

Zaina hovered between wanting to be that person and wanting to run, because this situation had far too many echoes with what happened with her and Xalia.

Jevaithi's eyes met Zaina's in an uncomfortably intense expression that set every fibre of Zaina's mind on edge. She rose. "Sorry, I've got loads of work to do."

This was a *bad* idea. She should go now before something bad happened.

"I understand."

Zaina crossed to the door.

"Zaina."

The pleading tone in Jevaithi's voice made Zaina cry inside. *Just like Xalia.* And she couldn't not look and not meet those innocent, beautiful eyes, and see those sweet soft lips and her flaxen, elfin-like hair. And she knew that she could fight this feeling that bloomed inside her, but she could never, ever, win.

A GENERAL ALERT for all the Knights and Apprentices at the eyrie went out later in the afternoon. Everyone, from the Senior Knights to the newest Apprentices, gathered in the big assembly hall downstairs, seated on rows of benches that occupied most of the room's main floor. There was not enough space on those benches, and some people had to stand at the back.

Rider Barton strode in from the side door. He still wore his riding harness, the straps of leather with the metal eyelets slapping against the leather protectors on his upper legs.

As soon as he took up his position at the front, everyone fell silent.

In typical fashion, he wasted no words. "I assume that everyone has heard the news by now. I've just been on a flight around the perimeter of the city and it appears we are surrounded by at least five Aranian units. It looks like each has about twenty men, although it also looks like they might have built shelters, so there may be more in hiding. They don't look particularly well-equipped, which means that whatever they are here to do, they will probably do it sooner rather than later because these men won't last in the cold of winter."

Some Knights laughed at this, and some others, who had seem the Aranians, were quick to point out that what the Aranians lacked in equipment, they would make up for in numbers.

Rider Barton continued, "As far as we have been able to establish, the reason they are here is because the troops that belong to Prince Denori want to root out the ones belonging to Prince Nayek who are in the city."

"So we are just caught in the middle?" a Senior Knight said.

"Yes, and no. Because the men loyal to both princes have had contact with our noble houses and many of our nobles are deeply involved with this struggle. And before anyone thinks that the simple solution would be to get rid of all of the nobles: these are the people who still hold the knowledge and technology to work with icefire, and who still believe in the greatness of King Caldor. They have been going to Arania in great numbers, taking their technology, and Arania has been experimenting with icefire and weapons related to icefire. While those weapons won't harm us directly, they will harm many of our workers, our citizens and our friends and neighbours, anyone who does not have Perian blood."

Some murmuring went on in the back of the hall. The Knighthood included other people of Aranian and Chevakian blood.

Someone said, "Icefire was supposed to be dead."

"True. It was our belief that since the Heart was destroyed, icefire would fade and die out. This has proven false. We don't understand where the icefire is coming from. I've been in contact with the Chevakian doga, and the skylights we used to see have moved to most of Chevakia, and now even occur in the north of Chevakia. The knowledge gathered by the noble class, the supporters of King Caldor, contains the answers we need to rid the world of this evil once and for all. I say this to all of you with a heavy heart, but the world has changed in a frightening manner. The Aranians are playing with knowledge they don't understand, and they seem intent on returning us to a situation akin to the rule of King Caldor. The princes rule by fear. The nobles have the knowledge. They've sold this knowledge to the prince who is the highest bidder or who has the biggest army."

Someone at the back of the room asked, "But I'm confused. I thought most Aranians weren't resistant to icefire?"

"They're not," Marek said.

"Then won't large numbers of soldiers get killed by their own weapons?"

"They do, and the generals don't care, because the foot soldiers are peons for the princes and their deaths serve the purpose of getting the master on the throne."

"That's just terribly screwed up," someone said in a low voice behind Zaina.

No one needed to tell her that.

"It is a strange country," Rider Barton said. "I cannot claim to understand the motives of the princes, but we appear to be caught in the struggle between two of them. In this struggle, they have captured and maybe killed two of our teams, and they have now invaded our territory. We're at a point where we can no longer ignore Arania. We also cannot fight them, because we are too few. We need to focus on hanging onto our knowledge and our citizens who have that knowledge: the nobles and the members of the Brotherhood of the Light. Ideally, we'd like to drive the Aranian troops from our city but, failing that, we can stop the nobles leaving by offering them a safe haven. I would like to believe that if we give them that safety, most would elect to stay. If we start listening to them, they may come to appreciate us."

Some mumblings broke out around Zaina about whether or not the nobles were worthy of protection. A young Knight behind her said, "Finally. I always wondered how long it would take them to realise that."

Rider Barton said, "We will be doing two things: I will assign some teams to Rider Carro to patrol the Aranian positions outside the city. These will be flying patrols only because we do not have the resources to engage them on the ground. The people in these units will be the scouts and hunter units. You will report to Rider Carro after this meeting."

Rider Carro rose briefly to show everyone where he was.

Zaina had seen him before and had never thought anything special of him. He was just another straight-laced Knight with short-cropped hair and an angled face. So he was the lady Loriane's son, huh?

"Most of our members will be dedicated to detecting the Aranian cells in the city, taking them into custody, interviewing them, and convincing the nobles that they need our protection. I will be doing some of the latter, engaging the houses in meetings and spelling out the situation for them, and offering our help. Those people will report directly to me."

He cast a look around the audience room, where not a single seat was empty and where people sat in the aisles and stood along the walls.

A feeling of pride swelled Zaina's heart. She had done well to join the Knighthood. All those Knights were good and honest people, and what was more, a lot of them were women, especially in the flying division.

"I will also contact Tiverius for help, but we will not be reliant on it. For one thing, we now understand why the mail has been intermittent for the last few days. It wasn't just the weather. If I contact Tiverius, they may not receive my message. If they do, they may not be able to send help. If they send help, they may not be able to reach us. Until they arrive, and they may never come, we are in this alone, and I want us to survive this. Take no unnecessary risks."

He dismissed the meeting at large, and the flying divisions left the room with Rider Carro.

Zaina remained behind, and so did Marek. She joined him when the Knight next to him left the room.

Rider Barton remained at the front of the room.

"Now, all of you, city team. While the other guys are just going to fly around, we'll do the real work."

Some people laughed at this.

"We absolutely need to stop Nayek and his men from getting their hands on any more ancient technology and taking it out of the city. We need to identify which families are still with us and which ones aren't, and we need to confiscate the collections of those that aren't. We are going to divide into small groups and systematically search every house, every shop, every alley of the city. I'm expecting that these teams will meet with some resistance, so I will allocate street fighters and sharp shooters to each team. Many of you will already have been allocated to either of these activities. You are as of now relieved from all non-essential tasks until further notice."

He then went into logistics, like who would be the leader of each group, and dedicated a part of the building to each. Zaina was to be allocated to a group led by Rider Taino, a Senior Knight who was still quite young for his position. He was of stocky build and wore his hair long, tied back into a ponytail at the back of his head. He normally led the mechanics division, and Zaina had met him a few times.

The team also contained another Apprentice, a young man named Prito, a female scout called Leya, a sharp shooter, Naran, and a Tutor, Wido.

They went to work quickly.

CHAPTER 7

KOTORI HAD BEEN cautiously happy over the past few days.

The southern woman had moved into the Mother's House. She had seen the king, and the king appeared happy, and what was more, he was still alive. That had to be a good thing, Kotori surmised.

Never mind that rumours had told him that she had since seen the king twice more—which was highly unusual—and that she had applied to use the Astrology library. The first time he had ignored her application, because she was *foreign* and a *woman* to boot, but the second time, it came with a recommendation from the king, and Kotori figured he'd better approve it unless he wanted to lose his head, or, worse, be sent on the boats to see the Mother.

Those boats had signalled a change in the mood in the city, because there were so many of them now. He was called to the harbour front almost every day.

He had to wait on the quayside, like today, while the prisoners were led out of the big shed, legs shackled, arms behind their backs, and taken up the gangplank before being forced to sit on the deck.

Lately, most of them had been Chevakians, stocky men with dark eyes and hair colour varying from dark brown to sandy. Many of them still wore their Chevakian military uniforms, and Kotori was *not* sorry to see them herded onto the ships. He was too young to remember much of the war, but he did remember the stories told by

91

his elders. Of unbelievable butchery, of blood-soaked streets, of the smell of burning bodies that lingered in the air for days. His old grandmother had never again been able to enjoy meat, knowing that three of her sons had died in warehouses set alight by the Chevakians who had stood watching as the flames devoured fellow humans. The women had heard the screams of those caught inside and had lived with those memories.

The Chevakians deserved the worst death they could get. Kotori thought that dying in view of the Mother was still too good for them.

They were proud, healthy, haughty, despite the shackles and chains that bound them. Just look at them walking onto the ship with smirking expressions on their faces. Some were even smiling, like they thought they were going on a trip or being taken to some prison camp from which they could escape.

Well, they were going to be surprised.

Kotori set his bag at the bottom of the little stone table that stood on the quay and unpacked his star chart and stones. He didn't understand why the general still asked him to make a casting for this filth. There were no Aranians in this lot, were there?

None were on the deck, but a small group of Aranian men were now being led out of a cart that had just arrived.

They numbered five. Three of them were military men, probably the minor sons of the king and his brothers: all those boys who, back when Orik was vying for the throne, had been born as proof of the virility of the contestants for the throne. Boys whose lives never had more purpose than to be a number on the number counter's sheets.

Such young men were never shackled. They didn't shout. They didn't swear at their captors. They quietly walked up the gangplank, and sat on their knees as instructed, faces solemn in the seriousness of the moment.

Most of them would have spent time at military camps since they were old enough to hold a weapon. Those were the men Kotori came here to make a casting for, because they had chosen to come here. They were usually too sick to continue serving in the army. Sometimes they had committed a crime and had shown remorse, which gave them the choice to see the Mother or spend awful years in jail.

All of them would have their names inscribed in the wall at Kotori's back.

The Acolyte of the Mother's Temple walked up the gangplank, swinging the bronze smoke dispenser. The contraption held wood soaked with oils so that it would burn hot and spread scented smoke over the prisoners. One Chevakian coughed and flapped his hand—the insolence of him—but like Kotori, the Acolyte was there for the Aranians. He touched the heads of the men, and each in turn, they reached up to his hand, pressing his fingers against their foreheads. So they would sit for a while, letting go of their worldly thoughts in preparation for their journey to the Mother.

When the Acolyte had attended all five men, Kotori made his casting, and it was favourable. The weather would be fine, the crew—dressed in their thick body-covering protective gear with facemask—would return safely. The men's names would be honourably inscribed on the wall.

He put away his stones and folded up his map, while the ship cast off and the crew hoisted the sails. A good number of people stopped to watch, hands on their chests to indicate the gravity of the moment. The Aranians on board stood proud, chin up, legs apart, unshackled, courageous.

Kotori's heart filled with pride. If ever he'd be sent to see the Mother, he would go like this.

The ship slowly glided out of the harbour. It would navigate the channel between the two large islands that lay in front of the coast, and would vanish in the Mother's Veil. When it next came back, perhaps two weeks later, the deck would be empty.

"Hey, astrologer, what's up with the king's southern woman?" a man asked behind him.

Kotori didn't need to smell the scent of tobacco to know that this was prince Denori. The dark voice, far too mellow for his personality, made Kotori's hair stand on end. He would recognise it anywhere.

"Southern . . . woman?" He turned around.

Prince Denori was almost a head taller than him, and twice as broad. He always wore a sleeveless leather jerkin that showed off every rounding and angle of the muscles in his shoulders.

Like so many princes, he shaved most of his head, and the skin there bore tattoos of vicious growling dogs, saliva dripping from their teeth as if they were about to attack his eyeballs.

"The king has taken this young thing, someone you picked out for him, I believe. I mean, do I even need to tell you this or are you just pretending to be thick?"

"I was lost in the serenity of the men's sacrifice."

"Please spare me the bullshit."

Kotori took in a sharp breath. The prince was really most insolent and rude, worse even than Nayek. "The king asked me to select a replacement for Selwa."

"What is wrong with Selwa?"

"She is too old to have children."

"Why is he still interested in having children? That is my point. He should be selecting his successor."

"He probably is doing that."

Denori's hand shot out, grabbing Kotori by the upper arm. His fingers closed around the too soft muscle like a vice. He pulled Kotori close to him. "Do not be smart with me." His breath stank of tobacco.

Then he let Kotori go again.

Kotori rubbed his arm. That was surely going to be a nice bruise tomorrow.

"My excuses. The king does things for reasons only known to him. I am not privy to how he makes his decisions." *Why don't you ask him, since he's your father?*

"Yes, you are. You are the only person in all of the kingdom who can tell him what to do."

What? Kotori stared at him. Denori was one of the princes who had succumbed to the terrible fad to have the whites in their eyes tattooed. His were black, which made his pale blue irises stand out in a ghostly way.

"You and your maps and stones and other nonsense. You can say to him, 'The star signs indicate that you will die within four months. You must appoint a successor if you don't want the kingdom to fall down in disarray.' " He even did a reasonable job of imitating Kotori's way of speaking.

And this was what Kotori hated about him: his slow, mocking way of speaking that sounded as if he owned the entire world. It reminded Kotori of another royal son, a bully in the Children's House who had made Kotori's life a misery and who was now the head of the railway service. Bullying got you places, if you could stomach it.

Kotori straightened. "You are mistaken. Appointing a successor is the king's decision, and he is not going to die within four months."

"Look at me." Denori thumped a fist on his leather-clad chest. His lower arm was criss-crossed with scars. The muscles rippled underneath the skin. "I am not an astrologer, but I don't need stones and trinkets to make this prediction. If I say that the king is going to die within four months, he will die within four months."

Kotori took a step back. Was that a threat? "You're not suggesting that I *lie* to the king about the star signs?" Seriously, he wanted nothing to do with this. He was *not* into threatening anyone, and most certainly not his brother the king, who had been a very good and strong king even if he had gone a little soft in his old age.

Denori snorted. "What difference does it make? Whatever you say, you're lying anyway. Don't tell me that you believe any of that star sign rubbish. You're always and forever weaselling around trying to back-pedal over some silly prediction you made that turned out to be not quite as people expected. 'Oh, but it depends on who made the request for a casting. The wishes of the requester must taken into account.' " Again, he did a reasonable job of imitating Kotori's voice. Then he bent close and shouted, "Bullshit!"

Kotori jerked back, away from the spit flying from Denori's mouth.

"If you could really predict the future, why didn't you see Nayek's misfortune? Why didn't you foresee that Selwa would have a misshapen child? Why did you, back when I became an adult, give me such a lame prediction instead of one that shows the great achievements I have made?"

Kotori's mind raced. He didn't remember what he had predicted for Denori. He was one of the oldest princes and his adulthood ceremony would have been a very long time ago.

"I didn't say anything bad." That was all he remembered. Denori would not have been allowed to stay in the citadel if his casting had not been favourable.

"You casted an Eagle for that runt of a brother of mine."

That had been Nayek. He remembered that well enough. But it had not been the birthstone but one of the coins that landed in the Eagle, and Nayek was not born in the sign of the Eagle.

Denori was still sore about that?

Kotori guessed it shouldn't surprise him. As Kotori knew from having grown up in the Children's House himself, most of the princes bullied their way to the best positions and bullies tended to have long and vindictive memories.

"And that brother of mine refused to die when he was supposed to, when that bitch stuck the knife in his chest, and somehow managed to miss all his important organs. Stupid woman."

"Did you order her to do that?"

"I wish. If I'd have thought of it, I would have hired someone who'd do a proper job. Now, instead, I have two competitors. Sferuk is just a dumb brute, but Nayek . . . you let him live."

"It is my duty to protect life."

"Fuck your duty, astrologer. Do you want to live?"

"I already live. I don't need anyone's permission."

"Don't be smart with me. You're going to tell the king to step down. You're going to tell him that he will die within months and he needs to choose a successor. That is if *you* want to have a place in the new citadel, when I'm finished with it."

Kotori's heart thudded against his ribs. "I can suggest to him that he may want to pick a successor."

"Not suggest, *tell* him."

He stared into Denori's light grey eyes surrounded by black-stained whites. He *hated* adult men who bullied. He wished he had the courage to tell Denori to go fuck himself, but since Denori was the most likely successor of the king, that would be a stupid thing to do.

"I know my *brother* well enough to know that I can *tell* him whatever I want, but he will do as he pleases."

Denori growled. He grabbed the front of Kotori's robe. "You. Will. Tell. Him. I don't care how. He will retire. Or he will die. And you will die, too. Understand?"

"Yes, yes." Oh, how Kotori hated himself.

"Good then. Go." Denori loosened his grip.

Kotori scurried back to the citadel clutching his bag.

WHEN HE CAME to his room in the astrology tower, another visitor waited for him: another giant of a man, this one broader in the waist than Denori, but probably just as strong. It was prince Sferuk.

Being Selwa's oldest surviving child was his single-most important virtue. He looked a lot like her, too, with a coarse-skinned face, thick waist and large nose. He wore his long hair tied back in a ponytail. As was customary for horsemen, he oiled his hair, which gave him a greasy appearance.

The best feature about him was his eyes, which were, again like Selwa's, clear and observing.

Kotori bowed. "Your Highness, can I be of assistance?"

"That's why I was waiting here."

Kotori's heart sank. Here came another request for a casting he couldn't make. But he could hardly refuse to see Sferuk, so he opened the door to his room and led the prince inside.

At least Sferuk didn't grab him by the throat, and that had to be a positive, right?

"I want my fortune told," the prince said as soon as the door had shut behind Kotori.

Sure enough, there it was.

But telling fortunes was the reason Kotori worked here. He set down his bag and pulled out the star chart and the little bag with the stones and coins. He spread the map out over the desk.

"Tell me what the casting is for."

"Well, I have this little project that I'm considering. It's not a very big thing, but it's important to me. I was wondering . . . before I start, whether it has any chance of success?"

That was typically Sferuk, as clear as the horizon under the Mother's Veil. "I will need to know a bit more than that. Is this a project in the north?" Both Denori and Sferuk had been building military bases along the Chevakian border. Denori held the southern positions, leaving the desiccated north for his half-brother. Having started later, Sferuk tried to catch up with his brother but excelling in viciousness. It was Sferuk's troops, he realised belatedly, who had brought him the half-Perian woman whose presence seemed to irk Denori so.

But Sferuk shook his head. "That's not a small project, and I asked your fortunes for it years ago, and your predictions have been very good."

Sferuk always struck Kotori as the most civilised of the three contestants for the throne, even if he *knew* of the atrocities the prince committed in those military camps. He'd heard of the parties where he and his senior officers abused young women—and men—until they died. He at least had the grace to do that stuff away from the capital, even though Kotori seriously would not want anyone who did things like that on the throne.

"So, to be clear, it's not about the camps?"

"No, it's a small project, in the capital."

Kotori didn't like the sound of that. Surely if it was an honourable thing, Sferuk would say more about what it entailed. But the prince asked for a casting, so Kotori took the stones and coins out of the bag. It was cold in the room and the metal felt cold in his hands.

He threw the coins and gemstones over the map.

The emerald and two of the coins landed in the Wagon, the ruby in the Horse and the sapphire and the last coin landed in between star signs. A perfectly fine casting.

He glanced at Sferuk.

He remembered Denori's words.

Sferuk had never struck him as being the brightest spark.

"Hmmm." He pressed his lips together.

"What, astrologer, is there bad news?"

"You may need to reconsider the project. The signs are not good."

"Oh?" He looked sideways at the stones and coins on the map. "Are those bad signs? That's the Wagon, right? I thought the Wagon was good."

"Normally it is, but the combination is rather . . . ominous."

"Oh?" The prince frowned.

Kotori's heart thudded. He hoped the prince wasn't going to ask any further because then he would *really* have to start making up serious lies.

The prince rubbed his upper lip. "I thought . . . the projects I have in the north are dangerous. You know, because of the weather, and some of the Chevakians are nasty. Their military is starting to discover what we've been doing up there and they're finally coming to the party. They've got balloons, and Denori has all of *our* balloons in the central region, so we have to make do with horses and quickly get out of the place after an action. I didn't think a small project here in the city would be dangerous."

"It looks like it will be."

"Yeah. I see." He scratched his head. "I'll see what I can do now."

He got up and left the room.

Kotori remained at his desk, leaning his head in his hands. With everything he did, every word he spoke, every prediction he cast, he dug himself deeper into the shit. But what else should he have done?

Sferuk was a highly superstitious man. If he wanted a casting for something he was about to do and he refused to name the project, however vaguely, then it couldn't be anything good.

Kotori pushed back his chair and went to the window. Sferuk was just coming out of the entrance to the astrology building, and crossed the courtyard below. At the same time, Denori came out of the opposite entrance.

Uh-oh. Those two never got on well.

But Denori stopped and Sferuk stopped and neither hit the other in the head. In fact, they exchanged some words. Sferuk shook his head. Denori said something that looked like he was angry. Then again, Denori could say "I love you" and it would still sound angry.

The exchange was short, and the two princes went on their way without having laid hands on each other, without even having shoved, or attempted to trip or push aside the other man. That had to be a first.

CHAPTER 8

SANDOR THOUGHT OF the strange phenomenon of icefire that didn't register on the Chevakian sonorics meter a lot during the next day of travel.

It seemed there were two types of icefire: the one that made the air cold and another, unknown one that made the air hot. It seemed to him that even Chevakia and their Scriptorium were unaware of that second type, and that their devices did not measure it.

But come to think of it, had no one ever wondered why it was so hot and dry in northern Chevakia?

They passed the bay of seals, which was considered the border between Peria and Arania, and were now coming close to Curack.

The landscape passing underneath changed gradually, with an increase in the number of houses and fields and tracks linking them all. Occasionally, a cart would move along the track, and once a large flock of sheep ran across the hillside as if there would be anywhere for them to flee had the eagles chosen to dive, which they did not.

The landscape was still without trees.

The silver ribbon of a river came into view, with the town of Curack at the mouth, hemmed in by the shore and the flood plain. The first forests appeared here: swathes of dark pines, similar to those that grew on the edge of the southern plateau at Bordertown and on the slopes above Fairlight.

The scout took the eagles further inland, to a wooded rocky outcrop, where they set up camp.

The clear skies were gone, to be replaced with a thick blanket of low clouds.

Because the mission relied on birds, they'd only been able to take their waterproof sleeping sacks, which had a little flap with two flexible whale bones that, when they were inserted into little slots on the bottom sheet of the sack, made a tent just big enough for one person.

They would need the tents.

Two of the Knights lit a fire. During the day, one of them had shot two plains turkeys and they now set about plucking and cleaning the birds. They were experienced, professional men and did all this with quiet efficiency.

The other members of the group gathered around the fire, scouring for something dry to sit on.

One of the older Knights unfolded a map and spread it on his knees.

"We're here." He pointed with a vein-knotted and scarred hand. "The town is over there. The domed building with the spire that you can see from here is the temple of the Mother."

Isandor could just see it, silhouetted against the last remaining daylight.

"Curack is, by all our information, nothing more than a fishing village. The interesting part of what happens here is to the east of us."

This was where the mist hung over the foothills of the mountains and everything except a few hilltops were shrouded in a blanket of mist.

"That's where the military camps are?" one of the Knights asked.

"Yes, but we will try to stay away from that area. Likely, Tamerane will be held in a Mother's House belonging to some important man in the town. They don't have Mother's Houses in the military."

"No *women* in the military?" Rider Nallayo asked.

There had always been women in the Knights, even if they dressed as men, behaved like men and had certain reputations. Now there were more than at any time in history.

"No women at all. Women in Arania are only good for one thing."

They discussed on how to proceed and agreed to leave the eagles here and go into town on foot the next day. Isandor had certain questions, but he kept quiet during most of the discussion. The Knights knew exactly what they were doing, even if he did not.

It was really cold and everyone was tired, so after the two turkeys had been reduced to a pile of bones, they went to sleep.

For a long time, Isandor just lay looking at how the meagre light from the town reflected off the clouds directly above him, wondering what Tamerane would be doing now. Would Ledor have sold her off in order to rescue his business? He couldn't imagine that any Aranian prince could offer a better deal for her. He couldn't even imagine that they would be interested. Southern women did have the reputation of having poor fertility after all.

He turned onto his belly. If he propped his chin on his hands, he could see the lights of the town over the top of the grass. It had started raining, if the miserable drizzle could be called that.

He became aware of a flickering light in the corner of his vision. He turned over and wormed himself out of the sleeping sack tent. Ugh, the grass made his trouser legs wet.

By the feeble light of the town's lights, he climbed up the rocky outcrop at the very top of the hill.

The mist in the valley to the east had taken on an eerie golden glow.

Isandor would have thought that it was moonlight—except there was no moon—or lights underneath the mist, but he noticed crackles of light flickering over the top of the mist.

It was icefire and it was coming from underneath the cloud cover.

THE MORNING DAWNED pale and blue, with the entire world softened by mist.

Some of the Knights were already active around the camp, making breakfast and tending the birds, which sat like mounds of fluffed-up feathers with their heads tucked under their wings.

Isandor crawled out of his sleeping sack and wished he hadn't. Everything was cold and wet, including his packs, his boots and his jacket. How soft he had become.

He joined the others at the fire, accepting a bowl of steaming porridge.

"All right, we go to work today," Rider Nallayo said. "We'll leave the eagles up here and split into groups to explore the town. Our first task is to find the family. We know that there is a garrison inland, but I very much doubt that any of the Aranian princes would allow Perian civilians to come there for more than a brief, controlled visit. In my admittedly limited experience, and from reports by people more knowledgeable than myself, the princes tend to keep their plans close to their chest, even from rivals within the country. We're not talking about national armies here. These are hired mercenaries who answer to their master only. This means that, initially, we will be looking for the family in town. He runs a business. He is said to have warehouses here. There may be signs and ships."

Rider Nallayo spread out the map on her knees. "Curack is a big enough town that not everyone knows everyone else. The garrison inland also means that there will be traffic of people from the harbour to the camp. These will be people unknown to the locals."

"I'm guessing we're going to be recruits?" a Knight said.

"That is the best disguise. I and Rider Kaithi will be disguising ourselves as young men. All their recruits are male."

She turned to the map. "The layout of the town is pretty self-explanatory. This here is the commercial harbour. Ships come in from the City of Glass and from the north, from Kadrish and many of the smaller towns along the coast. Most of the goods are stored in warehouses along the quay and on the southern side of the harbour. This is a place to investigate, since we know that Ledor uses a warehouse in town. Before we left, I asked one of the Aranian residents in the City of Glass to write out the names of businesses that Ledor is known to use or associate with. We made a couple of copies so each of our groups can have one."

She handed out the pieces of paper with copies of the text. The recipients studied and frowned at the Aranian script. Isandor got one, too. He did read a bit of Aranian and could speak enough words for the very basic life needs. He could read the names of the businesses if he spelled out the individual letters, so he memorised the "look" of the words, because Aranian script tended to have characters with distinctive loops.

After breakfast they divided into groups so that each group had someone who spoke at least some basic Aranian. That Isandor ended up being his group's "expert" was indicative of the lack of Knights with recent knowledge about Arania. The only Aranian Knight Isandor knew was Rider Farey and he had gone missing along with the very first expedition.

The plan was that the groups would leave their camp staggered over the morning. Each group would investigate the town and would reconvene in the afternoon in a piece of forest outside the town on the road to the garrison, but well short of it so as not to run the risk of attracting attention from the military.

Isandor waited with his two companions, both Knight hunters, by the names of Marlo and Naissa. They were, like himself and Jevaithi, twins, brother and sister working together as a seamless team. Seeing them work together and communicate without words made him realise how broken his relationship with Jevaithi was. He hoped she was all right. He hoped he had done the right thing to leave her, and that it hadn't thrown her into a deeper cycle of self-destruction. At least she had Rider Barton to fall back on, and he seemed to be her flavour of the month. Maybe he could talk some sense into her, because Isandor could not. Isandor wondered if Jevaithi would listen to anyone.

Isandor's group was the second group to leave, with two groups to come after. At first, the path was no more than an animal track probably made by wild deer, of which they met a few grazing on the dewy hillside.

The further they descended into the valley, the more misty it became, until the sky turned into a soup of light grey and darker grey, and the shapes of buildings, trees, dung heaps, barns, oxen, carts, horses and people were not immediately clear until they were quite close.

The mist also dampened sound. Not a bird squawked, not a cow bellowed.

Like so many of these towns, the outskirts were the home of businesses that both required proximity to a town and some space. They passed a sawmill with a giant water wheel. Despite the lousy weather, activity in the shed was in full swing. Men were singing and laughing while the saw worked and spread a scent of pine resin in the nearby air.

They passed a coach yard, where horses covered in blankets stood by the gate, obviously waiting to be fed, and curiously eying the companions walking down the road. The coaches all stood inside a large barn, where a young man was washing one of the vehicles.

As Isandor and the twins passed, another man came out of a barn with a wheelbarrow filled with hay. All the horses turned their attention to him.

The man greeted the companions on the road, and Isandor lifted his hand in greeting, not trusting himself with his limited Aranian vocabulary.

The houses became more densely packed, with a couple of mansions belonging to administrators or landowners and then the little houses of the workers and their families.

Black rock was a product of the area, and many of the men worked in the quarries digging it out. A few trucks passed the companions, their loading trays heaped with the stuff. Isandor even thought that the truck engines ran on it, judging by the amount of black smoke the vehicles produced.

The trucks in the City of Glass ran on peat bricks or grass bricks, and while that might not burn as hot, it was a lot less smoky.

The fog intensified the further into town they went. Was it because they were closer to the ocean? A warm current ran the length of the Aranian coast, and it used to keep this area free of sea ice, back in the time when the Heart kept the south frozen. Or was it so misty because of the foul air from those smoky fires?

Either way, it was miserable and cold. People went about their business hidden in the hoods of their cloaks, and that suited the companions well.

They found the harbour easily enough—the main road led straight to it. The road by-passed the market square, of which they could see glimpses through side streets. It did seem to be a bit busier there, but in general the activity on the streets was subdued and miserable.

Of course the thick mist also prevented larger ships coming into port. Apart from the poor visibility, there was also no wind, so engine and sailing ships alike lay uselessly at the quay.

The water was calm, the surface almost oily, and fishing boats lay on the shore with fishermen fixing their nets.

Isandor and the two Knights walked along the quay twice, taking in the signs on buildings and ships. Literally nothing was happening in the harbour. No ships being unloaded or loaded, no movement except for a pair of ducks chasing each other across the water. He didn't get the impression anyone watched them, but chose to play it safe and led the twins into a side street. Here, big warehouses occupied both sides of the street. Occasionally a door would be open, revealing a glimpse of the content within. Most of it consisted of crates or bales, but he spotted a business shipping black rock, and another where the warehouse contained a couple of shiny new vehicles.

This again brought the question that it had never become clear to him what type of items Ledor sold. They studied all the signs and inscriptions and came to the conclusion that Curack's business sector was a lot bigger than it appeared at first glance.

Around midday, they met another group of Knights coming the other way. They couldn't stop and talk of course, but their body language told Isandor that they probably hadn't found anything worth mentioning either. So the other group kept walking and Isandor kept walking. They came to the end of the road at a beach. A couple of fishing boats lay on the sand, as well as two legless lions. The animals lifted their heads, looking semi-alarmed. They were not the same type as in the City of Glass. These lions were smaller, and their pelts had more spots. One of them got up and hobbled half into the water, looking over its shoulder to see if the intruders were really going to invade their resting spot.

The three companions stood on the beach in indecision.

"I haven't seen anything that looks like those names on the paper," Rider Marlo said.

His sister shook her head. She had covered the bottom half of her face with a shawl and, in male clothes, looked like an adolescent boy.

Isandor blew out a breath. He hadn't seen anything interesting either. In addition, the weather was far too cold and miserable for them to sit down here and wait. And he already had a feeling that they were being watched, and that some of the locals in grey cloaks were spies.

Rider Naissa rubbed her hands. "Maybe we could go to the markets and buy something warm there. Surely there will be some eating house where it is acceptable to sit and watch?"

A seagull landed on the keel of one of the turned-over fishing boats, and started an argument with the seagulls already there, which had, up until then, appeared asleep.

While he watched the gulls, Isandor spotted a cart on the track behind the beach. It was pulled by two sullen horses, and steered by a single driver. On the back tray lay a pile of bags that looked like . . .

"By the skylights, are those bodies?" Naissa said.

That had been Isandor's thought, too. Not only that, but as the cart made its way along the road, a trail of golden sparks leaked from the bed on the cart, winking out as soon as they hit the ground.

Icefire.

Marlo gave a hand sign, one that Isandor knew. It meant *Let's follow.*

The horses plodded slowly, and the driver of the cart sat with his shoulders drawn up and the bottom half of his face hidden in his collar, probably unaware of the trail he left behind.

When the cart crested the top of the land tongue to the next bay, Isandor made his way from the beach to the road, followed by Marlo and Naissa. They could walk faster than the horses were going, and when they came to the crest in the road, the cart had just turned off the road into a track that led to an ugly, square building that stood on the hillside, lined by fishermen's houses, overlooking the next bay. The field surrounding the ugly building was free of trees. A plume of smoke drifted from the chimney and slowly dissipated in the surrounding air.

Did Isandor imagine it or did he smell burning hair? He definitely didn't imagine the golden strands of icefire fanning out from the chimney.

He felt sick.

Aranians were not resistant to icefire. The dead bodies in the bags had to be laden with it to leak this much.

He remembered seeing icefire magic at work: a young man, his heart cut out and his chest filled with icefire so that he became a servitor who blindly obeyed his master. He remembered the Sorcerer Tandor, his own father, begging him to use the craft to take control over the City of Glass. He had vowed to do everything in his power to make icefire magic a forgotten craft.

What did these Aranians think they were doing?

"Well," Naissa said when they turned back towards the town. "That's one way to get rid of the dead."

Marlo shuddered visibly. It was not the Perian way. People in the City of Glass abhorred fire. It was thought that if you burned a body, you destroyed the soul as well as the physical form.

"Each country to their own," Isandor said.

Marlo nodded and none of them said anything until they had reached the commercial quarters with the warehouses again, and had taken another turn at wandering around aimlessly.

But then Naissa said, "Look, there goes another one."

They looked, and she was right. A second cart filled with bodies, this one bigger. One of the sheets was stained with blood.

"Where do they all come from?" Marlo asked, his voice disturbed. "With a town this size, I wouldn't think more than one or two people died each day."

Isandor had never thought of such macabre numbers, but it did seem that this many dead people was not in line with the size of the town. It was . . . disturbing. He could only think of the army camp inland, but what were they doing there that soldiers died before they even got to battle?

They walked around for a bit, but couldn't find where the carts had come from, and couldn't find Ledor's business premises either. So they went to the market place, where there were lots of people selling food, and found a place at an eating-house under the cover of a shop awning. It was not entirely indoors, but the area contained a big fire bowl. People sat around it warming themselves and clutching warm drinks.

Isandor and the twins joined the crowd, but dared say very little for fear of being outed as foreigners.

There was a certain grimness about the townsfolk that suited the weather and the mysterious pile of bodies and the smell of burned flash that just wouldn't leave his nose.

When they met the others in the patch of forest outside town, Isandor could already tell by their faces that no one had found anything of note.

"This is proving harder than we expected," Rider Nallayo said.

This met with nods from the group. Most of the Knights looked gloomy, but that was hopefully just the weather. Surely they had faced more difficult searches than this.

"Worse than that, we're being followed," Rider Kaithi said in a low voice. Being a tracker, she would know the signs.

"Soldiers?" Isandor asked.

"I don't think so. Whoever it is made some basic mistakes in remaining unnoticed."

"Do you want to grab him?" Kill him would be more likely, especially when Jeito got involved.

"Not yet."

"Does this mean that the Aranians now know where we are?"

"They probably already knew that anyway, even if they don't know who we are. We need to make our move quickly."

They spoke for a bit about the plans for the next few days. Isandor's heart sank. It didn't look like this was going to be a quick mission after all.

Rider Nallayo outlined the next stage of the investigation, where they would station people on the main roads and in the harbour to check the movement in and out of town.

At that point, Naissa raised the issue of the bodies on the cart.

"Aranians burn their dead. Every town has a furnace, usually a bit out of town," one of the Knights said.

"Yes, but why would more than twenty people die on the same day in a town like this?"

He couldn't answer that question, but all agreed that it seemed a lot of people.

They agreed to put people on the main road to the garrison, on the road to the incinerator, in the harbour, on the road north, in the market square and keep two people to roam between those groups.

They made their way back up the hill, stopping every now and then and checking the surroundings for people following. The eagles were asleep and the single Knight guarding them reported that it had been very boring save for some deer invading the campsite and running off with half the bread.

"I didn't know deer liked bread," Isandor said.

Rider Nallayo smiled. "You learn something new every day."

At that moment, a few of the Knights jumped up and everyone

around the fire sat up, suddenly alert. Rider Nallayo slid her dagger out of its sheath.

A few of the Knights ran off into the darkness. They came back, a moment later, with a scruffy young man in a fur cloak, with his hands tied behind his back. Two Knights held him, one of them holding a dagger across his throat.

They pushed him down near the fire.

"Why were you following us today?" Rider Nallayo said.

"Please, don't hurt me. I can explain." He spoke Perian. "I have a message from Tamerane."

CHAPTER 9

THE GUARDS WAITED patiently in the hall downstairs to take Lana back to the Mother's House. The first thing she did was go upstairs and swap those horrible clothes for a more comfortable outfit.

Next she decided to wash the oil and jelly and other substances off her body in the bath.

Selwa came to join her while she sat there. She had brought a carafe of juice and two glasses.

"Sorry, no wine. You're not getting any until the day you give birth."

"You seem to be certain of that." She thought of Nashi's seeds.

"You're strong and healthy. You'll be expecting soon."

Lana sipped from the juice, thinking of the seeds that Nashi had given her and she faithfully bit in two and swallowed every three days. "I'm half-Perian. They have bad infertility problems in Peria."

"Your mother gave birth to you. Your father is Chevakian. I don't expect any problems."

"What happens if a mother fails to become pregnant?"

"There have been a few. Usually, the king stops seeing them as frequently, and he passes the woman to the junior princes. If they fail, too, she gets to work in some place like the laundry. That's not pleasant because the lower class men will know that they can jump on her without consequences and . . . those girls are usually found floating face down in the river within the year. I truly feel sorry for them. If you were ever thinking of taking something . . . to prevent pregnancy, I would strongly advise you to stop. He will find out. He will not take to it kindly. The discomfort and bother and pain of pushing out a child is nothing compared to incurring his wrath."

Lana's ears glowed. "I could be infertile because of my heritage. How many times does he try?"

Selwa grabbed her upper arm. "Look at me."

Lana did.

"Whatever you're taking, stop it. It's not worth it."

But . . . Lana's eyes pricked with tears.

"I didn't ask to have Sferuk, or Nayek or any of the others. I definitely didn't ask for this last cursed child that almost killed me. The king decides that you will have a child. You give him the child. Rest assured, he only asks when he needs it."

"But I understand he's about to retire?"

"That's what people want him to do, especially his sons. But it is up to him. Why he wanted to replace me, I don't know either, but it's not up to me to see into his mind."

"How old were you when you first came here? Was it your wish to be in the Mother's House?"

"Mine? Oh no. I had to be dragged here kicking and screaming. I was very young. My father died and my mother had no money to look after us."

"You're not a princess of some kind?"

"Heavens, no. My father was a small town administrator. I don't remember him very well, but it was said he always drank far too much and it was the drink that killed him. He didn't have a very large Mothers' House. I think there were just nine of them, and none of those women had anywhere to go when he suddenly died. So my mother put me on the register, and a king's scout picked me out. I was fifteen, still too young. Sferuk was born when I was seventeen. I had a girl before that, but the birth was very hard and she didn't survive."

"That's terrible." When Lana was that age, she led a happy, innocent life and was about to finish school.

Selwa spread her hands. "It's life. I was lucky. Only half my sisters are still alive. The ones who died did so from causes related to poverty. Diseases caused by filth or poor healing practices. When I first came here, Orik was much younger, much angrier and more violent. He frightened me. The first time I went to see him, he dragged me into his room, pushed me up against the door and was going to do the deed right there until I told him I wouldn't have it."

"You told him. . . ?" Lana laughed.

"Oh yes. He took pride in conquering his women, not pleasing them. He was violent and even if he tried not to, he would sometimes hurt me."

"He came to power after the war, didn't he?"

"Oh, yes. After the war, we went through a quick succession of many princes who killed each other in their search for power. Orik emerged from that chaos, and you don't do that by being nice to people. He had to learn to be nice."

"He *has* changed a lot."

"You can't even see half how much."

"Is that why he is upset?"

Selwa gave her a puzzled look, and Lana told her that the king had appeared to cry after having sex with her. Selwa listened, fingering her upper lip, while her heavy eyebrows formed into a deep frown.

After a short silence, she said, "I'm as puzzled as you are. To be honest, I haven't been with him since I conceived the last ill-fated child."

"Maybe he is sad about his decision to retire."

"Rest assured, if he had decided to retire, he would not have taken you on. I don't know why he'd want a child when he's got hundreds, but you better give him what he wants. Anyway . . ." Selwa climbed out of the bath. "I have a lot to do. I better get going."

She wrapped a towel around herself and left the bathroom soon after. Lana remained in the water and two young women came in before she decided to get out.

They wanted to talk about embarrassing details. Both had come into the house over a year ago and neither had been seen by the king. It sickened Lana that they were so keen to have their turn and it seemed to her that if you were keen, the king was less likely to pick you. Maybe she could pretend to be keen, and he would lose interest and she would not have to worry about whether or not she still took the seeds. But she also knew that was just a wishful thought. The king had taken an interest in her. She had two choices: escape or give him what he wanted.

LANA APPLIED to go to the library the next day. She sent her message to the astrologer whose name was Kotori, and spent the rest of the day waiting.

And waiting.

She hung around the garden, waiting for a return message, which didn't come. In preparation for her visit, she asked for a book and pens. That met with curiosity, because she had already been given paper and when she sat in the library, some women came to have a look. Lana already knew that her talk of the sun and stars and the Great Wanderer bored most of the women, but usually one or two remained. In the past few days, she had asked for their names and had written them on the last page of the notebook. Many women in Arania couldn't read or write, so they found this immensely interesting.

Lana wasn't sure what she was going to do with those names, except she promised the women that she would let them know if she found out anything interesting. She skimmed over that page: nine names of women who had displayed interest in her work. She must tell them what she found in the library.

She flipped to an empty page and started a list of things she wanted to look at in the library:

The history of the stars.

Rumours went that star maps went so far back that the changes in certain constellations were evident by minute differences, but measurable because of the accuracy of Aranian records. She was in particular interested in the passing of several star tails, and the fact that they were said to return every so many years.

Also the positions of the wandering stars over the years.

The history of astrology in general.

Records from fishermen or other seafaring people about other lands on the other side of the ocean.

The cause of the Mother's Veil clouds and other phenomena about the weather in Arania.

The existence of possible sonorics sources.

The list grew and grew. Maybe it was better to list what she did not want to look at.

But the response from the librarian remained conspicuous by its absence.

Two days of waiting later, the king called for her again. She repeated the first visit. They ate and talked about the differences between the two countries. He spoke of beautiful and wild places that made her realise that, like Chevakia and Peria, Arania was just a country with pretty places, ugly places, inhospitable places. Places where the citizens of Kadrish went for summer, places where they grew their food, places where they travelled on business.

After dinner she went first to the other room. She gulped the wine from the glasses on the little table by the door, undressed, washed herself and climbed on the chair, and then the king turned up for his part of the performance. Now that she knew that he wouldn't hurt her, she didn't even have to pretend enjoying it. He enjoyed it, too, rewarding her with a kind smile that she had never seen on his face before. He made a joking comment about loose Chevakian women, but the affectionate squeeze on her shoulder when he pushed himself off her brought home to her that he still wrestled with whatever demons tormented him.

This was not at all the man Selwa had described. It was not the man described in the Chevakian history books. It was definitely not the man Uncle Milleus and her father talked about. King Orik had laughed about the incident with the turd.

But when she thought about it . . .

Arania had badly lost the war, had been further knocked about by an even more brutal struggle between a couple of rival princes and then their enemy sent a letter saying that the person responsible for the defeat had died, so now was the time to become friendly again.

What would her father have done in Orik's position? What would she have done?

Certainly something not so very different from what King Orik had so clearly expressed with his package. Chevakia thought it was hilarious. Arania said: you can keep your friendship. We don't want it on your terms.

Arania was a proud and stubborn country. A country with a

terrible type of society with Mother's Houses that were prisons for the country's women and warring princes who held many of the citizens to ransom and in which so many children were born that no one cared about them, nor showed them any love.

While she got dressed, Lana knew she could not stretch her situation out forever. She had to get out and make her move before someone discovered the seeds, before they ran out or before he discarded her for being infertile.

The problem was: she had no idea what form her "move" was going to take.

The king looked sad and lonely.

He sat by the hearth holding a glass of wine. He gestured at the bottle. "Do you want a glass?"

Lana figured she was probably going to find it hard to walk straight, but she wasn't harming any unborn child, so she took a glass from the cabinet against the wall and held it up for him to fill.

"Sit here." He patted the couch next to him.

She sat. It was warm in the glow of the fire.

"Are you all right? Are the mothers giving you a hard time?"

"Selwa is good to me."

He smiled. "Selwa is gold. She is very honest, but she is gold." He sighed and stared into the fire. Then he shook his head slightly. "What about your study?"

"I applied to visit the library, but haven't had a reply."

"You wrote to Kotori?"

"I did."

He snorted. "Write again. Wait." He set his glass down, rose, pulled a sheet of paper from the little desk in the corner, wrote something on it and handed it to her. "Send it again on this paper."

Lana looked at it. The sheet had the royal seal on it, and he had written, *by order of the king.*

"That will work on that silly man."

Lana gave him a sharp look. "I thought . . . I thought I was the only one who disliked the astrologer."

The king laughed. "No, although he is one of the least obnoxious unlikable people in the citadel. Unlikable but harmless."

"I thought . . ." She hesitated. She *almost* got the feeling that he didn't believe in astrology either, but as far as she knew, the Aranian court was the heart of astrology, and mentioning her disbelief to the king would amount to treason.

He said no more about it, instead talking about the weather. He wanted to know what Lana could tell him about the strange cold snaps that the north of the country had experienced, where *snow* had fallen in places where it had never done so in written history. He talked about the skylights that had never been visible in Kadrish.

Through the fuzziness in her head caused by the wine, she remembered that once, what now seemed very long ago, in Tiverius, she had been worried by these phenomena, and she had been going to study dust devils in Ysherra. She and Viki—whatever had become of him?—had been on their way to look at disturbing changes in the weather.

Ultimately, she still was a meteorologist, and if the king wanted to know about those changes in the weather, she could help him. But not today.

Lana was now starting to feel sleepy from the wine and being warmed through by the fire on one side. When she almost fell asleep, he asked the guards to take her back to the Mother's House.

Lana almost asked if she could sleep on the couch by the fire. That was so much more comfortable than trying to find a spot to sleep in one of the large rooms upstairs, where the women who hung around in the house all day had taken all the good spots.

But she did not fool herself into thinking that the king really liked her, nor that this was a safe place. Surely, he was just pretending, trying to get information out of her, or trying to get her to confide in him.

So she went back with the guards through the darkness to the Mother's House, where most of the lamps were already out. Lana stumbled up the stairs in the dark, her head spinning from the wine.

As she had predicted, most women were already asleep, sharing beds and couches in one of the large rooms where the soft breeze came in through the open window.

Lana found a spot and lay down.

From her position, she could see the clouds gathering over the ocean. Lightning occasionally flashed within. Eventually, she drifted off to sleep, expecting to be woken by thunder, but that time never came.

❄

LANA WOKE up with a lot of chatter and noise around her. Ugh, she felt terrible, and she hadn't even bathed last night. Her pink outfit lay next to the couch where she had fallen asleep.

All around her, women were getting dressed and streaming out of the room. Did they have to make so much noise?

She lifted herself on one elbow and asked the woman who sat next to her, and who had also just woken up, what was happening.

A birth ceremony, apparently. A first time mother had started having pains during the night and had been moved into the room next door. Because she was a first-timer, it was an event only for the mothers in the house.

"Come on, get dressed. We need to be there to support her."

Lana didn't want to go, and her head agreed with her, but if Selwa told her she couldn't drink any wine at all, she could hardly admit to having drunk just a little too much last night. So she found her comfortable clothes and went into the large recital room. It was already quite busy with women carrying blankets, pillows, towels, water, firewood and a host of other items. She managed to find a spot at the back, out of the zone of attention.

The women there recognised her.

"Oh, you're the Chevakian one," one of the women said. "Have you ever attended a birth ceremony before?"

When Lana admitted she had not, the woman next to her, herself pregnant, explained the meaning of the music and the drums and the dancers as they came to the front of the room and surrounded the poor woman who sat on a stool in the middle, stark naked and dripping with sweat, her face a mask of pain.

Lana cringed. "If I was in that much discomfort, I'd want to hide somewhere."

"You Chevakians are really strange. It's acted, of course. Yes, there is pain, but the noise is the symbol of suffering that the Mother has to go through for her child."

"So, she has pain and has to act as well?"

"It comes with experience. First time mothers don't go on the big stage downstairs."

120

Still, Lana hovered between not knowing where to look and being morbidly fascinated. In the big ceremonies they used modesty sheets, her neighbour went on to tell her, because there were men and sometimes there was blood and it would be improper to expose the men to all the details. But they were all women amongst each other here, and there was no need.

So the poor mother wailed and cried and the actors wailed and cried with her. The music, wailing and drumming got increasingly frantic and so noisy that Lana's ears hurt—especially after the wine she had consumed last night. She could feel the drumbeats vibrating through the floor. The women in the audience cried and wailed. An older woman brought a light that she put on the ground so that everyone could see between the birthing woman's legs.

It showed way more detail than Lana ever wanted to see. You could see the flesh in her thighs move as she strained. You could see her private parts fill with the pressure from inside and could see the opening stretch as the child's head pushed the flesh aside.

Everyone was clapping and cheering. The poor woman was screaming her lungs out, her hair hanging in sweaty strands around her face, and everyone in the room was cheering as the child came out into the hands of the midwife.

Lana swore that she would throw herself off the tower before exposing herself like that in public.

The whole thing was over very quickly after that, and the servants put up a big breakfast which was attended by everyone, including the new mother, who basked in the glory of being told that she'd done very well. Prince Denori would surely favour her, because apparently he was the father of the child. Over the past few days, Lana had learned that the king had fathered very few children in recent years.

"You must count yourself lucky," one woman told her while glancing at her belly.

Sleeping with the king was, apparently, a subject that incited jealousy.

"I thought this was the king's house," Lana said.

"Oh, it is, but he's an old man, you know. He doesn't have to prove himself anymore."

What about the child, Lana asked, because she couldn't see the new baby anywhere. In fact she hadn't seen any infants since coming here, although she sometimes heard them.

"The children go to the children's house. The nursemaids come and get milk for a while until the mother has healed and is ready for the next one. The child grows up in the children's house. There are nurses and teachers and nannies to take care of them."

"Don't children grow up in families?"

She gave Lana a strange look. "Children belong with the other children. Only the women who are really poor look after their own children, and they'd probably be better off not having any, because those children never learn, never go to school, because no single person can do all that alone."

Lana thought children belonged with their mothers, especially when they were small. But she began to see the sickening truth: these women were focused only on pleasing their man. They saw childbirth as a punishment for having enjoyed themselves, and a culmination of an experience, to be repeated again as often as they could manage in order to increase their man's status. And yes, the king didn't need his status increased, having made it to the top, so he could probably take it easy.

The act of procreation was itself a performance. True motherhood, the nurturing and teaching of a child, was never an aim.

The thought made her sick. She did not want to play this game.

After the celebration came to an end, and women started to leave the room to go back upstairs for more sleep or games or music or any of the other things they did, Lana went to see the guards at the door with the letter to be delivered to the astrologer.

The same guard came to notify her while she sat at the midday meal in the large dining room that not only did the astrologer agree, but he was waiting for her. That brought her a few sharp glances.

"You don't get to see the astrologer until it's almost your time," a woman said, and several others nodded sagely, looking at her belly for telltale signs.

Another woman said, "But it is a bad thing having come in the Mother's House already expecting."

"Oh, yes."

And that met with more nodding, and more looks at her stomach.

"I'm seeing the astrologer to visit the library," she said, speaking clearly so that more women around the table could hear her. "When I come back, everyone who is interested can come listen to what I've found out and what I'm studying."

Most of the women weren't interested, she knew, but a few were. When she rose from the table, a young woman said to her, "I don't know if you know that many of us can't read or write. If you can, would you be able to teach us?"

Lana stared at her. She was going to object that she wasn't the right person to teach Aranians to read and write their own language —since she didn't know it all that well and she'd probably mangle up the grammar, but she could ask someone to help. She could teach the women algebra and calculus, and they could work on things for her. She didn't know what, but she was sure to find something for them to do that was more useful than embroidery and slightly off-key singing.

She said goodbye to the women and left with the guards, walking through the ground floor corridor and out into the courtyard.

The nice weather of the morning had made way for threatening clouds that usually marked the afternoon and the sun was about to disappear in the haze that surrounded these clouds, called the Mother's Veil.

Lana was glad to be out of the cloying atmosphere of the house, where every move was interpreted as a sign of pregnancy. Apparently another mother's pains had started, and she was glad that she didn't have to attend another ceremony, or see the sly glances at her stomach.

"Where are we going?" she asked the guards.

"The Astrology building."

"The astrologers have a whole building to themselves?"

"They do study the stars, don't they? There are a lot of stars and they have a lot of books."

The second guard agreed. "A shitload of books." From the sound of things, books were definitely not his thing.

Somehow Lana had expected the famous library to be part of some institution like the Scriptorium, which covered many different disciplines. This really brought home to her how important astrology was in Arania and how long it had been important.

She had to do her study of the stars by climbing onto the roof through the little sloping window in the attic of her house. People in

Tiverius complained about the cost of light plates. They complained that she was wasting her time. They said that the group she ran was something of a useless project.

Here they had an entire department devoted to the study of the skies. Imagine what Chevakia could do with those types of resources. Doing real research instead of making silly predictions. Putting the smartest minds to making bigger and better spyglasses and keeping more accurate records.

When they approached the building, Lana knew that she had seen it before: The building's facade, with its many arches, graced the front cover of her edition of *Star Signs and Their Meanings*. Somehow, she had never considered that it might be a real place. The gold-embossed image hadn't shown colour, of course.

The arches and walls were made from red stone. Panels at the top of each pillar and ornamental strips over each arch consisted of mosaic glass tiles in blue and white patterns. The shutters on the upstairs windows were painted blue, with a star in the middle, and the doors under the overhang of the arched entrance were also blue.

A couple of steps led to the porch, with black and white mosaic patterns depicting the star signs.

Two guards stood at the entrance to the building.

Lana had started to notice that Aranians employed people to guard just about everything. Not just the Mother's House and the king's private quarters, but also the administrative building, the kitchens, and even the dining room.

Maybe that was because they had so many useless princes who needed to be given something to do. Maybe the king and the important princes constantly needed to watch their backs.

Maybe a bit of both.

The guards accompanying Lana spoke to the guards at the building's entrance. Lana showed them the letter she had received from the astrologer.

The men at the door gave her curious looks. The gaze of one of them rested on Lana's thighs, uncomfortably visible through the ridiculously thin dress. Lana stared back, and he turned away, his cheeks red.

The men let her through, although their expressions were

reserved. But the astrologer's approval was the astrologer's approval, right?

And so Lana entered that hallowed building about which she had read so much in an outfit that, in Chevakia at least, would be more suited to a backstreet whore.

She came out into a big foyer, where people rushed into passages that led off it, or up a big stone staircase or occasionally a little creaky wooden one that wound around a central axis several times before vanishing into the ceiling.

The air was cold in here, as it was in all these buildings with their thick walls, with the stone radiating the coolness it had soaked up during the night. It was also very, very old. The white tiles in the mosaic on the floor were no longer white and clean. The passage of thousands of feet had worn paths in the tiles.

The guards led her across the foyer into a marble-tiled passage that led past many doors—some closed, some open—to a big set of double doors at the end. The doors stood open and a steady stream of people went in and out.

They were all *men.* Young men wearing green robes carrying books, older men wearing blue robes, sometimes with a few stars embroidered along the hems.

Some of them gave Lana curious looks. Others looked outright hostile or shocked.

The room on the other side of the door was huge, spanning at least three floors in height. Rows of tables stood in the middle. Many young men in green robes sat here to work. The walls, including two gallery levels of them, were all covered in bookshelves filled with thick leather-bound tomes.

The guards led her onto the floor, approaching what looked like an information desk with a clerk with long grey hair. The man's mouth fell open at the sight of Lana.

"We're here for the astrologer," one of Lana's guards said.

"Oh!" The man's eyes widened. He got up from his seat and shuffled across the library's main floor.

He came back not much later in the company of the king's astrologer, that terrible man who ruined people's lives with his lies.

His expression was blank.

He met Lana's eyes and Lana met his eyes. She kept looking at him until he looked away. Apart from a terrible haughty man, he held a powerful position. Many people looked up to him for judgement. Not someone she wanted as enemy, although she suspected her dislike of him was mutual.

"Thank you for allowing me to use the library."

He nodded.

Lana suspected that if it was up to him, she wouldn't be here at all.

"I have heard much of this famed library, and it's an honour to finally be here."

He nodded again. His expression remained closed.

"I would like to study the old star maps held in the library, and your books of observations."

"That is not appropriate attire to use the library. This is the reason why women don't come here."

"This is all I was given. If you want me to wear something less revealing—and I would love to wear it—then I need to be given something more appropriate."

"You will have to get dressed properly."

"The king said I could use the library." She held up the letter.

"You distract the staff and students."

"Are the students really so immature that the sight of a woman distracts them so much that they can't work?"

He snorted. His nostrils flared and he pressed his lips together. He turned on his heel and disappeared into a door in the wall. Lana frowned at one of the guards. He spread his hands.

A moment later, the astrologer came back with a dusty piece of fabric which, when he unfolded it and shook it out, turned out to be a grey robe. Lana draped it over her shoulders. The sleeves were far too long and she needed to roll them up several times. The collar was so wide that it immediately slid off one shoulder, taking that part of the dress with it, so that her naked shoulder was exposed. She hiked it up, but she could already feel it sliding again. Man, this thing was way too big for her.

The astrologer pursed his lips while he looked her over. "This will do for now. Come with me." He turned around abruptly and crossed the floor.

Clutching her notebook—and holding the robe so it wouldn't slide off again—Lana followed him.

He walked so fast and was so much taller and had so much longer legs than hers that she almost had to run. He wove between rows of tables, where students stared at her, nearly crashed into a librarian with a trolley of books and charged up a little winding staircase that went up to the first gallery level. He strode over the gallery with great speed and stopped just as abruptly at a set of shelves that held huge fat books bound in red leather.

"This section holds observation records." He flapped his hand at the shelves, five or six bays to the end of the gallery, all packed full of books. "Here is a table you can use." It was more of a tiny shelf than a table, attached to the railing of the gallery.

"Thank you," Lana said.

She waited until he had gone and walked along the shelves. The big books were all dated and shelved in order. But there were so many of them! It would take her a lifetime to study all this. Maybe, she thought, that was his aim, to give her so much old stuff that she became discouraged. She would have to focus on just one of her questions.

What question would that be?

She was reasonably satisfied that the question that the world was round had been answered.

She was also happy with her observation that the Great Wanderer was a—well, what was it? Another sun? And were the children worlds like the earth?

That should be her question: what was the Great Wanderer? She should find the books with the dates when it was clearest in the sky.

Of course she didn't have her notebooks that sat on the shelf in her bedroom in Tiverius, but with her interest in the Great Wanderer, she thought she remembered.

She put down her notebook on the little shelf-table and went to pull a giant book off the shelf.

Oof. It was so heavy she almost dropped it.

When she opened the book, it took up all the space on the little table, and there was no longer any room for her notebook. That was silly, so she went to sit on the floor with her legs crossed, and opened the giant book on her lap. That was better. The book on her lap had the added benefit that the leather was quite warm, because it was chilly in this room.

She leafed through the pages of lush, thick paper. Each page detailed one day of observations. Sometimes, there was hardly any text, and sometimes the text spilled over to the next page. Sometimes the page contained only text, and sometimes the observer had made drawings that were works of art in themselves.

He'd drawn the Great Wanderer as a star, with brilliant rays reaching into the night. Was it maybe a small star that gave only a little bit of light? Or was it a body like the moon, that did not give off any light by itself?

The moon was only visible low over the horizon in Kadrish, yet observers had made intricate drawings of its surface in more detail than Lana had ever seen.

On one page, the chronicler noted that there were no observations because a new lens was being installed in the spyglass, and "The workshop has outdated ideas about working times, so unfortunately the glass was not ready in time for my use."

That particular entry was made by the astrologer Sizek, who in his youth had travelled freely to all corners of the continent. She remembered reading about a trip he took to Red Hill in northern Chevakia to study "star trails" and had to resist the temptation to find the accompanying volume of notes. Lana leafed through the pages, falling from one wonder into another. All this history, all this amazing data locked up behind the facade of astrology. Making stupid predictions that had nothing to do with the way the stars moved in the sky. It made her brain hurt. What a monumental waste.

Then she came across a page with delicate drawing of the moon phases: from a little crescent to a disk.

No. It said *Red Wanderer.* Well, that was . . . interesting. Did that mean all the Wanderers were like this? Did none of them give any light?

She read the text.

With the new lenses in the spyglass we can now see that the stars go through phases like our moon. This is why their light varies in strength.

The observation was made over ten years ago. She should ask the astrologer if the department had spyglasses that could see the crescent shape of the stars.

She was scribbling furiously when footsteps sounded behind her.

There was the astrologer again, flapping his hand. What did he want now?

"Get up and sit properly," he told her.

"But that table is too small for the book. I might drop it."

"Get up. That's no way to distract my students."

Lana gestured at the gallery walkway, which was empty on her side of the room. Through the spokes on the banister, she could see two students in green on the other side, both gawking across the library space at what was going on.

"There are no students who can see me."

"Get up, insolent woman."

Lana struggled to her feet. The book was so heavy that she could no longer hold it open and keep it balanced in her hands. This was ridiculous.

She shut the book, tucked it against her chest and walked past him to the stairs.

"What are you doing?"

"Using one of the tables downstairs. That's what they're for, right?"

"You can't."

"Why not? Will the sight of my female curves hurt the poor students' eyes? Are they that immature?"

She knew she had gone too far the moment the words were out of her mouth, but she was so incredibly sick of this man and his obstructionist attitude.

He snorted. "Do you know that I'm a brother of the king?"

She could have guessed, since everyone was a prince in the citadel. She couldn't see why it mattered.

"You can leave this building. I cannot stop you coming back, but I can definitely stop you coming in looking like this."

"And whose fault it is that I look like this? Who put me away in the Mothers' House, hoping that I would shut up and be a good girl? What did you actually predict for me? I was born in the sign of the Eagle. In combination with the stone landing on the Great Wanderer, that, according to *Star Signs and Their Meanings* was a sure prediction that I was going to be trouble. Why then did you still recommend me to the king?"

His face went white.

He opened his mouth and closed it again. "How dare you talk to me like that? You insolent woman."

"It's true, though. I've read Sizek. I know what it means."

"And you think, having read *one* book qualifies you to do my job?"

"Tell me then, am I wrong about what I said?"

He snorted. "Out with you! I will protest to the king."

Lana turned on her heel and strode across the hall. All the students and acolytes and other silly hangers-on watched her.

CHAPTER 10

IN THE DAYS FOLLOWING Loriane's departure, Sady worked from dawn until he could no longer keep his eyes open. Nothing would stop him giving all the time he had for his country. During the day he was in his office.

To keep him busy at night, he took a box of books so big that Farius and his faithful guard Orsan needed to carry it into the house for him and spread them on the table in the kitchen, where it was warm.

The box contained weather records for the Watya, Tamyra and Ysherra regions for the past five years. He went through all these weather records, and made maps, tables and drew charts. He hadn't done this type of work for so long that he needed to look up his books to make sure he didn't make any mistakes. The work was relaxing and to his surprise, he enjoyed it a lot.

Once the maps started to take shape, he discovered alarming patterns of building storms similar to those that had existed at the time of the sonorics explosion twenty years ago.

But there were only brief flurries of elevated sonorics, nothing high enough to warrant warnings. Sonorics-wise, the threat came from the eastern border with Arania. Weather-wise, the Aranian machines didn't even make a blip on the charts.

But those storms in the north, those patterns . . . and snowfall on the highlands. Those were worrying signs.

It seemed there were two different issues at work. The Aranians were using sonorics. Yes, that was dangerous and they needed to be stopped. But something far more serious was coming from the north.

Every now and then, an academic at the Scriptorium would voice an opinion that the existence of a sonorics machine in the City of Glass might have been balanced by another in the far north. Those theories were often dismissed as silly, but Sady began to worry about it.

There *was* an area in the north called the Badlands, and rumours circulated that animals didn't want to go there. It was so hot and dry that no one had a reason to investigate. But what if there was another machine up there?

If that was so, the machine was far enough to the north that the elevated sonorics levels didn't register in places where people lived who could measure them.

Maybe.

Or maybe that was the reason why the telegraph lines in the north had always been so troublesome.

Sady spent a lot of time at night in the kitchen thinking about these things.

While that was going on, during the daytime he met frequently with General Selidas and less frequently in closed sessions of the doga. The military's call-up had resulted in many thousands of soldiers pouring into the bases. They had to be supplied, so factories for uniforms, tents, shoes, sleeping bags and weapons worked overtime. He located all the stockpiles of old sonorics suits and had them distributed to the frontline troops. He started the production of more suits. Much of the knowledge about sonorics damage was no longer taught in training, so he hired a group of scientists from the Scriptorium to bring everyone up to date.

One night, the entire western sky lit up with skylights. People came out of their houses. Doomsayers appeared in the street the next day, proclaiming the end of the world. And people believed them. At the same time, many people were pouring into the city from the north, but many others were leaving for the east coast. A lot of the well-off families had holiday homes there.

The weather went from unusual warmth to driving rain.

It was getting ridiculous. Over the past few days, Rodi had

supplied him with new prediction maps every day. Warm air cells popped up over the border with Arania and dissipated just as quickly. Sometimes they heralded rain, sometimes warm and dry weather followed.

Flowers came out, and died. Trees grew leaves and they froze off mere days later.

People were blaming it on the Aranians and their machines. Lacking more data, Sady had no grounds to refute those opinions. He failed to believe how those small devices could have that much influence, and over such a large area. Something else was happening, but he had no proof, and in light of the Aranian threat, obtaining proof was not a priority.

THE MILITARY WAS GETTING ready to ward off attacks from the Aranian camps across the border. Several garrisons had amassed in the region closest to Tiverius. They had a few balloons, but not as many as the Chevakians. Their numbers, however, were staggering.

Sady's ultimatum to the king for the release of Lana and the other women was fast approaching, and the lack of response from Arania had been astonishing, if not unsurprising.

Did they even have Lana?

He would have thought that the proctor's daughter would be an excellent prize for a ransom demand. Unless Lana had been stupid and angered them, or she had tried—and failed—to escape. Those were dark thoughts.

He had not given up such a large part of his life raising such a beautiful young woman to have her killed by Aranians.

With every day that passed without a sign from her, or a reply from Kadrish, Sady grew angrier about that terrible possibility.

If he found something had happened to Lana, he'd raze Arania to the ground, finish the job that Milleus had left unfinished. He felt *sorry* that he'd written that letter asking for closer relationships after Milleus' death. Arania didn't deserve closer relationships. They deserved to be burnt to the ground. At times, Sady stood in the hall, looking at the dried-out turd in the box, wondering if it might be better to smash the glass and burn it. Or better still: send it back to its owner.

Maybe he should add a fresh one.

But that wasn't his style. He'd rather cut the posturing and strike at the heart of the country.

Over the past few years, Chevakia had developed explosives that could be dropped from great height. The Balloon Division had done some tests with these, and the amount of devastation these devices wreaked was disturbing.

Up there, the balloons were unreachable. The military camps on the ground would be sitting ducks for a few well-aimed missiles.

When General Selidas visited, Sady authorised him to start using these explosives.

"That requires our troops to cross the border," the general said.

"Yes." The Aranians had crossed the border to capture Lana.

"And it is likely to lead to a high casualty count in the Aranian camps."

"Yes." The Aranians had shown no care about casualties of their own troops.

"It is likely to lead to war."

"We can't keep staring across the border at each other, with us pretending that we're fine with Arania's incursions. We've given the ultimatum. If it passes tomorrow without a word, send out the Balloon Division."

"Certainly." The general nodded, his expression closed, and then left the room to have it organised.

General Selidas was a much younger man than Sady. He would never have seen war, only trained for it in hypothetical scenarios.

Sady had expected to feel upset about ordering air strikes, but the reality was quite the opposite. He felt relieved that the process had been set in motion.

Hopefully air strikes would allow them to get started on the Aranian camps before Isandor and the Eagle Knights turned up to help with more targeted destruction of the sonorics machines.

Rodi came to all meetings now. He argued that he could tell from the weather patterns where the machines were. Except the data didn't seem to be terribly reliable.

Sady knew where some of the machines were and where they

definitely weren't. There were none in the Ensar district, even if a cell showed up there. There were also none on the central Chevakian highlands. There might be some near Watya, since Arania had invaded that region, but no cells showed up there, and while sometimes cells showed up over the central border and there were definitely machines in that region, the cells were not very stable.

And no one could find any reason why a huge cell developed over the northern desert. Limited records reached the capital that the desert had turned green, that even the plateaus that had not seen any vegetation in human memory had turned into endless fields. There was no evidence of elevated sonorics in any of that region.

The situation led to an extremely heated discussion in the doga one morning. A senator doubted Rodi's knowledge. "It has become painfully clear to me that the temporarily appointed Chief Meteorologist is uncertain about the developments and their consequences."

Another said, "Yes. Does he even know what he's taking about?"

"Are you questioning my science?" Rodi went red in the face.

"Well, yes, to be honest, because your predictions haven't proven to be worth the paper you so copiously use to produce all these pretty maps. I don't know what you're thinking, but we are not so easily fooled by pretty colours. You may be able to sway some of the doomsayers outside on the square, but we prefer reliable facts."

Rodi's mouth fell open. He turned to Sady. "Proctor! Did you hear what he said?"

"I have heard it."

Rodi spread his hands. "Then do something about it! That is an insult."

"Actually, he has a point, because I have spent the past nights studying weather patterns in the north and not once have I been notified by the department that those patterns are quite worrying."

Sady pulled out his own data and showed the assembly the maps he had made. Rodi watched all this, his face going increasingly red. He said nothing and did not object to Sady's analysis either. At the end of the session, he vanished before Sady could talk to him.

Sady would normally have gone after him to give him a piece of his mind, but there were too many other issues to attend to. He couldn't afford to lose the Chief Meteorologist, inept though he was.

※

THE ULTIMATUM to Arania to return Lana expired the next day without a word.

Sady watched from the headquarters of the Balloon Division as the balloons took off, more than twenty of them, heavily armed and full of soldiers dressed in modified sonorics suits.

They would fly into the dusk before discarding their load and returning. Unless Arania had developed a significant balloon program or recruited help from the Eagle Knights—and that was always a possibility—Sady didn't think that Arania would have a quick reply to the raids.

Indeed, they didn't.

In the evening, telegrams came in from several towns near the border where observers had reported hearing loud thuds and seeing the forest ablaze across the river that formed the border. One report even spoke of Aranian soldiers jumping in the river attempting to swim to the other side. The Chevakians had fished several people out of the water. The military reported that most of those captives would rather spend the rest of their lives in Chevakian camps than return across the border.

This gave Sady hope that the resolve of the Aranian army was not very strong—there were strong rumours that it consisted of surplus men—and that a couple of air attacks were all that was needed to solve this conflict. After all, if Aranian troops had deserted, nothing would stop Chevakia from marching into Kadrish for the second time.

And find Lana.

Sady did, however, remember one occasion where Milleus, gruff and cranky as he used to be in his last years, had told him that the words "war" and "easy" did not go together. Sady could still see him there at the table in the kitchen. Getting ever thinner, with dishevelled grey hair, shoulders stooped, knotted hands clutching his tea.

"Even if we could penetrate all the way to Kadrish and take the capital, the war was never easy. There is always a price to pay. Maybe now, maybe in the future."

Maybe the price was that Arania refused to talk, and that the world had missed out on important knowledge because of it. Maybe it was that Aranian princes had been allowed to run regimes of terror in the race for the crown.

In his office, Sady pulled out another sheet of paper and wrote a second letter to King Orik.

Release all Chevakian prisoners or we will continue air attacks on your country.

He sealed the letter and went to the mail office to arrange to have it delivered.

A scene of chaos awaited him there. Extra desks had been placed in the main mailroom, and people worked sometimes two to a desk. Mailbags and parcels covered every bit of flat space.

"Oh Proctor," said the postmaster. "I'm sorry about the mess. With the telegraph lines being out of action, we've been so busy."

"Out of action?"

"Yes, the north has been touch and go for a couple of weeks now, but the lines to the east are also affected."

That was new to Sady. "Affected in what way?"

"Sometimes the power goes out. Sometimes, we get shocks through the lines. A few operators have even become injured that way. Sometimes the line will continue to operate without power after we've shut it down. It's dangerous to our staff and we have to be cautious to balance the need for communication with the safety of our staff."

"Yes, I understand." Again, why hadn't he been informed of this before? "Any idea what is causing it?"

He shook his head. "I'm very sorry, Proctor. I wish I knew."

It was, in fact, something Sady had heard before, at least about the lines that operated by themselves. At one point, many years ago when the Eagle Knights had come to power in the City of Glass, there used to be a telegraph line next to the route that led through the mountains to the City of Glass. The line had only been built as far as the foot of the mountains on the southern side. Constant outages and line sparking had frustrated the engineers so much that they abandoned the project. He remembered people mentioning that, even though the line had never operated commercially and had not been powered for a long time, it would sometimes function.

It was, he surmised, a function of sonorics.

After giving his letter, he went to find the most recent weather station recordings.

As before, there were a fair number of little cells with isolated increased levels of sonorics, but nothing that warranted special notice. Yet this thing was still happening.

There was no reply from Isandor, which irked him, because Loriane had been away for a while and he wanted to know how she was.

Sady went home feeling unhappy, feeling like something was about to break. All the signs were that an unexpected disaster would happen, but as yet he had no idea what form it would take.

SADY CAME to his office the next morning, finding a letter on his desk. After his initial excitement, it turned out to be from a field station officer, asking for permission to send wounded officers to the capital.

General Selidas came in while Sady was reading it.

"I put that on your desk," he said.

"What sort of men are these?" Sady asked. "I don't understand why he needs permission or why they can't be treated in the field."

"They're contaminated with sonorics."

"Are they ours? Our men have suits. Their injuries would be minor."

The general shook his head. "They're Aranian. These are men with serious burns."

Sady had seen those burns twenty years ago and felt ill. "Do I understand correctly that the Aranian officers send these men to fight with sonorics weapons but don't even give them protection?"

"It looks like it."

This disturbed Sady more than anything. He went with the general to the field communication office to check it out. The officer would not let him talk directly to the field officer.

"We've had a lot of sparking on the line today, Proctor. I wouldn't want you to be hit by it. One of my staff will ask your questions. My people are all trained to deal with sparking."

There were not many prisoners, Sady heard in the second-hand conversation. These men had jumped into the river that separated the two countries. A few had died of exposure since, and it looked like a further couple would not make it.

Sady ordered the men to be brought to the city. He was very curious about why the Aranians would do this.

He wondered briefly if the Aranians had been hit by something other than their own sonorics devices, but the areas around the camps definitely showed elevated levels that were consistent with harm to humans.

He went home with even more books of weather data and ploughed through them while eating dinner.

Around him, the servants were chatting about daily life in the house.

"You hardly talk to anyone at the table anymore," said Myra.

"I'm too busy," Sady said without looking up from the books.

"That's all weather stuff, isn't it?"

"It is."

"I thought that was why the doga had a Chief Meteorologist."

Now he put his pen down and looked at her.

She was right. That was why they had a Chief Meteorologist. But he didn't trust Rodi's work. Or rather, he didn't trust that Rodi placed enough importance on the work the doga wanted him to do.

"We do have a Chief Meteorologist. But it is not the one I would have chosen."

"Then appoint another one. You can do that, right?"

"Yes, I can, but the Meteorology Department is very busy right now."

It was, however, a problem he would need to solve, because if important information wasn't making its way to the people who made decisions, then something was broken.

He missed Viki so very, very badly. Not just as a faithful hard worker, but as a friend. Rodi was not a friend. He was a typical academic: haughty, in love with himself and out of touch with the people of the city and unwilling to learn or compromise. Yes, he should be relieved of his position. The trouble was: who could replace him?

There was no one in the department who stuck out as particularly suitable. To be a Chief Meteorologist, one needed to be experienced, have an understanding of how the doga worked, be astute enough to detect when senators wanted to use you to further their aims and have a thick skin to weather their insults when you didn't want to play their game.

He'd done the job for many years. Life had been so much easier then.

He missed it.

Sady left the kitchen long after everyone had gone. He trudged up the stairs, feeling dark and depressed. He wasn't coping. The doga wasn't coping. No one understood the problem and, on top of that, no one, including in the City of Glass, was talking to him.

He lay alone in the big bed wondering why he had deserved to again be lonely.

He must have fallen asleep at some point, because he woke up with a shock. Someone was banging on the door. Sady jumped out of bed, walking barefoot across the cold floor.

Farius was in the hall, also in his nightgown.

"I'm sorry, Proctor, but Orsan is at the door. Apparently Arania has launched a counterattack."

CHAPTER 11

THE CAMELS FINALLY had names.

Javes' camel was called Zaylen, which meant "leader" in the old forgotten language of the north. Tali's camel was Shirra, which was a type of desert flower.

Javes didn't know if he imagined it, but he felt that both beasts walked taller and more proudly because of it. They often walked side by side now, not tethered to each other, and Javes and Tali would chat about everything. Tali, it turned out, had a gift for lame puns; one that, Javes feared, would get worse once she learned the central dialect, which offered many words suitable for puns.

By now, they had left the worst of the bad weather behind.

Because the telegraph lines were out, Javes never found out whether the storms up north continued, but after a few days of blustery weather with a few specks of rain, the skies cleared for mild autumn weather. They made good progress through the central heartland of Chevakia. They came through little farming villages, industrial towns and trading towns along the river. They passed the railway several times, but few passenger trains stopped here.

Some of these places Javes even remembered having visited before. When he was little, his family travelled a fair bit to establish his father's business empire of inns and eating-houses. He didn't remember much of the towns, but at least the names were familiar to him, including the inns they passed. His father had since sold his

141

regional business network, and it was good to see that a lot of the establishments flourished under their new owners.

Life here seemed disturbingly normal. People still farmed crops and went to work as if nothing had happened.

It made him angry, seeing this. It was further evidence—as if he needed any—that Tiverius cared nothing about the northern districts. He had known it; everyone knew it. But he had never *felt* it. He guessed *he* had changed more than anything. He cared about the north.

After many days of walking, Javes and Tali finally came to the hill with the lookout from where you could see, in the distance, the many roofs of Tiverius.

It was early morning, and the air was hazy.

Javes had known about this place and had known it was coming up, but it still hit him with surprise. That was his hometown down there, and he could not have felt more foreign.

Tali was looking at the city with wide eyes. She had thought that Watya and Lekata had been big towns. When he first came there, he had thought that Watya was a hole, and Ysherra had been an unimaginable dump of a place.

Being unable to read well, and not having had access to a library, Tali had never even seen pictures of Tiverius; and Javes had never even heard of Ysherra before he received the letter with his placing. He remembered being disappointed with where he was being sent. He'd wanted to go to a more glamorous place, like Solmeni.

And now he wondered how the people of Ysherra had weathered the storms.

Tali said, "I thought . . . I thought that people who drew these buildings made them up. How does a round roof like that even stay up? How big is it? What does it look like from the inside?"

"You'll see soon enough."

"Do you live in a house like that?"

Javes laughed. "No, my parents' house is big, but nowhere near as big as that."

"Those people must be so rich. Are you rich? As rich as the town administrator?"

"Something like that."

Ysherra's town administrator lived in a house that looked like a mansion compared to the other houses in town, but compared to the well-off in Tiverius, he would be considered quite poor. Javes saw no need to mention that to her. She was smart and would soon understand how much more power these people had than Ysherra's town administrator.

They rode down the slope to the city's market gardens and then across the bridge into the part of the city where the workers lived. Buildings of three or four floors lined the road. It was busy here, with many people walking down the street, waiting for the train, buying food from street vendors.

Javes was disturbed to see so many soldiers in the street. He couldn't remember ever having seen that many. They walked in groups, carrying bags. Some boys from his school year had signed up for the army, because it paid and they either had no desire or no money to go to the Scriptorium. Many of the soldiers patrolling the streets today were much older.

What was going on?

The two camels and their riders, accompanied by a dozen goats, attracted many strange looks.

Tali wanted to know how big people's families were because the houses were so big.

"They're not houses, they're buildings made up of apartments. Each group of two windows you can see there is a different apartment. Most of them have two rooms: one for living and cooking and one for sleeping. They're not so different from the houses in Ysherra, but they're all stacked up."

"But . . . don't you hear the people walking around and talking in the house above you?"

"Yes, you do."

She stared at the buildings with renewed horror. "But that's terrible. I guess these people are not rich."

"Nope."

Javes was getting nervous. Once they crossed the main road, they would almost be at his family's house. He hoped his parents wouldn't freak out too much about the animals and about Tali. There was a disused shed at the very back of the garden, and he could rig up a pen for the animals until he found a more permanent home for them.

They entered the administrative quarter, and then turned into his street. Everything looked so strange and clean. The houses were so opulent, and the gardens were ridiculous, with their clipped bushes and fountains. The trees had finally gone yellow.

A man came out of the gate of one of the houses. Javes knew him. He was that family's oldest son, about to take over his father's business. He and Javes' brothers were of the same age and used to play together a lot.

It was not until Javes greeted him that he looked at the pair of them. His eyes widened.

"Why, Javes, it's you. I almost didn't recognise you with this whole menagerie."

"We're just coming back."

"All the way from Ysherra?"

"Yes, the trains were crowded, so we walked."

"The camels walked," Tali said.

The neighbour gave her a strange look. Yes, she had a northern accent, and people were already wondering what she was doing with him.

The neighbour went into the yard of Javes' house and knocked on the door. "Mari, Clessa, look who's here!"

The maid opened the door and ran to the gate, followed a moment later by Javes' oldest brother Belo, laughing as the goats wormed themselves through the gate past the maid, or jumped straight over the garden wall, and went to drink from the fountain.

His mother came to the porch and gave a squeal. "Oh, Javesius!" She ran down the steps, insofar as a middle-aged lady with big hips can run, and came to the gate.

Javes made the camel sit on the garden path and slid off into the arms of his mother. "Oh, we were so worried about you. We didn't hear and then all these horrible things started happening in the north and—ugh, you smell. What's with all these goats and camels, anyway?"

The camel had taken an interest in the bushes. Javes pulled the animal's head away. "I'll take the animals to the back."

The goats had scattered over the garden and were sampling the vegetation, pulling on grass and bushes. One had dropped a handful of tiny round poos on the paving next to the fountain.

He cringed. The gardener his parents used didn't come cheap. "Tali, can you put them in the harness?"

That request earned him a puzzled look and a little headshake from Belo. Javes had said all of it in the northern dialect. The groundsman ran around, shooing goats away from the flowers. Tali tried to catch them, but the man scared the animals too much.

After having sat down, Tali's camel had gotten to its feet again, unsettled by the running goats.

Javes grabbed the rope before it, too, started demolishing the garden beds.

His mother yelled at the groundsman to keep the goats out of her lavender.

Javes called over the top of all the noise, "Everyone, calm down. Let us get the animals." He directed the groundsman and Belo to stand at the gates and everyone else to go to the veranda.

Once that was done, Tali could catch the goats, and they took the animals to the back.

The shed was smaller than he remembered it—and seriously, had it always been this small? There was no hay, but there was a heap of clippings that might keep the goats amused for a while, so he tied the animals to the fence in the shade of the neighbour's tree and hoped nothing would spook them enough so that they'd all want to take off in the same direction at once, because he didn't think the fence could withstand that.

He took the packs off the animals and set them to the side of the shed, where the goats couldn't reach them. The neighbour's dog was going nuts in its pen on the other side of the fence, barking and growling and jumping up against the sides of its cage. The goats crowded against the shed wall, the whites of their eyes showing.

There was no trough, so he filled the gardener's wheelbarrow with water and put it in reach of all the animals, rubbing the necks of the camels to calm them. Then he asked the groundsman to find a bale of hay for the animals. It was probably one of the stranger requests the man had received, and Javes wondered where one got hay in the city.

This was no place for camels and goats. Why had he even imagined that it would be?

He glanced at Tali, who looked nervous. Compared to his mother and the maid, she was incredibly thin. Her skin had gone deep brown from the long days in the sun on the back of the camel, her clothes were tatty and smudged with dirt, and flyaway wisps of hair had escaped her ponytail. He figured he didn't look much better. His trousers were covered in camel slobber, and the last time he had made an attempt at shaving was three days ago. His skin *felt* dirty.

"Do you think your family will like me?" Tali asked.

"To be honest, I don't think they will. But try to be nice. We'll figure some sort of solution." Although what form that solution would take he had no idea.

He led Tali up the back steps into the kitchen, after taking off their shoes at the door.

The entire household had gathered around the kitchen table, or at least the ones who were normally at home: his mother, the maid, the groundsman, the cook, the laundry maid and his father's secretary. Belo, Belo's wife, Reeza, and Belo's bratty eight-year old son lived a block away, and happened to be visiting. That was a stroke of luck, because Mother tended to go hysterical over silly things, and Belo could tell her to shut up. She usually listened to him, too.

Right now, they were all looking from him to Tali and back again.

"Well, I'm back," Javes said into the uneasy silence. Then he turned aside. "This is Tali."

His mother looked Tali up and down. They lingered on a rip in Tali's shirt, the dusty leather of her shoes, and her messy hair.

"Tali, this is my mother and this is my brother Belo."

Tali gave an awkward bow. Both Mother and Belo nodded but said nothing.

"Tali is from Ysherra. I looked after her because . . ." This was a long story and he wasn't sure he wanted to tell it now. He didn't want to embarrass Tali or answer questions about whether or not her parents were still alive. He didn't think he could lie. "She was left alone. Her parents were gone."

It was Belo who spoke. "Well, Tali, sit down. We're about to have a small bite to eat before we wash and get ready for dinner."

The operative word in that was probably *wash.*

Javes found Tali a chair to sit next to him at the table. Normally, guests would come to the reception room, but Javes guessed he wasn't a guest and both of them were too dirty for the chairs with the delicate floral patterned fabric in the other room.

So they sat around the table and the maid distributed tea and cakes. The kitchen smelled familiar, of hearty meals and bread. For a little while, the talk was about food.

Javes asked where his father was, and the answer was, as expected, travelling.

Then Belo asked about the trek and Javes answered as efficiently as possible. Ysherra already seemed so long ago and far away and, now that he was here, he wanted to present Karlen's map to the doga as soon as possible.

"We were pretty worried," Belo said. "With our army and the Aranians trading blows across the border and the lines to the north cut and then that dreadful incident where the meteorologist got killed up there, and the proctor's own daughter went missing—"

"Wait. Meteorologist? Who died?"

"The Chief Meteorologist."

"Viki?"

His voice had sounded so horrified that his mother gave him a strange look. "Yes, you hadn't heard?"

"No. What happened?"

"Apparently Vikius was on his way to Ysherra, and when they got stuck in the weather his bus got ambushed by Aranian soldiers out of Watya."

"But I didn't know he was coming." A feeling of total horror came over Javes. Was there anything he could have done to help Viki?

"The proctor's daughter was with him."

"Lana? What happened to her?"

"No one knows, but all signs are that she was taken to Arania."

"But they force women into Mothers' Houses in Arania."

Belo nodded, slowly.

"But that's horrible."

The groundsman said, "The proctor has written to King Orik with an ultimatum to return the women and stop the attacks on the north of the country."

"The ultimatum expired a few days ago," Belo said. "That's why the proctor ordered the air strikes across the border."

"Air strikes?" The feeling of horror grew ever bigger.

"Yes, the army has new explosives which they only need to drop from the balloons and—boof!" He spread his hands, mimicking an explosion.

Javes felt sick. He knew why the Aranians were raiding the north. The object in question felt like it was burning a hole in his pocket.

If he'd passed it to someone in authority, the Aranians would have stopped searching for this thing, and all this might not have happened. And now Lana was caught up in it as well? "All those soldiers on the street, are they all headed to the north?" He didn't quite see why that many soldiers were needed. The Aranians up there were just bands of rogues. Many of them didn't wear uniforms and didn't fight as such. They just came to search the place.

Belo shook his head. "Arania has launched attacks on Vesar and Haritius."

"But that is . . ." Javes' heart jumped. His father used to own inns in Haritius.

"Uncomfortably close to Tiverius, yes. The Aranians are on their way here. The proctor has amended the mobilisation call to include everyone who served in the military in the last ten years. He gave a speech about it yesterday. If Arania doesn't respond to the new actions, he will give the order for the ground troops to cross the border. You should have seen him, Javes. You know he's a very old man, but if I live to that age, I want to be like him. You could not find a single piece of ground in the hall that was unoccupied, and you could have heard a mouse scurry in that room when he spoke. And when he finished, the roof blew off with all the cheering. People who couldn't get in and were standing outside said they could hear it from the market square."

"He's really going to war?"

"What else can he do?"

A chill went over Javes' spine. He'd heard terrible things about the last war. "Belo, how long ago did you serve?"

"It was twelve years ago."

Javes met his brother's eyes. If this conflict didn't resolve fast, his brother would be called up next.

A moment of painful silence passed.

His mother was looking at Tali. "Javesius, what do you want us to do with this girl? Does she really have no family up there?"

"No, she doesn't."

"But do you really think it was wise to take her all the way to Tiverius?"

"What else would you have done?"

She scoffed. "I believe that the natives are best off staying in their own villages."

"There is nothing left up there. Dust devils are destroying the houses and the crops; they're killing the animals. Many people are getting spooked and leaving."

"Well, she could have left with people who weren't going that far, people only going to the next village."

He wished he could say, *Mother, just what is your point?* But he couldn't be that rude, and he knew what her point was: she was afraid that the neighbours—the ones whose dog was still barking its head off at the camels—would talk about the presence of a *northern* girl in the house. As if they would talk about that any more than they'd talk about the presence of two grumpy camels under the tree.

Thankfully, the cook brought fresh bread and soup for everyone. Tali looked unsure about what to do with the spoon. Javes demonstrated, but she held it awkwardly and spilled two drops of soup on the table. She ripped pieces of the bread and wiped the soup up because that was how she would have done it at home, and how Pashtan would have done it.

But that was *not* what his mother counted as "civilised" table manners, and to his mother, table manners were *very* important, and a major factor in whether or not she counted one worthy.

Tali failed that test on all fronts.

Belo's son thought it was hilarious, because Belo's wife also thought much of manners, and she spent the rest of the meal trying to get him to sit still and stop trying to get snippets of northern dialect out of Tali.

"My mother says I can't say cluey. I have to say smart or intellish ...intelli ..."

"Be quiet, you rascal," Belo said.

But the boy went on, and Tali looked ever more petrified.

Finally, Belo announced that he and his family were going home. "I'll drop past this afternoon with those jars of plum sauce." The latter to the maid. Belo's back yard had a large plum tree from which his housekeeper made beautiful sauce.

His mother accompanied the family into the hall, the maid started clearing the table and the groundsman, laundry maid and secretary went back to work.

"Sorry," Javes said, and he used the northern form of the word.

"I don't know what to say." Tali's voice was barley audible over the clangs made by the maid in the sink. "I don't understand what any of them are saying. If they ask me questions, I just don't know."

"That boy is a brat. You don't need to answer him."

"But what is he saying?"

The maid glanced over her shoulder, giving Javes a strange look. He and Tali spoke northern dialect between them.

His mother came back into the kitchen. "Now, about you."

"I would like to wash and have some clean clothes."

"Sure, you know where your room is."

"What about Tali? Can she use Belo's old room?"

"Does she have no one to go to?"

"No. Not in Tiverius, and nowhere else either."

"I thought it would be more appropriate for her to stay in the servants' quarter."

"Mother, she travelled with me all the way as a companion. She's not a servant. Besides, I need to stay close. She doesn't understand what people are saying."

"I suppose she could stay there. We don't have any girl's clothes, though."

"That's all right. She can wear some of my things. Come, Tali."

Javes escaped his mother's penetrating look. He led Tali down the hall and up the stairs.

She gaped at the chandelier with the many glittering glass pendants.

"Wow. They're like stars."

"Yeah." To be honest, Javes felt ashamed showing all this to her. His family was so rich that it was barely comprehensible from Tali's point of view. Having grown up in a dusty town with a scrap metal shop in the back yard, she wouldn't even have known running water, and the only bath available was the tub in the back yard, after which you had to be careful not to tramp mud all over the house with your wet feet.

He showed her Belo's old room which contained only a bare bed, a desk and a chair.

He found spare sheets and blankets in the cupboard and put them on the bed. By this time his mother had turned up and of course he was doing it all wrong.

She called in the maid who went on to ask Tali what size she was, and after Javes had to explain the concept of sizes to her she gave him a *one that fits?* look.

"We'll have a look through Javesius' clothes from when he was a boy," the maid said.

Javes let Tali know that it was all right to go with the maid, so that he could go in the bath.

He washed quickly, but there was no time to tackle the growth on his chin, because the doga closed late in the afternoon, and he wanted to pay a quick visit before dinner to hand Karlen's map to the proctor. Surely the proctor, having been Chief Meteorologist, would be worried about the dust devils and the storms. Showing him were to find the second sonorics machine would still be important; if not right now, then definitely after the Aranians had been driven back into their own country.

The face that stared back at him in the mirror was unfamiliar to him. His skin had gone dark. Sunlight had bleached the hair on top of his head. His previously sparse beard had become much fuller, and no longer looked like someone had smeared random spider legs over his face.

The timid, pale-faced student was gone, replaced with a weather-beaten young man with a strong face.

Maybe he wouldn't bother with shaving anymore. The beard didn't look bad on him. It looked *northern*.

Javes got dressed, grabbed Karlen's map and his notebook and, while the maid directed Tali to the bathroom, left the house.

He felt . . . strange to be going somewhere without the camel. Empty, naked.

As he walked down the street towards the dome of the doga assembly building, he clutched his treasure. After tonight, when he had given the map and igniter to the proctor, his task was over. What would he do tomorrow?

What would be going on at the Scriptorium with Viki gone? Who would have replaced him?

He went up the steps into the foyer of the assembly building and then to the first floor to the proctor's office. A line of people stood on the stairs, and a guard at the door informed him that if he wanted to see the proctor, he would need to join the back of that line.

"But there are at least thirty people in it. The proctor will never see me today."

"Then you can come back tomorrow morning," the guard said.

"Yeah, just like us," said an old woman in the queue.

"But how long is that going to take?"

"However long the proctor decides. We come back here every day. Your place will be behind old Saro. His neighbour built a big ugly wall in front of his living room window."

He looked down the stairs past all the people who were waiting. Most of the people were quite old, grandmothers and grandfathers, who, by the look of things, used this line as their social outing. "Old Saro" at the very end waved for Javes to come over. His expression was delighted, probably at the prospect of not being the last in the queue anymore. Or maybe he'd bored the people in the queue so much that he was looking for a new victim to hear his stories?

Javes had not come here to deal with neighbourly disputes. This didn't seem to be the right avenue to deal with the proctor directly.

He turned around and, under comments that "the youth of today have no patience," made his way back to the hall downstairs, left the building and went to the Meteorology Department in the Scriptorium.

Many people in the doga building had already gone home, but he was surprised at how busy it still was in the Scriptorium. The notice board in the hall said that there was to be a lecture tonight. Since when did they have night lectures?

The door to Viki's office was open. A light was on inside, and voices drifted into the hallway. As Javes approached, someone said, "Yes, I'll be back tomorrow."

The man came into the hallway—he was one of the office staff. He stopped. "Sorry, sir, if you're looking for the northern region meteorological representative, you've got to—my, it's you, Javesius! It didn't know you were back. I thought the train line to Watya was cut."

"I didn't come on the train. We walked. Well, the camels did, at least."

"All the way from Ysherra? You have to be the only person to have come out of that area recently."

"Yes, I need to speak to the proctor urgently."

"Then you're in the wrong building."

"I know, but I was hoping that someone here could give me a letter that convinces the guards to let me pass." He would have mentioned Viki's name here, and he still couldn't believe that Viki was dead. Viki would surely have written him such a letter. He had a very good relationship with the proctor.

"Ah, yes. Rodi may agree to do it, but—"

"Rodi? Is he the Chief Meteorologist?"

"Temporarily, yes. But go in if you want to see him. I was just on my way to the admin office."

Rodi raised his eyebrows when Javes came in.

"Did we have an appointment?"

"No."

"But you are a student, right?" His gaze rested on Javes' bronzed arms.

"I'm Javesius han Demerian. I was the fourth year student stationed in Ysherra for my fieldwork. I have important material for the doga that they need to see as soon as possible, but there is a long queue—"

Rodi squinted. "Oh, yes, I remember you. You're the lad who couldn't give his speech because the text had mysteriously changed into a picture of a naked female."

Javes cringed. Yes, that had been in Rodi's class, and everyone in his year had thought the incident hilariously funny, because Rodi had *no* sense of humour. He pressed on, "Please, I have important news for the Proctor—"

"For the proctor, yes. Don't we all?"

"I need to see him now, and I was wondering if you could sign a note that will get me past the guards."

"Me? I doubt the proctor will listen to me."

Javes noticed a set of maps on the table. He recognised the pressure bars that circled a deep low-pressure system over the north of the country.

"I was in that storm. I walked all the way through it to come and give this map and a device I found to the proctor."

Rodi shifted a sheet with readouts on top of his map. He gave Javes a stern look. "Boy, the proctor has very little time. He is in meetings about serious topics like war. The Balloon Division is engaged in attacks and counter-attacks along the border. He needs to take steps to protect all the citizens of Chevakia. He does not want to be disturbed with a student's fourth year study project."

"But it's not a study project. Listen and let me explain. You don't even know—"

"No. I'm busy. I'll be seeing students tomorrow. If you want to see the proctor, you can wait outside his office."

Javes went back to the doga building, seething.

The same people were still waiting on the stairs, and they laughed at him. No one had taken the position behind "Old Saro".

The old woman said, "That's what you get when you have no patience. My son would know that patience always wins, because I taught him."

Javes ignored all of them—seriously, why were these people even here? It didn't look like the proctor ever saw any of them—and went to the guards at the door again.

"I have a matter that the proctor needs to attend to as soon as possible."

The guard flicked his eyebrows. "I thought I told you to get in line with the others."

The old woman chimed in. "There you go, maybe you'll believe it when he says it."

"If I have something urgent. Like really, really urgent, and I believe that the proctor should see it right away, where can I go?"

"There is an assembly meeting on in the morning. Join the queue tomorrow afternoon."

"But I need to see him now."

But that didn't get him anywhere. If he had been angry when coming here, he was even angrier going back. He walked home in the darkness, with his hands in his pockets, the right hand firmly balled around the metal object, contemplating how he could do the most damage to someone's head with the metal globe.

He'd have to do something drastic tomorrow, or he would never see the proctor, or would see him only by the time it was already too late. When Arania had invaded the country and their soldiers were outside Tiverius and the storms had reached the capital and the whole world was being destroyed by this powerful remaining sonorics machine.

This was not why he had walked all the way to Tiverius, and part of him began to feel sorry that he had even bothered.

When he came to his house, he went to check on the camels and goats—they had been provided with hay. He stood in the garden with the camels for a while, rubbing the fur with one hand on each hairy flank, while the camels were eating and paying him absolutely no attention at all.

All around him, light radiated from windows in the mansions, each in their own yards. Voices drifted on the wind. Laughter, a child crying, someone walking along the neighbour's path of pebbles.

"Yes," he said after a while. "I don't think I fit here anymore either."

But the smell of cooking drifted through the yard. He was hungry. Tali would be out of the bath and feeling awkward without him.

He heaved a sigh, patted the camel's rump and made his way up the back veranda.

No sooner had he stepped into the house than his mother ran through the corridor. Her cheeks were red, her eyes were wide and she pressed her lips together in the way she did when she was really furious.

Whoa. What was going on here?

"Javesius. What. Did. You. Do?"

Javes stepped back from the bubble of perfume that surrounded her. "What do you mean? I went to the doga to present some important material—"

"What do I mean? What did you do to that poor girl?"

Tali? "Me? Nothing."

"Do you even know how young she is?"

"Thirteen, why?"

He became aware of someone sobbing loudly somewhere in the rooms off the main hallway.

He called, "Tali?" And when she didn't answer, he asked, "Where is she? What did you say to her?" He sidestepped his mother but as he walked past, she grabbed his wrist with a long-nailed hand and pulled him close. Javes could have wrenched himself free, but that would not be appropriate action to take against a parent.

Her gaze bored into his. There was sweat on her lip.

"That's right. She is *thirteen*. What is everyone going to say?"

An uncomfortable feeling grew in his stomach. "I don't know what you're thinking, but she came with me like a sister. I never did anything to her. I know how old she is, and I'm not interested in her in that wa—"

"Rubbish!"

"Excuse me?"

"The waif is *pregnant*. That just happened by itself, didn't it?"

Javes stared at her. Tali, pregnant? But she was only . . .

And a lot of things started to make sense to him. The teahouse owner in Ysherra had mentioned how the Aranians went about raping women. Tali had acted very strange in those days. Afraid of him, and afraid that, being a man, he might hurt her again. The bloodstained bandages.

He felt sick.

"Let me see her." He wrenched himself from his mother's grip and ran into the house's official guest room.

Tali sat stark naked in the corner on the couch. She held herself curled into a ball, her knees drawn up to her chest.

She wailed when her eyes met his. Her face was red and blotchy from crying, like a schoolgirl.

Pregnant? And his mother thought that he—how *dare* she even think that he would actually do such a thing.

He crawled onto the couch.

"Come on, come on. Calm down."

Tali squealed and threw herself in his arms, crying with wracking sobs. Her words were completely incoherent.

Over her shoulder, Javes met his mother's furious expression from where she stood near the door.

"What happened, Tali?"

"That woman . . . said I was a harlot and I was trying to steal your money and . . ." The rest of her words drowned in sobs.

"Please, mother, leave me alone with her."

His mother snorted. "I guess the damage has already been done."

Something inside Javes snapped. He let go of Tali and jumped off the couch. He ran to the door and faced his mother, who had the grace to look mildly alarmed. Since when had he grown that much taller than her?

"*What* did you just say?"

"I said it was all right for you to talk to her."

"No, you didn't. You made a vile slur on me. As my mother, where do you even get the idea that I would do such a thing?"

"You spent—how long—with her? I'm guessing it was just the two of you travelling. What else am I supposed to think? I am not crazy, in case you wondered."

"Mother, I swear I did *not* touch her, and if you don't believe that —" He *had* dreamed about her, and he'd thought that inappropriate enough. "If you don't believe my words, and you think less of a young girl who has been *raped* by Aranians, and you think that I . . ." He spread his hands. "I'm not your son, and you're not my mother."

She huffed. "Well . . . I didn't mean it like that."

Yes, she did. "I want you to apologise to Tali."

He stared at her and she crossed her arms over her chest. Javes knew his mother well enough to know that she wouldn't apologise.

He lifted his chin. "I'll say again, if that's what you think of me, then I'll leave."

"No, I believe you. You can stay, but I think she should go to one of those houses where they look after girls like this."

"You don't understand it, do you?"

"I understand what people will say about you and us."

"I don't *care* about what people will say."

"But I do."

She stared at him and he stared back. All of the petty things she had done in his youth went through his mind. The times she told him who he could play with, and who he couldn't. The times that she wouldn't let him attend parties because she thought friends' parents were beneath the family's standard, the times that she sent him out to school in foppish rich-boy clothes, the time that she had tried to stop him going to the Scriptorium because "real men go into business."

He had always been a nuisance to her. His brothers had always been the pride of the family. Belo was nice, but his oldest brother was a total dick, with his mother's character.

And Javes had enough.

"Come on, Tali, let's get you some clothes." There were no clothes in the room, and the wet footsteps indicated that Tali had run here straight from the bath.

Tali's clothes in the bathroom were disgusting, so Javes ran upstairs, grabbed an old tunic and trousers from his wardrobe, went back down and threw the bundle next to Tali on the couch.

His mother remained in the hallway, her arms crossed over her chest.

Tali slowly unwound her legs and stepped into the shorts. She was very skinny, but her figure did seem rather full for her age. He *had* noticed that before. The button on the shorts barely closed. He had not noticed that before, but he hadn't been looking for it either. She threw the shirt over her head.

"Come." Javes held his hand out to her. She took it.

"Where are you going?" his mother said. "It's dinnertime."

"We'll be having our own dinner. I don't have to tell you where I'm going. I'm an adult, and I'm not putting up with your insults anymore."

She did not reply.

He took Tali into the back yard where the camels and goats were pulling at a fresh bale of hay.

"Brother." Belo ran after him.

"I thought you had gone home?"

"I came to bring Mother some firewood. I heard about the girl."

"Don't you start as well. I took her with me because she has no one else in the world. I treated her like a sister. I might have been stupid, but I didn't know any of this. I doubt she knows what's wrong with her."

"I believe you."

Belo did. He was much older than Javes, and he might be a hard-nosed businessman, but he was also fair.

Javes sighed.

"What are you going to do?"

"Find somewhere for the animals. We've got a tent, we've got food."

"There is a barn just on the other side of the railway bridge."

Javes nodded. Belo owned the land.

"It's dry, there is some firewood. I'll come around with the truck and bring you some stuff."

"Thank you."

They saddled the camels, tied the goats in the harness and set off again into the evening sun.

Javes knew where the barn was, and when they arrived there, Belo was already waiting with the truck. He'd brought mattresses, sheets and blankets, a huge selection of dried fruit, bread, beans, sweets, cheese, a baskets of eggs and even some wine. He'd also brought a midwife.

While Tali lay on her back and the woman was feeling her stomach, the true story, or something close to it, finally came out. The Aranians had set fire to Arukat's house while Tali was out selling milk. When she came back, she found the goats gone and the men plundering her father's store of ironware. She had tried to chase them off, but they had taken her into the truck. Javes didn't think Tali understood what happened there, except that it hurt and made her bleed. To the midwife's questions as to whether she had bled before that happened, she said, "A little bit, sometimes."

The midwife rose and faced Javes, shaking her head. "It's far too late for me to give her herbs to abort the child. It has started growing, and I can feel it move. It's due in less than five months. She is very small. It will not be easy."

"I'll look after her," Javes said

They had walked from Ysherra together. They could do this.

AFTER BELO and the midwife had left, Javes made a fire and cooked dinner which they ate while seated on the mattress. Tali was still weepy and had grown very tired. She fell asleep with her head on his knees. He took off her shoes and tucked her under the blanket.

Look at them now, two northern outcasts, about to have a family. He had no money, no job and nowhere permanent to live.

Tali would say, "We have the camels. We could sell wool."

Yes, they could, but he needed a job that paid better than that. They needed a house. They needed a stable for the animals. He needed to pay for Tali's visits to the midwife. She needed new clothes and whatever one needed for an infant.

Well, wasn't that just great. He got a student placement that completely changed his life, and everyone in the city, including the meteorology department, tried to wash their hands off it.

That thought made him angry. He was going to make sure that they could live well, and that the proctor got Karlen's map. And then, possibly, he would leave Tiverius and never come back again. He thought of Pashtan and how pathetic his life had seemed. He'd learned Pashtan had fallen out with his family in Watya. No, he didn't want to do that. If he moved to another place, he'd lead a *better* life there than here. He would not hide. He would *not* turn away in shame. He needed money to buy things. A house, land, camels, businesses. Maybe he'd start a service to properly maintain telegraph lines, or one to collect and distribute weather data, or deliver parcels. Or he'd bring machines to work the massive riverbed in Lekata so that farmers could grow crops on the northern bank of the creek. He'd build aqueducts and channels to irrigate the crops. That would pour money into the town and Tiverius would finally extend the railway. He could even tell the Scriptorium about the strange bowls in the desert, and they'd send students and tutors to study the history, and they would build roads, and they'd need places to stay, and they needed to eat, and if more people wanted to go there, they might even push to have the railway built to Ysherra.

And then if the big sonorics machine could be destroyed, the dust devils would stop, and all that land would become suitable for crops again.

He went to sleep seeing green fields and shiny red and black puffing trains, where hordes of camels and goats watched the traffic in lazy indifference.

He woke up in the morning knowing exactly what he would do to get the proctor's attention.

CHAPTER 12

KOTORI TREMBLED WITH ANGER from head to toe. He went into his office to put on his official astrologer's cloak, his mind going over how this *woman* had insulted him, daring to suggest that his predictions were flawed and that he knew nothing. He, who had studied for years, who had passed many exams, who had the respect of everyone in the citadel.

It would be funny if it weren't so deeply scandalous.

With his official cloak over his shoulders, he left the building for the king's quarters. It was now midafternoon and the king would be resting. He disliked being disturbed during this time, but always said that emergencies had priority.

This was an emergency.

Kotori walked quickly, holding himself straight, his nostrils flaring. He strode past the guards at the entrance, who saw him coming and didn't dare question him. He crossed the foyer, went up the stairs, taking them two at a time, crossed the landing to the king's private quarters . . . and found the room empty.

Well . . . that was . . . odd. Normally, Orik would be dozing by the fire. The fire burned, but no Orik.

A small sound, like knocking of wood on wood, came from the next room where the door stood ajar.

"Excuse me? Your Majesty?"

There was no reply.

Kotori disliked going into that room. The purpose of much of the furniture in there was far too blatant for his liking. Kotori prided himself on never having desired a woman in that way. Pleasures of the flesh were weak. Women only existed to tempt men and lead them astray.

But now more noises of hammering or some such came from that room, so Kotori had no option but to go in.

He found the king on his knees on the carpet, unscrewing bolts that held together the waist-high chair that allowed him easy access to a visiting woman's private parts.

"Your Majesty?" Had he decided to give in to his flagging interest in women? As far as Kotori knew, the king had at least seen the southern woman with the sharp tongue.

Orik turned around, holding a screwdriver.

There were also, Kotori noticed, some loose pieces of wood in the room that looked like part of a set of bookshelves. The books themselves stood in a crate next to the door.

"I'm a bit embarrassed by these lewd pieces of furniture," Orik said.

"Oh?" Kotori didn't know what else to say. *I agree* would sound hypocritical.

"With women like Selwa, she was used to this thing, but for a new woman to come in here and have to lie on this thing . . ." He spread his hands. "Life is about more than screwing. The one and truly attractive part of one's being is the mind."

"So that's why you're putting up a bookshelf?"

"Precisely."

Er, all right? "Let someone else do that for you. I can order a carpenter to come."

"I'm healthy. I can do this."

"As you wish."

The king continued to undo screws and the chair slowly came apart. Kotori remained near the door.

"Astrologer, is there a reason you're here? Do you have a matter to discuss?"

"I do."

The king sighed and put the screwdriver down. He heaved himself to his feet. "Let's briefly go into the other room then."

Kotori heard *but you better not waste my time* in every word, and he was less and less sure of the wisdom of his decision to come here. All right, the southern woman had made him angry, but running to the king to complain was an overreaction. Maybe he'd be better off broaching a different topic, because the woman was in the library by the order of the king, and complaining about her would just make Kotori look silly.

In the other room, the king donned his cloak, because it was quite chilly. He took the poker from the side of the hearth and stirred the half-burnt logs in the ashes, grumbling something about servants having let the fire die. "You have to be on your feet all the time, astrologer. Do not let people take advantage of you or do their job poorly because they think you're not looking. Now, what was it that you wanted to say?"

Every shred of Kotori's resolve left him right there. "Well, I was. . . ." *Speaking to Denori.* No that would be a dumb thing to say. "I was thinking that . . ." *You're getting old, Your Majesty.* No, no, no, he couldn't say that either. "I would really like to see you leading a happy life."

Well, crap, that was a terrible way to start the conversation.

King Orik laughed. "Yes, me, too. I *am* very happy. Thanks for your concern."

Kotori breathed in deeply. "It seems to me that life in the citadel could become . . . dangerous for you."

"Tell me something new, astrologer. The citadel is forever a dangerous place, and none more so than for the reigning king. I've lived with that all my life."

"Maybe then it is time for your retirement." There, he said it.

Orik laughed again, long and loud. "If the citadel is a dangerous place, you are the single-most transparent dishrag that graces the bottom rung of its drying rack. Astrologer, Kotori, no, *brother* of mine, which of my illustrious sons exhorted you to bother me with words like that?"

"Well . . . it was a thought I had."

"You have *one* thought, brother, only one. That is: how do I get out of here with my head on my shoulders?"

Kotori let his shoulders slump. While Orik had, all those years ago, won his position through strength and brutality, he had managed to survive in it because he was very, very shrewd.

He placed a hand on Kotori's shoulder. "I *will* leave your head where it belongs, because I happen to be *very* happy with the woman you have brought me. She is vicious. She is smart. She does not spread her legs readily and makes me work to satisfy her. She makes me feel alive again. The sweetest fruit is the one you have to climb highest to obtain."

So? Was that why he was changing the room next-door into a library? Because that was more arousing to her?

"But if you retire, you can pursue all the knowledge in the world without having to worry about the running of the country."

"Have you not looked around and listened, Kotori?"

"Of course I have."

"No, you haven't. When I retire, *that* is when I need to worry about the world."

"But you would leave the country in the capable hands of one of your sons?"

Orik fixed Kotori with his old, grey eyes. "Then tell me this, astrologer, which of my sons would you judge 'capable'?"

Kotori didn't understand, but he did understand that the king had no interest in retiring and that trying to push that angle of the conversation would do interesting things to the angle of his head on his shoulders, so he left the room after having given a lame excuse of being busy.

He walked through the corridors of the citadel wondering what he was going to say when Denori came to see him, as he inevitably would.

He knew what Denori would say: just predict the king's death; but according to Sizek, his old venerable mentor, an astrologer should never predict the futures of people unless specifically asked, either by the person themselves or by the authorities, such as the king, military leaders or acolytes of the Mother's Temple. The king, infuriatingly, wasn't asking for a prediction—he hadn't asked for a prediction regarding himself for a very long time—so Kotori couldn't make one, not even to please Denori. He would adhere to that standard, because otherwise he might as well get himself a stall in the marketplace amongst the trinket-sellers.

Above all, Kotori just wanted to survive. He wanted to buy a nice house on the coast and spend the rest of his life fishing, and would be happy if the king did the same and they could both leave the younger generation to run the country.

DENORI DID NOT COME BACK the next day. Kotori was teaching and didn't leave the Astrology building. Here, at least, he was safe from Denori who, if his memory served him right, had never set foot inside this building since he was an adolescent, probably not since that prediction that he was still sour about.

His class of first-year students had heard of the commotion in the library from older colleagues, and they were discussing this as he came in.

A young student was saying, "I don't see why it should make any difference."

And another student said, "Because they're *mothers*, that's why. They have their tasks, and we have ours."

"But imagine if mothers could study or work while they're waiting."

Several students called at the same time, "That's blasphemy!"

"You don't get mothers to work," another added. "That's like . . ." The boy spread his hands and noticed Kotori in the doorway. "You have to agree, astrologer, that mothers are too delicate for study."

"They are." Kotori put his books down on the table in front of the classroom. "They are also too valuable to waste on such things as study. If I had a Mothers' House, I would not dishonour them to subject them to tasks such as reading and calculus."

"But the king seems to think it's all right."

"That woman is extraordinarily stubborn. If I have anything to do with it, she will not be coming back into the library to distract you."

"I don't mind the look of her," a student said. "Especially when she climbs up on the ladder."

Kotori snorted. He grabbed one of his books off the pile, strode to the boy's table, and whacked the book on the surface with such a thud that the whole classroom shook.

The boy retreated, mouth open, eyes wide.

Kotori spoke through clenched teeth. "If I catch you once more talking about the pleasures of female flesh, you're out of this classroom."

The student nodded, his face pale. The other students, too, acted timidly, and started on the work he set them.

When the lesson was over and he dismissed the class, the students walked out in groups. As they were going down the corridor, he caught one student saying, "I still don't understand. Why have I done such a bad thing by teaching my sister to read?"

Kotori was about to call the student back and explain it to him, when the student's mate said, "Shhh, don't worry about it. He's just living in the past."

Kotori stopped just inside the classroom. The two students reached the end of the passage without knowing that he was there and had heard them.

Was he living in the past? He was older than the students, of course, but he was not *that* old. Younger than his brother the king.

Well, that was a disturbing thought.

Kotori went back up to his room to dump his books and his official cloak. Why would a woman want to study in the library anyway? Look at those dry books with observations? Was she checking out star signs at a particular date?

No, Chevakians didn't believe in predictions. Perians didn't, either. Most of their star signs would be wildly different anyway.

He couldn't comprehend it and because it bothered him, he went down to the library.

As soon as he came into the hall, the librarian rushed to him. "Oh, astrologer, I am so sorry, but I couldn't help it."

"Couldn't help what?" But Kotori had already seen it: that *woman* was again in the library.

But this time, she was wearing a skirt of plain, non-transparent fabric and a blouse with long sleeves. She also wore a loose scarf over her hair, wound snugly under her chin and around her neck so that it didn't slide off. This type of dress was typical for the central-south region, where Selwa came from. In fact, he wouldn't be surprised if this outfit belonged to Selwa. Did that mean that this woman was here with the knowledge and approval of most of the Mothers' House?

That was even more disturbing.

She greeted him. "Good day, astrologer. I hope this outfit meets with your approval."

Kotori let his gaze go over her. He tried very hard, but could not find anything amiss with her appearance. In fact, the snug blouse made her look attractive. A lot more so than all that blatantly naked female flesh.

He nodded, and she went on her way, back to the section from which he had banned her during her previous visit. She took out the giant book, and brought it to one of the tables in the hall. A few students looked at her, but most went back to work quickly.

During the rest of the afternoon, whenever Kotori stole glances in her direction, she was busy working and scribbling.

A couple of times he walked behind her in an attempt to see what she was writing. She had made drawings of moon crescents. She had drawn circles and had written formulae of Perian algebra, something outside his field of knowledge.

And one time when he walked past her carrying a pile of books just for the sake of having a look, she turned around.

"It's all right just to ask me."

Well. She was not just a little bit rude.

"Ask you? I was just . . . taking these books to the shelf over there."

"Hmm. They must be very special books, that you carry them around a lot."

He had been carrying the same pile all afternoon. He huffed. "I am just doing my work."

"What are you working on here?"

"I . . . We're researching interference patterns between the major star signs."

"And interference is where the characteristics of one star sign mix with another, kind of like unorganised chaos."

"No, not like chaos at all. There are patterns."

"Do you have formulae or ways to calculate?"

Why did she bring everything back to formulas? "Astrology is not a discipline of numbers."

"Then how do you take measurements?"

"Astrology is about knowledge and feeling. It requires a lot of experience to interpret the signs correctly."

"So that is what all these students are learning? I talked to some of them. They learn to name the stars. They learn the properties of metals and stones and other materials. That's really interesting. You could use the knowledge to make better spyglasses, make the lenses more precise. You have much better lenses than we have in Chevakia. I don't understand, though, how one goes from knowing the names of the stars and the properties of metals to making predictions that affect people's lives."

Kotori snorted. He could not possible explain the soul properties of the star signs to someone so unbelieving. It had taken him years to fine-tune his knowledge. He said, "The first line in *Star Signs and Their Meanings* is 'In order to understand, one must first believe that it can be understood.' "

"I agree with that, but I suspect that your interpretation of it is very different from mine."

Kotori didn't think there were different interpretations. He thought this woman was insufferably rude, but he didn't want to have an argument in front of all his students. She was the type of person who would go into the minute details of predictions and he was feeling fragile enough in his confidence. As with every bit of research, people could always pick it apart. Interference was not a precise art and involved a lot of interpretation. "We're not talking about inter-ference. I wanted to know what *you* are doing."

She moved aside so that he could see her notes. "I'm trying to solve the question: what sort of thing is the earth?"

That surprised him. "What do you mean, what sort of thing?"

"When you compare the earth with the Great Wanderer and its children, is the earth like the Great Wanderer or like one of the chil-dren? We know that the world turns around because of the images we made with the light plates." And she went on to explain how she had left a light plate on the ground at night and how someone else had done the same thing in the City of Glass, and how the one at the City of Glass showed the stars moving in circles and the one in Tiverius showed she stars moving in stripes. She also showed how she had worked out a system for all the different phases of the moon

—and there were many—and that they repeated over two days and that they slowly cycled over a period of a year, and those were things that Aranian observations had also confirmed.

And it slowly occurred to him that she was not using star signs and the soul and character of parts of the sky, but merely the things that human eyes could see to determine and calculate where in the big space that she called universe the world was.

It would help very much, she said, if she could use the much better Aranian spy glasses, because she wanted to see if she could find the moon in the sky at daytime, because it would help her solve a problem.

And very slowly, Kotori began to see why she didn't want to call what she did "astrology" because it wasn't, but how all the data Arania had collected was useful to her.

It frightened him, because a lot of what she said went directly against the long-held beliefs of what the world was. If it was, in fact, round, that meant there was another side of it, and it meant that there might be land beyond where the ships went to meet the Mother, and it might be full of angry people or dangerous creatures who could live in places where humans could not.

But those thoughts clearly didn't frighten her. "Think of it, if we understand where we are and what we are, we could begin to understand many other things, because mistaken beliefs about how a thing *should* work are barriers against properly understanding it."

And oh, to him this sounded like she was shouting *Astrology is nonsense* with every word, because none of the things *she* believed were based on anything like the great musings of Sizek and astrologers before him. She wanted to *measure* everything, and that went against the magic of the great minds.

Yes, he could see how her way of thinking could unsettle the populace, and could undermine the authority of the great minds and cast the people adrift spiritually. That was it, the woman had no spirituality. She did not trust the guidance of people much smarter than her.

The stars had been right. She was dangerous. That in itself was proof that *his* way of thinking was correct.

All he could hope for was that she would be pregnant with the king's child soon, and she would no longer be able to come here.

But, once, Kotori had aspired to be a scholar, and he was now curious about the things she had said and agreed that she could use the big spyglass on the tower. It was too late for her to use it today, and as the bell for dinner rang, she scurried off with the guards who had been sitting at the door looking extremely bored all afternoon.

Kotori went to his room where he made some quick notes of the things she had told him as well as he remembered them.

After a while, he became aware that someone was at the door, watching him.

Kotori turned aside and did a double take. It was Nayek. Seriously, why was everyone after him all of a sudden?

During the prince's stay in the hospital, the hair on the sides of his head had grown, hiding those fire-red tattoos of creatures spewing flames and making him look much more like a normal, reasonable man, save for the whites of his eyes, which he had tattooed red.

Now that he had recovered, he had shaved his head again, and when you saw him from the front, it looked like flames were coming out of the back of his skull around the sides of his head. He had also added a couple of golden studs with sharks' teeth on his heavy gold necklace.

Kotori had never seen him set foot in this building. None of the princes were remotely interested in art. His heart skipped a beat, because the prince must certainly have come to see the astrologer and seeing how "well" Kotori's casting had gone last time, he must certainly be on probation.

He was also quite hungry, having missed the midday meal, but he couldn't try to get rid of Nayek with a lame excuse. "Can I assist Your Highness?"

Nayek snorted. "What's with this southern bitch?"

"The king asked me for a replacement for Selwa."

"What does he need to replace her for?"

"Her body is too tired to have more children."

"Why does he want more children? I thought he was done with fuckholes. Last time I spoke to Selwa, she said he could hardly get it up."

Kotori took in a sharp breath. That was not the way one spoke about Mothers, about *his* mother, or about the king. Nayek had always been rude and brash, but lately he had become so much worse.

"How is your health, Your Highness? It's a pleasure to see you have recovered."

"See this?" Nayek balled his fist and this made all the muscles in his arms bulge so that the veins corded under the skin. "I'm ready to kill that bitch who stabbed me, and anyone who sent her, *and* anyone who failed to warn me that it would be a bad trip."

Kotori's heart jumped. He took a calming breath and then another one.

Nayek laughed. "Got nothing to say? You weaselly coward. You can't predict anyone's fortunes. You just tell everyone what they want to hear, huh? You made a casting for my trip and you said it would be glorious or some other rubbish. Instead I almost died. Or would that have been the good outcome, dear astrologer?"

A deep breath, and another one. "I saved you." It came out like a squeak. "If I hadn't been there you might well have been embalmed alive. If I'd have wanted you dead, would I have taken you to the infirmary?"

Nayek's hand shot out, grabbed Kotori by the front of his astrologer's robe and whacked him against the doorframe so hard that the air flew from Kotori's lungs.

Nayek's ugly, scarred face was closer than Kotori had ever wished it to be.

His breath stank of liquor. "You've tested my patience more than enough already. You sent me to my death. *You* pretended that everything would be fine."

Spit flew into Kotori's face.

"What do you want from me, then? Why are you here?"

"I want to know what that bitch said to you, and what she says to the king when she is in his room. She has bewitched him with her strange words and drawings."

"I don't understand why you care so much about her. She is just a Mother."

"You don't understand it, do you? The king is supposed to announce his succession. He's been tired for years, and we've waited and waited patiently. He was clearly getting ready to hand over power to his successor. The only woman he still saw was Selwa. Now, he's taken this young thing, who will probably give him another son soon. Yes, she may be 'just a mother', but she is *his* mother. He should be retiring. What is his game?"

"I honestly don't know."

Nayek grabbed Kotori's robes again, pulled him close and growled in his face. "You useless piece of shit. If you were not the king's astrologer, I'd belt you over the head."

CHAPTER 13

ZAINA DIVIDED HER TIME in the next few days between combing the area immediately surrounding the palace for prince Nayek's supporters or their activities, and interviewing Aranians who had been picked up by other teams.

Many of the Aranians she had seen before; some she had spoken with; and by far most of them were, like herself, refugees who wanted nothing to do with the struggle between the two princes and had no interest in icefire or dealings with the nobles. They were let go as soon as the interview was done.

A few had activities labelling them as suspicious, and she passed these off to Marek and his team, who questioned them more thoroughly. The work was, for the most part, pretty boring. At night, at dinner, the Knights exchanged stories of fights and chases, but Zaina's team managed to avoid trouble. But maybe that was also because they had been allocated the area immediately surrounding the palace. Most of the trouble took place in the Harbour District.

The area covered by the team contained many of the grand noble houses.

Zaina had never known much about history, and she was amazed how old the City of Glass was. The houses were blocky structures made out of the same smooth stone and glass of ancient origin that also made up the palace. Some of the houses were in the old tall buildings, where the family lived on the very top floor and the servants lived on lower floors. Apart from stairs, there would be mechanisms that took a cubicle from one floor to another. Many of those no longer worked, because they had used icefire to do their job, but as she already knew, many families had moved to use steam engines for this purpose. Some houses even had lights that ran off a generator driven by steam propelling a wheel.

The families were understandably suspicious when finding Knights on their doorstep demanding answers to questions.

But Zaina could also feel the fear that radiated from some of these people. Many even fixated on her, because she looked obviously Aranian.

She told Rider Taino when walking between houses, "It's like in Arania. No one knows what's going to happen next, so no one commits to anything or makes definite plans for anything. Everyone is afraid of the people in power and the people who *might* be in power next, and those people sow fear in families who have something to lose."

He nodded. "Yeah. The nobles are afraid. There was another murder last night, also rumoured to be committed by prince Nayek's supporters. The victim was a well-liked person in the noble community, Milandor of House Vandri. A nice, honest, moderate fellow. Never stood in anyone's way."

"I bet they had financial dealings with Arania."

He gave her a searching look.

"The Aranians are all over the shipping companies. They give generous deals and then reel in the favours. The recipient of the deals is caught. If they complain, their business suffers. If they try to get out of the deal, people get killed. It's how the princes operate."

The family's house was one of the ones on the main street, where a young woman opened the door a tiny crack.

"Can we talk to you for a bit?" Rider Taino asked.

"Talk about what?" the woman said. "You're too late. You should have been here to talk yesterday or the day before."

"We can help bring the killer to justice."

"You can't. You have no idea what you're dealing with. You can't fight them."

"Open the door and we can talk freely."

"No." The door shut with a click. A bolt was drawn shut on the inside.

Rider Taino knocked. "If you're afraid, we can offer protection in the eyrie or palace."

The door opened again. "You have no idea!" And it shut again. Further knocking by Rider Taino yielded no response.

They walked around the house, but the curtains were closed.

The team only managed to talk to the family by threatening to break the door, and even then they learned little. The man's surviving family were all women and, as would be the case when dealing with Aranians, the women had been kept out of the negotiation. Many honestly didn't know what their husbands, fathers and sons had been doing. When Rider Taino explained that they were serious about offering protection for citizens who were under pressure from Prince Nayek's men, they were grateful to accept.

The team looked around the house, but if there had been anything that Prince Nayek wanted, it was no longer there.

And so they moved from building to building.

Sometime in the late afternoon they came to the last house in their allotted area. It was an ancient building that stood in its own yard. The surrounding tall buildings dwarfed the mansion, even though it was quite large. The path to the front door was lined with clipped bushes, but they didn't look healthy. Surely they didn't get enough light, Zaina thought.

There were no lights on anywhere in the house, and the front gate was shut.

"House Mara," Rider Taino said.

That, Zaina remembered from having studied these families, was the home of Ledor, whose business she had briefly dealt with in the workshop, but had ditched because it was hard to get payment out of him.

"Doesn't look like anyone's home," Rider Naran said.

"There isn't. This is the family of Isandor's lover."

"The one he has gone to bring back? They even sent their servants home? No one to look after the house?"

"Oh, don't think no one's watching." Rider Taino looked up at the buildings that surrounded the house on all sides, with dark windows that looked like hollow eyes. It must be depressing to live here knowing that thousands of people could see into your yard and dining room window.

Rider Taino lifted the latch and opened the gate with a creak.

Zaina and Leya were the first in the yard, followed by Prito and Wido, the latter holding his crossbow at the ready. They walked across the yard with a crunching of footsteps in gravel.

Rider Naran knocked on the door with predictable result, so Rider Taino went back down the veranda and led the group along a path past the side of the house, between the fence and the wall. The paving was bouncy with moss that, Zaina assumed, had grown since the family left in autumn. People in the city were always scrubbing moss off their porches, roofs and walls.

The moss was blackened and dead now that it was winter, but it still dampened the sound of their footsteps. Zaina hid deep in the collar of her cloak, her breath steaming in the cold air.

The path opened into the back yard, lit by the golden glow radiating from the windows in the tall building on the other side of the back fence.

Rider Taino stopped abruptly. He gestured, *Someone here.*

They stopped and listened. Zaina behind Rider Taino, with Leya, Prito, Naran and Wido making up the rear.

Zaina couldn't see much from behind his back, but all of a sudden, a shape climbed over the fence next to her. She barely had time to reach for her dagger. Leya behind her yelled out.

Zaina didn't pay attention. The alley was narrow and it was hard to see what was going on. She only saw the glittering of a blade in the attacker's hand. She hefted her dagger up—and he landed straight on it. The heft was wrenched from her hands by his weight, but not before the blade had cut deep into his flesh. She could feel the softness of it and the stickiness of blood seeping through her gloves.

He fell with a thud, face-first, on the paving between her and Leya.

"Good work," Leya said. She sounded disturbed.

While this was happening, a few men had attacked Rider Taino from the back yard. He was holding them back by swinging his sword in broad sweeps. Somewhere in the back yard, out of Zaina's vision, someone loosed a crackle of icefire that hit the sword and lit up Rider Taino as if he'd been struck by lightning.

Zaina held her breath and pressed herself against the mossy wall of the house. If that was how they were going to fight, she was gone. The Knights were impervious to icefire and, belonging to the Pirosian clan, couldn't even see it, but that blast would have killed her.

Rider Taino ran into the yard, icefire still dancing over his clothes. The other Knights pushed past Zaina.

"Make sure no one comes through here," Tutor Wido said while pushing past her.

Well, that was easier said than done.

Zaina clutched her dagger, still wet with the dead man's blood. He lay slumped next to her.

While the fight raged in the house's back yard, and icefire flashed but didn't stop the Knights, Zaina stood in the space between the house and the fence, nervously looking in both directions. The day had not been as cold as it could be because of cloud cover, and now it started snowing, big, fat snowflakes that made it impossible to see.

She knelt at the body of the man she had stabbed. He lay on his side, his face slack. He carried a second dagger on his belt. She couldn't see the design of the weapon, but it felt smooth and well-made. He also carried a powder gun of some description. She found the buckle of his belt and pulled with all her weight until it came free and the weapons fell on the ground.

The dagger sheath had two loops that fitted her belt, but the gun—or whatever it was, because she wasn't sure it was a gun—was too unfamiliar for her to know how to handle it in the dark.

"Anything interesting?" Rider Taino said behind her. He was breathing heavily and exuded a scent of singed hair.

"Can't see very well. It's dark. I got his weapons." She wiped snow from her face. "He was carrying a strange type of gun, I think, but I need to wait until we get back to see what it is."

"There is light in the house. You can have a look in there."

"Is the house safe?"

"Yes. The family appears to have left a while ago, and it looks like Aranians set up some sort of base in there."

They walked around the side. The back yard was one of those traditional designs, with clipped trees—now leafless—straight paths and statues of stone and glass.

The glow from the lights inside the house showed at least five or six bodies strewn across the yard, one surrounded by a big pool of blood.

Prito sat on a garden wall while Leya bandaged his arm.

"Who were these men?" Zaina asked.

"No one familiar to us, but probably Prince Nayek's lackeys. Come and have a look at what we found inside."

Rider Naran and Wido were in the back room. At some point it must have been a living room, but the most recent occupants of the house had moved the family's heavy wooden furniture to one side—a round table, a red velvet couch and chairs all stood bunched up against the window. Half empty cups stood on the table, the tea inside still steaming, and a cutting board lay in the middle of the table with a hunk of bread.

"We disturbed them in the middle of dinner," Rider Taino said.

Zaina put the gun on the table.

Rider Naran whistled.

The golden light made the metal surface gleam. It was made not of bronze or copper, but a much lighter-coloured metal that also didn't weigh as much.

The barrel was quite short—roughly twice the length of Zaina's hand—and tapered from the handgrip to the end. The handgrip itself was set in a recess, moulded into the metal. A little panel on the left hand side had four buttons.

"Where did you find this?" Wido asked.

"The man who first attacked us at the side of the house carried it," Zaina said.

"Does it work?" Prito asked, walking into the room.

Rider Naran rolled his eyes at him. "He wouldn't have been carrying it otherwise."

Leya looked over Zaina's shoulder. "How does it work?"

Zaina shrugged. She picked the weapon up. She couldn't even see how to reload the weapon or where to put the bullets. She studied the buttons at the back. There was a sign next to each, but she had no idea what any of them meant.

"I thought you were the mechanic here?"

Zaina snorted. One day she would make a cutting comment, but unlike this bimbo, she was professional enough to see that having an argument while at work was not going to be helpful.

"I'm going to test this thing."

In the back garden, she made sure that the weapon didn't point at any people or important structures. She pressed one of the buttons. Nothing happened.

When she pressed the next one, a pinprick of light started flashing. Then she pressed the top one and it stopped. She pressed the bottom one again and the light came up again, but it stopped by itself. The bottom two buttons also did nothing.

There was also a raised button on the inside of the handgrip. That would probably be the trigger. She pointed the weapon at the ground and pressed it—

—And a sizzling beam of light shot out. It hit the pavement of the garden path, leaving a scorch mark the size of a boot print.

"Whoa!"

Zaina pressed the button again, but nothing happened. Well, this was interesting and strange. She wondered how to put the catch on so that it didn't go off accidentally.

When turning the weapon over in her hand, she noticed a thin groove across the bottom of the barrel. There was a little notch in it, and when she put her nail in there, the two halves of the barrel moved apart ever so slightly. So that was how it came apart.

She went back inside the house, put the gun on the table while making sure that it didn't point at anyone, and levered the two halves apart. She had expected to find some kind of loading mechanism or one of those metal rods with stones on top, but this was . . .

It was full of tiny *things*. Wires, tiny little metal bits shaped into precise filaments and fashioned into patterns. She had no idea what all of this meant, save that she knew no one who could make this sort of thing, and she was familiar with the level of technology in all the different parts of the world.

This reminded her of the times she used to correspond with the man in northern Chevakia called Shen Mani, and he'd send her detailed drawings of stuff like this, and she sometimes wondered how much of it he made up.

Not nearly enough, it seemed. This was real. It was ancient.

"What is all that?" Rider Taino asked, staring at the tangle of wires and metal filaments.

"That is a very good question."

Not only that, but all the boxes stacked against the back wall of the room were filled with stuff like this.

There was a lot of metal: strange objects with wires and levers and buttons. Many of them had fallen apart, were tangled up and bent.

Zaina pulled one of the objects out of a box. It had an arc shape, and had broken off at the end. The material of the outside was very smooth, but weathered and cracked on one side, where it might have been exposed to the air or heat. Inside the bent shape of the thing was a hollow with metal rods. A bunch of wires, some coated with coloured material, ran down the side, held out of the way of whatever mechanism was inside the thing by eyelets on the inside of the outer shell.

"Where does all this come from?" she asked.

"It seemed the group we interrupted used this as a collection point," Rider Taino said. "I found some books with shipping dockets on the desk over there. Some of the boxes have documentation that is *really* old, like from before the time of King Caldor. It seems that noble families have been collecting this stuff from all over the known world for centuries. I'm guessing this stuff is being taken to Arania."

Zaina understood. "To Prince Nayek's camps. And Prince Denori doesn't like it and has sent the troops stationed outside the city to intercept his rival's shipments."

"What are the Aranians doing with this?"

"Nothing good. What worries me more is why they're collecting it. These things are from a technology so old that it has become lost. I know that some of these items are being found in the northern desert of Chevakia."

"Some of it is found locally, too," Rider Taino said. "It's made by the people who built the towers of the City of Glass. I guess the cold weather here and the heat of the north preserved the artefacts better than they would have been preserved in Chevakia, where *rain* and *plants* will destroy mountains over time."

"Where did those people go, and why?" Zaina asked.

None of them could answer that question, so Zaina went to investigate further into the house.

A long hallway ran the length of the house, ending at the front door. On the little cabinet by the door lay a letter.

Zaina almost ignored it, because it was *familiar.* Then she realised that it was familiar because the paper was of the glossy parchment type that Aranian high-class families often used.

On the front, it said *Tamerane of House Mara* in Perian script. The seal at the back was of the citadel in Kadrish.

Zaina slid her finger under the seal and broke it.

She unfolded the rich parchment inside. The letter detailed all manner of star observations. At the bottom it said, *Please tell my parents I am in the Mother's House in Kadrish and am safe.*

There was no name.

Zaina folded the letter and tucked it in her pocket before continuing to look through the house.

Room after room was filled with boxes containing ancient material, such a wealth of technology as she had never realised existed.

It should never fall into the hands of Arania, because it would be used for some silly game of rivalry between stupid princes and would be lost forever.

Imagine if she could work on this kind of technology in her workshop. Steam engines were beautiful things, but this technology was another level altogether.

"What are we going to do with all this?" Wido asked.

"We've got orders to take everything we find interesting to the eyrie," Rider Taino said. "Leya, run to the eyrie and get someone to come pick all this up with a wagon."

Zaina was in the front room of the house and saw Leya come out from the side of the house and walk through the front yard.

She was almost at the gate when Zaina spotted a glint of metal in the open window of the stairwell in a building on the other side of the street.

She ran to the window. "Watch out! Watch out!" She banged her fist on the glass.

Leya turned around, searching the façades of the surrounded buildings. Her gaze darted from one side to another, and an expression of horror came over her face.

Zaina yelled, "Get out of there!"

Leya ran. Something flashed on the other side of the street. A beam of light hit the gate. Leya just managed to duck behind a bush.

Yells and shouts broke out in the back room of the house. A couple of people ran past the front room to the porch. Someone else went up the stairs. Leya ran across the yard, up the steps and into the front door.

She stood in the hallway, panting. "They're up in all the buildings surrounding the house. We're completely surrounded."

Zaina met Rider Taino's eyes.

Well, crap. So this had been a trap after all.

CHAPTER 14

TAMERANE WAS BEING WATCHED. She knew that of course, but until now, she had assumed that the watchers were paid by General Pakori who worked for Prince Denori. Now she understood that they were paid by her father instead.

Her father thought that he knew what went on in his own house, but he didn't know about Zeiro in the shed. Zeiro, who had been out in the town at her request, looking for ways in which the two of them could make their way back to the City of Glass, and who had, when she ducked into the back yard to visit the outhouse, let her know that he had news.

So she returned to the yard after dinner and went to the shed.

Zeiro had made a little shelter by stacking a couple of crates on top of one another. His blankets and supplies were stacked in a hollow behind the crates and the back wall.

When Tamerane came in, he sat hidden under the fur cloak. His eyes lit up.

She passed him the cup of warm soup that she had taken to "work on some calculations" in her room. He clutched it in both hands.

"You wanted to see me?"

"Yes, I've got some news for you."

Tamerane sank down on her knees on the bed of straw and blankets he had made for himself, so that they could talk quietly.

"I climbed over the fence before dawn this morning, and walked

183

all over town. I found a group of people who looked like strangers and when I saw them a few times, I suspected that they were also looking for something. I followed them when they left town. They have a camp on the hill at the back of the town, and it turns out that they are looking for you."

"For me?" Her heart jumped.

"They're Eagle Knights, and they have some huge birds with them."

"Really?" She dared not hope.

"One of them is a man called Isandor. He asked me to give you this."

He handed her a small piece of paper. It was folded in half. In the familiar, loopy handwriting were three words:

I love you.

Isandor! Tamerane clamped her free hand over her mouth. Oh, Isandor was here.

Her eyes misted over. Oh, that was . . . so romantic . . . and so dumb.

She so badly wanted to see him and fly away with him on his eagle.

But did he even know the size of the Aranian army that lay in wait just over the crest of the hills behind the town?

"He wants to know which is the best place and time to collect you."

Tamerane opened her mouth. She was going to say *What about right now?* but that would not solve anything. She could escape, but her father would know where she'd gone and the Aranian army would simply barge into the City of Glass, overpower the Knights and kill both of them. Maybe they'd even kill the queen for good measure. Only Chevakia had any hope against that military force, and Chevakia *would* send help, but there would not be time to contact them.

No, she couldn't rely on help from others.

She alone had the means to do something bad to the military camp and Prince Denori's forces. Those books on the table contained all kinds of ways to make big explosions and kill lots of people, if she could get close enough to the machines. That would be a problem.

The machines stood in tents uphill from the camp in well-guarded locations. The Aranians died from too much exposure, and the general made sure that not too many people came close.

She would have to think of something.

She told Zeiro to wait. She went upstairs to her room and spent the rest of the evening writing a long letter. If her father had come into the room—which he hadn't—he would have seen her working, with maps and sheets of paper with calculations all over the desk. When she was finished, she rolled them all up and brought them to Zeiro, who sat in the shed in the dark, asleep.

Tamerane shook his shoulder, holding the roll of paper under his nose. "Take that to him, and he'll understand."

She watched him stumble out of the yard, still groggy with sleep.

TAMERANE KEPT Isandor's note folded up inside the top of her dress and, during the next day, took it out several times to look at it.

She was embarrassed to admit that seeing that familiar writing made her melt inside. She *remembered* so much: his wonder at all the things she told him about the stars and the sky, his long-fingered hands, his sincere blue eyes, and peeking at the long eyelashes of his closed eyes while he made love to her.

That feeling she had, the temptation to put her chin in her hands and stare at the ceiling while dreaming of him, scared her.

She was supposed to be rational. She would never do anything without thinking. She would certainly not do anything because of a pair of blue eyes or a smile that made her go all funny inside. Or the chance to feel the whisper of his naked skin against hers again.

The two afternoons that he had visited her had been so good. She'd been surprised that he had been interested in her books. She had thought he'd be like her mother: all show and frilly dresses but nothing on the inside.

But he was intelligent and encouraged her to work on her science.

That was what mattered most, right?

Because she couldn't possibly do anything for the simple reason of wanting the pleasure of making love to him again?

Come on, girl, admit it, you're in love.

Love scared her, because it meant she had something to lose, something that people who wanted to hurt her could take away from her. People like her father or the general, or that horrible prince, who had left for Kadrish, but could come back at any time.

Zeiro had a response for her that evening. He had, in fact, received the response in the morning because Isandor had made him sit in the camp while he wrote it, a long letter in his beautiful loopy handwriting.

Tamerane almost cried when she opened it and saw the little love heart he had drawn in the top corner of the paper.

Please, don't, because they'll try to break us.

She sniffed the paper, as if she could detect his male scent.

But the content of the letter was much more serious.

He said that recent events in the City of Glass had made him aware that a lot of the noble families had been forced or coerced into going to Arania, either through business interests or to "preserve the old ways of life", and that the Aranian princes were actively recruiting supporters, finding fertile ground in the city's nobles. He was hoping to find a way to set back the Aranian efforts as well as free her.

She replied that escaping the house would probably not be too hard for her, but she would want to destroy the icefire machine before leaving town because she didn't want any people to die because of something she helped make. She told him of the dacon and the dead bodies.

His response the next day was short.

If they want to play with the magical phenomena of icefire, let them play, because I know the rules better than any of them. Get ready tomorrow night.

HE DIDN'T SAY what he meant by that, and Tamerane could barely sleep. Get ready for what? Several times, she got up to look out the window, but she'd seen nothing unusual in the past few days, even if she knew that he or one of the Knights in his group watched.

She pulled all her warm clothes out of the wardrobe, and stacked her books next to them on the side of the bed. She slept in her underclothes with her warm clothes spread over the cover so that she could get dressed quickly. Lying on her back in the bed, it worried her that her stomach, normally soft, had firmed up a lot. If she poked with her fingers, she could feel a hard ball inside. She felt no movement yet, but that wouldn't be too far off.

She must have dozed of, because she woke up with a shock to the sound of the door opening downstairs. Male voices sounded in the hall.

And then her father called, "Tamerane!"

She jumped out of bed, threw her dress over her head and opened the door a crack. "Yes, Father?"

He called in the downstairs hall. "Get dressed. Commander Lakrey is here for you."

No. She didn't want to go. What had happened to Isandor's plan?

In a moment of panic, she saw him captured by the Aranians, tied to a chair, *tortured* by that horrible commander.

She shut the door and leaned against it, her heart thudding. What was she going to do? If Isandor turned up here, he would find her gone, and then he would risk being discovered for nothing.

"Tamerane!" Her father knocked on the door.

"Yes, I'm getting ready." What should she take?

She buttoned up her dress, put on her stockings and boots and her coat. Then she collected her books in a satchel. Wherever she went, she didn't want to leave those for people to pry at. With the satchel slung over her shoulder, she left her room and went down the stairs. Would there be time to grab something to eat from the kitchen?

Her father waited in the hall. The front door was open, letting cold and humid air into the house. A truck waited outside.

"Where are we going?" she asked her father.

Please, not back to that dungeon and the dacon boy, and the dead bodies.

"They want us to come to the camp."

Something about the way he said it made her wary. Going to the military camp and then what?

"Can I go to the outhouse first?"

"Hurry up."

Tamerane ran down the hallway to the back door and into the yard. She did visit the outhouse very quickly before ducking into the shed.

"I'm being taken away somewhere. If Isandor comes, tell him that—"

Zeiro's hiding place was empty, the blankets neatly folded on the straw mattress.

Oh, no.

She stared, mouth open in horror.

She had no time to find out where he had gone. She had to go. Could she write something? She dug up a pen from her satchel, found a piece of board and wrote *The general has taken me to the camp.*

Hopefully, that would be enough to help him find her.

She scurried back through the yard and into the hallway, where her father was looking very impatient, muttering something about women taking so long getting ready.

"Can I get something to eat?"

"We'll eat at the camp."

That was a good drive away, and her stomach was so empty that she felt ill. But drawing attention to that might make him think that she was expecting, so she followed him out the front door to the truck.

Commander Lakrey waited in the cabin. Apart from the driver, two guards were with him.

While she sat by the window and her father climbed in, Tamerane glanced at the nearby houses, the yards, the alleys between them and the roofs, but saw nothing out of the ordinary.

The guards shut the door, climbed into the front cabin and the truck set off. Tamerane clutched her satchel. She really did feel quite ill and faint.

Her father and Commander Lakrey talked about the weather. Tamerane thought that her father looked tense. She looked out the window, leaning her head against the cool glass. It was so stuffy in the cabin, and the smell of damp coats did nothing to make her feel better.

In the distance she saw the hill where the Eagle Knights camped, a rocky outcrop on the edge of town. The sides were too steep for building, even for roads. Pine forest covered the back of the hill, and the side that faced the town was rough with huge boulders. She hoped Zeiro would find the note. She hoped that Isandor knew where the camp was.

The first part of the road out of town was very good. A lot of agricultural and army traffic used the road. But when they came to the turnoff, the road veered off over the hill, through a barren field with boulders and down the grassy slope on the other side. Sheep grazed in the paddock by the side of the road.

The road crossed a little creek here, with clear water burbling over round stones. A low log bridge crossed the stream—and the truck came to an abrupt stop just before the bridge.

The commander peered through the window in the front of the cabin. The driver and two guards were talking in the driver's compartment. Someone opened the door to the driver's compartment. One of the men left the cabin.

"What's going on?" Tamerane asked her father.

"One of the logs in the bridge is loose."

Did that mean it was going to take even longer before she got something to eat?

Tamerane pushed her nose against the glass trying to see the road ahead. She spotted movement from the corner of her eye, something flitting behind one of the boulders that dotted the riverbank.

Could it be. . . ?

The guard yelled for another to come to help him. The man left the cabin. Before the door had shut behind him, a crack went through the air, followed by a hard thunk that made the truck shudder. The remaining soldier shouted.

Another thunk, and the clack of crossbow being fired. A giant bird flew up from behind a few boulders. On its back sat an Eagle Knight, riding only with her knees in the saddle pouches, because she was firing autoloading crossbow bolts in rapid succession. They went *thwack, thwack, thwack* into the side of the truck's cabin.

Then it fell eerily quiet.

The Commander held his dagger, pressing himself against the cabin door.

Another thwack made the cabin shudder. The Commander's face drew into a grimace. He felt down his side, and his hand came away wet with blood. The sharp point of a crossbow bolt protruded from the inside of the door. A trail of blood also ran down the wooden panelling.

She felt sick.

The Commander pushed the door open. He dropped to the ground, while the bloodstain spread on his shirt.

Another thunk and then silence.

Then footstep in the puddles.

Tamerane's father sat frozen, his hands clamped between his knees.

A man climbed into the cabin, silhouetted by the light outside.

"Tamerane?"

Oh, she knew that voice better than any. For long nights alone in her bed, she had longed to hear it. Tamerane got up—and dark spots danced before her eyes. She stumbled. Her knees gave in. She fell sideways against the bench where her father sat. He gave a surprised cry. Tamerane landed hard on her side and one hand. Pain shot through her arm.

"Tamerane, what's wrong?" Isandor grabbed her under her arms and hauled her up.

She squinted at him through the fog. "I . . . didn't have any breakfast."

Black spots were still dancing in her vision. She now also noticed the guard on the ground just outside the cabin, with blood seeping into his grey jacket.

Isandor closed her in his arms. "Come on, calm down. Don't look. It's not pretty. Rider Nallayo takes no prisoners."

"Are the guards all dead?"

"They didn't put up much of a fight. Let's get out of here."

"We're really close to the military base."

"I know."

Tamerane met her father's eyes. He sat pressed with his back straight against the bench, eyes wide. Sweat pearled on his forehead. "What are you going to do with him?"

"I think the Knights' normal practice would be to kill him, but I can't kill a father in front of his daughter."

"Do you know what he's done?"

"Yes."

"I don't think you know the full detail of it."

"I've seen some evidence. However, if he's been trying to make servitors, he has no idea how to do it."

"They have a *dacon*," Tamerane said.

Her father's expression hardened and his lips formed into a thin line. She wished she could order Isandor to kill him, but she couldn't do that, and she knew he couldn't do it either. King Caldor might have dealt with dissenters by killing as many as possible, but his crimes must never be repeated.

Isandor said in a low voice, "If he thinks he can control a dacon, he's going to be disappointed. Worse, he'll disappoint his masters and creditors. I think we'll just leave him to face his failure and punishment. I'm sure it will not be nice."

Her father made a concerted effort not to look at her. "The ancient art must never be lost." His voice was low. "We are the magicians and guardians."

"I have no interest in playing your games. I'm going my own way. If you stop wanting to sell out to Arania and want to help the City of Glass instead of betray it, you know where I am. If not, I think Prince Denori will have interesting things to say to you."

His face remained blank, but his flaring nostrils showed his distress.

Tamerane moved towards the door. She had to go, and getting forgiveness from him would involve more than a simple "I'm sorry." Even if he said it, she wasn't sure she would believe it. So she just said, "Look after Mother better than you looked after me."

Then she was out the door. Isandor pulled the hood of her cloak over her head, but she couldn't help seeing the dead bodies on the grass. Commander Lakrey lay on his back, staring at the sky with empty eyes.

So much death.

Isandor took her hand and pulled her in the direction of the bridge.

"Hey, you," her father called behind them.

He stood in the opening of the cabin door, holding a metal object.

"Get behind me," Isandor said.

At the same time, a crack split the air. Standing behind Isandor's back, Tamerane couldn't see it, but she could feel the *foomp* in the air. A net of golden light strands crackled through the space between Isandor and her father.

Her father held this metal rod with a stone at the tip. Isandor just held up his hands. The net shimmered and moved. The golden light strands *oozed* through the air, slowly moving away from Isandor. They wove into a shape like a fishing net that settled over the truck.

"Hey!" her father called.

He ran up to the golden strands, tried to grab them but a crack split the air before his hands could touch the cage made of icefire.

"Hey, how am I going to get out?"

"It will fade eventually," Isandor said. " But it will last long enough to keep you from damaging our chance to escape."

And he whistled hard. A moment later, a giant bird glided down from the hillside. It landed in front of Isandor. He grabbed the reins that dangled loose from the harness and pulled the bird's head close. "This is Tamerane. She's going to come with us."

The bird glared at her.

Isandor helped her onto the bird's back and climbed up behind her. Then the eagle took off, with much flapping of giant wings. The cold wind bit into Tamerane's cheeks, but she was free.

Another bird joined them soon after, and a second one, and a couple more. On the back of each sat an Eagle Knight. They were not in full uniform, but she recognised the shorthair cloak.

"Where are we going?" Tamerane said. "I need to—"

She had been going to say she needed to find Zeiro, but there he was, riding with another Knight. His eyes burned with excitement, and his cheeks were red. He bravely let go of the saddle with one hand and waved to her.

"How did he get here?"

"He came back overnight because he was going to help us get into your house."

The eagles flew over the forest, *away* from the ocean.

"Where are we going?" she asked.

"We have a little job to do still," Isandor said at her back. "You said you helped them make their icefire machines. I guess you know how to destroy them?"

"They're easier to destroy than they are to keep running." Feed more power in, and it set off a chain reaction. It was, by all records, how the Heart had been destroyed. "We're not going to the Aranian camp, are we?"

But they were doing precisely that.

CHAPTER 15

*L*ANA **RETURNED TO** the library the next day, again wearing the dress she had borrowed from Selwa. Apparently Selwa had worn it in her youth, although the slender sizing made it hard to believe that it had ever fitted her.

At first, the astrologer wasn't there and she had a good look through the old observations, going back much further than the time of Sizek.

Those books were extremely old, and some had pages so brittle that she needed to be extremely careful that they didn't fall apart. She made a lot of notes.

In the very old days, the astrologers did a lot more drawing of stars than writing. She assumed that not as many people could read or write in those days, and loosely-bound books of artworks were popular. It amazed Lana how these very early works included detailed measurements on where in the sky to find certain phenomena, even if sometimes their writing was hard to read.

Going back even further, the books consisted of thick sheets that had been preserved much better than the thinner, more recent, ones. These maps had been hand-drawn in exquisite detail, although the handwriting was hard to read.

The very oldest observation books consisted of loose sheets. Some were made from vellum, others of a thin smooth material that people in the City of Glass sometimes used. Most of those were ancient maps of the Aranian coast, some extending into Chevakia. She recognised none of the markings on the map. She didn't even recognise the script it was written in. How old was this?

One map was a beautiful hand-drawn representation of the entire continent, complete with mountains and rivers drawn in. It appeared to have air flow streams marked on it, curved lines with arrows indicating movement in arcs linking a few places along the Aranian coast. But the main movement of air was from the north to the south. It reminded her of a weather map, except she had never seen those patterns before, and she didn't think meteorology existed as a discipline that far back, since no devices were available that measured any of the weather data that long ago. But the map intrigued her. The lines with arrows were especially close together just offshore from Kadrish and showed two dips at the position of the two offshore islands, another one north of Curack, one along the northern coast and then a pronounced dip at the City of Glass and the very northern tip of the continent.

She made a crude copy of the map, and put the original book on the bottom shelf where she could easily find it again.

By now, the astrologer had arrived in the library, and she didn't want to annoy the man again. She had more important work to do.

Lana went back to the Mother's House, where everyone was in the reception room downstairs for the celebration end of a birth ceremony she had missed. It had been for the young woman she had first met in the small library upstairs on the first day she had come here. She sat in the middle of the adoring women, talking about how happy she had been to be allowed a big ceremony. It had been her second child, a boy, a son to Prince Denori.

Lana grabbed some of the food on offer and mingled with the women.

She didn't ask about the child, because it was not important. He would grow up in the children's house, and then, when he was an adolescent, he would become one of the soldiers sent out to die in battles against rival princes' armies. He would grow up bullied and angry, or bullying and angry, hacking other people to pieces with big swords and talking about women as being "fuckholes", and those women would willing come to him in flimsy outfits, in the hope that giving him sons would better their lot.

What surprised her most about this whole revolting system was that none of these people had ever mustered the courage to stand up and tell the royal family "enough". That was a measure for how much this country was ruled by fear. She knew no parallel in the modern world. It was almost like Peria in the days of the rule of Rider Cornatan. Sure, both the modern Chevakian and Perian systems had imperfections where some people got a better deal than others, but that was nothing like this.

Whoever could plant that seed of revolution could change the entire world.

"What have you been doing?" a woman asked next to her. Lana turned around and found one of the women on her list, a timid girl called Jela, next to her.

"Come to the library and we can talk about it without all this noise."

Lana loaded some more food on a plate and led the way out of the room. She still wore her modest outfit and drew some disapproving glances from some of the mothers in their gauzy dresses.

On the way to the library, someone else was coming down the steps: a tall woman with curly hair, carrying a big pile of laundry. "Nashi!"

She stopped, dropped the bag of laundry and hugged Lana. "Oh, I'm so glad to see you."

"You work in the laundry now?" The Chevakian words felt strange but familiar on her tongue.

"Yes, some of the others are also there. It's hard work but we get good food, and none of the men are interested in us because we're 'dirty Chevakians'." She laughed. "We were wondering about you. I told the others that I saw you. Do you live in here?"

"Yes. It's not so bad. Except I can't leave the house without an escort." And that, she surmised, sounded worse than it was. She *had* made some progress and was happy to be allowed to go to the library, a privilege she could never have achieved working in the laundry.

"Has . . ." Nashi hesitated. "Has he seen you yet?"

The king, obviously. "Yes. Thank you for the seeds. I may need some more soon." But Selwa's words burned in her memory.

"I think I should be able to get them. There is a woman who sells them at the markets. I can get some for you."

Lana felt a pang of jealousy. The women of lower status were obviously afforded a lot more freedom to move around than the Mothers. Maybe she could use Nashi's freedom.

"Come upstairs with us," Lana said.

"No, the boss is waiting outside with the cart. I can't stay. We're doing all the laundry and ironing for the king's big celebration tomorrow night."

"Celebration?"

"Yes, or whatever it is that is happening. It's big. All the tablecloths and hand towels and serviettes need to be folded into shapes. It's a lot of work."

Lana didn't know about anything planned, but Nashi didn't have much time, so she picked up her laundry and left.

"Do you know what's going on?" Lana asked Jela when Nashi had gone; and because Jela didn't understand any Chevakian, she had to explain Nashi's words.

Jela shook her head. "The only thing I could think of is that the king will finally announce his successor."

A chill went over Lana's back. According to everything she had heard and read, the succession of the king could mean civil war. The king might choose his preferred prince, but that didn't mean that the princes would be happy with that. In fact, history showed that to be the rare case.

"I thought he would only do that when he stepped down." From Selwa's words, she understood that it was to the king's advantage to announce his successor as late as possible.

"The king can do whatever he wants."

Upstairs in the simple library room, Lana and Jela sat on the couches, which were usually occupied by the same group of women who liked being in the library but had no interest in books. Those women were all downstairs now.

Soon after they sat down, another two women came in, with the announcement, "We saw you leave. This will have to be more interesting than that braggart downstairs."

The speaker was another of the women on Lana's list of the ones who had shown interest in her astronomy observations. She sat down on the couch, her cheeks red. Her friend, who was beginning to show signs of pregnancy, followed, out of breath from walking up the stairs.

"So, what are we talking about today?" the first woman said.

"A lesson in getting your way," Lana said. "Never speak ill of your opponent, because you never know who hears it and will repeat it." She had heard her father say this so many times that she feared she was speaking in his voice. Unfortunately, she knew full well that she didn't always follow this advice.

The young woman blushed. "Well, she *is* a braggart."

"Maybe, but one day she may control something that you want and if she remembers you being nasty to her when you thought she was unimportant, she will not help you."

The woman cheeks deepened in colour.

"We don't have to like everyone, but if we want change and want people to help us, we should at least be polite to everyone."

Jela said, "I just want to know what it means for us when the king appoints a successor. Will the prince take over the Mother's House?"

The pregnant woman snorted. "Most of us already serve the princes. I don't think much will change."

"Well let's ask a different question: who of the princes would you prefer to become crown prince?" Lana said.

"What does it matter? We have no say in the king's choice."

"I think we have a lot more influence than you think."

"How so?" Jela asked, and the other women looked at Lana, too.

Lana told them about the king's interest in her library work, and how, last time she visited his rooms, he had set up an entirely new library for her. The women's eyes grew wide as she spoke. And she didn't even mention how the king had seemed embarrassed by the lewd nature of the old furniture and how fragile he seemed.

"But I still don't see what that has to do with choosing the crown prince," Jela said.

"The king wants to see what I have to say. If I find something that he finds interesting, he will listen. He will make changes if they seem insignificant enough. When a man likes you, he will do a lot to please you. It's like finding a loose thread on a garment. Start pulling it, and the hole you make might look small, but if you keep pulling gently, you'll unravel the whole garment."

Someone at the door said, "Some of our men are not knitted from yarn. They are made of rock."

Selwa. She strode into the room and plonked herself on the couch opposite Lana. "A lot of those men become favoured princes. They can't show any weaknesses because the fellow princes would kill them. They often do anyway, especially close to the time when the succession is announced. I don't know where you learned all this type of talk, but you're playing with fire."

"I can't watch all these dreadful things happen before my eyes. In what other place are children discarded the moment they are born—"

"They're not discar—"

"I don't know what you want to call it, but growing up in Children's Houses makes people mean and hard. They're either a bully or a victim, suffering constant pestering. No one cares. The girls can join the Mother's Houses to produce more worthless children. The boys can get killed in reckless experiments or fights of one prince against another. There are far more children than this country can use, and the people in power play games with the lives of lesser-born. It's disgusting."

Selwa's eyes narrowed. "You're not just a Chevakian peasant girl, aren't you?"

Lana almost shared the secret of who her father was, but that news would go straight to all types of people she didn't want to know, who would blackmail her father. "My history matters little. The king chose me, and either he made the biggest mistake in his life, or he wants change."

NASHI WAS RIGHT; something big was being planned. Lana asked the king about it when he called for her that evening. They'd had dinner in the sitting room, had spent some time in the library, where he showed her new acquisitions, and had moved to the bedroom for business.

"I have to make a choice some time," he said, leaning on the pillow, staring into the fire.

He looked at her.

"I'll ask you a question. I don't expect an answer, but think about it for a while: if you had to choose between the three of my sons who have positioned themselves to succeed me, which would you choose? You can choose only between them, because if you were to choose another one, he would be killed immediately."

Lana met his eyes. What did this mean? He hadn't yet made up his mind?

She didn't know any of the princes particularly well. She couldn't say that she liked any of them more than the others, or that she liked any of them at all. In fact, they kind of frightened her. But he probably had his favourites, so she would be better off not saying anything. "I wouldn't know any of them well enough to make that decision."

"It's an important decision, right?"

"Yes."

"One that will affect the entire country for the next thirty or forty years."

"Yes." Where was he going with this?

"And if I were to choose someone nasty, vindictive, or someone who would seek to go to war, the people of Arania would suffer."

"I guess."

"You are too timid. You understand what I'm saying."

"I guess." Lana's heart thudded in her throat. There was an important undercurrent to this discussion and she had no idea what he was getting at.

"So, let's go back to the question. Given the choice Denori, Sferuk or Nayek, who would you choose? Would you choose Denori, who has giant armies and is not afraid to use them? Denori, who I might add, has been experimenting with icefire and has killed hundreds of his own people. Would you choose Sferuk, who has his horsemen and has been raiding the northern part of Chevakia, and who is probably responsible for your being here. Or would you choose Nayek, who always uses violence to intimidate people who don't agree with him, and who talks about women as 'fuckholes' and regularly murders his own children as a way to spite the mother?"

"Well . . ." Was she meant to agree or disagree? She truly didn't know any of the princes terribly well, and to be honest, *all* Aranian men came across as domineering haters of women and people of lower rank.

"Choose."

"I can't," she burst out. "I don't know why you describe them like that. You make them sound like they are horrible people."

He gave a short nod, as if he wanted to say *they are horrible people,* but stopped short of saying it.

A moment of heavy silence passed between them.

Then he blew out a heavy breath. "Then you understand my choice."

LANA HAD an appointment at the astrology tower the next morning.

She had also been so bold as to ask the king whether she would be able to visit Sizek.

He'd found that amusing. "He's an extremely old and confused man, a shadow of his former self. His mind is wandering, most often to the much-reduced function of his private parts. All the nurses complain that he makes lewd comments."

"I'd like to be able to say that I met him. His book is known all over the world."

It was pure flattery, but it worked. He signed a permission for her to leave the citadel. She wasn't sure what she was going to do with it yet—nothing, probably, at this stage, to build up trust—but it was a step forward.

Of course she was still assigned a guard, but she had asked the king for Kento. He was one of the minor princes, and a very proper choice. Moreover, Lana liked him because he at least replied to her questions.

So after making early morning observations of the Red Wanderer above the dawn horizon, followed by breakfast, she got dressed in her modest clothes and left the citadel with Kento.

It was the first time she had been through those gates since coming here, and Lana found it hard to hide her excitement.

She drank in the colourful scenes in the street, and the sights of cramped houses, colourful washing hanging from balconies, temples hidden in alleys to the sides, and carts and people with animals going to market.

Walking through the narrow alleys, Lana spotted the occasional glimpse of dark blue beyond the crowded houses.

"Is that the ocean?" she asked Kento, and he said it was.

"Do you think you could take me back by a way that gives me a better view of it?"

"We can walk past the waterfront. It's not far from here."

"Thank you so much!"

She was playing an act, of course. Another painful lesson she had learned in the past year: people are more likely to help you if you're always nice and thankful to them.

Sizek lived in a hospice for the infirm and elderly on the slope to the western side of the citadel.

He had a large room to himself and, when Lana arrived there, sunlight streamed into the window, which looked out over the bay.

The man himself sat in a big chair, his skin impossibly wrinkled, hanging off his bones as if there was no muscle underneath. He had almost no hair and his skin bore many flecks and warts that came with age.

Lana had read every page of *Star Signs And Their Meanings*, probably more than once. She thought most of the interpretations were nonsense. But she had also seen the meticulous observations made by this man and knew that he had genuine dedication to his discipline, and that his work had helped her a lot. She could not deny the great influence he'd had on the field of astronomy, even if he made his studies for a different purpose.

She bowed. "Good morning, great Sizek."

He looked up at her with clear eyes. "Hmmm, I didn't order any candy, but I can sure use it. It comes well-wrapped, I see."

Lana ignored the comment. The king had warned her. "I study the stars and have been working for the king."

"Hmmm, so the king has a girl astrologer now, does he?"

"I'm not an astrologer."

"Oh? That's a pity. What is the point of studying the stars if you're not going to do anything with the study?"

"I am an astronomer and meteorologist."

"Ha! Chevakians and their meteorology. The stars do not influence the weather."

That was at least something that he and her father would agree on. "I'm wondering if you could help me."

"Help you?" He laughed. "I'm an old man. Your methods have become all so fancy. Women should stick to the Mother's House, though. What will happen if women need to study as much as us men? There would be no more time for producing the next generation."

Lana itched to give him a piece of her mind about this, but held her tongue, because if she started to argue there would be no end of it. She dug in her bag for her notebook. She flicked through the pages until she came to the map with the arrows she had copied. She held it up to him. "Do you have any idea what this means? I copied it from a very old book in the library. It was a beautiful map, but it looked so old that I couldn't even read the language it was written in."

He frowned at her drawings and didn't say anything for a while.

Then he said, "Sit down."

Lana did.

Then he said in a low voice, "I will tell you something you may not like to hear. Not many people do, which is why it is a secret: there is *magic* out there. Those lines you see are the ancient magic lines. Many of them are broken now."

Lana clamped her jaws. She could probably have guessed that he of all people should talk about *magic*.

"I know you don't believe me, because Chevakians never do, but look here." He pointed a trembling hand at the map. "Look at these lines. You see how they bunch together at the tip of the continent? That's where the City of Glass is. That place is full of *magic*. You can see the lines going into it."

"It's not magic, it's sonorics, and we can measure it."

"Bah! Chevakian words. You try to demystify everything, explain it away as if it is a mundane thing. In the City of Glass, people used it to perform unnatural deeds. Cutting out people's hearts and filling them with blue light, people that grow old within a few days and that can change into flying creatures and listen only to their parents. Tell me that isn't magic. How would you Chevakians explain that?"

Lana ignored his barbs. Thanks to her mother, she probably knew more about these phenomena than he did, and no, she couldn't explain them either. "These points here where the arcs touch the earth, is there a sonorics machine at each of them?"

"Used to be no doubt, but many have broken, because of neglect."

Her father had wondered if there were machines other than the one in the City of Glass. He'd suspected there might be one in the mountains. According to this map, there wasn't. The machines were along the Aranian coast, on the two islands off Kadrish. There was another one in the far north, a big, powerful machine like the one in the City of Glass. But surely it had to be broken, because there were no sonorics in the north—

Not entirely true, because what about the dust devils?

Sizek went off on a tangent about all kinds of rumours that he had heard about things that used to happen in the City of Glass, as proof that magic existed. Some Lana had heard before, others she hadn't.

A bit later, Lana left the apartment, when Sizek's attention drifted and the nurse said that he was tired.

"But I don't see him as lively as this very often. Come again, if you wish."

Lana said she would—it would be another excuse to leave the citadel, after she'd had some time to think about what he'd said and looked at the original map again—and left the hospice with the guard.

She reminded him: "You promised we'd go to . . ."

"Yes, I haven't forgotten. Come this way."

Lana followed him through the narrow alleys, down several flights of stairs until they arrived at the quay.

By now it was midafternoon and the sun was sinking behind the threatening cloud banks that always hung over the western horizon. That was another phenomenon she didn't understand. The Aranians called the clouds "Mother's Veil" but why did those clouds sit out there and why did they never move inland?

In any case, Lana understood why Aranians would travel to northern Chevakia to study the stars. The sky in Kadrish was never completely clear.

Lana had been to the ocean only a few times, and was surprised how well she remembered the tangy air that always hung around ships and harbours. There was a lot of activity on the quay. A fishing boat had just returned and men were unloading big boxes full of slippery silver fish.

Lana never ate much fish. The only ocean fish sold in Tiverius was the dried variety. It was chewy and salty. Trout caught in the rivers was expensive and the river lungfish, though cheaper, was not as nice.

She also saw ships that looked like they carried timber and big blocks of marble.

Kento explained what sort of ships went where, and where what type of business was conducted.

Lana studied the ships on the waterfront: big ships, small ships, sailing vessels, steam boats, fishing ships with nets and ships with oars. To right, the quay was empty except for a single ship. It was not as big as the others and quite pretty, with flowers carved into the side panels. The maroon sail was neatly folded and tied to the boom. The deck was empty. It didn't look like a ship for heavy freight.

Behind that ship, at the back of the quay, in front of a wall of solid smooth stone stood a little stone pillar. Oil burners on stands stood at regular intervals along the wall.

Lana walked past the flapping flames, looking at rows and rows of names engraved in the stone.

"What is this?"

"All the people who go to meet the Mother have their name inscribed in the wall for honour."

"What do you mean 'meet the Mother'?" She had heard that expression, but thought it was a euphemism for when someone died—

Wait . . .

"Is this like a graveyard? All these people who have died?"

"These are people who have gone to meet the Mother."

"Yes, you said that, but I thought it meant that they died."

"It does."

She stared at him.

"Then . . . it's a graveyard."

"No, it's a wall of honour. These are people who chose to go out on the ships and set eyes on the Mother before stepping out of their bodies and joining Her."

"On the ships?"

"Like this one over here." He indicated the pretty ship at the quay.

"Wait—how does this work?"

"It starts with people who commit an indiscretion. They might have stolen from their master, or cheated on their wife or disobeyed their military superior. When the district court finds them guilty, they suggest the sentence, but if it's a long one and the prisoner shows remorse, he is given the option to meet the Mother to clear their name and that of their birth mother. They come here and go out on the ships directly west. They enter the Mother's Veil, set eyes on the Mother and die in honour."

"To go out in a boat and have someone kill you is an honour?"

He gave her a sideways glance. "You think that's what happens out there?"

"The people who go out on the boats are prisoners, and once they're out at sea, the crew kill all of them."

Kento shook his head. "Oh no, they die through no human hand."

Lana frowned at him. "How do you know what happens? Have you seen it?"

"As a matter of fact, I have. I spent a short time working on the boats."

"You—what?" Lana stepped back. *He* had hacked people to death?

"You can't go out on the ocean without getting killed. The crew wears thick suits, but still, if your supervisors want to keep you on, they only let you work on the boats for half a year or so, because otherwise you get sick as well. The Mother burns the skin off people's bodies. Their bodies turn liquid from the inside out. It not a pretty death."

"You have seen the Mother? It is a real thing?"

"Oh yes. She surrounds herself with the Veil, but once you enter the Veil you can see her through the mist. She is big and fat and takes up most of the sky—much, much bigger than the moon. Sometimes she is round, sometimes she is a massive crescent. She is grey with bands of blue, and sometimes she turns our way and observes us with an orange eye. When the sun hits her side-on you can see the trails of her magic through the sky. They're golden strands that reach for us through the sky. Where they hit the ocean, the water boils, and steam rises. That's how she cloaks herself in a veil. And you can see how she heats the ocean, and the ocean reaches for her with trails of mist. I have seen these things with my own eyes. Still, you unbelievers will say we're stupid and the Mother is in our imagination, but you will never see it, because if you did, you'd die."

Lana's cheeks glowed.

She thought she understood.

The earth and the moon were children. The Mother was a type of Great Wanderer, which they never saw in Chevakia because only the ocean side of the Earth ever faced it, like she had noticed that she only saw one side of the Moon.

The Earth was one of the children. The Moon was another. That was why the Moon grew bigger and smaller and wasn't visible in the sky for months on end. *This* was the world's position in the sky, and the great unseen thing that Chevakians had denied because they couldn't see it from their country affected all of the world.

CHAPTER 16

"WE NEED TO FIGURE OUT a way to get reinforcements," Rider Taino said.

They stood in the hall, only side-lit by the faint light that came from the front room where Zaina had been looking at the collection of ancient artefacts with the view of taking all of them to the eyrie for investigation.

That now seemed an unimportant, trivial activity.

"Do you have any idea how many people they have out there?" Rider Taino asked the scout Leya.

"I had a look upstairs, but the vantage points from which to observe this house are endless. There could be any number of people out there, and there will be, depending on how important this house is. To be honest, it looks like it is very important, with all this stuff here. I don't think any of us can risk trying to leave the house to find out, no matter how dark it gets outside."

"How can we call for reinforcements?"

The scout shrugged. Zaina felt like saying, "Aren't you supposed to know this?" But she thought that was childish.

Leya met her eyes and Zaina could see that Leya half-expected Zaina to say it. She didn't.

Prito, the other Knight Apprentice said, "We could write something in the snow in the yard."

Wido said, "Everyone would see it, not just the people we'd want to see it."

Yes, that was a problem.

They then mused about writing something that only a few people would understand, but that discussion didn't give any solutions.

Zaina was thinking in another direction. She said, "We're sitting on the largest depository of weird technology I've seen. I'm sure there has to be something we can use to escape."

They all looked at her.

"Use, how?" asked Rider Taino.

"I don't know yet, but I can look around to see if I get any ideas."

She went into the room and let her gaze roam over the many boxes with their strange content.

The great idea, however, proved elusive. A lot of the material in the boxes was of very poor quality, with parts missing or broken, metal and wiring eroded, dirt caked onto or even into the machines. A lot of the dirt, too, didn't look anything like the dark soil around the City of Glass. The soil was much lighter in colour, sometimes even pink or red.

She suspected these items were found somewhere in the north of the continent, in the desert. Shen Mani always talked about all this stuff that was everywhere in the desert. Were these the things he had found? She had never kept in contact with him, because he started asking if she could sell his finds for him. Zaina didn't like the idea of trading in things she didn't understand; besides, at the time, she'd had no money to invest, and he stopped writing to her.

Zaina took items out of the boxes, studied them, tried to figure out what these things had been used for, and how she wanted to escape.

In an ideal situation, she would have something that sent a message straight to the eyrie. The Knights used gulls for this, but she had none.

They could probably attract some gulls to the yard. But catching one and hoping that it was trained would take too long. Trained gulls usually lived in cages and were only allowed out for a short period.

Prince Nayek's men would surely do something to rat the team out of the house before morning, because they couldn't just start shooting at people while the citizens of the city went about their daily lives.

It was quite amazing that this went on right under the noses of the palace and the eyrie anyway. This house was only a short walk away from all the other Knights. All she needed to do was attract the attention of the guards at the gate to the eyrie and they would come.

Or maybe she could create a distraction, an explosion or some such. She went to hunt for ideas.

In the cellar, she found some oil and paint.

She also found a pile of black rock in a barrel.

In General Pakori's household, she and the boys used to make bombs from flour, and there was some of that in the kitchen.

All right, she could create a fire. She could even cause an explosion. How was that going to help? The Aranians would simply see it as excuse to rush in, pretending to help. That would not let the team escape. They were trapped here, surrounded on three sides by tall buildings, with the only entrance through the street at the front, which Prince Nayek's men would be watching.

She again went through all the things she had picked out. She kept coming back to the black rock and the oil which she had put on the porch. There had to be a way to put that to good use.

Maybe . . .

She went back into the house. In one of the rooms, she had spotted sheets of the translucent protective material that people in the City of Glass sometimes used to cover their wares. She wasn't sure what the material was made of and how it was made, and she had never seen it before she came here, but Jadan used to use it in the workshop to protect seat upholstery while working in dirty overalls, or to protect parts of the truck when painting.

If a sheet was too small, Jadan would stick it together by heating a piece of metal in the fire and pressing it onto the sheets. What if she could . . .

That was it! Surely she could find some rope and something they could use for a sling. Bed sheets or something.

Zaina bundled up all the material she could find and took it to the porch. There, she put a good deal of the black rock into the barrel and lit it. It burned with fierce heat. She punched a couple of big holes in the barrel's lid with a pick.

She rolled out the transparent material, and because she couldn't find anything else to do the job, took down a set of curtains and used the metal curtain rod to melt the sheets together.

The Knights became curious, and she instructed them how to help her fashion two sheets of the transparent material into a longitudinal bag and then two more sheets into another.

"Be careful they don't rip," she said, wiping sweat from her face. It was getting hot so close to the fire.

Then she found the fire barrel's lid. She used a piece of metal pipe and shoved it in one of the air holes. It didn't close off nicely, so she found some gum to seal the gaps. She tied the gasbag to the pipe.

Then she told Prito and Naran to get the bellows from the fireplace in the living room and fan the fire in the barrel through the little air hole in the side. She found a jug from the kitchen, filled it with cold water and poured that into the top of the barrel. Then she slammed the lid on top. The metal pipe spewed a gout of hot gas which started filling up the bag she had tied over it.

A look of understanding came over Rider Taino's face. He went into the house while Zaina manoeuvred the inflating gasbag out from underneath the porch roof. She tossed a fishing net over the top and tied it to the porch railing stop it flying away.

Rider Taino returned walking backwards while dragging a large rug.

By this time, Zaina had sealed up the first bag and had started on the second one, while Leya stood on the table, which she had dragged to the porch, to seal a couple of little holes.

While the second bag filled, Zaina helped Rider Taino tie the carpet onto ropes.

The second bag was full, too. Zaina sealed it up. The fishing net went over the top and they tied it onto the first bag and then the ensemble onto the carpet rig. Zaina untied it from the porch railing.

Whoa!

Rider Taino, Wido and Ley had to jump onto it to stop the ensemble flying off.

"Bring some heavy things!" Rider Taino yelled.

Naran and Prito hung off the side. Naran chucked a stone statuette into the carpet-basket.

Wido yelled, "Ow! You idiot!"

But the rig stabilised.

Phew. It looked like her silly idea would actually work. It was still quiet in the street, but soon the shop holders would come to set up for the start of the day, and then the shoppers would follow. Prince Nayek's men were not going to risk being discovered by shooting at Knights in full view of the citizens.

Zaina climbed onto the rig. Whoa! Everyone slid into the middle in a mess of legs and bodies. They managed to all find a position while sitting on their knees and looking out over the rim of the carpet. Rider Taino held his crossbow ready. Wido held a powder gun. Naran also had a crossbow, and Zaina wished she had a better weapon than a dagger.

She leaned over the side to untie the rope and pushed the construction off.

For a moment it looked like it would sink but then it started rising. Zaina pushed off from the porch railing and then the gutter.

Slowly, the gasbags pulled the ensemble up.

Something whizzed past her.

Wido yelled, "Come on, hurry up , they're shooting at us." He picked up the stone statuette and tossed it over the side.

The balloon's ascent quickened.

They huddled together in the hollow of the carpet. A few times, Zaina felt something hit the carpet, but either the projectile was harmless, or it had lost too much speed to be harmful.

The gas balloons rose and rose.

"It's working," Leya said, and she grinned in the almost-darkness inside the rug. "I admit I thought the idea was pretty stupid."

It's not the idea that's stupid. You are stupid. But Zaina didn't say it. After all, it was some sort of compliment.

And they were not out of trouble yet. While Prince Nayek's men had not caught up with them yet, a breeze now threatened to blow the gasbags into one of the buildings.

Leya, who stood on that side of the carpet-basket, yelled, "Watch out, sharp edges up there!"

Zaina's view in that direction was blocked by the gasbags.

Rider Taino used his unsheathed sword to push the balloon away from the building. People inside the apartments ran to the window to look, astonished faces behind the glass.

They were rising higher and higher. A couple of men had entered the yard of the house below, but their arrows and bullets could no longer reach the makeshift balloon.

They weren't clear yet. The wind again pushed the balloon up against the side of that building. The top of that building consisted of broken shards of stone and glass with jagged edged that glittered in the low light. A metal rod protruded from the side of the building.

Zaina managed to grab it as they passed and shoved off, into the middle of the open space. But the wind became stronger as the gasbags cleared the top of the building behind them.

"Watch it!"

Jagged shards of glass came far too close to the fragile gasbags for her liking, and the bags themselves were losing gas. They were going to get stuck on this tangle of metal and glass.

Wido, on the other side of the carpet, had turned himself feet-first over the edge of the carpet, using his feet to kick off any surface his boots could reach.

A gust of wind made the gasbags slap against the glass side of the building.

Wido kicked off again, but now they were on the same level as the jagged glass, and the gasbags didn't have the lift to carry them over.

The wind became stronger.

Wido hung half off the carpet, pushing off whatever surface he could reach with his feet, but there was no point. The balloons were not rising anymore.

Wido called out, "I'm the heaviest. I'm going to go. I'll see you all later." He let go, jumping the sort distance to a ledge below the tallest part of the building.

With his weight gone, the balloon lifted immediately. It cleared the jagged metal and the glass shards.

Rider Taino yelled at him, "We'll send an eagle over to get you!"

Zaina and the others cheered, but he was already out of hearing. The wind carried the balloon over the top of the building into the open and then they couldn't even see him on the ridge anymore.

The Knights often trained on top of these buildings, so Zaina hoped that he knew the way down and that he would be able to stay out of the way of Prince Nayek's men.

They drifted over the city in the eternal dusk in eerie silence, much slower than an eagle would fly. The sky was dark blue above, with a glimmer over the horizon and a faint orange tint. The sun would not rise above the horizon, and the day would get progressively darker as the sun went behind the cloudbanks in the west.

The wind whistled in the ropes that tied the gasbags to the carpet, but few sounds from below reached up here.

Rider Taino peered down into the darkness between the buildings.

"I don't see anyone in the streets. That's odd."

Rider Naran agreed. "The shops should start to open around now."

But there was almost no one in the streets, and the shops were dark.

The balloon drifted over another row of buildings and they could see along the street that ran down the hill to the Harbour District, a wide avenue with street lamps on both sides.

Most of the street was also strangely empty, but a group of people stood about halfway down the incline, blocking the road. A tram stood downhill from the group.

"What's going on there?" Rider Taino asked.

It was too far away to see, but there seemed to be some sort of hold-up, where someone was preventing the merchants and shoppers from coming into the centre of the city.

The wind was carrying the balloon in the direction of the bay, to the north side of the palace. A group of people stood in front of the palace gates, and a couple of others, who clearly wore shorthair cloaks like worn by the Knights, were inside the palace grounds. The gates were shut.

Rider Taino swore. "Look at the eyrie."

Zaina looked. The bad weather shutters that protected the birds from wind, rain and blizzards were all closed. Zaina knew that the shutters existed, but had never seen them closed.

A couple of men who clearly *weren't* Knights stood outside on the path from the eyrie to the palace. The gate into the palace was shut, too.

"Prince Nayek's men forced their way into the eyrie?" Prito's voice was horrified.

"Looks like it," Rider Taino said.

"How did they manage to do that?"

"Heaven knows, it was low-staffed enough. If only we'd known there were so many Aranians in town."

But they had known; at least Zaina had. She had seen the Aranians in the bars, working for the guards. What they hadn't known was just how many Aranians had ties to Prince Nayek. And how vicious they were.

Rider Taino swore. "And the administration office across the street, too. It looks like they got into everything."

Everywhere except the palace. The first loyalty of the Knights was to the queen, so at the first sign of trouble, they would have run to the palace.

"What are we supposed to do?" Prito asked.

No one replied to that question. What *could* they do, only five Knights, two of them Apprentices, against an army of Aranians.

The balloon was drifting in the direction of the bay, but it was also losing height at quite an alarming rate.

Zaina did some quick mental calculations.

If they landed in the city, they were likely to fall into the hands of Prince Nayek's men. And she had escaped him once, but didn't want to bet on being able to do it a second time. If they somehow managed to clear the city, they would land in the bay, where there was little shelter, and it would be wet besides.

"We have to get to the palace garden," Zaina said. "Otherwise we'll be outnumbered and have no chance."

And already, the wind carried them further away from the palace. The makeshift balloon had no way of steering. Had Zaina known that the rest of the city was in the hands of Prince Nayek's men, she might have added one, but now she could only hope that they could land some place safe enough.

The balloon was losing height rapidly, and was not going to clear the next row of buildings.

Rider Taino directed everyone to sit face out and grab onto whatever they could get hold of. Likely, they would be on the ground after this obstacle. This was their one chance to get it right.

The wind blew the balloon against the side of a building with a smooth façade of stone and glass without any places to climb off or hold on. The gasbags were now deflating ever more quickly, and the carpet was sinking to street level.

Zaina peered into the street. There was nowhere nearby for the team to hide, and Prince Nayek's men would soon be here.

"Watch out!" Rider Taino called, as the carpet missed a lamppost by less than a hand's width. The ropes got tangled in the top of the lamppost, and the carpet was drawn up on one side. The top of the lamppost ripped through one of the gasbags.

Zaina fell off the listing carpet on top of Prito and Leya and Rider Naran fell on top of her. The second gasbag deflated and covered everyone.

Zaina wrestled herself free, cutting through the fabric with her dagger. Rider Taino pulled the material up to help free the others. "Quick! Get out of here before anyone comes."

Prito started running. Zaina ran after him, followed by the others, with Rider Taino bringing up the rear.

They had landed in a street below the palace, and Prito charged up one of the narrow alleys that ran between buildings, consisting mostly of stairs.

His legs were much longer than Zaina's and he reached the top before she did. From around the corner, it was not far to the palace gates, but he stopped. When she came up, panting, she saw why: there were men in front of those gates. Aranians.

"Let's go through the side door," Rider Taino said.

He ran back down the stairs, but three men were coming up from the lower level. They were also Aranians, with their dark leather jackets.

Zaina drew her knife. Rider Taino aimed his crossbow.

The men stopped.

Rider Taino loosened the bolt with a click and a twang. It whizzed through the air. The men had no time to run.

The bolt hit the first Aranian square in the middle of his face.

Zaina gave a little involuntary gasp. She had heard that some Knights could hit a jackrabbit while flying on the back of an eagle, but had never seen that kind of deadly precision.

The force of the hit toppled the man backwards, blood streaming down his face.

The other two Aranians decided that was enough and ran back down the stairs.

Rider Taino's crossbow went *clack* and *twang* and again *clack* and *twang* in close succession.

Both men fell face down on the steps.

Prito ran down, holding his dagger, and crouched at the bodies to retrieve the bolts.

Ew.

Zaina could almost feel the sensation of the blade of her dagger sinking into soft flesh. She felt sick, and was glad she had been allocated a position in the flying division, so she didn't have to pull arrows out of dead people.

When Prito came back, his face pale, Rider Taino led them at a quick pace into a narrow passage that ran off a section of the alley between two flights of stairs.

It ran between two tall walls, one of which was the back of houses that stood along the lower street, the other a natural rock wall. If Zaina was correct, the palace garden ended at the top of that wall.

They ran along it for a while, footsteps echoing back at them in the narrow space. Then Rider Taino stopped.

Everyone else stopped, too, except Leya, who put her hands onto the rock wall and heaved herself up.

Very slowly, she climbed up the wall.

Zaina couldn't see where she held herself. She hoped with all her might that she didn't have to do the same.

Leya reached the top of the wall, disappeared for a bit, and then one end of a rope ladder tumbled down.

Rider Taino grabbed it and gestured for Prito to climb up, then Zaina.

The ladder was wobbly despite Rider Taino hanging onto the end with all his weight.

Prito and Leya helped her over the wall at the top. They had come up in the private garden at the back of the palace.

Zaina had only seen this from the back of her eagle, a little oasis with a pond and clipped bushes. Because it was winter, the bushes had no leaves and a thin layer of ice covered the pond.

Light radiated from the back windows, edging the garden in gold.

A number of Knights ran from under the porch carrying weapons.

"Stop where you are!" one of them yelled.

"It's only us," Rider Naran said.

"By the skylights, at least one group made it!" a Knight called out.

A few others came out of the building, and the ones who could not leave their posts watched them from across the yard.

A Senior Knight came to Rider Taino and clapped him on the shoulder. "Good to see you back. It's been quite a night, and things are grim. You must tell the queen what you have found out."

"Not much, I'm afraid. I don't think we are much wiser than any of you, except that a lot of the city appears to be in the hands of Prince Nayek's troops. Is Rider Barton here?"

"We don't know where he is. He went out and didn't come back."

"Rider Carro?"

He shook his head. "We think he's outside the city."

Rider Taino's face turned dark. "So who's in command?"

"One of the Knight tutors, but he doesn't have much experience."

Then he finally asked the question that had been on Zaina's mind. "What about the queen? Is she safe?"

"She is. For now. I don't know how much longer we can hold out."

CHAPTER 17

*J*AVES WAS STILL ANGRY the next morning.

His youth was no excuse for those stuffy men in their stuffy offices to brush him aside. He'd never had anything to do with Viki's deputy but had no idea why Rodi had gotten that job. The man was an academic, and had no interest in the doga and in the political processes that influenced the Chief Meteorologist's job.

Since it seemed to be Rodi's intent to protect his own importance, Javes wasn't going to get anywhere with him. He was also not going to see the proctor by patiently queuing up.

He got up early and started a fire for cooking breakfast later. Tali was still asleep. She lay on her side, her face relaxed. One hand lay draped over her stomach, the other hung off the mattress. Her hair, dark and thick, spread out over the pillow.

His mother had treated her terribly yesterday. That was what you got when people were obsessed with status and what other people thought of them. That could only happen in places where life was safe, where people had enough food and had time to think about things like what others thought of them. Only among the rich in Tiverius.

It was not how he wanted to live his life.

He went outside, where the two camels were grazing in the lush grass. Dew coated their fur and made their long eyelashes look like strings of tiny diamonds.

He took both animals under the shelter of the shed and brushed the knots and burrs out of their pelts. Then he put the saddles on and unpacked the ornamental headdress that had come with the female camel. He draped it over her head so that the strings of metal disks hung down both sides of her ears. He dug into his pack and found a reasonably clean *temuz*. In the cold air of the shed, he took off his shirt—brrrr—and pulled the cloth over his head. Being traditional wear for a warm climate, the fabric of the *temuz* was much thinner than his shirt, but he also had a leather vest that went over the top.

The he removed his pants and pulled on the loose trousers that went with the *temuz*. It was too cold for sandals, so his leather boots would have to do. Then his hair. It had grown a fair bit since he first left Tiverius.

Northern men usually wore their hair loose or tied in wraps or veils if they needed to wear those against dust or glare. It was neither hot, dusty nor glary in Tiverius, so he undid his hair tie and teased out the kinks with his fingers.

There.

"What are you doing?" Tali stood in the doorway into the barn.

How long had she been standing there? "Today, we are going to be the voice of the north."

She gave him a blank look.

"Get dressed in your best clothes from home."

"I'll be cold."

"I'm cold, too. We'll get changed later. It's just for the effect."

"I thought you were going to give the proctor that thing you got from the windwalker."

"I tried to. I went in yesterday to see the proctor, but no one would talk to me because I'm just a student, and no one cares about the problems of the north."

"Pashtan always said that, too."

"It's been enough. Today, the problems of the north are going to come to the doga."

"So we're getting dressed up to make them listen."

"Yup. And we're dressing up the camels as well."

In that last visit Javes had paid to Arukat's house, when he had found the burned bodies in the kitchen, Javes had grabbed some useful-looking clothes, including a burnt-orange dress that Tali had never worn. He'd thought about leaving it behind on several occasions, but it looked nice, and would be a memory of her youth. When she put it on, it transformed her from a skinny boy-girl to a young woman. The colour brought out the olive complexion of her skin.

"Is this all right?" She turned around so that Javes could see all sides of her.

"You look fine. Very northern." Very mature and, now that he knew, the slight rounding of her stomach was obvious. How had he missed that before?

"We look like we're going to a feast. Some of my friends got married in dresses like this."

"You have friends who are married?"

"Yes. Girls get married when they bleed." She said it without flinching, as if it was the most common thing in the world. And then she added, "I think we should get married."

What? He was only . . .

"You can't marry until you're seventeen." His cheeks burned.

"Why not?"

"Because . . ." Why not indeed? If you lived together and shared responsibilities and weren't family, you might as well be married, because that gave more protection if something happened to one of you. "Because the law says you can't."

"The people here have so many silly rules."

While they were eating breakfast, Belo turned up in the truck. He did a double take when he saw Javes and Tali. When he had brought in the supplies of camping gear, Javes offered him a mug of tea.

"That looks . . . rather cold," Belo said, glancing at Javes' *temuz*.

"Believe me, it is cold."

"It's a bit esoteric. I guess you're getting ready to make point."

"You got it."

"Mother is beside herself. She's afraid you'll do something to embarrass the family."

"Is that why she sent you here?"

Belo shrugged. "I hate it when people make fools of themselves."

"Belo, this has nothing to do with what people think of me or our family. I've had enough of trying to please Mother, because she hates whatever I do, and always has. My entire life is a nuisance to her.

Well, I don't need her anymore. I thought she'd be happy to see me, but if she's not, I'm happy to stop pretending. I've had enough."

"So what is this with the doga about?"

"Someone gave me a map that shows where to find the sonorics machine that's causing the upheavals in the weather."

"Like the one in the City of Glass?"

"Yeah, like that. It's in the northern desert. It's what's causing the strange weather."

"Rodi says that it's caused by the Aranians messing with machines."

"He is wrong. Yes, they're messing with machines, but those are too small to have much influence on the weather. This machine is huge. It needs to be destroyed before the crops die and the forests die and towns are overrun by dust devils. But all of the people who control access to the doga are too much obsessed with my age, with following protocol and whether or not I embarrass them. Yes, I probably will do something that embarrasses Mother, but if that's all she's worried about, I don't have much to say to her."

"I saw her this morning. She said she barely slept and she's really upset about yesterday."

"Good. By the way she treated Tali and refused to believe what I said, I don't think I have to apologise to her. She can come to see me when she wants to apologise."

"Fair enough. But I'll still come. I don't want to lose contact with my brothers."

"Belo, my place, no matter how small, will always be open for you."

Javes and Tali mounted the camels. A moist wind had come up that did nothing for warmth. Javes shivered in the saddle. Tali's lips were blue and her teeth were chattering.

"The sooner we get this done, the sooner we can get changed into something warm again."

He kicked the camel into motion. Tali's camel followed through the grass to the gate. Belo watched from the door to the barn, and then got into the truck.

The two camels and their colourful riders attracted quite a bit of attention on the way into town.

After crossing the railway bridge, Javes stuck to the main roads.

He heard the first goat whistle while crossing the workers' quarter on the other side of the bridge.

The man who had whistled came running up to the camels. He was a dark-skinned northerner. "Hey, brother, what's going?"

Javes raised his fist. "Railway and justice for the north. We're riding to the doga to make our claims."

The man pumped his fist. "Justice and an equal share to the north! I'll march with you."

Soon enough, more people joined them. They came out of side alleys and out of the entrances to the big blocks of apartments. They were old people and young people, mostly poor people. They were dark-skinned and olive-skinned. Some brought their children or their Chevakian families. Some brought husbands or wives of Perian blood.

They all had a different reason to protest, but that was unimportant. All their reasons were about the north's disadvantage. All Javes needed was a big enough crowd to overrun the security at the gates to the doga building.

Javes talked to a few of the people. One man was a builder trying his luck in the big city. He'd come six years ago and had never left. A young couple had eloped when they didn't like the choice of partners chosen by their families. A man with a dog had taken his entire family to Tiverius because crops were dying and so many people were leaving town that his business was about to collapse. He was from Ysherra, as Javes guessed, and listened, horrified, to Javes' story about dust devils overrunning the town.

The man knew Arukat well. Javes caught him saying to Tali, "And you're his little daughter, all grown up. That's a good man you have there. Keep him."

This made Javes' ears glow. He'd intended to tell everyone that Tali was his sister, but as her pregnancy became more obvious, that would be cruel to her. Like his mother, they would think less of Tali and might call her names behind her back.

There was no way that he would send her to one of those horrible homes as his mother suggested. He'd have to think about the issue. Not now, though. Besides, somehow he already knew what the solution would be.

The ever-increasing group of northerners had now reached the market place, where the day's trading was in full swing. A stall on the corner was selling puppies, stacked three high in cages, and they all started barking at the camels. The stallholder yelled at them to shut up, and then, when his yelling increased the barking, at Javes to takes the camels out of his sight. Then the rest of the group of northerners entered the crowded market aisle and no one could move anywhere, in particular because people came running from between the stalls to see what the commotion was about.

And as Javes wrestled through the crowd—and the camel took a few swipes at people who annoyed it too much—the crowd grew even more. Why hadn't he guessed that so many northerners made, sold and traded things? It was in their blood. It was how they survived in that harsh country.

Javes finally reached the gates to the forecourt of the doga building.

Two slightly alarmed guards watched the group. The only weapons these guards normally carried were their batons, and they were no match for the large group. One of the men ran off, presumably to get reinforcements.

The remaining man placed himself in the middle of the entrance, planting his fists at his sides. In this way, his hand was also close to the handle of the baton in case he needed it.

"Halt. What is your business?"

"We come in peace and don't wish to create trouble, but I have to see the proctor immediately about a matter of great urgency."

"The doga is in session," the guard said. "But you can go in and join the queue to see him. If you leave your animals here—"

But Javes had enough of that.

He whistled to Tali, and both slapped the camels on their backsides.

The animals jumped into action, one squeezing on each side of the guard into the forecourt. The man ran after them. "Hey, hey! Stop! You can't go in with those beasts!"

Javes laughed. "You're lucky I didn't bring my goats." In hindsight, he should have.

As soon as the guard abandoned his post, the crowd of northerners surged into the forecourt.

Javes yelled at the group to follow him.

A couple of other guards came running out of a door to the side, but they, too, were far too few to stop the group.

The camels ran between the stately trees and up the steps to the front porch. Two young men were close behind Javes' camel.

"Careful! Mind your head!" Javes ducked when his camel ran through the open double doors into the building.

The foyer exploded with echoing shouts.

Javes' camel showed signs of alarm: the tossing of its head, the white in its eyes. There was nowhere for it to go, so it ran in circles around Tali and her camel, which had, much more sensibly, stopped in the middle of the hall.

All the guards were running after Javes and his camel, and trying to stop the group of northerners coming into thew building.

They left the door to the assembly hall unguarded.

Javes yelled, "Open that door!"

The guards realised their mistake, but it was too late.

A young man flung the door open so hard that it bashed against the wall with a clang.

Javes and Tali rode . . . onto the floor of the assembly in full sitting.

People started yelling. Guards poured in, surrounding the pair of camels, trying to get hold of the head rope while staying out of the reach of the camels' teeth. Tali's camel had had enough, scattering guards with growls and bites.

Javes let himself slide from the camel's back without getting the animal to kneel, even if it was long drop down. The animal was much too agitated to sit. He clutched the map and the igniter to his chest while wrestling through the commotion. The proctor stood at the dais, watching with mild bemusement all the goings on.

From close up, he looked much older than his proud, straight-backed figure suggested.

"You have caused quite a stir, young man. I hope it's good for something."

"I'm sorry, sir. I tried to see you in the usual way, but the guards wouldn't let me through. It is extremely important that you see this."

The proctor took the map and the igniter. He weighed the metal globe in his hand. Javes could see him thinking that it was too light to be made of solid metal. Then he carefully set it at the dais so it didn't roll off. He unrolled the map, raising his eyebrows. His eyes moved as he studied Karlen's notes.

Meanwhile, Javes' camel was running circles on the central floor, with a couple of guards trying to catch it. A whole group of northerners had come into the hall and were standing at the doorway, looking around in wonder.

Some of the members of the assembly tried to shoo them out, and one man held his fist up, yelling, "Justice for the north!"

And others took up his chant.

The proctor lifted the little hammer on the dais and hit the golden bell that stood in the corner. It produced a single *Biiiinnnngggggg!*

"Quiet please!" one of the guards yelled.

Javes whistled to the camel. It ran to him with the rope trailing behind.

The hall returned to a semblance of quiet.

He said, "Thank you." As if he'd simply asked for someone to sit down or shut the door, or some other small activity. "This young man here has given me a very interesting piece of data that I need to examine with some urgency. To the rest of you who have forced your way illegally into this room, please make your way outside in an orderly fashion. The staff out there will hear your complaints. The meeting is adjourned."

A woman in the audience protested, "But Proctor, we need to discuss the supply allocation—"

"Yes, we do and we will. But this piece of data may change everything. I will notify you all when this assembly is ready to reconvene." He gestured to Javes. "Come, young man."

Javes handed the camel's rope to Tali. "Look after him. Stay with the others."

She nodded, a slightly terrified look on her face. Behind her, the other northerners were being herded out of the room by the guards.

Javes followed the proctor out of the hall. He felt *angry* on behalf of these people. He was sure that the proctor only made time to see him because he came from the Tiverian high class. What about those people who had worked hard in this, for them, strange city all their lives and got nothing in return, not even the long-promised railway to Lekata?

"You quite know how to make an entry," the proctor said while walking through the hallways.

"I'm truly sorry. I did try to see you the normal way, but I thought the map was important." He was not sorry at all.

"Indeed."

They walked up the stairs, went past the queue that was still waiting, with Old Saro still at the very end. The old woman saw Javes. Her eyes widened. "Look at him, guys. He cheated!" She stepped forward. "I was here first, Proctor. You have to see me first!"

The proctor's guard pushed the woman aside so that his boss—and Javes—could walk unhindered into the foyer and through the door with the guards who had refused Javes entry—twice—yesterday.

The proctor's office was large and airy with a big desk and lots of bookshelves. The far wall was mostly windows that looked out over the marketplace and the roofs of the city. The view was to the south, with the blue hazy mountains on the horizon.

The proctor sat down at the big desk in the middle and bade Javes sit on the chair opposite him.

"You're Viki's student from Ysherra, aren't you?"

"I am. I'm so sorry to hear about Viki. I had no idea that he was on his way to visit. I might have stayed had I known. Maybe I could have prevented . . . what happened."

The proctor shook his head. "They were ambushed just out of Watya. The weather made it impossible to cross."

"We came through that storm."

He went on to tell the proctor all he had learned at the Windwalker camp and from Karlen about the ancient artefacts in the desert.

The proctor listened, interrupting only to ask questions.

He didn't have many questions about the weather. He was a meteorologist and had seen the signs.

"Thank you," he said when Javes had finished. He rose and pulled two maps from a table behind him. Both were large sheets of paper and encompassed the whole continent. One of the maps was recent, the other was drawn in an achingly familiar hand—that of Viki—on yellowed paper. Both featured a large storm cell, one in the north, one in the south.

The proctor turned the old map upside down. It featured the bad weather in the south. The recent map—made by the proctor himself —was almost a mirror image of the other, with the storm cell hanging over the north of the continent.

"I don't have to tell you about the similarities of these two maps."

Javes could see that. He could also see the alarming size of the system.

"This here is the pressure map that Viki made in the days before the machine exploded in the City of Glass. We know that sonorics causes low-pressure cells to form. The higher the level, the deeper the cell."

"We've never measured that much sonorics over the north."

"No, that's right, we haven't, but all the indications are that it's there anyway, and, like that machine in the south, it's getting stronger."

"But why now?"

He spread his hands. "Maybe because it has a problem. Maybe because someone touched it. Maybe because the Aranians are messing with sonorics. We don't know. It is clearly time to investigate. I will get into contact with the Knight Council in the City of Glass so that they can send people to help us. Thank you for this, young man."

"So . . ." Javes hesitated. That was it? Time to investigate? Somehow, he had expected more urgency. "What do you want me to do? Go back to the Scriptorium and finish my studies? What about all those people whose livelihoods have been ruined by the changes in weather? I think they deserve to have us do something about this machine as soon as possible."

"We will do something, but, unlike the Aranian meddling with sonorics, we will not risk lives to do it. We will get knowledgeable people from the City of Glass here to help us."

"And what about support from the doga to the northern regions? Many of these people have lost everything. What will the doga do to rebuild the region? Will they finally get their promised railway?"

A little flicker of *something* danced across the proctor's eyes. Clearly, the subject of *northern railways* was a sore point.

"The field placement was the last thing you needed to complete your education as meteorologist, right?"

Javes nodded.

The proctor produced a sheet of paper from the corner of his desk. He took a pen and scribbled on the paper, then stamped the paper, affixed a ribbon to it with the colours of the proctorial office—blue and yellow—and signed the stamp, too.

He handed it to Javes. It said *Javesius han Demerian has successfully completed his study in meteorology and is qualified to work as a meteorologist.*

Javes' ears glowed. "Why, thank you." That saved him writing a report of his experience in Ysherra.

"Don't thank me too soon. That piece of paper comes with a price. Or rather, a job."

CHAPTER 18

ETRIEVING TAMERANE had been easy enough, Isandor considered.

Too easy, he feared.

He held the reins of the eagle while it flew over the rugged terrain, traversing occasional shards of cold mist. The other Knights were behind him, each on their birds.

Tamerane sat as a warm presence against his chest—pregnant with his child. He wanted to take her home, but he couldn't go back home and leave the Aranian icefire weapons intact. Her long letter to him had confirmed what he already knew: that Aranians were experimenting with icefire, that they had devices that made it and they were trying to revive the old skills of making servitors and breeding dacons. He'd seen a dacon once, and had even flown on the back of one. They were creatures not meant to live peacefully on this world. They were creatures of destruction. They were part of the ancient icefire magic that he wanted to make sure never returned.

He had learned that Tamerane's father Ledor had a major hand in passing this knowledge to the Aranians. He had attempted to subvert Tamerane, too. She had been sent to Brotherhood of the Light schools so that she could learn to wield the powers of icefire.

And here he was, thinking of Brother Veshi who sat on the Knight Council, and he had been under the impression that the Brotherhood was of the same opinion as the Knight Council: that no one should ever use the same power as King Caldor had. And now he wasn't so sure anymore, but one thing he knew: icefire should be banished forever.

These Aranians didn't know what they were playing with.

And now he would have to use that same power to destroy this project by the Aranians.

"Are you cold?" he asked Tamerane, who was shivering. She sat before him, so caught most of the cold wind.

"Yes—no. Nervous."

"I love you," he whispered in her ear from behind.

The mountains loomed on the horizon. Snow covered the rugged slopes. The camp came into view in the distance, over the crest of a hill.

After crossing the stream and the bridge the Knights had sabotaged, the dirt road wound through a pine forest. Isandor could see no traffic.

The scouts had said that the track from the camp to the main road was little used, except for the trucks that went to the incinerator very early in the morning, and that picked up new batches of fresh-faced soldiers from the harbour every day. It would be a while before someone discovered Ledor in the cage, and longer still to find a person who could do something about it.

The icefire net might have weakened by then, if they could find the source and destroy it.

Rider Nallayo, at the front of the group, turned around and pointed.

Isandor squinted against the biting wind to see the collection of buildings that lay in a valley in the foothills of the mountains. Some were tents, others more permanent structures. Curls of steam rose from the chimneys of the taller buildings.

He couldn't see any obvious signs of alarm. The camp looked peaceful.

Rider Nallayo had taken the lead, and she kept the eagles low to give the group less chance of being spotted. They skirted the treetops. Isandor's bird was so heavy that it threatened to fly into the trees a few times.

"See anything yet?" Rider Nallayo called.

Isandor squinted. His eyes were watering from the cold.

Yes, a few golden strands shimmered around the perimeter of the camp.

"It's warded," he shouted back. Being of Pirosian blood, Rider Nallayo couldn't see icefire.

"What can we do about that?"

"Nothing. Ignore it. Be quick." And hope that the Aranians didn't have the skill to make wards that did anything more than warn of intruders approaching.

"We've been seen," another Knight shouted.

It was true. A couple of soldiers stood on top of the guard tower, pointing in the direction of the approaching group of Knights.

A very *small* group of Eagle Knights, in a very *large* hostile camp. Isandor hoped that the Aranians hadn't developed any additional weapons besides icefire ones. Up here, they were out of the range of arrows or powder guns, in case they used those, but in order to disable the icefire machine that was a blazing spot in Isandor's vision, they would need to come down. That would be a huge risk.

They had now crossed the wall to the camp. Rows and rows of tents and cabins spread out underneath them. If Isandor had ever doubted stories about the size of the Aranian army, he could doubt no longer. It was huge. No wonder the princes were so careless with the lives of their soldiers.

"Do you know how many people they have stationed here?"

"About ten thousand," Tamerane said. "There are a lot of useless princes in Kadrish."

The scale of the camp was overwhelming. There was no way the severely depleted ranks of the Eagle Knights could fight this force and win. Maybe not even Chevakia could fight this force, certainly not if they used icefire.

Yet, if no one could stop this army, then the whole world was at risk.

"Do you know if Prince Denori is in the camp?"

"Not that I know. People say that he is in Kadrish."

Isandor half-closed his eyes as the eagle soared over the tents. The golden light strands wound between the tents, sometimes encasing them, sometimes avoiding them. Isandor guessed that this behaviour depended on the ability of the tent's occupants. The Knights, for example, being of Pirosian blood, did not attract any icefire strands, but he and Tamerane . . . that was a different story. There was so much icefire in the camp and so many strands all woven together that it was hard to see.

He spotted a group of soldiers running from one tent to another, and here and there soldiers stood and looked up at the Knights flying overhead. They appeared to be wearing normal gear that would not provide adequate protection, even if the uniforms were quite thick. Had some Aranians developed resistance?

"Where to?" Rider Nallayo called.

"There!" Isandor called. It was inconceivable to him that she couldn't see the source of the icefire threads: a big grey tent that stood in a field, a little apart from the others. There was a fence around the field. A couple of soldiers guarded the gate in the fence, which was closed, but the enclosure itself was empty of people.

"It's so bright!" Tamerane called.

Yes, she had been young when the Heart exploded in the City of Glass. She might never have seen the brightest glow of icefire.

"We need to be quick going in. The longer we give them to put on protective gear and reverse our damage, the more risk for us."

The eagle swooped down over the enclosure and landed on the trampled grass next to the tent. The guards at the gate were shouting and an alarm started ringing.

Isandor slid off the eagle and lifted Tamerane off.

The other Knights had also landed.

The Aranians had opened the gate. A group of men ran in, all of them in thick, cumbersome protective gear. They carried crossbows, still out of range.

Rider Nallayo yelled, "Free the birds!"

She whistled and all the eagles took to the air in a huge flapping of wings. They were trained to stay close by.

Isandor took Tamerane's hand and drew her into the tent.

Blinding light hit his face.

Whoa! He shielded his eyes with his hand. The thing in the middle of the tent produced so much light he could barely see.

"Come." He pulled Tamerane further in.

The contraption in the middle of the tent looked similar in design to the Heart, although he had only seen that in pictures. It looked a little smaller, but was still bigger than a house.

It was a square thing, consisting of plates of metal and tubes.

The entire thing blazed with icefire.

"Is that it?" Rider Nallayo had come into the tent and stood next to him, staring at the machine. "Doesn't look very appealing."

As one of the Pirosian clan, she didn't see icefire, so wouldn't see the blazing light radiating from the machine.

"We need to increase the current that goes into the machine," Tamerane said.

Rider Nallayo said, "Be careful. I don't want it to blow up while we're still here."

"It won't," she said. "The power needs some time to build. It may not even explode today."

Damn it. That meant even more risk that none of this would work.

"Quick, let's do it."

Tamerane was the first to reach the side of the machine. "Can someone come here? Someone who can see normally."

A Knight joined her. Against the glare, Isandor couldn't even see who it was. Tamerane opened a panel and instructed the Knight to cut and reconnect wires.

Behind Isandor, Rider Nallayo said, "We've got incoming."

Isandor turned. The first of the suited Aranians had reached the entrance of the tent. One of them raised a weapon, but Rider Nallayo's crossbow bolt hit him square in the visor of his helmet. He fell forward and didn't get up.

More soldiers ran in. None of them got any further into the tent than a few steps before falling to the ground, sometimes over the top of another. Sometimes a crossbow bolt stopped them, but most of them just fell.

Isandor felt sick. Aranians clearly weren't resistant to icefire. They might have set up shielding around the machine so that they could keep it inside the camp, but this was dangerous territory for them. Yet, a senior in a suit was still yelling orders for the men to go in, and they obeyed without question. Many of them had no protective clothing. They fell. Their skin burned and peeled, their eyes bled. And still, they came.

Isandor was horrified. "What sort of people are these, sending the poor men out to die like that?"

Rider Nallayo snorted. "They think it's an honour."

"Like this, bleeding from their eyes? He's going to have no men left."

"Believe me, Arania *always* has more men."

Tamerane came back. "Done." She looked, horrified, at the bodies. Her face went pale. Isandor wished with all his heart that he could have kept her from seeing that.

"What happened to them?"

"The commanders are sending them in to stop us. They're not resistant to icefire. They never had a chance."

"These people are animals."

"Worse than animals."

"Are you done?" Rider Nallayo asked.

"Yes," Tamerane said, but she sounded disturbed.

"Then let's get out of here." Rider Nallayo ran to the other side of the tent and with her dagger, cut a hole in the fabric and held the sides apart so that the others could get out.

"We must stop this," Tamerane said to Isandor.

"I agree, but I don't know how. Leaving is probably the best thing we can do."

"But these people . . . how can they obey their commanders so blindly?"

Isandor looked over his shoulder. "Even that could be a result of icefire. I don't know. I don't claim to understand Aranians."

They left the tent, and Isandor whistled. His eagle sailed down, uttering a shrill cry.

He ran to grab the reins, and lifted Tamerane onto the saddle and jumped up after her. The air was turbulent with flapping wings.

Isandor clamped his arms around Tamerane's waist. "Hold on."

The eagle launched into the air.

Aranian soldiers ran around the tent, but even the ones who made it were too late. They fell over each other as icefire spilled out of the hole that Rider Nallayo had made in the fabric.

Isandor clamped Tamerane close to him. "Don't look, don't look." The icefire called out to him, but he resisted the temptation to use it to raze the camp. Tamerane was right. The soldiers deserved better. They didn't need his help to die. Their commanders already killed them. Let the men see that and revolt, if they had the courage.

He spurred the eagle on, but it needed no reminding.

Only after several minutes did he dare look over his shoulder. An expanding cloud crept over the hills behind the town. Strands of icefire flickered within. The process was set in motion. People who moved quickly could still get out. Whether they would was another matter entirely. Once he was back in the City of Glass, he would think about a way to reach out to the common soldiers of Arania to entice them to stand up against their superiors or escape.

The eagles flew south.

AT NIGHT, Isandor, Tamerane and the Knights came to the underground den which they had discovered on the way here. Everyone was exhausted. There was no sign of followers, and of course no news from anyone. The presence of icefire would protect them from Aranians.

A couple of junior Knights went out and collected some shellfish which they made into a hearty soup. Several times, Isandor spotted Tamerane nodding off.

They took the large bedroom. The bed was comfortable and she slept in his arms, too tired for anything else.

He lay in the dark, listening to the talk and laughter from the kitchen over the top of the hum of icefire from the basin below. They'd have to destroy it later, once he could get people here to empty the water from the basin. All these machines would have to be destroyed. There would be no more evil deeds done with icefire. But for now, it kept them safe from Aranians.

Isandor finally fell asleep when the other Knights stopped talking in the kitchen and went to bed as well.

He woke up when Tamerane stirred in his arms. It was still dark, but voices sounded in the hall.

"What's going on?" he whispered.

"I don't know. I was just going to ask you."

Isandor got out of the bed. The floor in the room was warm under his feet and that reminded him that he needed to show Tamerane the chamber downstairs.

A couple of the Knights stood in the office, looking out the window in the dark. Isandor recognised Rider Nallayo with them.

It was just dawn, which, of course, came pretty late at this time of year. The rocks and the beach showed up very dark blue. A pale mist hung over the water.

"What's going on?"

"A ship just put into the jetty," Rider Nallayo said.

Well, damn it. "Any idea who it could be?"

"One of the ocean traders from the City of Glass, judging by the ship."

"Do you think they've seen us?"

"They're probably not expecting anyone to be here."

The eagles might give them away. They'd not thought to hide the animals.

"What do you want to do?" Isandor asked.

"See how many there are and ambush them if they come inside."

They were going to wait just inside both doors. Isandor went quickly to put on some clothes. Tamerane already sat in bed, getting dressed.

She wore only her underdress, and the faint light that came in through the window silvered the distinct rounding of her stomach.

He longed to get home where he could take her in his arms.

From further down the hallway came the noise of a lock being opened. Then a cry and a thud.

People started talking.

"You can come out now."

Isandor went to the corridor, where a group of Knights surrounded the man who lay unconscious on the floor. They were all talking.

"Was he alone?"

"We have to assume there are others."

Someone lit a light and looked at the man's face.

Isandor recognised him. He was a junior assistant in the Brotherhood, working with Brother Veshi.

Isandor knelt.

The man opened his eyes and squinted into the light. "Please." His voice sounded rough.

"What are you doing here?" Rider Nallayo asked.

"Please. I'm with the old captain of the ship out there. We came from the City of Glass to look for help. We put in here because of the swell."

Isandor's heart jumped. Jevaithi was alone in the palace. "What happened in the City of Glass?"

"Take him into the kitchen," Tamerane said. "We can question him while someone looks after his head, because he's bleeding, and someone can make him some tea."

It surprised Isandor how easily the Knights organised all that. Tamerane had that quality of voice and confidence that made the Knights obey her. It probably came with having grown up in a house-hold with servants even if, he realised, Jevaithi *didn't* have that confident tone. She was still looking for approval from the people around her.

His heart ached. Jevaithi was in danger.

Not much later, they all sat around the table clutching bowls of porridge and cups of tea.

The man started his story.

"Soon after you left, Aranians started causing trouble in the Harbour District. Oh, we didn't know that at the time, and I don't know the exact story, but apparently the Aranians who supported Prince Denori came to root out support for Prince Nayek and managed to trap the prince in the city. All we knew was that there were a lot of fights in the Harbour District. I work for the City Guard, so I heard all the stories. My superior called in the Knights, but the more people they sent, the more Aranians appeared, like they came out of nowhere. The Knights tried to separate the groups of Aranians, but they failed because they were outnumbered. When Prince Nayek came back, he brought a lot of men. I heard rumours that the eyrie was taken over and all the eagles locked inside."

Several Knights gasped.

"The guards managed to close off the area of the city directly surrounding the palace, but a lot of the city is open war between the Knights and guards against the Aranians, and between Prince Denori's and Prince Nayek's men. The citizens are locked in their houses. Many have been killed or—especially the natives with resistance to icefire—taken prisoner. My superior asked for people to go and get help. I volunteered because I've got experience in sailing. We were going to go down the coast to Chevakia, but the weather was too bad, so we came this way on the off-chance that we could find either you or any other Knights."

"Well, you found us," Isandor said.

"But what can we do to help the city?" a Knight said.

"We have a post outside the city," Rider Nallayo said, and she went on to describe a hideout which they always kept stocked and Isandor had not known about. They would arrive there tomorrow, and take stock of the situation, and then decide whether a group as small as theirs could do anything or whether they needed to go to Chevakia for help.

"But certainly someone would have already warned Tiverius?" Rider Naissa said.

Rider Nallayo agreed.

Isandor and Tamerane left the kitchen to pack up and prepare.

Tamerane snorted. "Isn't it disgusting that the choosing of one single person, a man, I should add, should upset the entire world? Let the Aranian king choose an heir already. I'm through with accidentally being a victim because the sons are bickering over the throne."

She was right, and by the skylights, this conflict amongst Aranians would have been building for years. "I don't think the Aranian invasion is an accident or simply a conflict between princes. They're interested in the City of Glass, because we have technology they want. They're after all the ancient artefacts. We expected them to go after Chevakia, but they may think Chevakia is too much of a risk. They've been pretending that they were going for Chevakia, but I think that *we* are the focus of the Aranian attack."

Tamerane nodded. "The generation of my parents had lots of all that ancient stuff, and King Caldor did a lot with it. The Aranians like playing with icefire, but they don't understand it very well."

"Who does? Did King Caldor even understand it? Talking about that, do you know the purpose of this rather nice apartment? Have your parents ever told you about this?" Isandor asked.

"My father told me that it used to belong to a prominent member of the Knight Council, but that was a long time ago. It has recently been used by the sailors travelling to Kadrish, especially those who are used to luxury."

"And these travellers are all from the noble families of the City of Glass, I'm guessing?"

"Yes." She frowned. "Why are you asking that?"

"Don't you feel the warmth?"

"It's nice in here, but that must be the warmth of the earth. It's very humid here, so I guess there might be a hot spring below this house."

"Almost right. I'll show you."

He took her to the storage room and through the little door that gave access to the underground passage, while explaining what he had seen here previously.

"So," she said behind him, "I noticed that it's unusually warm in this house and even in the bay, but you're saying that is because of some icefire device that produces heat instead of cold."

"That's the best way I can describe it."

"It *is* very warm and stuffy in here."

It was even worse in the chamber. By the time they stood next to the basin, Tamerane had taken off her jacket. Like him, she saw the strands of icefire that blazed out of the water and disappeared into the cavern's walls.

"Wow. I can't even see what's down there," she said.

Isandor produced the sonorics meter that years ago, he had been given by Sady. The needle still sat solidly against the left side of the dial, indicating a reading of zero motes per cube.

Tamerane frowned at it. "It is very odd indeed."

And then she said nothing for a while, still frowning. Isandor watched her, knowing that she was thinking and that her brilliant mind would come up with possibilities for why this might be happening.

But she said nothing, and shook her head. "I'm not sure. I would need to check my books, which are all still in my room at home."

"I guess the same applies to destroying this machine?"

"Yeah. We'd need to get to it first, drain the water so we can see what sort of thing we're dealing with. I often wonder what sort of people built all this. They must have been very smart."

"Me, too. I wonder why they died out."

"Or left."

"Left? Where to?"

"I don't know." But she looked at the ceiling of the cavern where, if they weren't under the ground, they would have been able to see the stars.

CHAPTER 19

IN BIG STRIDES, Sady walked through the corridors of the doga building.

The guard who had come to get him sounded disturbed, as if on top of Lana's disappearance, on top of the fact that he'd received no reply from the Knight Council about his request for assistance, on top of the lack of correspondence from Loriane, on top of the fact that all telegraph lines were out to the south as well as the north, there could be any worse news to relay.

Sady had been interrupted in a meeting with General Selidas who detailed the state of affairs with the increasingly bold border incursions by Arania and the increasingly heavy replies necessary to repel them. The word was that a southern eagle had arrived with a rider.

The door to his office stood open.

He couldn't decide if the person waiting on the chair opposite his desk was male or female, but he—or she—was an Eagle Knight.

She, he decided when he came in and she rose in a graceful, cat-like manner. She wasn't very tall, but she was whip-thin and all sinew and muscle. She wore her greying hair in a ponytail. Her cheekbone bore a scabbed-over graze.

"Welcome. Sit down."

She gave a polite little bow. "My pleasure to meet you in good health, Proctor." Her voice was surprisingly deep.

"Well, yeah. Good health is all I have these days."

243

She nodded. There seemed no need for an explanation.

"How can I help you?"

"It's a really long story."

"If it's important, I've got time."

The Knight's name was Rider Jeito. She had been sent into the mountains between Arania and Peria to look for a team of Knights investigating elevated sonorics who disappeared. She and other members of the expedition had been captured by Aranians. They were mostly locked in cages in tents, made to do maintenance work like mending uniforms.

"It was cold in the mountains and many of the troops are poorly equipped. They don't have much heating, not even for their own troops, let alone for prisoners. Your fingers go numb from the cold and you can't do your work. If you don't work, they beat you until you work or fall down. I saw many prisoners die that way. They were mostly local shepherds and prospectors who accidentally ventured too close. I picked up the fur cloak of one of the young fellows who came with us, a young fellow named Daro. He was a good sort. Didn't deserve to die like that. The lower-ranked Aranian troops in the camp were just as afraid of the leaders as the prisoners were. There was a fellow named Tirek I got friendly with. He was a minor prince, apparently, and he said that whether he lived or died depended on which prince secured the succession. Prince Nayek, who owned the camp, was stabbed by one of our group. They thought he had died, but it was that cold in the mountains that his body cooled enough for his wound not to be fatal. He came back. That was good news for my friend, because if Prince Denori would have gotten his hands on the camp, he and other minor princes like him would have been killed. I told him we supported prince Nayek—"

"Does the City of Glass support him?"

She snorted. "No more than we support any of the other princes. Frankly, I think this race for the throne is ridiculous. It's all right if they want to have a fight over who gets to succeed their father, but let them keep their fights within their borders."

That, in a slightly blunter wording, was what Sady thought, too.

"Anyway, when I said that, and I gave him poor old Daro's cloak, he 'forgot' to lock my cage one night and that was how I got out."

"Why did you come here rather than the City of Glass?"

"Oh, I went there first. It was a long way through the mountains. All our trucks were gone so I had to walk—admittedly, the trucks are not much faster on that terrain, but they offer shelter. I had no food so I had to take time to hunt. But when I finally came to the City of Glass, I found my eagle waiting for me. It looked healthy and well-fed, unlike me. Someone must have released it. I was looking forward to going home and telling the king about the camps, but instead I found that I'd been the lucky one, having escaped the siege of the City of Glass."

Sady's heart jumped. "Siege?" He felt faint. The first thing he thought was *Loriane.* He had sent her to the City of Glass specifically to keep her safe, because all the signs were that Arania was going to attack Tiverius . . . while in reality they had been after the City of Glass.

He asked, "Where . . . where is the king?"

"He went to rescue his lover, who is from the noble Perian class, from where she was being held in Curack."

The sick feeling increased. "So the City of Glass is held by Jevaithi alone?"

"Rider Barton is there, but a lot of our good men are not. The Knights don't have great numbers even if we're at full strength, and we're not. From what I could tell from above, the troops of one of the Aranian princes have trapped the supporters of one of the others in the city. The young fellow Tirek told me that it's all about the trade in those ancient things that people have been finding for years and that the Brotherhood of the Light considers itself an authority on. Aranians have been after that stuff forever, too. And like everything else, the princes turn it into a blood sport."

Sady made sure that the Knight got a good meal and comfortable place to sleep. He wanted to send her back to the City of Glass with his men. He wanted her to check on Loriane.

His staff found her a room in the guard quarters, and he accompanied her there.

Walking back through the hallways, he tried to order the thoughts in his mind.

Aranians had made sonorics machines.

They were combing the known lands for ancient artefacts in the hope of finding an igniter to help them control their machines.

An igniter could possibly control *all* the sonorics machines.

The Aranian machines might be dangerous, but they were also small. The big danger was that machine in the north that absolutely needed to be destroyed.

And now that the City of Glass was under siege, who knew when he could get help from the Knights with this task?

Much as Sady ached to help free the City of Glass, he knew that he had a more important task to do, a task that would be unfair to give to a younger man.

THE DOGA ASSEMBLY met and General Selidas agreed to send a contingent of soldiers to help break the siege in the City of Glass. To Sady's question if they could spare the people, the general said, "We'll have to make do. The sea route from the City of Glass is a back door into Chevakia that could prove dangerous to us."

"But you're already tied up in the east and north."

"Yes, and now the south. Yet no one has an army as massive as Arania. If we don't stop them at the border, we will never stop them."

Ignoring Arania for all that time was the major mistake everyone had made. "I also request that a few of your men come with me on an expedition."

"With you, Proctor?" The general looked at him with wide eyes. "Where would you go?"

"To the north to destroy the second sonorics machine of which the young man was so kind to tell me the location."

"But I thought we agreed to do that once the Eagle Knights could help us."

"Looking at the current situation, that may take a long time. Also, the Aranians are in the City of Glass to look for old technology to control their machines. We need to destroy sonorics once and for all, before they figure out how it works. This machine is destroying the farmlands of the central highlands and the north. It's destroying our forest. If we do nothing, it will soon destroy the world."

"But . . . you? It's dangerous."

"That's why I should go, and not a younger man. I'd wear a suit. Whatever leaks through if the suit is not up to the job won't harm me as much as it would harm a young person. If I were young, I would go with you to the City of Glass, but at my age I'd only get in your way. Besides, I think this is the most important task we face, and one of the most dangerous ones without any fighting involved. I'll go with a small team to assist me. Send one of the strong young men to free my wife instead. I'm too old to fight, and if sonorics kills me, I don't leave a young family behind, like many of the soldiers I could send."

AT NIGHT IN THE KITCHEN, Myra and Farius were outraged. "But you can't go. What if something happens?"

"That is why we have a vice-proctor. Senator Shara can deal with it. She is very experienced and will do a good job."

They still didn't like it, but Sady went to pack anyway. He stood for a while staring at the empty bed. What if he never saw Loriane again?

His eyes misted over. He had to do this, for the sake of Chevakia and all the people who trusted him with their lives, for Viki, for Lana, for the people in the north, for that young man Javes and his young girlfriend and their two camels, who had walked all the way from Ysherra to give him the map. If nothing else, he owed this young man the attempt to do something with that information.

They prepared over the next few days. Sady compared the map he had received with the maps available to the Balloon Division. The windwalker map showed several landmarks that were absent from the military maps, so Sady had the mapmakers copy those landmarks across. He wondered what the marking "bowl" meant. There were several, scattered through the northern half of the desert, and a few south of Ysherra.

He went to speak to Javes, whom he had installed in the northern division of the meteorology department. He had ideas for the young man's future, but would not implement them until the north was safe.

Javes' eyes went wide. "Are you going up there? That's dangerous. Let me go instead."

"Don't you think that hasn't crossed my mind, young man? But won't there one day come a time when you want children of your own?"

"Well, yes, but what does that have to do—"

"My *wife* was a breeder in the terrible society in the City of Glass under the rule of Rider Cornatan. It was a time that few women could have children; and those who could, rented themselves out to rich men. And even the men sometimes couldn't have children, because their bodies were damaged by sonorics. It is one of the effects. I would not want to do that to you."

"Oh." The young man's cheeks went red. "Well . . . thank you."

"I came to ask you about this." Sady rolled out the map and pointed at the "bowl" markings.

"I've seen those," Javes said. "The windwalkers live underneath one, and they seem to think that they're for collecting water. However, we came past others and they weren't pointing straight up at the sky. They're much bigger than a house and look like this." He formed his hands into a bowl. "Then there is a pedestal underneath."

"If they're not for collecting water, then what do you think they're for?"

"Well . . . I don't know. They were made by the old people. Maybe they were a kind of sonorics barrier for these people? Maybe the ones that don't point straight up have been broken. When you go up there, you'll surely see them and you can make a guess. I truly don't know."

"Would you like to find out?"

"I think we *should* find out."

"Agreed."

Sady packed his sonorics suit and his instruments. No way was he going to travel all the way up there without taking notes on the climate and landscape.

He even read about the Badlands. The signs of sonorics had always been there: people's skin burned and peeled and animals refused to go there. All the signs except a positive measurement of any level of motes per cube. He didn't understand why, but there was no time to investigate.

He packed the suit, including the inner suit that he used to wear when he travelled to the City of Glass in his youth, when it was still under the rule of Rider Cornatan. He shuddered at the memory of how uncomfortable that suit was. Did it even still fit him?

He tried it on, and yes, it still fit him, and it was still uncomfortable.

He went to Shara, who listened quietly to all his notes about his job and what needed to be done.

After a while, she said, "Hey, I can manage."

He smiled, nervously.

They had been through a lot together as colleagues and he figured she was a competent senator and although she was not him, and wouldn't do things exactly the same, people would get used to her.

The hardest thing was to write a letter to Loriane, which he would give to the commander of the group going to the City of Glass. He sat in his office staring at the empty sheet of paper for a long time before writing anything, hoping she would understand.

They left Tiverius the next morning.

Watya was considered too dangerous and train services to the town had been severely cut.

The military had set up a base to the south of the town. The train stopped there, in the middle of nowhere, in the very early morning.

A couple of trucks waited by the side of the rails, accompanied by men in dark clothing. They wore long sleeves and hoods against possible sonorics, but no suits.

Sady and the other got into the truck, and the men in the cabin gave him wide-eyed looks when they saw him.

The truck bumped over the uneven road in the treeless plain. The sun came up through dusty haze, lighting a surprisingly green land- scape. Great tussocks of formerly dead grass had sprung to life, and the ground between them, normally bare, was covered in low plants, many of them with flowers.

The base became visible when they crested a hill. It lay halfway down the slope in a gully which contained a few puddles of water. The tents had been disguised to look like boulders, but there was no doubt about their purpose. The tracks and crates with folded balloons alone gave it away.

The truck stopped in front of the largest "boulder", where Sady was met by the local commander. The commander was also surprised to see Sady there.

Most of the day and night was taken up by planning the trip. They would take three balloons. They would probably take at least three days to travel and needed to bring all supplies.

"I need to take into consideration that the Aranians can attack at any moment, and I need to keep men in reserve for dealing with that possibility."

"I understand."

It was to be a very quick trip: up there to destroy the thing and back again to make sure the troops could be here in case Arania attacked.

It hurt Sady because there was so much still to be discovered about this ancient civilisation. He'd much rather have waited for someone from the City of Glass to disable the thing, if they had the time to find someone who knew how to do that. But there was no time.

The enormous extent of the rainfall became apparent the next morning when the balloon rose over the landscape.

They could see the silver ribbon of the Aramys River in the distance and, in the haze, the railway bridge across the expanse of water.

The captain made sure that they weren't going in that direction.

The balloons crossed the Aramys River upstream from Watya, where several brown streams merged in a messy floodplain with many snaking riverbeds, a huge flat area full of sediment that dried rock hard in the dry season but, when it rained, easily became a treacherous ground of mud, quicksand and ever-changing river courses.

Sady remembered coming here a long time ago, when the bridge at Watya had been nothing more than a cobbled-together floating log bridge that washed away and had to be rebuilt after every flood. He'd come here to study the composition of the sediment to find out where the sand came from and how far mud was carried off the desert plateau.

He didn't remember ever measuring any sonorics levels back then, and of course he should have measured them. Having been carried here from most of the platform, there would have been sediment with a high level of sonorics.

But they were in the north, and sonorics was a southern thing, so there had been no need for sonorics measurements. Or so his teacher had told him.

Well, the teachers had been wrong. Everyone had been wrong for so many years.

So he measured sonorics now, recording his precise location.

And the levels . . . varied.

He'd made everyone on board the balloons wear their suits, and mostly the soldiers had been annoyed because the suits were hot and cumbersome. And sadly, he didn't find much justification for their use, not even as they went further north.

The country below was majestic. Rough rocky outcrops in a sea of green and flowers. Sady knew this was an unusual occurrence, but to see the desert in bloom was a magnificent sight.

They passed the outcrop called Red Hill that was mentioned as a go-to place for people studying the skies. Its main attraction, besides being a point of elevation, was the oasis with the palm trees at the bottom, said to be a tranquil pond during the driest of times. It had expanded to a lake, encompassing most of the valley. The palm trees stood half in the water.

There wouldn't be much study of the sky tonight, because it looked like there would be more rain. The clouds hung low, wind was squally and changed direction often.

The first spits of rain hit Sady in the face late in the afternoon. They had intended to fly through the night; but the captain chose to spend the night on the ground, because the wind picked up and there were no known landmarks they could use for navigation, as there would be with clear skies.

The night was not particularly comfortable. The wind picked up, the cloth that was strung down from the balloon's basket to form a tent flapped and the ropes whistled, and maybe Sady was just getting old and soft and wasn't used to being in the field anymore. The last time had been more than twenty years ago.

The weather didn't get any better overnight.

After breakfast and packing up, the crew got the balloons inflated.

They had camped on the side of a gentle slope. To the north stretched a somewhat elevated plateau, an ancient land form pushed up from the desert floor. The top was cracked and jagged, with valleys and rocky plateaus devoid of any kind of vegetation, a truly hostile landscape.

A scout called out that he spotted activity on the ground.

Indeed, when Sady used the spyglass, he could see a group of four camels with riders making their way up the slope.

It seemed that this was a well-worn path, because he could see it snaking up the hill. One of the riders pointed up. His arm—indeed, his entire body—was covered in cloth.

Windwalkers.

Then the balloon crested the top of the platform and—

"Whoa, what is that?" the scout yelled out.

That had to be the installation young Javesius had told him about: a huge bowl on a pedestal, pointing up at the sky. It was covered in a thin, transparent cloth and, as Javes had said, the camp was at its base. It consisted of about forty or fifty large tents. If the number of camels in the pen was an indication of the number of people in the settlement, there would be a few hundred.

"There are people down there," the scout told him, unnecessarily.

"What do you want us to do, Proctor?" the captain asked.

"We'll have to warn them that there might be an explosion," Sady said.

The captain yelled the order for the "bag boy" in the rafters to let air out of the vent at the top of the balloon, and they descended slowly.

By the time the balloon touched the ground on the northern side of the village, all the people in the entire settlement had come out of their tents to watch.

They were true desert folk, with sun-beaten faces and loose, all-covering robes. Some of them wore cloth wrapped around their entire bodies, including their heads.

Sady stepped from the basket, feeling ashamed of the fact that these people were Chevakians in name, and Tiverius had never done anything for them. There was no road and no telegraph lines; no one recorded the weather here, and no one looked after the health or education of these people.

A man detached himself from the group and came towards him.

At seventy-six, Sady considered himself pretty old, but this man was positively ancient. He walked slowly, bent over. His skin was deeply wrinkled, his hands gnarled and the skin covered in spots without pigment. That appeared to be a common thing in these people. Some even had patches of white hair or one blue eye.

"Well, this is an interesting show," the old man said.

Of course Sady had to come inside one of the tents. The old man's name was Tiraa and, as elder of the settlement, he had seen a lot of years. Never had he seen a drought as severe as the past few years, never had he seen as many dust devils going as far south. Never had he seen as much rain as had fallen in the past few weeks.

"It grows unusually cold, too. When the sky is clear at night, green and purple bands of colour creep across the sky. The world is going bad."

Sady asked about the bowl that towered over the settlement, which, as Javes had said, was used for collecting water from moist soil.

"Funny that in the last few weeks, we could have taken the cover off and collected rainwater as it was intended to do."

To Sady's warning that they should seek shelter further south in case the destruction of the machine led to another explosion of sonorics, Tiraa was sceptical.

"The Badlands will be the Badlands, no matter what you do. It's in the soil. Nothing grows there, and whether this thing that you say is there or not, doesn't matter. If it doesn't rain, nothing grows there."

But these people's lives were influenced by the machine. Sady would bet that the skin pigment patches were a direct result of living with a higher than usual sonorics level.

His meter still didn't register anything out of the ordinary, but every other indication was that the sonorics level was quite high.

When they set off again, he made sure that all the crew wore their suits.

The landscape grew even rougher.

Towards evening, the balloon rose over a ridge, and a line of the rain bowls, or whatever they were, lay before them.

They were quite a distance apart, each on the top of a ridge, and Sady spotted no evidence of people at their base.

These installations did not stand straight up, but all five of them, made of weathered metal covered with flakes of white paint, were directed at the same point in the sky.

As if they were watching something up there.

But all Sady could see was blue sky.

CHAPTER 20

*L*ANA WENT BACK to the Mother's House with the intention of having dinner in the dining room, getting changed into a dress the king liked and visiting him. He was the only person who would care about her discoveries.

But she found the dining room virtually empty, and all the women upstairs in one of the dorms on the citadel side of the house. The window looked out over the courtyard, and you could see into the top windows of the great hall. If there was ever any light in the hall at night, it was a single lamp near the door.

Today, however, the windows radiated a golden glow, and on the floor inside stood many tables where people in colourful attire sat at dinner.

Oh, drat. She'd forgotten about the ball. The one where the king was supposed to announce news about his succession.

She wondered what he had decided, and then felt a pang of jealousy that she had not been told what it was. But, peeking into the hall, she didn't see any women at the tables at all, and maybe it was one of those things that men in power didn't share with women.

"Does anyone know what's happening?" she asked in a low voice.

Women at the front shushed her.

"They can see the king down there at the front," a mother whispered to Lana. "He's giving a speech."

"No one from the Mothers' Houses can attend?"

"A succession ball? Certainly not. All the king's sons are there. There is no room for anyone else."

Lana had walked past the hall a few times. She knew how big it was. It would seat hundreds. Imagine having that many sons—and not being enamoured with any of them. She felt sorry for King Orik more than anything.

A few women gasped at the front.

Other rose and crammed to the window.

Cries went through the room. "What's going on? What? What?"

A couple of women pushed their way out of the throng and ran to the stairwell. Lana followed them, picking up bits of information on their way down two floors. Apparently, according to the servants who went in and out of the room to bring food to the tables, instead of announcing his favourite, the king had set his sons a series of tasks to be completed to his satisfaction, involving outrageous things such as reading a book and doing a good deed for a less fortunate person and paying a visit to an elder.

When she heard those things—and the outraged reactions—she felt a glow of warmth inside. *Something* she had done or said to the king had made a difference. She had found a thread by which she could unravel his harsh reputation. She didn't know if this was solely her doing—she didn't think so—but she should use that change in the king's mindset.

Even the guards at the door to the Mother's House were looking at the hall, not paying attention to their charges. People were yelling inside the hall. The door was being flung open and a bevy of royal guards came out. They lined up in two rows, carrying flaming torches.

King Orik walked in the middle in a splendour of blue and gold. He wore his hair loose, a circlet on his head and gold earrings. The weasel of an astrologer ran after him, protesting about something.

Then one of the guards was pushed forward. He almost tripped, but stepped in the king's path. Men shouted. A couple of guards sprang before the king.

A stocky man ran forward. A metal blade glinted in the torchlight. Shouts.

Clangs of metal on metal.

The struggle lasted only briefly, and when the royal guards

retreated, a single man lay on his belly on the ground, while his blood seeped into the paving. His face was turned in Lana's direction. It was prince Sferuk.

The king paid him no attention. He sidestepped the body and went in the direction of his private chambers while all the guards and courtiers and other servants broke out in talk and activity. Someone brought a cloth and another had a stretcher ready.

Apparently this was not unexpected.

"Pssst!" someone called.

Lana looked around.

"Pssst!" It was Nashi. "We're going to escape." In Chevakian.

"Have you got money?"

"No, but we'll hide on the train. We're going home. Are you coming?"

Lana hesitated. No one was looking at her.

She could slip into the ever-growing crowd of servants and workers in the citadel and run away. Except she had no money for the train. And even if she did, the station guards would find her suspicious. And no trains crossed the border. She would have to walk across the forest and swim across the river. And then it was a long way to Tiverius. There might be soldiers; there might be robbers, slave traders and pimps looking for girls.

Here she was, a favourite of the Aranian king, having his ear and at least part of his mind. Which of the two options offered more influence? No question, really.

She also admitted that she rather *liked* the new Orik. Oh, she understood that he hadn't always been such a wise, wryly humorous man, but he seemed to want to make real change. The court didn't understand that. His sons didn't understand that.

"You go," she said to Nashi.

"What? You want to stay here?"

"It's not—" She shook her head. "Just go." She couldn't quite explain it. Because *he likes me, he pleases me and I've grown fond of him* would never be an acceptable answer.

Nashi left, and Lana eventually managed to get the rest of the story on the banquet. The king had set his tasks for his sons. Sferuk had expected a decision about the king's successor. He had accused the astrologer of lying to him about a recent prediction, and he and the astrologer had argued across the hall, because apparently when Sferuk came for the prediction, a few days ago, he hadn't wanted to say what the "project" was, and the astrologer said that for that reason, he had never predicted anything—the man had a tad more resolve than she would have given him credit for.

The king had then ordered Sferuk to leave the room for insulting the astrologer, and Sferuk had waited outside to attack the king as soon as he came out.

"The king was lucky that both Nayek and Denori are in the City of Glass," the guard said. "Or it would have been a three-way fight."

"I would like to see the king," Lana said.

"Right now?" He sounded horrified.

"Yes. Is that a problem?"

"He won't be in the mood to see visitors."

"He will be in the mood to see me."

The guard was still hesitant, but Lana had found that Mothers had the authority to order guards as long as it involved business, so he waited while she dressed, and took her to the king's quarters.

Lana put on the thinnest, gauziest dress that she still liked. She loosened her hair and combed it so that it fell over her shoulders in glossy curls. She opened the locker in the bathroom where, in the very back corner, she'd hid the pouch with the seeds that Nashi had given her. She should take one today to avoid falling pregnant, but rather than putting one in her mouth and biting it in two, she tied the pouch to her belt and tucked it under the fabric.

Like this, she went with the guard into the night. There was still a lot of activity in the courtyard, mainly from royal guards checking every alcove, every window for suspicious activity. The guard led Lana to the king's private quarters, where the guard had been doubled.

At the top of the stairs, Lana met two familiar faces. One was that horrible astrologer, who waited with his little table by the doorway. The other was Kento, standing guard at the door. He smiled at her.

The astrologer unfolded his map.

"What is this for?"

"When the king is in danger, I check all his contacts."

"You've already done this for me. The king doesn't know that I'm coming, and so he's not asking for a casting and I'm not, either. That's the rule, isn't it? The subject of the casting or an authority must ask for it. I didn't ask it. He didn't ask it. So who asks?"

"Are you telling me how to do my job?"

"You seem to be in need of telling."

"What?" He turned to Kento. "Did you hear what she said? I'm going to make a casting, whether you want it or not."

He threw the contents of his little bag over the cloth. One of the stones fell off and fell with a clatter to the ground. It was a clear one, the birthstone. Lana picked it up and put it on the cloth.

"Here you go. Look at that. You were born in the sign of the worm."

"It was the snake, actually."

And he even took her seriously!

Kento met her eyes. He pressed his lips together to keep from bursting out in laughter.

Kotori met her eyes. "You think you are so wonderful and you know everything, right?" He rose and went to the door to the king's private quarters. "You remind me of those bullies who always found me to tease me in the children's house. No matter where I hid, they would find me, laugh at me, play pranks and get me in trouble with the tutors. Similar things still happen. I don't know why people pick on me. But this time, I have a reply. The king received some letters from one Sadorius han Chevonian, the brother of the hated butcher of Kadrish. Apparently this insolent and arrogant man is looking for his daughter. The king is interested in talking to you about her."

Lana's heart jumped.

Kotori pushed the door open. "Go in. It will be a very fruitful talk, *Mala*."

Lana went into the room, her heart thudding. Now she wished she had not been so smug. She should have taken the opportunity to run with Nashi. And she also felt horribly embarrassed.

That had been a very childish thing to say to the astrologer. And he'd been right to put her in her place. This was no place to be smug. She might be smart, but these men had a lifetime of experience in working out their smart tricks and they could deliver much more crushing blows than she could.

King Orik sat in his usual spot by the fire, looking at the door when she came in.

Lana crossed the room and sat down on the couch opposite him. She felt stupid. Why had she ever thought that she could manipulate a man as powerful as this?

He said in a slow, deliberate tone, "Lana han Chevonian."

"I'm the daughter of Proctor Sadorius han Chevonian of Tiverius and Loriane, heiress of the Pirosian clan of the City of Glass." Whatever he was going to do, she was going to keep her back straight and chin up.

He chuckled. "I should have known that you were no peasant girl. Sometimes, I should spend more time listening to my own astrologer. He warned me."

"Would you have done anything different? Put me in jail, given me to your sons to rape and murder as payback for my uncle's crimes?"

He let a small silence lapse, a silence in which Lana could hear little except the beating of her own heart. And the silence lingered on.

Lana said, "I heard you started the process to find your successor."

He gave a short, sharp snort. "And lost one son already."

"I'm sorry."

"Are you, really?"

What a strange question. "I am, for you. Losing a son is a bad thing."

He sighed. "If my own succession is anything to go by, I will lose a good number more. This is why I chose to make the announcement now, while Denori and Nayek are in the City of Glass."

"Which son do you want to win?"

Again, he said nothing for a while. And then he bounced the question back at her. "Who would you choose?"

"I . . . honestly don't know. I don't know any of them well enough."

He chuckled. "Well enough to know that they're brutes, I bet."

Lana stared at her knees. She agreed with him, and she thought the whole system of raising children in Arania, of locking them in children's houses, was to blame. But saying something about it would get her into trouble.

"You're right, I was going to make a speech, and Sferuk got belligerent halfway through and I was not brave enough to make the full announcement. I told my sons I intended to test their statesmanship, rather than their prowess in violence or in the begetting of children. But Sferuk expected to be chosen. Denori expects to be chosen.

Nayek expects to be chosen. They expect to fight each other. Two of them will die, maybe some of their brothers, too. No, don't look at me like that. It is how *I* got to where I am. Back then, we were at war, we needed angry armies and an angry king. I was angry. My anger ate at me. It kept me awake at night; it gave me stomachaches. It made the women in my house terrified of me." He met Lana's eyes squarely. "And it achieved nothing. Chevakia ignored us. Peria rebuilt the entire country from the ground. They asked Chevakia for help, not us. No one wanted to talk to us. We were too angry."

He looked into the fire. His eyes glittered briefly, before he blinked and met her eyes. "Look at me today. I'm an old man. I've spent my life making people unhappy, ruining their lives, *killing* them in huge numbers, and I'm talking about our own people, not even Chevakians. We—Arania—are broken. We can't keep going like this. My sons are broken. All their lives, they've learned to be cruel. It has to stop. I have to make it better, or at least do my very best before I die."

Lana's heart was thudding.

He rose and went to the desk in the corner of the room. He pulled open the drawer and took out a sheet of paper that, when he had handed it to her, turned out to be a messily written letter. "After I discovered this, I don't think I can ever make it up to anyone."

She took the flimsy, stained pages from him.

Lana could read Aranian, but the handwriting was so messy that she had trouble with the first sentence.

"I found it a few years ago, and it hit me right here." He put a hand on his heart. "It keeps me awake, it tears at my soul. You can't read it?"

"A bit, but it would take me a while."

"It's a letter from my eldest daughter, eldest child, born to Yala, who is also Denori's mother, and who still works as midwife."

Lana nodded. Yala came around to the Mother's House quite a bit. She was gentle, grey-haired, unassuming in all the ways Selwa was loud.

"My daughter was a bright little girl who used to make everyone smile. She was friendly, gentle, perhaps a bit too trusting . . ." His eyes glittered again. "She was the oldest girl in the Children's House, and she was beautiful. I was very happy that General Pakori wanted her in his Mother's House. I thought she was happy. But about five years ago, she became very ill suddenly and she died. Her possessions stood in the attic of the house until the General moved to Curack two years ago. One of the General's mothers brought me a small satchel, and it contained this letter to me, which she never managed to send. It tells of . . ." He took a shuddering breath. "Horrific treatment at the hands of her man, who was, she said, jealous of the attention that she gave one of his own daughters. She admitted to having a greater interest in women than in men. She found men *unnecessarily violent* even when showing affection to a woman. The general mistreated her, and not just her, but others in the house. It described . . ." His voice wavered. "Things that we all thought were standard practice that happened to these women. And the bad thing is . . . those things were happening in my house, in the citadel, all over Arania. Not only that, but I helped keep those practices in place." He hid his face in his hands. "The letter was a call for help that she was too afraid to even send. She held on and avoided him until one day, someone told me, he cornered her in the garden, raped and strangled her. They were not solely his hands that killed her. They were mine, too. I killed the beautiful spark in her eyes. I killed her spirit and everything she could have been but never was. Her name was Xalia."

He let out a heavy breath.

"And I was trapped in a place where I would have to do it again, and again, and again. And I did, for many more years. And then Denori started to experiment with icefire. Terrible things he does with it. We have, between all of us, so many sons that his army is full of young men with no purpose in life except to die. And I understood that if Denori became king, Aranians would suffer far worse than they have in the past thirty years. If Sferuk became king, they would suffer. If Nayek became king, they would suffer. *I* have created these monsters."

He took a deep breath. "I planned to announce that in order to be chosen the princes need to convince me that they are capable of running a country with people other than soldiers. I planned it for when Denori and Nayek were in the City of Glass, so that they would hear about it second-hand and would fight each other over there. I assumed that Sferuk, who is not that much of a fighter, would at least be willing to try, but I might as well announce immediately that I'm changing the rules by which I'll choose my successor."

"Do you have anyone in mind? One of the younger princes?"

He looked down and shook his head. "I intend to stay on until I find one."

"In all of your hundreds of sons, there is not one you like?"

"They've all been taught to fight and be as mean as possible. The killing has started and the whole lot of them will pounce like hungry alligators on a stray chicken."

Lana wasn't sure what an alligator was, but it sounded vicious.

"Well . . ." Her heart was thudding. She knew that what she said next would affect her entire life, and that of many people in the world.

"Well," she said again. "I have a proposal."

He said nothing, then he spread his hands as if he wanted to say, *Go ahead, it can't possibly get any worse.*

"My mother's foster son is King Isandor of Peria. The Brotherhood of the Light in the City of Glass has a lot of knowledge about sonorics and how to fight it. My father commands the best-equipped army in the known world. I'm sure Arania has seen some of their fireworks already."

He gave her a suspicious glance.

"If you reached out to King Isandor and my father and told them what you have just told me, they will help you."

"Against my own sons, huh?"

Lana shrugged, although sweat was rolling between her breasts. "You confessed to not liking them much."

"I hate all of them. But I have to choose one, unless I'm lucky enough to live forever. I'm not a young man."

"You're healthy. You can live another fifteen years. King Isandor and Queen Jevaithi were fifteen when they came to power."

"With a lot of support from their people."

"Fifteen years is a good amount of time to build support. You could start by teaching women to read. And then give women a much more important reason to join Mother's Houses. They could become institutes of learning, and research. We have already made some great discoveries. There is so much more to be done, observations to be made, ancient artefacts to be chronicled, put together, studied. Arania has an incredible wealth of astronomy observations. It could become the centre of knowledge in the world, if only everyone could study. If

women could read and study, if low-ranked men could have func-
tions beyond being expendable foot soldiers, if the worth of princes
was no longer counted in the number of sons they have, they'd have
fewer, and all children who are born could grow up in loving homes
where their parents care about them."

He laughed, not in a happy way. "You can't change all that in
fifteen years."

"I think I can, because I'm prepared to put myself out there and
lead by example. I can teach, I can research, I can talk to my father
and King Isandor and the Knight Council."

"Why would you do all of that?"

"Because your part of the deal will be to get your sons out of the
City of Glass and out of Chevakia and out of experimenting with
sonorics. You do have men who are loyal to you?"

"Every soldier in Kadrish is loyal to me."

"Well then, you can stop your sons waging war."

"I could kill all of them if I wanted, and heaven knows, I've wanted
to do that so many times, but one of them will have to become the
crown prince."

Lana said, "I propose that you have the child who will succeed you
grow up in a loving family and be taught skills of negotiation, such as
how to win people's favour through deeds of kindness. The child who
will succeed you, a boy *or a girl*, has not yet been born."

Lana returned to the Mother's House very early in the morning,
with the scent of the soap that the servants used to wash the king's
bedding still lingering in her hair. There was much to be done,
including packing for a trip. She stopped in the yard, kneeling at one
of the garden beds. She pulled the pouch with seeds that Nashi had
given her from under her belt. She emptied it on the palm of her
hand, and dropped the seeds in the warm soil.

She whispered, "Go, Nashi. I hope you make it home safely."

CHAPTER 21

THE LOWSUN DAYS were the darkest in the City of Glass, and this day was darker than ever before.

Zaina followed Rider Taino and the team into the Knight Council chamber, where she had been once before, although it now seemed many years ago, when every seat at the table was occupied and daylight had played with the sheets of glass in the ceiling.

Today they were few, the public gallery was empty, and the sky was dark.

Jevaithi sat at the far end of the table. Dressed in a dark colour, and with her hair tied in a ponytail, she looked like a ghost in the low light. Her eyes looked dark and sunken, her face much sharper than before.

She met Zaina's eyes, and the corner of her eye crinkled with the faintest smile, making Zaina's cheeks glow.

She looked almost as frail as the woman in the wheelchair, the breeder Mistress Loriane, who sat next to her. From close up, her skin was very pale, almost grey. Her hair was grey and curly, but it was so thin that the light fell through it and showed her scalp.

She nodded a greeting. It was a solemn gesture that made Zaina feel almost ashamed of being young and healthy, ashamed of not being able to get rid of all those horrible Aranians outside the gates.

She recognised some of the others at the table, like Brother Veshi, the meteorologist from the Brotherhood of the Light. He wore a black robe and looked like the scarecrows that would stand in the cornfields at General Pakori's country estate.

The Knight Tutor who was in command of the remaining Knights was called Rider Willan. He was in command by virtue of being the most senior Knight, even if his regular job was teaching new recruits about hygiene in the eyrie and the dorms. Zaina had been through his class, and "didn't have much experience" didn't half begin to describe his expertise. Leading the meeting fell to Jevaithi, and she did so with a cool manner which Zaina hadn't seen from her before.

Willan gave a brief description of what had happened the previous day. After all the Knight teams had dispersed to check out various parts of the city and the plain outside the city, a large and highly organised group of Aranian fighters had taken possession of the eyrie. They had closed the doors and stationed themselves in the stable on the top floor, grabbing each Knight team as they returned. From the back room of the palace, guards had spotted at least three people being thrown from the top floor entrance of the stable.

Zaina shuddered.

Rider Taino then told the gathering what happened to the team from the moment they came to the yard of House Mara. He told them of all the items stored in the house and that it looked like the material might be readied to be transported to some other place.

Rider Willan asked about the improvised balloon and looked appreciably at Zaina when Rider Taino explained.

She blushed. It was getting so warm in here that she was feeling sleepy, not having slept at all during the night.

But the city was under siege. Prince Nayek's men were outside the gates. They needed to bundle their efforts and find a way out. Jevaithi had already sent a gull to Chevakia, but there was no way of telling whether they had received the message.

For now, they were on their own.

And Zaina remembered something. She pulled out the letter she had in her pocket. "I found this in the living room of the house. It was addressed to someone called Tamerane."

She handed the letter to Jevaithi, who opened it and glanced over the pages of observations on stars and the moon. She glanced at the line at the bottom, which said, *Please tell my parents I am in the Mother's House in Kadrish and am safe.*

"Who is it from?"

But mistress Loriane held her hand over her mouth. "It's from our daughter Lana. She was captured by Aranians."

In the Mother's House in Kadrish. The *king's* Mothers' House? That was one of the most dreadful places to be. Just the memory of the General's house made her shudder.

Zaina knew that at some point in her life, she would need to come to terms with her past in Arania. It was part of her and she couldn't keep running from it. She would have to face it, and hopefully help those people who worked to make the horrible lot for women in Arania a thing of the past. Failing that, she would have to help start such a movement. Because wherever she moved, Arania would always be part of her.

The Knight Council made a map of the city and drew in what they knew about the position of Aranians. The information was limited, with large area on the map having no markings. They simply didn't know what was going on there. It could be that Rider Barton and Rider Carro held out in parts of the city.

"I'm worried about the eagles," Rider Taino said. "Since the Aranians closed the shutters, they won't be getting fresh air. Do they even know how to look after them?"

"The stable hands are also in the eyrie," a Knight whose name Zaina didn't know said.

"But can they hunt for meat?"

No one knew the answer to that question. Probably not. Hopefully at least the Aranians went to hunt so that the eagles could be fed.

The alternative didn't bear thinking about.

"How have the palace stables coped so far?" Zaina asked. Everyone around the table looked at her. She didn't think she had ever spoken up before without having been asked a question.

The stable hand said, "The bears may become a problem, but we have a small supply of frozen meat."

His expression was dark, and he no doubt considered the same options as Zaina did: when that meat ran out, did they kill one of the other animals and feed it to the bears, or did they kill the bears? That was a terrible choice to make.

"What about the other animals?"

Jevaithi replied, "We have enough hay to last a while. The dogs can eat scraps from the kitchen. We have enough stores to last us a while, too. Fire bricks might be a bigger problem."

Rider Taino put his hands on the table. "I'm not happy to sit here and wait to be rescued by Chevakia."

Brother Veshi said, "I'm not happy for all of us to take excessive risks. We have the *queen* here, as well as the wife of the Proctor of Chevakia. They *will* come to our aid."

"If you don't mind me asking, why did your husband send you here?" Zaina asked of Mistress Loriane.

"Because there are Aranian camps all along the border between Chevakia and Arania. Given the history of the earlier war, it seemed logical that Arania would attack Tiverius first, so my husband has stationed balloon units along the border. They are well-equipped with protective suits, and the doga encouraged all people who didn't need to be there to leave Tiverius."

"Except Arania attacked us instead," Rider Taino said. "We were the much easier target."

Mistress Loriane said, "They probably still want to invade Chevakia but will have a better chance when they can attack from both sides. Ever since my brother-in-law rode into Kadrish, they have been threatening this."

Whoa, the Butcher of Kadrish was her brother-in-law?

But yes, she remembered that the current proctor was his much younger brother.

She looked at this sickly and frail woman with new eyes. How could she marry into a family like that? She didn't look stupid or evil, and the fact that Jevaithi looked after her meant that she *wasn't* evil. Many things she'd been told in Arania had turned out to be a lie. All she knew for certain was that a lot of people had died after the fall of Kadrish. Some people said that many Aranians had died by the hands of their own people.

Meanwhile, Brother Veshi said, "I'm not sure that Arania will attack Chevakia until they have sorted out the succession. The City of Glass has become a competition ground over which of the sons can pull off the most impressive victory so that they get chosen as crown prince."

Much as she hated to admit it, Zaina agreed with that assessment.

The meeting ended. Zaina lingered in the room, wondering if

Jevaithi would speak to her, but although Jevaithi met her eyes several times across the room, there were too many people and too much needed to be discussed.

Rider Taino said that he'd take the team to freshen up.

They could have some rest and clean clothes, and that sounded awfully attractive.

Zaina got an unmarked guard uniform because it was the only thing that would fit. She rinsed out her Knight uniform and hung it to dry. It would be unacceptable to walk around in a shirt marked by hauling black rock.

She slept for the best part of the morning, not even hearing Leya come in after her.

When she woke up, the sky had gone completely dark. It was not that late, because the smell of cooking hung in the air. Every year, this dark period in the middle of winter still confused her.

She found everyone in the council chamber, where all the tables had been arranged into several rows. The domestic staff had brought the chairs down from the public gallery and everyone in the palace, from the queen to the laundry maid, sat in that hall. Zaina sat with the other Knights, Rider Taino opposite her and Leya to her right. To her left sat one of the Knights who had been able to escape what looked to have been a massacre at the eyrie, and who could not stop talking about it. How many people Prince Nayek's men had pushed down from the top floor of the building no one knew. Zaina shuddered at the thought that they had come up through the alley where they would have fallen and might have seen the bodies had they continued around the rock wall instead of climbing up to the palace.

The Knight said, "What disturbs me most is that the birds are still in there. They struck at the heart of the only useful war asset the City of Glass has: the eagles. First they lured many of us away, with patrols gone missing in the mountains, and the patrols sent after those patrols gone missing, too. And then the king left and then, with our numbers depleted, they attacked us. And we're a force that is normally not even a tenth the size of the Aranian army."

"I don't know that they planned it that well," Zaina said. "If this was an attack just by one of the princes, maybe, but this is about Nayek getting as many people as he can before Denori comes in. He'll be in a panic, because Denori's army is much bigger."

"Would those princes actually fight each other?"

Zaina shrugged. "I've never witnessed a race for the throne before."

"Yes, they do," Rider Taino said from across the table. "Much of the trouble that arose before the crowning of King Orik was due to two major princes going head to head. One of them was killed, then the victor was killed by Orik. They were brutal battles."

Zaina felt a bit ashamed that she didn't know anything about this, but it was not exactly the type of material that the women in General Pakori's household had access to. Reading and writing was not for girls. She had done well just by teaching herself, but discussions like these made her feel dumb and inadequate.

After dinner she went to check the animals in the palace stable.

The sky outside was already pitch black and only one lamp burned in the stable. For now they had enough oil, but in winter, when you used it all day, it didn't last very long.

The dogs were going nuts in their cages. They hadn't been out all day, and normally they got to have a run through the yard even in the very worst weather.

Their barking made the horses nervous.

One of the bears was pacing through the enclosure, making growling noises and keeping its nose to the ground.

The stable hand watched it, leaning against the horses' pen. He was a silent kind of guy and he and Zaina used to work together, sometimes not saying anything to each other for a whole day.

He shook his head, still watching the bear. "It's no good."

Zaina noticed a chunk of meat in the pen, untouched. The other bear was throwing its meat against the back wall.

"It's like they feel that something is up," Zaina said.

"They can smell the Aranians. They can hear their voices of gibberish. They don't like being inside all day."

"Can we let them out and just run around the yard?"

"Not if we can't get everyone to safety or stop the bears running mad into the palace. If they get it into their heads that they want to go and break things, they're hard to stop."

The bear that was pacing lifted its head and glared at Zaina with its little black eyes. The angry look in them chilled her.

These bears were angry and they would kill if something got in their way.

The night was crisp and cold. Zaina went back into the palace, where everyone had moved into the kitchens where it was warm. They debated ways to escape, especially to get to the eagles. Leya suggested that she could scale the outside of the building, but Rider Taino said that the big shutters had bolts on the inside which were likely to be closed. They had to think about how to break the Aranian hold on the eyrie, investigate all the materials at their disposal and make a plan.

The first people were about to go to bed when a guard came in from outside. "There is action at the gates."

"Everyone to their positions," Rider Taino said.

The defensive positions had been determined earlier in the day. Each Knight had been assigned a position in the yard or the entrance or down the side or the gate to the eyrie, in case of an attack.

Zaina's was at the front under the overhanging roof of the porch.

A couple of Aranians were trying to break the palace gates from the outside, ramming the gate with a piece of wood and the weight of a couple of men.

Yells and shouts in Aranian echoed in the street.

"Open in the name of the prince!"

"We'll rape the bitch!"

"Cut her tits off!"

Zaina grabbed the hilt of her dagger. So, the ultimate victory for Nayek was that there was no woman left in the world that he hadn't stuck his dick into?

She knew for sure, she would die before he would touch Jevaithi. She was the last bit of pride and hope the City of Glass had. Without an escape, Zaina's life would be forfeit.

The Aranians rammed the gate. One tried to climb over, but he was dealt with by Rider Taino and his crossbow. He'd waited long enough to shoot so that the body fell inside the gates and Prito could retrieve the bolt.

It looked like the Aranians gave up, or at least the shouts stopped.

They waited, listening for voices.

The cold seeped under Zaina's cloak. Already, her feet were so cold that she could barely feel her toes.

The Knight next to her tried to rub his arms to keep warm. His teeth chattered.

Then all of a sudden, a flash of golden light sizzled along the gate.

One of the Knights yelled, "Icefire!" This was for the benefit of those who couldn't see it.

The gates opened. A group of men streamed into the yard.

Rider Taino took care of a couple of them, but there were too many. Other Knights streamed forward. Soon the courtyard became a chaos. Still more Aranians streamed into the yard. It was too dark to see if Prince Nayek was one of them, but there were too many to fight, even if all the people in the palace came to defend this side of the building, leaving the other side unattended.

The Knights would lose this fight.

She could do only one thing.

She ran to the stables. All the animals were agitated, the dogs barking. She set them free first. They ran outside. While a volley of barks and shouts went up in the yard, Zaina went to the pens at the very end. Previously, she had only handled one bear at a time. Bears were known for mucking up parades when walking next to another type of animal or a bear who wasn't related. But she took both the bears out, and by now both were growling and restless.

Bears were not the smartest of animals, mostly motivated by food. Being hungry made them dangerous. They could listen to simple commands, but mostly handlers left the bears alone if they were upset.

Zaina walked two angry bears through the stable. The horses went crazy. *They* could smell the anger. They weren't crazy enough to come anywhere near those bears.

When she was almost at the stable door, the male bear yanked the rope out of Zaina's hand and bolted for the door. Zaina tried to grab the rope, but the female bear jumped, too. The male ran outside before she could warn anyone. The female followed. Both animals ran though the yard. The Knights called out. Most of them ran to the cover of the porch. The male bear bounded to the middle of the snow-covered yard, and stopped there snorting. It sniffed the air and ran off in the other direction: to the broken gate. The Aranians had seen the animals, too, and they had seen how the Knights ran. Now they decided to run, too, much too late. The male bear grabbed a soldier by the leg and swung him aside, like a rag doll. A couple of others decided to fight the bear. Bad, bad idea.

The female bear had caught up with the male and she ripped into the Aranians, quite literally.

Zaina didn't want to watch that or deal with the bears while they were still angry.

She joined the others on the porch.

"Brilliant move," Rider Taino said; then he added, "Someone needs to shut the gates when those animals are done."

"Yeah." Zaina did not look forward to cleaning up the mess.

Both the bears ran out the gate.

"Now might be a good time."

Prito and another young Knight ran across the yard. Zaina followed them. Fortunately, it was dark enough to hide the true gruesome nature of the dark humps in the snow. A few more lay outside the gates, where every other building was dark.

Zaina whistled, hoping the bears would return, but instead, she heard something else: a truck engine. That could not be good.

"Quick!" She yanked one of the gates, but the force applied by the Aranians had bent the metal. The lock was completely destroyed. There was no way it would keep out anyone.

"Go back inside," Rider Taino said. "Get the queen and find a safe shelter."

Zaina ran back through the yard and into the palace foyer, while a number of Knights were taking up positions at the front. With the gates gone, the building would be hard to defend.

Whatever truck was coming up the hill, it wasn't looking good.

Inside the palace the domestic staff were running around in panic, carrying boxes of food into the council chamber hall.

"Where is the queen?" Zaina asked.

A maid replied. "In her room upstairs. She was getting changed into sensible clothes."

Zaina had never been to the top floor of the palace. It was, she understood, where the private quarters were.

Several doors opened into the airy walkway with a glass ceiling that would be light-filled had there been any light. Most of the doors were open. She spotted a bedroom and a sitting room, both dark.

Faint sounds of shouting drifted from outside.

"Jevaithi?" she called.

A female voice came from behind a closed door to the right.

Zaina opened the door—

Jevaithi was standing before the mirror with a dagger. She hefted it to her throat—

"No, wait!"

Zaina ran into the room—and Jevaithi turned around. She wore a red tunic, trousers, gauntlets, a belt with a dagger and a shorthair cloak. She held her honey-coloured plait in her metal claw hand, the dagger in her real hand. Her hair was uneven, hacked off.

"Well . . ." Zaina staggered back.

"I'm fighting, too," Jevaithi said. "I'm not sitting here, expecting to be saved."

Zaina took a few deep breaths to calm herself. "Give that to me." She held her hand out for the dagger. "Let me cut it properly."

"It doesn't look good, doesn't it?"

"Nope. It looks terrible."

"Do you know how to cut hair?"

"I've done it before." Xalia and her pixie-like appearance with her short spiked-up hair. That was a painful memory. "But we don't have much time. I'll do it when we're done fighting."

"All right." Jevaithi went to the cupboard and took out a riding harness, which she slung over her shoulder. Then she buckled on a belt with a dagger and a Chevakian powder gun.

Zaina felt dumb. It seemed she had badly underestimated Jevaithi's resolve and abilities.

Jevaithi looked at her, looked away and met Zaina's eyes again. "Anything wrong?"

"No. It's just that . . ."

There was a lot of noise outside the window, of banging and men shouting. Zaina didn't like their chances of survival. Nayek was coming for the queen and if he found Zaina in the palace, he would rape and kill her as well.

There might not be another day in her life. She might never see sunlight again.

And she was not going to die like this, without having said the words she had wanted to say ever since that very first awkward conversation with Jevaithi.

She crossed the room.

"There is nothing *wrong*, except . . ."

She reached up and touched Jevaithi's cheek, holding her breath, prepared to face anger or confusion. It was a risk that might backfire badly.

At first, Jevaithi didn't move. She looked shocked, so Zaina withdrew her hand. Had she been so wrong about the signals Jevaithi gave?

But then Jevaithi took Zaina's hand, and pressed her palm back to her cheek. She stroked the back of Zaina's hand.

Zaina's heart thudded like crazy. Somewhere outside a man yelled.

"We should go and help them," Jevaithi said.

"Yes."

A moment of tense silence hung between them. Zaina could barely meet the intensity of Jevaithi's eyes. A wave of heat exploded in her cheeks, but she couldn't bring herself to say those three little words, *I love you*, for fear of being rejected.

So she jerked her head. "Come on, let's kick some princes' butts."

Kick princes' butts was something Jevaithi understood, and it seemed, in light of the dangerous precipice of memory that brought Zaina's thoughts to Xalia's death, a safe thing to do.

They left the room and ran through the hall.

The front yard was a chaotic mess. A group of men were fighting near the gates. A couple of dogs ran around barking. Bodies lay on the grass. No Knights, she hoped.

Zaina stopped, Jevaithi close behind.

"What can we do?" Jevaithi said.

It was all very well wanting to fight, but just running out there and joining in would be stupid.

"If we can get to the stable, maybe we can get onto the horses," Zaina said. "Can you ride?"

"A bit. Probably not well enough to escape this, but I'll try."

Zaina led the way out of the entrance. The Knights under the porch were so intent on watching the fight that they didn't even notice Jevaithi slipping out of the building.

They ran along the wall to the stable entrance. A variety of alarmed animal noises greeted them there. The horses were unhappy.

Zaina lifted two saddles off their hooks. Jevaithi took the headgear, and climbed into the pen.

"Whoa, calm down," she said in the darkness of the box, out of Zaina's vision.

"Careful," Zaina said. She was unfamiliar with this type of saddle. It had a lot more straps than the Aranian saddles she was used to.

Footsteps, behind her, and a chuckle.

She froze.

And then a familiar voice said, "Well, if that isn't my fighting bitch. How about we finish something we started a while ago?"

Prince Nayek.

Zaina had learned and was no longer stupid. She carried her dagger everywhere she went. Her hand found the grip and she pulled it out of the top of her boot while whirling around to face him at the same time.

He wasn't stupid either, and grabbed her attacking arm, twisting her around. With his arm around her neck, she could barely breathe. She kicked but her feet might as well be hitting rock. He was wearing leather armour, and her heels slid off without making much impact.

"You're not escaping me this time," he hissed in her ear.

"I don't care about you."

"You will. No, I'm not going to kill you. I'm going to chain you up naked in my house. I'm not going to fuck you. I'm going to watch as my slaves fuck you as much as they want. And you know what? Not being allowed to have a woman makes them want it, badly. And you will die, before my eyes, very slowly. And I'm going to watch it."

He laughed, and then his laughter broke off suddenly. And his head jerked. He leaned backwards. His grip on Zaina loosened and Zaina pushed herself away.

And then he fell, with a dull thud. Blood spouted from his neck.

Jevaithi stood behind him, holding a razor-sharp dagger, her arm and front of her uniform drenched in blood. She trembled, but she coolly wiped the weapon on her trousers.

"I used to be quite good at slaughtering chickens," she said. "Isandor hated doing it, so I would. One cut . . ." She slashed her hand in from of her throat.

Zaina scrambled to her feet, weak with relief, giddy with love. She crossed the distance to Jevaithi in a few steps and kissed her on the lips.

Jevaithi uttered a surprised squeak, but then her hands were on Zaina's shoulders and she was replying to the kiss. The blood roared in Zaina's ears. She wanted to go back inside and strip off Jevaithi's clothes, or even do it here.

Zaina had to let go when she was out of breath. She and Jevaithi faced each other, wordless.

Jevaithi's mouth was open, her face streaked with blood, her pixie hair messed up. She whispered, "I've wanted you to do that ever since I met you."

"You did? Why didn't you say so?"

She shrugged. "Not proper. I have to pretend I like men. I'm supposed to be making babies."

"Me, too."

They both laughed, and kissed again, while the horses snorted and outside the stable, the fight raged, and while Prince Nayek's body started to cool.

"We'll probably die out there," Jevaithi said. "But we should help them."

"Yes, but we'll die free and happy." She took Jevaithi's hand.

The situation in the yard was even worse than she had feared. The gate had not held, the truck had indeed been full of Aranian reinforcements, and another truck had just arrived. The bears were nowhere to be seen, and the yard was full of bodies.

"Get the horses," she said.

They went back inside, saddled the horses and led them by the reins out of the stable.

By now the Aranians had come into the yard, a contingent of heavily armed strong men. Within moments, Zaina and Jevaithi and the two horses were surrounded.

One of the men laughed and drawled in a rough Aranian voice, "My brother lets himself be killed by a woman. Rest assured that I won't be so stupid. Let me show you what I do with a woman. Come here, little queen."

CHAPTER 22

THE GROUP OF EAGLE KNIGHTS with Isandor, Tamerane and Zeiro arrived in the secret hideout outside the City of Glass on the evening of the second day. Of course, evenings meant little in the land of eternal dusk.

They were tired and cold. A thick blanket of snow had fallen the previous day. They sky was still overcast, heralding more snow. This made the night warmer, but dramatically decreased visibility. From the roof of the shelter—disguised as a rocky outcrop—you could just see the glow of lights from the city. In a couple of places between the shelter and the city, smoke curled up to the sky.

"Aranian camps," Rider Nallayo said in a low voice while she stood next to Isandor. The hideout's equipment included a spyglass and she was peering through it. "They're careless. Thinking they've won the battle already."

"Maybe they have. Who is going to challenge them? Not us. Even Chevakia may not have the capability, or they may need their army to defend their own country."

"Careless leaders lose battles," Rider Nallayo said.

True, but Isandor didn't see who was in a position to challenge that many soldiers, no matter they were fighting each other. As soon as a non-Aranian force turned up, he had no doubt that both camps would unite to defend Arania.

Rider Nallayo sent Naissa out to investigate. Isandor watched her leave, a small speck against the dusky sky, one young woman to spy on an entire army.

She came back not much later, when the Knights sat around the simple wooden table in the shelter. The fire blazed in the hearth, but the winter cold that had seeped into the stone breathed clammy humidity that needed a much longer period of heating to be dispelled.

Even when she was taking off her cloak at the door, the expression on her face showed that the news wasn't good.

"The whole city is surrounded," she said while sitting down. "There are two camps between us and the city, and one to the south and two that block entrance to the city via the train line from Chevakia and via the harbour. The city itself looks quiet, and there is hardly anyone in the streets. I can't come close enough to see if there is any destruction."

Rider Nallayo produced her maps and Naissa showed her where the Aranian camps were. Yes, they were careless, she confirmed.

"Is there any sign of help from Chevakia?" Isandor asked.

"A train has stopped on the tracks, but it looks like a regular train. That's all for that side of the city."

Damn. "We need to send someone to Tiverius," Isandor said. "The only hope we have is that no one discovers us."

Naissa said she would go, being the scout of the team. They discussed who would accompany her and settled on a junior expedition member, a slight young man. Tiverius was a long way, and the eagles would get tired if they were too heavy.

Isandor watched them leave, standing on top of the rock mound with his arms around Tamerane. She leaned into him, but neither of them spoke. Isandor glanced over her head to the faint glow of the streetlights of the City of Glass. He worried about Jevaithi. Was that orange glow fire?

The team settled in for a restless night. The shelter held a number of cramped bunks. Isandor took the top bunk so that Tamerane could have the bottom, but she clearly couldn't sleep either, and each time she shifted, the bunk creaked.

He woke up in the pitch dark when the door to the shelter opened, letting in a waft of freezing air. The Knights who had slept closer to the door were already on their feet, talking to the people who had come in. It was Naissa and her companion.

Isandor's heart sank. What was she going to say? Chevakia had also been attacked and there was no way they'd ever get help?

Naissa sat at the table. She accepted a cup of tea and clutched it in her hands. "The Chevakian army is underway. We came over the ridge at Bordertown and the sky was full of balloons. I spoke briefly to their commander. They're on the way to the City of Glass. They received a warning from Rider Jeito, who is with them."

Jeito! Isandor's heart flooded with hope. He had quietly grieved for Jeito, not expecting to see her again. He pushed himself up from the table. "We'll make sure we're ready to assist them when they arrive."

They went to pack up, doused the fire, put blankets and pillows in the dry cupboard. Isandor went out in the dusk to call the eagles. They were out over the ocean, looking for animals to hunt. The birds were well-trained and came at his whistle.

The group backtracked and flew in an arc over the foothills of the mountains, while constantly keeping the lights of the city to the right. They met up with the railway line to Bordertown, where the train stood lonely and forlorn on the rails. Isandor hoped that the passengers were all right.

"Look," Tamerane said.

Isandor looked where she pointed. In the dusk-tinged air, silhouetted against the orange glow where the sun hid below the horizon, flew a row of little dots. Balloons. Hundreds of them.

Rider Nallayo whistled and raised her fist.

The closer the line of eagles came to the balloons, the more impressive they looked. They were huge balloons, with many soldiers aboard, all dressed in thick furs. Stacks of supplies and various pieces of equipment lay on the decks, sometimes over multiple levels. It was a while since Isandor had seen the prowess of the Chevakian army, and it impressed him every time.

Someone waved on the deck of a balloon. Isandor steered the eagle in that direction.

The soldiers manning the deck shied away from the eagle when he landed. He slid off the saddle, helping Tamerane down. She rubbed her hands. It was very cold indeed.

A man strode over the deck towards Isandor. He was middle-aged, with short-cropped hair. His uniform bore a good number of stars on the collar.

He bowed. "Your Majesty the King?"

"Isandor. This is Tamerane of House Mara, my fiancée."

"I'm Commander Tarinius, commanding officer of the fleet. Welcome aboard our vessel."

He led Isandor into the cabin at the back of the deck. The rooms were as Isandor imagined they would be: cramped and tiny. The one where the Commander led him was a meeting room where benches stood on three sides of a table. There was just enough room to walk around it.

They were about to sit down when someone else came into the room: a woman in her late middle age. She was thin, with greying hair and sharp eyes.

"Jeito!"

Isandor rose.

Jeito was not someone he'd normally hug, but this was not a normal time. Yes, she was even thinner than usual. "How did you manage to escape?"

"The Aranians are all shit-scared of each other, waiting to see which prince rules them on which days. I managed to make an Aranian friend and he gave me a knife, and that was why I could escape. I can tell you, it's a bad idea to let me face a single soldier who has only basic blade skills."

Isandor could imagine the blood bath that she so casually glossed over. And oh, he was so glad to have her back. "How did you get back here?"

"I walked."

"From the mountains?"

"I only need a weapon and warm clothes. I made sure I had both."

There was a story under that statement as well. Jeito might have sat on the Knight Council for the last few years, but that hadn't softened her one bit.

"I came back and found the city under siege. I was lucky that my eagle came to me. It was healthy and well looked after, so it must have escaped from the eyrie. Or someone let it go." And the eagles could sometimes feel their riders from a long distance away. "I took one look at all the Aranians swarming in this area and went to Tiverius to get help."

And she had brought a lot of help. Isandor reflected that this would never have happened had Chevakia and Peria not shared a friendship and free traffic across the border. Ultimately, friendship was the only thing that stopped wars breaking out.

The Commander excused himself, saying he had to get the troops ready for arrival. Isandor briefly spoke to Rider Nallayo. She said the team had gotten word of another small team of Knights who had escaped the city. They requested to be given assistance to free the eagles from the eyrie.

More and more of the crew appeared on deck wearing thick, all-covering grey suits.

That brought back memories of terrible conditions in a refugee camp, of being herded into tents by men dressed like this, shouting words he couldn't understand.

Isandor shivered. Never, never would the world suffer the effects of icefire gone rampant again. He would get rid of these Aranian machines and all the Aranians who defended the machines.

The Commander's quarters became a hive of activity. A couple of more highly ranked officers came in. Maps were spread on the table. As the conditions were reported, they were drawn on a transparent sheet that lay over the map. Isandor sat in the meeting.

The protective suits were only effective against a certain level of icefire. The balloons and their crew had to keep out of the range of the Aranian icefire weapons. The officers agreed that freeing the fighting capability of the Eagle Knights had to be a priority. No one knew whether either the birds or the riders were still alive, but if the shutter doors could be opened from the outside, any birds would come out, and they would find their riders. Rider Nallayo suggested Naissa for the job, because she was fast.

The Commander insisted that she couldn't go alone, in case something went wrong.

Rider Jeito got up from table, her hand on her heart. "I will go with her."

Isandor ached to go as well, but he had to stay to coordinate the Knights, *his* Knights, while more and more of the city became visible.

The mist over the water, the colony of Legless Lions on the rocky island in the harbour, the tranquil water, it all looked so *peaceful.* But the trams stood at the harbour station. No passengers waited at the tram stops, and no one went into the eating-houses. Many of the street lamps, in fact, had gone out, not having been supplied with oil.

With a whistle and shout, Rider Jeito and Naissa took to the air. Isandor watched from the top deck amongst the ropes and out of the way of the frantic activity of the suited crew.

The eagles glided under the balloon for a while, before diving and flying over the harbour. A guard on the quay saw them, pointed and shouted, and then saw the army of balloons with flaring burners and archers and grenade throwers leaning over the side.

He ran.

Why Arania had never developed decent balloons, Isandor didn't understand. Maybe they thought icefire was the answer to everything. Maybe they were all going to ride dacons, never mind that they were rare, dangerous magical creature that led extremely short lives. Maybe it was true that the Aranian princes truly didn't care about the lives of their men.

They flew right over the Harbour District now, no longer unnoticed by the Aranians. Men ran into the streets, pointing. Some fired futile weapons at the balloons, well out of their reach.

Men in the balloons next to the Commander's were throwing grenades into the ranks of the Aranians. Isandor cringed. There would be more rebuilding after this.

But the battle could not be fought from the air.

Another familiar place now came into view: the palace, with bright lights shining through its roof of many angled glass plates.

A fight raged in the palace's yard. Bodies lay on the grass. Isandor tried not to look, in case he knew any of them. He must have hope that this was going to work, but there were so many Aranians. People in shorthair cloaks were trying to secure the gates. More Knights ran out of the palace entrance. A group of Aranian soldiers streamed from a truck in the street.

Tamerane cried out, horrified, "Look how many soldiers are coming up the hill."

She was right, a whole army was running up the street from the Harbour District.

"I'm going to help." Isandor whistled.

His eagle had been sitting on the edge of the deck, fully saddled. It hopped towards him at his whistle. While he climbed in the saddle, Rider Nallayo soared past on her bird. Rider Jeito and Naissa had already reached the eyrie. They stood on the outside ledge of the stable, trying to wrench the door open.

Isandor's bird took to the air. The shouts from the palace yard grew stronger the further down he went. The Aranian troops had pushed open the palace gates. The Knights were fighting them hand-to-hand in the front yard. Rider Nallayo flew over, firing her crossbow. One Aranian went down and another, but far too many were streaming into the yard.

An eagle's cry made Isandor look up. It was Naissa on her bird, in the company of at least twenty saddled and kitted-out but riderless birds. They swooped down and landed in the yard. The Aranians tried to drive them off, but the birds wore armour plates and the arrows bounced off. Their icefire staff weapons did nothing against either the birds or their riders.

Rider Jeito landed in the yard. She had jumped off the bird before it even hit the ground. She ran across the lawn, now joined by a few other Knights who had been in hiding. They were Perian, and immune to icefire.

Fights broke out everywhere.

Two female Knights at the palace stables climbed on their horses.

But they couldn't leave, because a huge group of Aranians ran into the yard. Two explosions rocked the ground, close to the gate. Sand, bushes and bodies flew through the air.

One of the horses reared. The rider just managed to cling on.

"We have to land," Isandor shouted to Rider Nallayo.

The Chevakian balloons were coming in closer, too. One of them was already on the ground in the middle of the lawn, now covered with snow.

Chevakian soldiers streamed into the palace garden. Guns went off. Further explosions rocked the ground. Isandor had trouble controlling his eagle. It decided it had enough of the noise and swooped low, but didn't land. He pulled the reins to steer it back in a sharp turn over the garden.

A shrill voice rang through the air. "Isandor!"

As his bird glided low over the roof of the foyer, he saw what he hadn't noticed before. One of the Knights with the horses was Jevaithi. The front of her shirt was covered in blood—and who had hacked off her pretty flaxen hair?

Facing her was a high-ranking Aranian fighter, a tall man with broad shoulders, raising a gun at her head.

Isandor steered the eagle down. Like Jeito, he jumped off and hit the ground running. But Jevaithi was surrounded, and the entire yard was full of Aranian soldiers. The Chevakians had been pushed back to the gate, and they were trapped by another contingent of Aranian troops who had come up from the street.

"It's Prince Denori," a Knight said next to Isandor.

The prince gave a mock bow to Jevaithi.

"Your Majesty, it is rude to face a victorious prince while in the saddle."

Jevaithi laughed. "Victorious? You will never win this town. My people are too proud to obey you."

"Just like their stubborn queen, huh? Maybe I should teach you some manners." Without warning, he grabbed her leg and yanked her off the horse. She clung onto the saddle, but the prince was too strong. He held Jevaithi, struggling, against his chest.

"I'll take this one home as trophy." He laughed. "When I'm king, she can have my sons."

And then a strong male voice behind Isandor said, in Aranian, "And who says that you will be king?"

The prince froze.

Isandor searched the yard for who had spoken.

While the fighting had been going on, a small truck had entered the yard unnoticed. Its blue-liveried driver had come out and opened the door for a grey-haired, bearded man in splendid outfit, who was just coming down the little steps.

Isandor had never seen King Orik but he didn't know who else this could be. With the king was a young woman, splendidly dressed, long dark curly hair over her shoulders.

But . . . wasn't that . . . Lana han Chevonian?

Her eyes met his. She recognised him. A smile danced in her expression.

What on earth was *she* doing here, with the Aranian king no less? *Holding his arm?*

Isandor wasn't the only one watching in absolute astonishment. Even the Aranians had forgotten what they were doing. Weapons were lowered, and the soldiers stepped aside for their king.

While the absolutely splendid pair walked over the path to the palace, another truck had entered through the gates. Heavily armed soldiers in blue livery streamed from it, driving Prince Denori's men aside.

Two of them positioned themselves between the prince and his father. They gestured at the prince to let Jevaithi go. He did, scowling.

And Jevaithi whirled around and hit him in the face with a slap that reverberated around the yard. Denori didn't bat an eyelid, but it must have hurt. His cheek was growing red. Every single soldier in the courtyard held his breath for Denori's reaction, which didn't come.

"Let that be a lesson, son," King Orik said.

Denori stared at his father, his nostrils flaring. "What games are you playing, old man? Your days are numbered."

"Not the way I see it. Yes, I'm supposed to announce a successor, and for the last few years, you, my merciless sons, have terrified the people, Aranian and foreign alike, with your schemes to win my favours. My favours have moved in an entirely different direction lately. We can either keep murdering, terrifying, producing hundreds of children no one wants, invest no time in them and hope they turn out all right, find that they don't and send them on missions that will kill them . . ." He spread his hands. "Or we can join the rest of the world. You, my sons, any who are still alive, are absolved from your obligation to please me. You can call yourself princes—although you'll find that the title has little currency—but I will no longer accept the tallies of your sons or wives. In fact, your sons, daughters and wives can help us become a greater nation, by becoming educated."

"But you can't . . ." Denori's face was red.

"I am the king, so I can put right what I made wrong. I am an old man, but I have a few more years to live and raise an heir who has not been beaten or bullied, or learned to become a bully. I will appoint an heir, but he—or she—has not yet been born."

With a growl, Denori yanked himself out of the guards' grip and lunged for his father. Isandor grabbed for his dagger, but it wasn't necessary. The prince had walked straight into the dagger held by another of the king's guards. He fell wordlessly to the ground.

Isandor stared at Lana. He had no doubt about who was in charge here. However she had done it, she had the old man around her little finger.

By the skylights, mention the word *mother* to an Aranian and he fell to his knees.

And then someone shouted under the porch. One of the kitchen staff wheeled out a woman in a chair.

She cried, "Lana!"

And Lana ran across the yard, undignified, gold coins glittering. She threw herself into the woman's arms.

Only then did Isandor recognise the woman in the chair. It was Loriane, his own foster mother. He hadn't seen her for a long time. He knew she was ill, but he hadn't expected to see such a hollow, emaciated wreck of a woman. Her beautiful hair had gone thin and white.

"Look at you," Loriane said to Lana. "You look like a princess."

"Not a princess, a queen," Lana said.

"Child, you're not saying that you're part of that dreadful man's harem?"

"I made a deal with him," Lana said. "I'm not a prisoner, and I'll be honouring my part of the deal. I think it will make the world a better place."

CHAPTER 23

*T*AMERANE WAS NO FIGHTER. In fact, the view she had of the struggles in the palace yard from the commander's balloon on top of one of the surrounding buildings was as close as she ever wanted to get. She was liable to cut herself with knives in the kitchen, let alone in battle, and the sounds and clangs and screams made her want to throw up.

There were even some women in the battle. She counted three, one with the front of her shirt soaked in blood. The ever-growing ball in her stomach that was her womb hardened uncomfortably at the sight of that. She was growing a new life, and down there, people were taking lives.

From her position she noticed, well before any of the people in the palace yard did, how a group of sleek balloons had landed in the Harbour District, and how a small convoy of trucks came up the hill. It was the oddest thing ever, because wherever the trucks passed—preceded by a couple of runners on foot—the fighting simply stopped.

The fighters were mostly Aranians fighting each other, she surmised from discussions between the Chevakian commanders who had remained at the top of the building with her, while the men had gone down to assist the Knights defending the palace.

This small group of trucks simply cut a swathe through the

Aranian street fighting. It went right up to the palace, and entered the gates. It stopped, and a man and woman came out, surrounded by guards in blue.

The Chevakian next to her swore, perhaps thinking that she wouldn't be able to understand him. "Am I crazy or is that King Orik?"

The fleet commander came over, took the spyglass from his assistant and looked down. The man and woman had come into the garden. There were a few scuffles at the edges of that group before the garden was under control.

Isandor was down there. He whistled, gesturing for her to come down.

Tamerane still felt sick, but she descended from the roof, following the Chevakian commander and his men, everyone, in fact, who was not needed to guard and maintain the position of the giant balloon. They went down the ancient stairway on the outside of the building. At the turning points furthest away from the building, she had a view into the street below the palace, and it was full of people. Many of them were common citizens, watching as groups of men were being frog-marched in the direction of the harbour. Some of the minders were Knights, but others wore Aranian uniforms, all of them with blue. The king had brought a loyal army.

The first thing Tamerane had to do when coming into the palace garden was step around a body lying face down on the ground. The surrounding snow had turned pink from the blood that had spilled from his side. Tamerane didn't look. She felt sick just thinking about it.

The group in the middle of the garden contained mostly Knights. She recognised a few. Rider Jeito, whom her father had always considered an enemy, and Supreme Rider Barton; another woman with broad hips in Knight uniform, but who was clearly Aranian; and the woman with blood down the front of her shirt was none other than Queen Jevaithi. She looked . . . feral, vicious.

And then the Aranian king, a man with silver hair and silver beard dressed in a splendid cloak. He wore a gold circlet, and gold also glittered in his ears and around his neck.

The woman with him wore a dress richly embroidered with gold, a gauze-thin shawl and gold earrings.

Tamerane didn't want to talk to all these brave and beautiful people. She was frumpy, ugly and, what was more, her family was the cause of at least some of this trouble, and her father was still out there in Curack creating more trouble.

But Isandor had seen her, and gestured her closer.

"This is Tamerane, of House Mara. When all this is over, she will become my wife."

All those brave and beautiful people looked at her, and Tamerane wanted to sink into the ground. She looked down, because her cheeks burned, and that would never do. Her dress was so dour and *practical* and her boots were scuffed and worn.

The beautiful woman with King Orik said, "Tamerane, I've looked forward to meeting you for so long."

Tamerane had to look up, meeting the woman's surprisingly blue Perian eyes. "Lana?"

"Yes, I didn't know you were here."

"We escaped from Curack. Isandor came to free me." That was the story of her life: waiting for someone else to help her. She would read and study, things she could do without talking to people or upsetting an established relationship, but once the time came to stand up and say something, she would shrink away. And the king wanted to marry her?

Not only that, now the queen was looking at her with interest. Tamerane had never seen Jevaithi this close up. Beyond the blood on her shirt and her hacked-off hair, she looked much older, her face bearing weary lines.

"I hear my brother is rather fond of you." Her tone sounded to Tamerane as if she had trouble believing it.

"I'm sorry. I would not take your place. He asked me to have his child, and I will."

The queen's eyes narrowed, looking Tamerane up and down. She turned to Isandor. "Is that true?"

"It is."

Another look.

Isandor continued, "You will never have to suffer idle hope and lost children again."

Jevaithi swallowed. She blinked. Did Tamerane imagine it or did her eyes glitter? "Well," she said and she cleared her throat. And then again, "Well. We seem to have a lot of guests and I'm afraid this place is in a mess."

"Jevaithi," Isandor said. His voice was serious. "I'm going to marry Tamerane and she will live in the palace. We will have a separate wing, either upstairs or we'll build one. I want you to say that you understand this."

"I do."

The expression in her eyes showed that Jevaithi was just as uncomfortable talking about personal things as Tamerane was.

"You won't need to suffer trying to have a child anymore."

"I know." And then she looked aside—where to, Tamerane didn't know. "If you are happy that I bring someone into our house, too."

Isandor's nostrils flared. "Certainly you're not going to ask—"

But Jevaithi held out a hand covered in drying blood. And the Knight Apprentice who had been standing nearby—who Tamerane had assumed had some sort of guard position—the *female* Knight who was clearly Aranian, took Jevaithi's hand, and the two moved together until their bodies touched in a way that was far too intimate for friends.

Isandor's mouth opened. And closed again. He swallowed. And then he said, "Yes. I'm happy with that."

So while the Eagle Knights cleaned the garden of bodies and herded out the remaining Aranian rebels, while King Orik's men collected those Aranians and frogmarched them out the gate, while the Chevakians went to find more permanent anchorage for their balloons and the junior Knights looked after the eagles—most of which were cranky after having been locked up—the party of dignitaries moved inside, leaving wet, muddy, bloodstained footsteps in the foyer.

Tamerane walked hand in hand with Isandor. Lana pushed her mother in the wheelchair, King Orik talked to Rider Barton, and the servants ran around trying to please all those people, the likes of which had never been seen in the City of Glass before.

King Orik had never left his country, he admitted, and appeared to be enjoying himself.

Tamerane finally managed to find a spot next to Lana at the improvised dinner table. She had to force herself not to feel intimidated. Lana was so well-spoken, confident, outgoing and pretty that she didn't seem the type to climb onto the roof of her house in Tiverius in the middle of the night to put down light plates to observe stars.

"You should see all the rows and rows of books with observations they have in Kadrish. The library is such an amazing building. And oh, do you know that old Sizek is still alive? I met him. Mind you, he's a bit nuts. I've got some maps I really have to show you, and I found out what the Mother is. It's a world like the Great Wanderer."

"A world?"

"Yes, when you use the big spyglass on the top of the astronomy tower, you can see how its children go in front of it or behind it, and how the second child moves half as fast as the inner one, and that set me thinking about why the Moon grows bigger and smaller and why it sometimes disappears, and why it has a cycle of two days. We are one of the children. The Moon is another of the children."

She took her empty plate and drew circles in the remains of the gravy with her finger. "See, if we go around the Mother twice as fast as the Moon, then if we're here, and the Moon is there—" She stabbed at the plate. "—then we can't see it. Because the continent faces outwards, and we are looking at the stars and the Moon which circles outside us."

"That makes a lot of sense." Even in her correspondence, Tamerane had gotten the impression that Lana was always much better at thinking about the questions to do with the world's position in the sky.

A couple of people at the table were now giving them funny looks. Lana licked the gravy off her finger. "Anyway, I can prove it all, if you'd like to look at my calculations, because I think I did it right, but I'd like you to check them. I can also show you the notes I made, and if these men can get together and bury their egos and stop bickering, you can come to the library and we can study together. I have a whole generation of young people, mainly girls, hungry to learn. I'll get them to make observations and take measurements. But I want them to take the right measurements in the right way. I've taken some of the most important discoveries. Do you want to see them?"

"Of course I do."

"The thing that puzzles me most is a map in a really old book that's in the case I've brought. The astrologer wasn't too happy that I wanted to take it, but he's never happy about anything. It's in our room. Do you think we can go there?"

"Probably." Tamerane judged dinner close enough to being finished.

Lana turned to King Orik on her other side, and said something in Aranian. The tender look on his face said volumes about their relationship, but Tamerane still asked about it when they were in the hallway.

"I came to Kadrish as a prisoner," Lana said. "But even if I don't believe in astrology, the stars apparently decreed that I satisfied the criteria for the King's Mother's House. Once I was there, it took me a while to realise what an opportunity I'd been given, purely by accident, because I think the Aranians thought I was just going to be timid and spread my legs out of fear."

"Are you really the king's consort?"

Lana played the question back. "Are you?"

And yes, Tamerane was a king's consort, the mother of his child and his future wife. Lana had King Orik around her little finger. And her father was the Proctor of Chevakia.

They looked at each other and started laughing.

"These men haven't worked it out yet, have they?" Lana said.

Lana and King Orik had been allocated a large room on the top floor of the palace. It looked out over the harbour and the bay, where only a blue glow indicated the position of the sun.

There was a young male Aranian servant in the room when they came in, and he had been adding little items of comfort to the room: an Aranian bedspread, a few embroidered cushions, a thin shawl and a jewellery box.

"Do you want some wine?" Lana asked. She picked up a sparkling glass carafe from the table.

"No. I'm expecting. The king has waited long enough for an heir that I don't want to risk anything."

"True." Lana put the bottle to the side. She asked the servant in Aranian for tea. He left the room.

She opened a chest and took out a pile of clothes and then, from underneath, an ancient-looking book. Tamerane recognised the type.

Her father had a couple of these really old books. They were mere curiosities, made from sheets bound together, with diagrams of strange things. No one knew what they were for.

Lana put it on the table and opened it at a page with a beautiful map. It showed the entire continent in a beautifully coloured image. There were curved lines drawn over the top with arrows that indicated some kind of flow. A concentration of such lines met in the position of the City of Glass, another in the very north of the continent, and a few smaller spots in between, but especially along the Aranian coast.

"What does this mean?" Tamerane asked.

"That's what I don't know," Lana said. "As you know, I've studied meteorology, and I'm unfamiliar with this type of pattern. It seems to me that this is about sonorics."

"Could be." Tamerane squinted at the map. "What do we know about the other places marked on the map? Are there elevated levels out there?"

"The obvious location would be the north, and we don't know, but apparently a man told my father about another machine there, and he has the means to turn it off and destroy it. But no one has measured any sonorics in that area until very recently."

There was a spot on the map, too, north of Curack, and Tamerane thought of the machine in the basin below the hideout that Isandor had found—the one that didn't register on the Chevakian instrument that measured icefire, and that produced *heat* instead of cold. And then she looked at the map again and the fact that the north was hot and dry, and that, according to rumours, big storms had been forming there, and that snow had fallen in places where there had never been any before.

The flow arrows went *from* the City of Glass to the north, and from the City of Glass to the locality on the coast. That spot north of Curack also drew icefire from a spot on one of the islands offshore from Kadrish where she had been surprised to find that no one lived.

There were another few spots on the coast to the north of Kadrish, mostly on offshore islands.

"There are—or were—icefire machines in all these places," Tamerane said. "I know that this area here—" She pointed. "—is a favoured holiday spot, so I don't think this machine works anymore, but some of the others definitely do. They channel icefire in some way. Icefire is polar. It is attracted by these machines like the ones in the City of Glass. It is probably driven away by the others." But no, that made no sense, because down in the cave where the machine lay in the water, she had seen icefire. "Or at least in some way, these machines make it move from here to here." She pointed at the two large machines. "Or hop, hop, hop along the Aranian coast."

"Wait—" Lana said, and then she frowned. "You are saying that it is *attracted.* We always said that the machine *produces* icefire."

"No, it is everywhere. The machine is like a big magnet. It just pushes icefire in a certain direction."

"And magnets have a pulling and a pushing end. That makes sense. It also makes sense why our instruments don't measure the machine in the north. Because they only measure the pulling type."

"Exactly."

"But if the machines don't produce icefire, then where does it come from—" Lana clamped her hand over her mouth. "The Mother. In Arania, they have this horrible way of punishing people, mainly low-ranked soldiers. They are sent out on a boat to what they call 'meet the Mother'. I always thought it was a roundabout Aranian way of saying that someone died, and it is, but it's also a real thing. Those men go on boats out here." She pointed at the sea beyond the islands. "It's an area ruled by bad weather, mist and poor visibility. I thought that the crew of those boats would kill the men out at sea, but I spoke to a soldier who used to work on a ship. He said they wear suits and can only go out for a few months before they become ill, even with the suits. He says that the sea boils and the clouds rise up to the Mother, and that—" She clamped her hand over her mouth again. "He must be one of the rare Aranians who can see sonorics rays. He says the filaments reach all the way to the Mother's surface."

"Now *that* makes a lot more sense," Tamerane said. "But then . . ." She looked at the map. "Those machines form a network. They direct icefire from one point to another, around the continent and our cities —except for the anomaly of the City of Glass. There are the smaller machines on the Aranian coast because there is more icefire to be directed. The network isn't some society's idea of evil magic power. It's there to—"

"To protect us!" Lana said, and she rose so quickly that she banged here knee into the table and upset the tea. "And we destroyed the machine in the south and now my father has gone to the north to destroy the only working large machine we have left. He's days and days travelling away from here."

Tamerane gasped. And then she said. "The eagles."

CHAPTER 24

FOR TWO DAYS, the balloon drifted northwards, making a decent pace for a balloon, helped by a stiff breeze.

Sady studied and mapped the country below, rediscovering the wonder of travel and fieldwork, which he had loved as a young man.

It was ancient land, rust-red rock with outcrops in brown. It was wild, rough, inhospitable. He could see no vegetation from the balloon's height, and no animals. No rivers had ever marked this land.

He imagined that normally the sky would be mercilessly blue, and the air hot and dry. But the growing cell of low pressure had brought low clouds to the sky. It looked like it might rain soon. The barren soil that would normally be orange looked brown in the muted light.

Few humans had ever seen this land. Fewer still had seen it in overcast weather.

It was menacing, alien country.

Sady had taken the precaution to wear his sonorics suit, and kept it on and made sure that the crew wore theirs, even if the sonorics meter didn't justify the suits. The sonorics level remained very low. Occasionally, when a dust eddy passed underneath, it would increase, but not by much.

Sady felt a bit silly, but he had seen the white patches of skin on the windwalkers, and had heard of the growths on the skin of people who came here unprotected. Animals did not want to come here, and that meant something was amiss, even if his instruments did not record it.

In the afternoon of the second day of flying over this desolate landscape, the cloud cover opened up. Instead of low-hanging clouds that chased each other through the sky, a huge bank of nearly black clouds hung over the horizon. They reached into the sky as far as he could see, petering out like skeins of cotton wool pulled up by an invisible finger and thumb. Lightning flashed almost constantly within the billows.

The temperature had dropped alarmingly. The wind that whipped over the highland was moist and biting.

"Look there; the ocean," one of the balloon's crew said. His voice sounded muffled in the suit. He pointed a gloved hand at the horizon.

He was right. An endless flat space peeped over the jagged top of the rock plateau, dark blue and brooding with the menacing clouds above. It stretched endlessly towards the cloud mass and to the west and north.

Sady was painfully reminded of Lana. She would have loved to see this.

The balloon's navigator was studying his maps at the little table by the railing. The wind worried at unfastened corners of the map, making them flap, or making the paper billow when sneaking underneath.

The navigator peered through his spyglass, keeping one hand on the map, to compare the rocky features with those marked by early explorers, which had all come by sea.

"Lower the craft!" he yelled, and the crew opened vents to let some air out of the gasbag.

The balloon lost altitude. It drifted silently over the majestic coastline.

The red cliffs looked like they were cut out of a thick sheet of rock. They were so sheer and forbidding, it was a wonder that anyone had ever climbed up here. There would not be many places where one could do so. Or, for that matter, places where you could safely anchor a ship without being smashed against the rocks. Yet, once in the past, a ship had sailed around this part of the continent and a small group of men had climbed these rocks. They had been Aranians, back before Arania existed, and in the time where Aranians were still inquisitive people and Kadrish was the centre of knowledge.

Today, the coastline lay deserted, without a ship or any sign that humans had ever been here.

The navigator compared landmarks with names such as The Dog's Head, White Cliff and Needle Point. He seemed to know where they were, even if the cliffs all looked the same to Sady.

The landscape was majestic, and alien, and scary. If they got stuck here, there would be no rescue.

"Further to the east!" the navigator yelled.

The balloon's engines came on, and propellers whirled, bringing them back over the land, where the other two balloons still hovered.

The craft flew much lower now so that the navigator could pick out smaller features. He now had young Javes' map on his easel.

The cave had to be around here somewhere. Sady checked his sonorics meter, but the needle sat dead against the left hand side of the dial. No sonorics at all, but there was a strange hum to the air that rang in his ears and messed with his ability to think. Clearly, *something* was going on that the meter didn't register. Sonorics did some strange things to people. At least, if it affected him, he was in the twilight of his life.

The sun was fast going down. Of course it had long since vanished behind the cloudbank, but now the light was turning murky. The red cliffs turned dark. The sea changed to almost black.

Sady did not want to get stuck out here overnight. They would probably have to land to make sure that the balloon didn't drift over the ocean in unexpected and unfamiliar breezes.

Someone yelled at the prow of the ship.

Sady struggled between the ropes and railing to have a look. His suit made it awkward to move in the narrow spaces.

Ahead, a rocky outcrop stuck out of the featureless terrain. "Is that it?" Sady asked.

"The map says there has to be a path from a small rocky beach nearby."

There was no rocky beach. There was, however, something that looked like a path. The balloon went down a bit to investigate, and yes, someone had attached some kind of railing to the rock wall.

Also, a piece of stone clung to the rock in that spot, weirdly suspended over the cliff face. Coloured stains on the rock showed where the rest of the walkway had been attached.

Sady imagined how a staircase would have been clinging to the cliff, and perhaps a jetty below, and in a time beyond memory, people might have come here regularly to look after their machine. Whatever they used their foul machines for.

And the beach was no longer here, because when the machine in the City of Glass had been destroyed, the sea ice in the south had melted, and the ocean had swallowed small islands off the coast in Chevakia, so the beach might have disappeared as well.

This had to be the spot.

The navigator yelled directions to the balloon's crew. They went back over the land. The staircase that was no longer a staircase vanished from Sady's view, replaced by rugged rocks. The balloon went lower still.

"Did you find it, or are we stopping for the night?" Sady asked the navigator.

"We're definitely in the right location," the man said. "We're putting down for the night so that we can spend the remaining daylight looking for the cave. We won't be able to find it from the air."

Sady's heart sank. He'd spent days inside these suits in the time he travelled to the City of Glass, but those were not his best memories. It was uncomfortable, hot and, above all, smelly.

The balloon's gondola touched down on the barren soil not much later. The crew jumped out to secure the craft to the ground before Sady was allowed out. He stepped onto the ground, which looked like sand but felt hard under his feet like rock.

He opened his notebook, where he had copied the drawings from the map Javes had brought. According to it, the cave entrance was at the base of an outcrop that was recognisable by three pointed rocks on top.

But the landscape around him was full of jagged edges and pointed rocks. And now that they were on the ground, they had no way to get a quick overview of the land. Finding the cave might take some time. And, damn it, now he was worried about what was happening in the rest of the world. Lana might come home to find both her parents gone. The City of Glass was under siege. Loriane might die and there would be no way for anyone to contact him.

Darkness approached fast. The activities of the balloon's crew changed from finding the cave to setting up a safe camp. They had their beds in the gondola and would be sleeping there, but eating in the suits was hard. It involved removing the visor and replacing it with a cap that allowed the wearer to reach his mouth. It was dark and hot inside the cover, and Sady used to always come back from trips to the City of Glass thinner than he had left.

They ate in the cramped galley of the gondola, where it was now hot as well, because they kept the doors shut.

Then the maps came out, and the crew was divided into a few groups, each of them with the task of searching a certain area. If they found nothing, they'd move on to the next rocky outcrop.

It sounded like it might be a long process.

Everyone was tired, and darkness fell fast. They went to bed early to conserve lamp oil.

Sady was tired, but found it hard to sleep with the buzzing feeling inside his head. Having seen the ancient bowls in the desert and the glass and stone structures in the City of Glass, he knew that those people possessed much more advanced technology than they had today. It bugged him that he didn't understand the purpose of these dangerous machines. Were they weapons? Were they for keeping out enemies who were not resistant to sonorics?

They were up early the next morning. It was impossible to stay in bed long when people started moving in the gondola. It wobbled— whether in the air or on the ground—and the wood creaked and foot- steps reverberated through the structure.

After a quick breakfast, the search started in earnest. All morning, Sady walked up and down the valley, checking each nook and cranny, occasionally looking over the landscape to see other teams doing the same. They used ropes to indicate where they had been. The sonorics meter, which Sady had thought to use to locate the device, was utterly useless. Yet one of the men made the mistake of taking off a glove to pick up a pen he dropped, and was rewarded with red skin on the back of his hand.

After a quick bite to eat in the now impossibly hot gondola, the search continued. They'd be finished with this area soon and would move to the next valley. But that was a job for tomorrow, as they would have to move the balloons.

Sady was sweating in his suit and taking a break when a jagged ridge of rock caught his attention. Three peaks stood on the top, looking like broken pillars.

The outcrop was just outside the area he was supposed to search, but he walked towards it anyway.

"Hey, what are you doing?" asked the soldier who had been working with him.

"Look at this: three pointed stones. I'm going to check it out."

"But we're not supposed to—"

"I'm going to check it out anyway."

The soldier remained behind, not sure what to do. The man was right, they had been instructed not to leave the allotted search area. It would be easy to get lost in this desolate landscape. If you fell down a crevasse, the others might not be able to find you. But Sady wanted to go home. For days, this igniter thing had burned in his pocket. He had memorised the instructions. He wanted to use it and wanted to get out of here.

Sady plodded up the hill, increasingly certain that he had found the right spot. The three sharp rocks at the top were quite distinctive. This had to be the place the maker of the map had described.

The rocks looked out of place, *artificial,* and when Sady reached the top of the hill and looked back in the direction of the cliffs, he spotted a couple of flat stones in the valley. Remnants of the path that led to the staircase that used to run down to the water?

He rounded the peak of the hill.

There was a depression on the other side, but it was full of loose sand, probably deposited there by a recent sand storm. Sady waded through, more sliding than walking, until he hit the stone wall at the bottom. He followed it where it disappeared between two rocks that were also not natural—they were far too straight for that. There was also the rusted remains of a sign that had once been attached to the wall.

"Proctor!" the soldier called.

"Get the rest of the people here," Sady said. "I've found it."

The passage between the two stones was narrow, but he managed to squeeze himself through. Around a corner, the passage disappeared into a dark maw underground. He'd come this way alone, but he wasn't quite so stupid that he was going in there alone and without a light, so he waited for a few others to turn up. That took longer than he wanted. They'd been spread out all over the area.

But finally a few people arrived, and he progressed into the cavern.

At first Sady saw nothing except the back of the soldier who had insisted on walking in front of him. The needle in the sonorics meter was jammed up against the side of the dial, almost as if it wanted to break out of it case. That made him think: if they'd allow the needle to go further to the left, would it do so? Was there one half, a *negative* half, of the sonorics measurement spectrum they missed?

That was a disturbing thought.

The soldier in front called out, "Careful! Stairs!"

A moment later, Sady went down the eroded and uneven steps of those stairs. Someone in the back of the group produced a light.

They had arrived in a cavern. In the centre of the floor was a circular pit about two floors deep, and inside it stood the machine. It was a big and ugly thing, a square shape consisting of metal plates mounted on a rack with tubes running through the spaces between them.

A waist-high box stood to the edge of the pit, and a few pinpricks of light burned on the panel that formed the top of the box. Sady remembered reading about this. He knew what to do.

He fished in his pocket for the igniter device. He knelt next to the box and found a second panel. It contained a small door which he opened. The inside of the machine was pristine, gleaming metal. A round hollow in the back wall had precisely the right snap for the globe-like igniter to fit. He would need to slot it in, and then turn up all the dials on the top panel. The balloon team would then have a decent amount of time to get to safety—from a few hours to two days, according to the man who had given this information to Javes. It was easy.

But Sady hesitated.

Where did this man get that information, and why was he so keen to have the device destroyed? It had sat here for hundreds, maybe thousands, of years, doing whatever it was designed to do.

This amazing device would explode into a heap of metal beyond recognition, taking with it the intricately made globe and this panel and the traces of the old civilisation that had once lived here. Surely, there had to have been some sort of *point* to the existence of these machines other than to produce sonorics?

He ran his hand over the smooth surface of the panel. Little white pinpricks of light shone through the dust-stained glass surface.

No one knew anything about these ancient people. What could today's people still learn from them?

But on the other hand, sonorics killed. Machines like these allowed the Aranians to use their weapons. Sady had lived through the frightening times of the rule of Rider Cornatan, when Chevakian women were taken to the City of Glass in an effort to solve the City's infertility problem, and all died horrible deaths. He'd lived through seeing thousands of burned and sick refugees arrive in Tiverius on a train. He'd seen some of the darker features of sonorics. He'd seen people perform *magic* with it, and he'd seen the legendary dacon shapeshifter.

Those things could not be allowed to return.

All traces of sonorics should be destroyed.

He fitted the igniter in the panel and shut the door.

Someone shouted outside. A few of the soldiers in the cave stirred.

"Go and have a look what's going on," someone said.

Sady climbed to his feet. He studied the panel on the top of the box, and slid all the levers up. The pinpricks of light turned orange.

"Let's go."

The first of the soldiers were at the top of the stairs when someone burst into the cave.

"Let me go, let me go." A clear female voice, not muffled by a suit. *Familiar.*

One of the soldiers yelled, "Get out of here. It's not safe."

"Of course it isn't safe. Where is he? Dad? Dad, where are you?"

"Lana?" Now he saw her, at the top of the stairs that led into the room. And it was Lana indeed, not wearing any protection. This had to be a hallucination. She would be dead if she didn't wear a suit—

Hang on, she was half-Perian and she didn't need it. And if she was a hallucination, then Isandor in his riding gear was a hallucination, too.

He strode into the cavern and yelled, "Quick!"

Lana ran to the panel, pushed all the levers back down that Sady had moved, opened the side panel and pulled the igniter back out. "How long has this been in here?" Her voice sounded urgent.

"I just put it in. What's going on, daughter of mine? Where did you come from? What are you doing here?"

She held up the igniter. "This machine is the only reason we're still alive."

They went back outside, where a young female Eagle Knight was making a valiant attempt to control five birds, all of them agitated and flapping their wings.

"You came here on those birds?" Sady asked.

"Yes. We took extra ones so that we could cover the distance as quickly as possible."

He preceded Lana and Isandor into the cramped gondola of the balloon, where she showed him drawings and calculations and explained how the network of machines protected the world from sonorics. "Sonorics is a type of light that is produced by the Mother, except we can't see it and it kills us. The machines form a network that has been falling apart for the past couple of hundred years, because we were not aware of how it worked and why it's necessary. We've destroyed half of it, with the machine in the City of Glass gone. We can't afford to lose this one, too, because the whole world would fall under the influence of sonorics. These ancient people built the network with two main stations and smaller booster ones on the Aranian coast so that they could live on the land. We must learn about it and repair it."

Her words resonated with him. Whether or not things were as she said, he never liked the idea of destroying something when he didn't understand how it worked.

"Look at you, Lana. You were taken as a prisoner, and you've grown into a confident woman. What did they do to you in Arania? How did you escape?"

"That's a long story and you'll be surprised when you hear all of it."

CHAPTER 25

ON THE SLOW DRIFT back to Tiverius, Lana explained to Sady what she had found out about the world.

He listened in quiet wonder. Was this genius mind really his daughter?

"Not just me. It's me and Tamerane," she reminded him. "We should set up a place for study of this sonorics network so that we can repair, understand and maintain it."

She proposed such a study centre in Kadrish.

Sady surmised that she had fallen in love with Arania.

"Not with what it is now, but what it could be," she said when he asked about it.

And, as it turned out over the next few days, Lana had big plans.

It took much longer for her theories about the sonorics network to be proven. This required the cooperation of the nobles in the City of Glass, and the chief astrologer in Kadrish, an unpleasant, whiny and selfish fellow called Kotori.

During Sady's visit to Kadrish—the first in living memory by a Chevakian proctor—he complained about having so many *women* in his library. Heavens above.

Those women in Kadrish were doing important work, sifting through thousands of old records that had been stored and filed in the magnificent building for many, many years, and had been forgotten there. Lana explained to him that the women were so keen because they had only learned to read and write a few months ago, and had always been locked up in the Mother's Houses.

"But you live in a Mother's House," Sady said. To be honest, it surprised him that she had elected to stay in Kadrish—until he saw the extent of this library. Someone like Lana would love it.

Her relationship with King Orik also disturbed him. She treated him like a favoured uncle, and Sady remembered the stories of the brutality of the Aranian war all too well.

"He's changed a lot since then," Lana said, but Sady was still doubtful.

He guessed this wasn't his problem anymore. It wasn't his world anymore, and it wasn't up to him to carry old preconceptions into new situations.

He had taken steps to resign from his post and had asked to be reinstated as Chief Meteorologist for a few years while training a younger person for the position. He had intended to eventually offer the position to young Javes, but Javes had refused, asking instead to be posted to Ysherra. It was not a request Sady ever remembered having heard before, but it was the time for rapid change.

The new knowledge about sonorics, about the Mother and about the Earth's place in the sky had changed the sciences enormously, and a lot of young folk had become interested.

In a historic meeting between himself, King Isandor and King Orik, the locality of the new, to-be-built sonorics nodes was determined. The existing nodes on the islands off Kadrish were in an excellent position, and so were the islands off the City of Glass. It was decided that these new nodes would be built on floating platforms that were to be towed to sea and anchored there, so that no single land would suffer the burden of having the machine on their territory.

It would mean that Peria would get colder again, but increased snowfall would re-fuel the rivers that fed the Chevakian agriculture. The northern half of Chevakia would become wetter and, in this light, Javes' request didn't seem so odd anymore.

THE MONUMENT for all those people, Perian, Chevakian and, as it turned out, even Aranian, who had died when the Heart exploded twenty years prior was unveiled in the old part of the City of Glass in the early spring. Loriane was getting ever weaker, and they could not postpone it any longer.

The unveiling was a solemn ceremony on the waterfront, the closing of a dark chapter in the history of the world and the opening of a new book.

It was once again an occasion where everyone came together. Isandor and Jevaithi presided over the ceremony. Jevaithi made a moving speech. In all the years Sady had known her, she had always seemed distant to him, and her comments were often disturbing, but during this visit, she seemed to have found some kind of inner peace.

Lana was there as well, representing Kadrish.

Of course she had written letters with her news, but it still disturbed Sady to see her *pregnant.*

"I hope you know what you're doing," he said to her when saying goodbye to her at the balloon station.

"This prince or princess will be the first to bring together the blood of all three nations. That alone reduces the chance of having another war."

Yes. Maybe.

Lana had grown up so much. She was no longer his little girl. Some people called her the Queen of Arania. She was smart. She was determined. The world belonged to her.

After the ceremony, he took Loriane back to Tiverius on what would probably be her final journey. He spent most of that trip holding her hand while they looked at the land passing underneath, knowing that, elsewhere, people were working hard to produce better machines with igniters that would complete the protection of the land from the harmful rays of the Mother.

It was time for him to take a step back and spend the last days of his wife's life with her.

THE TRUCK CRESTED THE HILL, and stretched out in the valley through the dusty window was the place Javes had never thought he'd see again: the blocky houses and dusty streets of Ysherra. The autumn and winter rains had caused lots of growth and the hillsides were golden with dried grass swaying in the warm summer breeze.

Tali's eyes shone. "Home." She held Renko clutched to her chest. Fortunately, he had slept most of the way, his little arm dangling down Tali's chest.

The house the doga had made available for his use was familiar to him. It used to belong to the town administrator, a useless man who had abandoned his post when the dust devils came. Javes could live in the house indefinitely, Senator Shara of the Ysherra district had told him, as long as he maintained it.

Now, he led Tali into the house, two young people seemingly far too young to own such a majestic place, even if there was sand everywhere and the garden was a mess.

"It's so big," she said.

"Lots of room for Renko to run around. Look." He threw open the door to a huge garden room with glass. "We'll make this the sitting room and that room over there will be the library."

Javes' task would be to collect, buy or excavate material from the ancient society. To find out what they did here, where they came from, where they went and how they used the artefacts. The doga had allocated him money to buy camels and hire people.

Jobs and money, something the ravaged town needed badly.

But first . . .

"Tali?"

Javes faced her, putting his hand in his pocket. His fingers met the smooth wooden surface of a little box which he pulled out and gave to her.

Tali's eyes widened. "For me? What's in it?"

"Open and you'll see. Here, give him to me."

She handed Renko to him and he balanced the boy on his hip. His raven-dark hair marked him clearly as half-Aranian, but Javes couldn't look at him without his heart melting. He wanted children, a whole bus full of them, to run over these hills, to play in the dirt, to milk the goats and ride the camels.

She opened the lid. On a bed of blue velvet inside the box lay a pendant of light-coloured metal on a silver chain. She took it out. The light glittered in the clean metal surface, showing up the mysterious characters that, ages ago, people had engraved in the surface.

"It's very pretty," she said.

Javes took the chain from her and fastened it around her neck.

"I took this thing from your father's house. I have no idea what it is, but I kept it in my pocket all the time, thinking I might sell it if we needed money."

"But we didn't."

No, they hadn't. They'd been lucky that Belo had helped, had even turned the shed into a little house. He'd given Javes little jobs so that he could pay for food and the midwife when Renko was born. Tali had even had to go to the hospital. That had been scary, seeing her in so much pain.

"Why are you giving this to me?" Tali asked.

"It's a present."

Javes let his gaze glide over Tali's dark hair, her olive skin, her dark eyes. "Because I like you."

"Does it mean that when I'm old enough, you'll marry me?"

"Yes. If that's what you want."

"I do. But why wait?"

"Because it wouldn't be appropriate." But he bent forward and kissed her gently on the top of her forehead, smelling the scent of her hair.

FAR AWAY, in Kadrish it was the hour before dawn, but the reception room in the Mother's House buzzed with people. Servants brought around food on trays and poured cider.

King Orik sat on the couch surrounded by women and guards looking at the bundle in his arms. He looked oh so awkward. Just as awkward as Lana felt but she was sure she'd get used to looking after a child.

Lana felt dizzy and exhausted, but she was relieved.

For the first time in history, Arania had a crown princess, and little Loriane had the blood of all three nations in her veins. Her face was scrunched up and blotched red from the birth. Her eyes were hazy still, but time would tell what colour they would be: her own blue, her father's brown, or the king's grey.

Lana's mother Loriane had finally sunk into eternal sleep a month earlier. Lana had been there, heavily pregnant.

After the funeral, she had made sure her father was looked after. He had finally stepped down, the longest-serving proctor in the history of Chevakia, and had gone back to his old job of Chief Meteorologist. With all the things that were going on with the weather, it looked like he would be busy for a while. He would be all right, he had assured her, although she hated to leave him alone in that big house.

She had been so incredibly reluctant to give birth in the Mother's House that she had avoided the subject for as long as possible, teaching women to write instead of discussing her ceremony plans. In the end Selwa had forced her to make some decisions, when the pains had already started.

The agonising process had taken two days, although for the first day she had lain upstairs with stomach cramps, thinking she had caught some disease, and barely able to hold any food down.

In the end, she had appreciated the other mothers' presence, for she could let the noise roll over her and concentrate on her task, which had, after a night of pain and hard work, resulted in the little girl.

So she sat in the middle of the celebration, exhausted but relieved, grateful for the wheelchair.

The women brought her little cards with messages they had written, some with spelling mistakes. The children came to bring flowers and the king smiled and made jokes.

Oh, the danger wasn't entirely gone. A few princes still thought they might have a chance at the throne if only they could kill the king. But the king's guard was loyal, especially since Lana had convinced Orik to increase their pay.

Lana hoped the time of safety would last long enough to bring about real change in Arania, until the next generation took the throne.

IN THE PALACE in the City of Glass, the next generation had just started exploring the world. Tamerane and Isandor stood, hand in hand, while Selinor crawled through the upstairs hallway of the palace's living quarters, squealing at the top of his lungs. Zaina sat on her knees, hands outstretched as he crawled and crawled towards her, lost in the joy of being able to move. Soon, he would add *running* to his arsenal.

Jevaithi stood in the doorway to the living room, the low sun gilding her pixie hair. She wore the Knight Commander uniform with pride these days, as she and Rider Barton organised the cleanup of the Harbour District.

Tamerane had told Isandor only a week ago that she was again expecting and she was already wearing wide clothes. It would be twins, Isandor joked, but it might be true. Twins were common in the royal family.

She still spent a lot of time reading and making calculations. Although a lot of the work was done in Kadrish, the new icefire machine would be assembled in the City of Glass. The giant floating platform already lay on one of the harbour's outer piers, where the Legless Lions would occasionally manage to climb on it, no doubt wondering what it was.

IN THE ASTROLOGY tower of the citadel, Kotori was already at work. In the past few months, he was grateful to have retained possession of his head, but privately disgusted at the developments at the citadel.

His domain had been invaded by lots of *women*, chattering and laughing and giving him strange looks as if he were some piece of quaint furniture.

That southern woman came with them a lot, always bossing the others around, wearing increasingly wide garments and not making a secret of her expanding figure at all.

Kotori found it both fascinating and disgusting. She should be resting in the Mother's House, but the one time he told her that, all the women started laughing at him.

Since then, Kotori would listen to what she had to say from behind a nearby bookshelf so that the women couldn't see him.

The things the southern woman taught made his head spin.

Where in the world did the bright minds allow women to study *calculus*?

But he had to admit that he had no idea what they were talking about half the time, and so at night, he would take the books they had been using and would study.

He had plenty of time.

By decree of the king, boats with prisoners no longer went out to sea, so his work had become much quieter.

He also didn't seem to get as many requests for castings. Maybe it was because Arania was more peaceful; but maybe, too, it was because people had less faith in astrology, something in which that woman had surely had a hand. If there was one thing Kotori had to admit, it was that a lot of people were smarter than he was.

He had tried to argue what he believed about the world and about astrology and on all accounts, he had to admit that the southern woman was right.

The world appeared to be round. The stars did not revolve around the world. They were not pinprick holes in the sky's canvas. The icefire machines diverted icefire and didn't produce it. That was why Denori's machines had messed with the flow of icefire in the air so much.

And star signs . . . well, he refused to let go of the belief that they controlled a person's life, even if many other people did.

A lot of information had been gathered the last couple of months, and he was sure there would be a lot more. It would be information that scared him, that upset him and showed the world just what a useless lump of human flesh he was. And one day the king would understand that, too.

But the king appeared to be so disgustingly *happy* with this woman who was far too young for him.

But just in case Kotori would be required to prove his usefulness, he'd gone back to taking regular observations of the stars, because it was something in which he was still an expert.

And standing here on top of the tower in the predawn morning cleared his mind. No one was awake yet, the city was dark, the sun still well below the horizon. His favourite time of day.

The Great Wanderer with its children was high in the sky, and the Red Wanderer hung low above the eastern horizon.

But hey, what was that? He peered through the spyglass.

A speck of light moved high overhead across the sky path. It wasn't a tail star, because it went in the wrong direction, and wasn't a flash star because it didn't wink out.

Kotori followed it with his spyglass until it vanished over the horizon, always going at the same speed, and, if he was right and the spyglass didn't fool him, *blinking*. Well . . . that was strange. He didn't think he'd ever seen anything like that before. Maybe some *woman* could tell him what it meant.

Bah. It was time for breakfast.

Thank You

. . . for reading *Moon & Earth*. While the series is finished here, I have written many other books, including the Icefire Trilogy, prequel to this series. If you haven't read that series yet, you will recognise some characters. If you are interested in hearing about new books and specials, register for my mailing list. At some point in the future, there may even be a sequel series.

ABOUT THE AUTHOR

Patty Jansen lives in Sydney, Australia, where she spends most of her time writing Science Fiction and Fantasy.

Her story *This Peaceful State of War* placed first in the second quarter of the Writers of the Future contest and was published in their 27th anthology. She has also sold fiction to genre magazines such as Analog Science Fiction and Fact, Redstone SF and Aurealis.

Patty has written over twenty novels in both Science Fiction and Fantasy, including the *Icefire Trilogy* and the *Ambassador* series.

pattyjansen.com

BOOKS BY PATTY JANSEN

More information:
PATTYJANSEN.COM

www.ingramcontent.com/pod-product-compliance
Lightning Source LLC
Chambersburg PA
CBHW061056190726
48286CB00006B/1769